Acclaim for the Dana Hargrove novels

Forsaken Oath is "clever, immersive... Kemanis, a talented weaver of scene and exposition, keeps the reader engaged with each new twist and bit of evidence. There is a lived-in feel to Bureau 90 that sets this work apart from lesser legal thrillers..." — *Kirkus Reviews*

"Riveting reading... V.S. Kemanis's compelling legal thriller *Deep Zero* distinguishes itself with its powerful blend of vivid writing, legal expertise and insight, and finely and compassionately drawn characters." — *Foreword Reviews*

"By far the best of the e-book originals under consideration is V.S. Kemanis' *Homicide Chart*... Besides being a well-written novel with interesting characters and strong narrative impetus, it is a law buff's delight, with intelligent discussions of unusual legal situations and excellent courtroom combat. Kemanis is an excellent writer..." — Jon L. Breen, *Mystery Scene Magazine*

Thursday's List is an "engaging and thought-provoking account of financial crimes, money laundering and the workings of a drug cartel... A stunning portrayal of the deep bonds of friendship and the complexities that are encountered when that friendship is threatened... Well written, with a plot that is complex and presented in a way that will keep you captivated..." — *The Kindle Book Review*

Homicide Chart is "a page-turner, expertly written and well crafted, deftly plotted with characters that portray real, human emotions... Kemanis is a writer of high caliber worth noting, and this is a novel well worth reading." — *The U.S. Review of Books*

"Kemanis writes in a style that adeptly dramatizes legal arguments while also finding moments of stark lyricism... [*Deep Zero*] is a well-drawn legal thriller." — *Kirkus Reviews*

In *Homicide Chart*, "Kemanis meters out the suspense in compelling fashion... A well-paced, polished, and highly enjoyable read... Highly recommended." — Carmen Amato, author of *43 Missing*

Forsaken Oath "really shines. A powerful book..." — *Mystery Sequels*

In *Thursday's List*, "Kemanis draws on her experience as a prosecutor at the county and state levels and brings her personal knowledge of the investigation process into the story. Her overall attention to detail makes the work a true page-turner." — *Kirkus Reviews*

"In *Homicide Chart*, V.S. Kemanis weaves three separate plot lines into a compelling tale. Her characters are well defined, very authentic,... painted with a deft hand. This is Ms. Kemanis' real talent. She makes us care for the characters." — *Online Book Club*

Forsaken Oath is a "legal thriller meets murder mystery... The reader is thrust into the dizzying world of the legal profession at a running pace and never slows down." — *The U.S. Review of Books*

"In *Deep Zero*...we return to the complex world of District Attorney Dana Hargrove, who, once again, in her line of work, is dealing with several unusual cases... There are no quiet moments, the plot is extremely suspenseful, and drama abounds as well... I was literally on the edge of my seat..." — *Mystery Sequels*

"*Forsaken Oath* is a terrific legal thriller, written by a prosecutor who knows her way around the legal trenches. Kemanis's expertise brings wonderful authenticity to a twisting plot." — Allison Leotta, author of *The Last Good Girl*

"*Thursday's List* has some qualities of mystery, legal thriller, and the police procedural... A plot that is different, with qualities that would appeal to fans of any of those genres." — *Books and Pals*

"*Forsaken Oath*...is informed, thrilling action in and out of the courtroom, and few can portray it better than V.S. Kemanis. Highly recommended." — *San Francisco Review of Books*

In *Deep Zero*, Kemanis "vividly portrays the difficulties of balancing the intricacies of the practice of law with the intimacies of the practice of parenthood. Her principal players seem particularly real... This is a confident author as at home with courtrooms, legal briefs, and summary judgments as she is with bedrooms, term papers, and adolescent anxiety." — *The U.S. Review of Books*

Also by V.S. Kemanis

Dana Hargrove Legal Mysteries

Homicide Chart
Forsaken Oath
Deep Zero
Seven Shadows

Story Collections

Dust of the Universe, tales of family
Everyone But Us, tales of women
Malocclusion, tales of misdemeanor
Love and Crime: Stories
Your Pick: Selected Stories

Anthology Contributor

The Crooked Road, Volume 3
The Best Laid Plans
Me Too Short Stories

Visit
www.vskemanis.com

Thursday's List

a Dana Hargrove legal mystery

V.S. KEMANIS

2020 edition

Cover art by S.A. Hunt
Paperback cover design by Valdas Miskinis

ISBN-13: 978-0-9997850-6-5

ℒ Opus Nine Books
• New York •

For the Lit Chicks,
my steadfast friends and voracious fiction aficionados,
with love

CONTENTS

1 » *GRAVEYARD*

"PEOPLE OF THE State of New York against Bernardo Rios. Step up!"

Rios didn't budge, didn't seem to hear. He'd fallen into a slump, head dangling from a loose neck, much like the five strangers surrounding him on the prisoners' bench. At four in the morning, mid-graveyard, every player in the courtroom was blinking grit, battling the nod.

Tilted upright behind the prosecutor's table, Dana Hargrove evaluated the case. Through sheer will and frequent sips from a tall coffee cup, she snubbed the empty chair and remained standing. In a stiff-armed lean, hands grasping the table edge, she scanned the papers laid out on the surface below. The faint print on tissue-thin paper was nearly illegible.

This had to get better. A new computer system was promised for the summer of 1988, a few months from now. Until then, the district attorney's intake clerks still typed the criminal complaints on multiple-sheet carbon forms, replete with black strikeovers. The police reports usually weren't any better. This one was hand-written.

Dana's large, brown eyes were red rimmed and burning. Squinting hard under the buzz of fluorescent light, she tried to make sense of the swimming text. Never enough information and

1

never enough time to formulate a strategy. Graveyard shift in arraignment court was the worst, an assignment dumped on new hires and a rite of passage for every rookie. With it came the absurd responsibility of making crucial, split-second decisions on zero sleep—plea bargains and bail applications in cases as serious as murder and rape.

But this one? Incredulous, Dana confirmed what she'd seen at first glance. Farebeat. Why was a farebeat in the system at four in the morning?

"Bernardo Rios, step up!" barked the clerk. This time the defendant snapped alert, suddenly aware that the name, spoken with a New York clip, was meant to be his. Bleary eyes searched the room and fell upon the uniformed court officer striding into his face, coaxing him up with a twitching finger. Rios straightened his legs, uncertainly finding his balance. Nothing restrained him. Unlike some of the prisoners, he wasn't considered dangerous enough to be handcuffed or shackled.

"We need the interpreter, Your Honor." Seth Kaplan of the Legal Aid Society addressed the Honorable Morris Chomsky.

The judge scanned the courtroom, rolled his eyes and growled, "Get the Spanish interpreter." Hadn't she been here a minute ago? Inexplicably, she'd disappeared. "Second call!"

Chomsky didn't appreciate obstacles to his relentless pace, which he maintained even on graveyard. His normal state of irritability grew with lack of sleep, along with his habit of blaming everyone in sight—particularly the defendants—for his inability to avoid a temporary assignment to night court.

Rios, already halfway to the defense table, stopped dead against Kaplan's upheld hand. "Esperas un momento," the attorney stuttered, whirling his hand in circles, miming a command to turn around.

"How do you spell that?" asked the droopy stenographer, hands poised over her machine.

"Don't take that down," Seth told her, then to Rios: "Esperas ...vamos a...well...otra vez." A light went on in the defendant's eyes, and he turned toward the prisoners' bench. The judge, behind his obelisk of gouged, dark wood, swiveled his chair to the side and beckoned the court clerk, who came up to receive an instruction.

"Very *good*," Dana whispered to Seth out the side of her mouth, keeping her head bent over the papers. She was practiced in a level of voice just beneath Chomsky's hearing, loud enough to reach her adversary a few yards away at the defense table while the judge was distracted.

"Not bad for one year of college Spanish," he replied with a wink.

"Trying to avoid the bologna and cigarettes?"

Seth understood her meaning and grinned, pushing a friendly set of quote marks into his cheeks. Earlier, he'd been allowed a two-minute conference with each of his prospective clients in the close quarters of the lockup, a breeding ground of singular odors on the breath and bodies of arrestees. Anyone held in the pens longer than six hours was entitled to bologna and American cheese on white, followed by a smoke.

"Just bologna on that one," he whispered, keeping an eye on Chomsky, who was giving a final directive to the clerk.

Seth was likeable, a pleasant distraction from Dana's nocturnal hallucination. His grin and lively blue eyes always tugged out a response, and his regular features made a welcome contrast to the grim vision of endless unsavory characters in the night. Some Legal Aid attorneys—those blindly overzealous champions of the accused—could make Dana's graveyard shift completely miserable, but with Seth in the opposing camp, she could count on a comrade against Chomsky's unpredictable wrath.

The shuffle of hard-soled shoes and scrape of a wooden chair floated in the cavernous space. The judge, now turning to face them, ran a palm over the half-dozen gray hairs on his head and dropped the hand to his desk. His fingers drummed the wood, sending audible vibrations into the unacceptable emptiness. "Let's go! Call the next one."

Meanwhile, out the corner of her eye, Dana saw Rios hesitate before resuming his seat, as if he'd just noticed his bench companions for the first time. Street people, three prostitutes and two disheveled, grimy men. Rios was a small cut above them with his clean, discount store clothing and a decent haircut. A sense of neatness. She wondered at this. The transit police usually didn't arrest people like Rios for jumping the subway turnstile. Instead, they issued a ticket directing the accused to appear in court to answer a charge of theft of services, a low-level misdemeanor. On the books, the maximum sentence was six months, but standard practice was to impose a fine.

"People against Velvet Desire," called the clerk.

Two court officers stood ready to escort the red-wigged woman as she slithered upward, giving Rios the extra space he needed on the bench to maintain some distance from the others. "De-zir-*ray*," she corrected the clerk, stumbling toward Kaplan on stiletto heels. The officers exchanged amused looks and took up positions behind her at the defense table to prevent the possibility of an escape through the empty audience section and out the door.

Assistant DA Hargrove had no need to examine the thick stack of carbon paper on this one. Ten years of pross convictions marred Velvet Desire's past. A raid early yesterday morning had sent more than two dozen prostitutes through the system in the last few hours. Chomsky wasn't fond of hookers and always offered them an impossible choice: five days for a guilty plea or an extortionate bail for a not guilty plea. Either way, the punishment was unprofitable for their pimps, who took it out on them when they returned to the street.

Chomsky's tough stance was out of line. Most judges would offer time served, anywhere from twelve to thirty-six hours between arrest and arraignment. But Dana didn't have a hope of changing the judge's mind. Neither did the defendants. At about 7:30 a.m., any prostitutes left over from the raid would stir up a scene in the courtroom, hoping to delay their arraignment until the day judge came on the bench. For now, there was nothing Ms. "De-zir-ray" could do but take what was coming.

Dana listened with one ear while continuing to eye Rios's papers, trying to unfurl the mystery of his arrest.

"Waive the reading of the rights and charges?" asked the clerk.

"So waived," responded Kaplan in between low, fast talk with his client. Velvet wasn't a stranger to Chomsky and knew the game well. Nevertheless, she shouted for effect: "Five days. Sheee-it!"

"Keep it closed," rapped the judge. "An extra day for the next outburst. You have fifteen seconds to give me your plea." He set a timer on his watch. "After that, another day for every fifteen."

Dana flipped up the Rios complaint and examined his yellow sheet underneath. Here was the answer. The transit cops must have recognized him. Rios had a recent conviction for theft of services and another for petit larceny. He was a small-time thief. He also used different aliases for each arrest. No wonder he hadn't responded immediately when his case was called. "Rios" might not be his name at all.

"That's bullshit," spat the large purple mouth. For all her legal experience, Velvet hadn't wised up. Seth pumped his hands up and down and whispered hoarsely, hoping to stem the overflow.

"Okay. That's six days. You don't like it? Get out of the business." Chomsky turned to ADA Hargrove. "Hear the People on bail."

Dana looked up. The judge didn't want a speech, and in fact, anything more than a few words would aggravate him further.

"The People recommend $250," she said simply.

"Mr. Kaplan?"

"My client has community ties and isn't a flight risk…"

The court officers snickered.

"Bail set at $1,500, cash or insurance company bond." The judge lifted the gavel.

"One moment, Your Honor," said Kaplan with an ear open to his rasping client. "Ms. Desire wishes to enter a plea of guilty to the charge."

Stifling a grin, Judge Chomsky flew into the necessary litany to assure the legality of the plea. Dana shut her ears to the proceedings and concentrated on the Rios police report. In the box for "personal property," the arresting officer had written "$3,300 cash, bank papers." Dana reached the logical conclusion: poverty was no excuse for the defendant's larcenous behavior.

With a crack of the gavel, Judge Chomsky imposed sentence.

"Seven days. That ain't the deal!"

"Go back to school, Ms. Desire. Six plus one. The bail application took fifteen seconds."

Velvet turned to her lawyer and screamed demands while Seth tried to convince her that the judge wouldn't allow her to withdraw the guilty plea. The court officers stood at the ready.

"Let's go," demanded Chomsky, cracking the gavel again. He stood, and with a look of disgust, swiped the air with his hand to erase the sight. "Take her out. Court stands in recess. Ten minutes. Don't go anywhere." He descended from his fortress, shrinking into a surprisingly small, gray and ordinary man as he scurried toward the side door, on his way to chambers.

Court officers removed a kicking Velvet Desire while the defense and prosecution exchanged looks. With Velvet gone, a moment of dead silence fell. Dana looked down at the table, now a morass of disorganized papers. At the beginning of her shift, she'd fanned them out like a magician's deck of cards, stretching the overlapping papers straight in a line with just the docket numbers and defendants' names showing. Periodically, a clerk or paralegal from the district attorney's office would enter the courtroom to deliver new papers and take away those already arraigned, challenging Dana's neat organization.

Underneath the line, she'd placed an alphabetically organized row of notes from various assistant district attorneys concerning the most serious crimes or high-profile defendants. "Second call this case," was a frequent message. "I want to appear on it." The ADA's office phone number or whereabouts would be noted. "I'm OT in 52," for example, was code for "on trial" in the courtroom for Part 52 of the Supreme Court.

Of course, it was impossible to predict the exact moment when a particular defendant would be arraigned. There were too many variables. The assigned ADA couldn't appear if the arraignment occurred on graveyard. So, every note included a backup set of specific instructions, including the amount of bail to request, the details of a plea offer, or a directive to refrain from plea bargaining—instructions intended to avert sure disaster committed by a rookie ADA like Hargrove, dizzy with fatigue and naïve with inexperience.

Eyeing the jumble, Dana smoothed her crown back down to the nape of her neck where a gold barrette neatly gathered her shoulder-length dark hair, shiny and thick as mink. She sat and quickly reorganized the papers, assuring herself in the process that nothing had been missed. Then she rose onto her low heels, the comfortable shoes she reserved for night court. Otherwise, her manner of dress was the same as daytime office wear—a gray, business skirt suit. She never wore a pantsuit, unlike some of the female Legal Aid attorneys she'd seen.

Dana pulled together the lapels of her jacket, buttoned it, and turned to go. There was just enough time to splash cold water on her face, among other things, in the ladies' room.

"Wait." Seth stopped her.

"I have to go."

"Just a sec. What are you looking for in the Rios case?"

"The farebeat? He has to plead to the charge."

"Yeah, but you're recommending a fine, right? How much?"

Dana lowered her brow and peered at her adversary like he'd just landed from Mars. "Sure, I'll recommend a fine. You know me, Seth. I just love to hear myself talk. I mean, where else can I be such an effective advocate?"

Seth grinned. "Don't be so sure about the judge. Even Chomsky can see that Rios isn't your common street punk."

"If the judge is giving prostitutes five days, he's giving time to a farebeat with a record." Both attorneys turned, as if on cue, to regard the defendant, now reestablished on the bench in a cross-armed, sideways slump with his eyes closed.

"You know," said Dana pensively, "if the judge wants to give your guy a few days, it's all right with me."

"Are you serious? He's been locked up since noon. No farebeat should get more than a fine."

"I don't know…"

"Besides, not that you care, but he didn't do it. Says he dropped his token, it was rolling away, and he had to jump the turnstile to get it."

Dana raised her shapely eyebrows. "He told you all that, back in the pens? Without the interpreter? I'm impressed."

"He was straight with me."

"I mean, I'm impressed with your Spanish, not your client."

"I understand a lot more than I speak."

"So, he dropped his token. Very original."

"I believe him."

Seth's earnest expression said it all. He didn't often admit to a belief in his clients, so Dana took him at his word. He had spoken with Rios. She had not. And while intuition counted for a lot in this business, Dana's intuition had been known to fail her at moments when she really needed it. In her nine months at the DA's office, many people—witnesses, cops, defendants—had lied to her, and had lied well. Now she was more inclined to stick to the record and form her beliefs about an individual based on his past habits instead of the words out of his mouth.

"He has a record," she declared. "He's a thief and a liar. Why do you think he was arrested? The cops recognized him. Listen, I've got to go..." She picked up her purse and stepped away from the table.

"If the judge wants more than time served, we're taking it to trial."

Dana halted and swung around to face him. A snappy retort would have been perfect just then, and her tongue might have found one if it weren't for Judge Chomsky, who banged open the side door and strode up to the bench. "All rise," intoned the clerk.

"Damn it, Seth," she hissed under her breath. "Now I have to hold it in."

"That weren't no ten minutes," he quipped with a shrug of apology and a parenthetical grin, almost making up for her lost break.

As the judge took his seat, a small, middle-aged woman entered the courtroom, scurried through the rows of empty pews and pushed through the swinging gate into the section reserved for the participants. Out of breath, she panted in a Spanish accent and glanced up at the judge but said nothing to explain her disappearance twenty minutes ago.

Judge Chomsky pointed to the court clerk. "Call that case with the interpreter."

This time Rios jumped to his feet when the name was called. Before he could reach the defense table, Kaplan spoke. "May we approach, Your Honor?" He was angling for a private, off-the-record conference at the bench to learn the judge's position on sentencing.

"Hold it," snapped Chomsky, thrusting out a hand. "There's nothing to talk about. Ten days, take it or leave it."

Dana's jaw dropped. Tough, even for Chomsky.

"Your Honor—" Seth began, in protest.

"The man got nothing for the other two raps. It's time to do some time Mr. Rios, or whatever your name is. Clean up your act!" The color rose in the judge's pallid cheeks as he geared up for a lecture. He always delivered one or two during his eight-hour shift, although Dana never knew when they were coming or which defendants would inspire them. Oddly, Chomsky more often unleashed his fury against the small-time thieves and street dealers than the kidnappers, rapists and murderers, for whom he clothed his tongue in solemnity. The serious criminals were beyond his help and therefore unworthy of his pearls of wisdom.

The Spanish interpreter rattled every word into Rios's open ear. He stood mute behind black, emotionless eyes, protected by an invisible, impermeable wall against the judge's harsh attention. His figure was so still, the air around him seemed to vibrate. Who was Bernardo Rios? Decidedly not a New Yorker. His past had trained his response, or lack of it, as he listened intently to the translation of Chomsky's ranting with an unreadable expression. Behind that mask lay any number of possibilities: acceptance, worry, fear, indifference, or seething rage.

"You're a liar and a cheat, Rios. Two thefts this year. How many others did you get away with? Do a few days at Rikers and see how you feel then! Money in your pocket and still won't buy a token. In this great city people who barely make it are still paying the fare. Nobody gets a free ride, Rios. Who needs you? Go back to Panama." The judge held up and slapped the case papers with the back of his hand. "Or is it Peru or Colombia?"

Dana looked at the defendant's yellow sheet again, and sure enough, Rios had given the police a different native country each time he was arrested. "You're a liar and a cheat. I don't want you in my courtroom again. Do your time and learn a lesson and go home. We don't put up with this kind of crap here!"

The judge paused for breath. The balls of his cheeks and rims of his ears were purple and a thin layer of white foam lined the inside corners of his mouth. "All right. Fifteen seconds. Give me your plea."

Kaplan knew better than to comment on the judge's lecture for fear of spurring a new tirade, aimed at him, not the client. He conferred briefly with Rios in hushed tones through the interpreter. Dana caught only a few words but grasped the understated outrage in Seth's voice. A plea of not guilty could mean an impossibly high bail, enough to lock the door on Rios for the full ten days while awaiting trial. Still, Seth might be able to pressure Dana's office into advancing the case. Almost any other judge would be more lenient. Rios could have his trial in the next day or two and win immediate release, even if convicted.

The trick was to finagle a short adjournment in a system jammed with cases. Dana decided she wouldn't create an obstacle. After all, the outcome seemed fair. She would have recommended a sentence of a couple of days for this defendant—if Chomsky had asked for her opinion.

Rios looked at Kaplan while listening quietly to the interpreter. A smoldering passivity was palpable, a reluctant acquiescence to fate. Within the allotted fifteen seconds, Seth gave his response: "Your Honor, Mr. Rios wishes to enter a plea of not guilty and requests an immediate trial."

Chomsky raised his eyebrows in boredom, his rage sated by his own recent outburst. He turned a blasé eye on ADA Hargrove. "People?"

The judge didn't want to hear it, but Dana needed to make a

record if the People were requesting bail in a farebeat case. A man with a larceny record who regularly lied to the police and now faced jail time was unlikely to return for trial, argued Dana—unless the court set a significant bail. Figures whirled on a roulette wheel in her head, the blurred numbers reflecting a world of differing opinions about the value of her words. The ball landed uncertainly in a slot. "The People recommend a bail of $1,000."

Chomsky raised his eyebrows again, whether in disdain or surprise, Dana couldn't be sure. He turned to her adversary. "Counselor?"

"That's an outrageous amount!" spurted Kaplan, clenching his fists in midair. Dana took no personal offense at his keenly felt sense of injustice. While some defense attorneys put on a show for every defendant, Seth was choosy and therefore genuine. "Mr. Rios was falsely accused. He bought a token, it slipped out of his hand and rolled under the turnstile..."

"All right, all right," Chomsky muttered, turning his head to the side and drumming his fingers.

"My client should be released on his own recognizance. He wants to return to court and testify..."

"Wants to tell his story, does he? A fine story indeed, but I don't buy it. Bail is set at $1,500."

"That's unconscionable! It's..."

"Watch it, counselor."

"Your Honor, he can't pay it. He'll stay locked up before he's found guilty of anything. At the very least, the court should order the DA to release my client's funds. A sum of money was seized from him at his arrest."

The judge turned to the prosecutor. "Your office will be forfeiting that cash, right Miss Hargrove?"

Dana was taken off guard. Forfeiture? She knew little about the law but assumed nothing could be forfeited unless related somehow to the defendant's crime. Nothing in her papers suggested the $3,300 was related to any crime, much less farebeat. "Well, Your Honor, certainly I'll discuss it with the attorneys in forfeiture. I'd request that the cash be held until then."

"Listen to me, Miss ADA." The judge turned a squinting eye on her. "You take *this* back to your forfeiture unit! The man here has $3,300 and won't pay his fare. Deliberately won't pay, even though he has enough for a ten-year supply of tokens. It proves his intent. It's a forfeitable instrumentality of crime. Take that back to your office and thank me for doing your work."

Dana had barely registered this far-fetched theory when the judge said, "Enough of this. Bail is set at $1,500." He turned to the clerk. "Call the next case."

"Judge," interjected Kaplan. "We need a trial date. Later today or tomorrow at the latest..."

"May 18. Let's go."

"That's a month from now."

"Listen, Mr. Kaplan, I know your game, and don't think I don't. 'Give me a trial, give me a trial.' Come clean and tell us what you really want! Your guy here wants to wait until to-morrow to plead guilty, after you find a judge who gives fines, not jail sentences. I have news for you, Mr. Kaplan. I won't be a party to your shopping expedition. If you really want a trial, you want motion practice—"

"Mr. Rios waives motions—"

"—if you're serious about a trial that is. This case is adjourned for defendant's motion papers, May 18th. You want it on earlier? Talk to the DA and see if you can get it advanced. May 18. Next case. Let's go!"

2 » *FAREBEAT*

LATER THE SAME day, at three o'clock, Dana walked into her office in Trial Bureau 90. On her desk she found the expected stack of clean manila folders enclosing the new cases her bureau chief had assigned to her. All were misdemeanors of course, since she wouldn't be graduating to felonies for another year.

A familiar name jumped out from the top folder: Bernardo Rios. Next to it lay a messy pile of pink telephone slips, the most recent one taken at 2:45 p.m., bearing Seth Kaplan's name and the message: "Re: Trial, B. Rios." She picked up the scrap of paper, fell into her chair, and burst out laughing.

If there'd been anyone around to hear, she might have restrained herself. She'd closed the office door behind her, relishing the privacy. It was such a rare thing. Her three officemates, fellow rookies, were across the street in court or elsewhere, leaving behind the relics of their existence. Tom's desk was buried under a mountain of paper, decorated with half-full Styrofoam cups and soda cans. Ellen's desk was freakishly dusted and annoyingly bare except for the Rolodex and framed photographs of her nieces and fiancé. Jared's desk, like Dana's, held a reasonable amount of clutter, something between the two extremes.

Maybe it was haziness from lack of sleep, but Dana found it hilariously funny to see the Rios case again. In the seemingly random assignment system (which she still didn't quite understand), most of the misdemeanors she'd arraigned during the night were destined for other bureaus. Only six of them, a small fraction, wound up on her desk after each of her graveyard shifts. Just her luck to get a ridiculous farebeat case that had consumed more time and energy last night than any of the serious cases she'd arraigned, a murder and three armed robberies.

Seth was driven, to be sure. He wanted this trial bad enough to miss a half day of catch-up sleep so he could call the DA's office, find out the assigned ADA and start badgering. In this respect they were pressed from the same mold. Like Seth, Dana shouldn't even be at work; she was entitled to a full day off to recuperate from graveyard.

When she'd gotten home at 8:30 that morning, she ate a piece of toast and fell into bed fully clothed to wrestle through four hours of fitful sleep. Even with the curtains closed, her apartment was filled with light and the sound of morning traffic filtering up from the street, contributing to a string of lifelike dreams in half sleep.

Drug dealers, pick pockets and pimps circled the bed, offering colorful insults of her business attire as she surveyed the courtroom and court officers, looking for reassurance that, *no they can't hurt me.* In a matter of seconds, the courtroom became a city sidewalk, her skirt suddenly molten, squeezing her thighs into skin-tight jeans, transforming her into one of them, jawing natural about the best crack, the best con, comparing neighborhoods, Times Square, the alphabets, the Bowery, Spanish Harlem, Hell's Kitchen. A hard-talking thug pierced her with sharp glints of eyes, prompting a flash of paranoia and a thought, *What's behind that grin on his face? What did I ever do to him, except recommend serious time?*

Her eyes shot open. She sat up in bed, heart beating wildly, blouse and skirt crumpled and sweaty. A few minutes were needed to reestablish her professional identity apart from the characters lurking in her tiny studio apartment—with "sleeping alcove"—in the Village on a weekday afternoon.

Professional identity, such as it was. Awaiting her at the office was a file cabinet stuffed with thin manila folders, more than two hundred misdemeanor cases bearing her name. Was she really a lawyer? She couldn't have fathomed this vision a year ago, back in law school. A more apt job title might be Chaos Manager, entrusted with passing seat-of-the-pants judgments on little lives, seriatim, without time for reflection.

That last thought was unfair. Never had she objectified the defendants or their victims, caught in a web of petty crime. They weren't so terribly different from her in the basic animal ways of human beings. Everyone shared the honor of belonging to this great mess of humanity and inhumanity composing the city. And so, she'd given up her day off and was back in the office, thinking she could put in a couple of hours at least and get good and tired for a proper eight (or ten) hours of sleep that night.

For just another moment, she sat staring at the pink message slip in her hand, feeling the building urgency of a call to action. 2:45. She'd just missed Seth's call. She didn't really mind this assignment to the Rios case. It would be her fourth trial, a simple bench trial, just the cop and Rios testifying, another chance to practice direct and cross-examination.

Nor would she resist Seth's push for an immediate trial, tomorrow if possible. She was a person who set her mind to things and got them done. A million obstacles were in the way, and sometimes they could be overcome, sometimes not. She'd come to respect the single overriding principle governing the life of a misdemeanor prosecution: the longer the delay, the more bollixed it would become.

She riffled through the remaining pink message slips and smiled. Two earlier messages from Seth, 1:15 and 1:57. Besides these, she had three or four messages about other cases, and one more "re: B. Rios," from an "ADA Reichert." Dana didn't recognize the name—not unusual in an office of more than four hundred fifty attorneys, many of them in offices across the street, in the Criminal Court building. She pulled out her office directory and found Reichert, listed as "Senior Trial Counsel, Financial Crimes Bureau." Immediately, Rios's $3,300 cash came to mind. But, no, this kind of small change would be of no interest to a senior ADA handling big financial swindles. Reichert's phone call remained a mystery.

She opened the manila folder, just to make sure she hadn't missed anything. No new secrets were revealed in the same few pages she'd seen at four in the morning, now two-hole punched at the top and inserted through a metal fastener in the manila folder labeled with the docket number, defendant's name, and "ADA D. Hargrove."

She was reminded of the property taken from the defendant and decided she wanted to see this evidence now, before the trial, not as she was walking into the courtroom. If the "bank papers" revealed money, she could use it on cross-examination: *Isn't it true, Mr. Rios, you have ten grand in the bank but couldn't spare a buck for a token?*

Or the opposite could be true. Maybe Rios had been on the way to the bank to make an overdue loan payment, $3,300 exact, and couldn't afford the fare. Either way, she had to see the bank papers to avoid last minute surprises.

Quickly, Dana jotted the docket number and defendant's name on a piece of scratch paper and walked to the door. Just outside, in a partitioned cubicle, sat Eric Trumble, the TPA she shared with her three officemates. Eric's job as Trial Preparation Assistant was to retrieve and organize documents and evidence, contact witnesses, and anything else needed for trial. As a practical matter, Dana ended up doing most of this work herself.

There was only so much one TPA could do when his time was divided among four attorneys.

Eric's flaxen head popped up at the first sign of Dana. For several months now, she'd suspected he had a crush on her. Twenty-two and fresh out of college, he was four years her junior. He'd taken the job at the DA's office to "get the inside story" on the criminal justice system. Immersed in the milieu, he emulated the cops and the grittier ADAs by peppering his speech with foul words—a stilted sound at odds with his innocent fair looks and suburban upbringing. Eric's plan was to decide along the way whether he wanted to go to law school. "Smart move," Dana and her cohorts would joke. "After a year in this place, no sane person would ever want to be a lawyer!" But Eric wasn't daunted. Most days, he could be seen at his desk during lunch break, consuming law school catalogs along with his bag lunch.

"Thanks for that stuff on my desk, Eric." She was well aware that his little elf hands were responsible for collecting the manila folders and phone messages from her box in the reception area and personally delivering them.

"Sure, no problem." His attempt at an offhand air was transparent.

"I have a defendant who was arrested yesterday at noon, and I arraigned him at four in the morning. Do you think his belongings are at Police Plaza?"

Here was Eric's chance to impress Dana with his area of expertise. He wrinkled his baby-soft brow and cleared his throat to add effect. "Depends on the precinct. Some of them really drag their asses getting the shit downtown. It can take forty-eight hours."

"This is a transit case."

"Pretty good chance it's there. You need something?"

"Yeah, kind of right now. If you could. I have to see some papers, then you'll have to lock them in the bureau safe for the night."

Eric jumped up. "Okay, I mean sure. Oh, fuck, sorry. I can't. I'm doing something for Denzel. He's OT tomorrow."

"Mine is on for trial tomorrow too."

"But Denz has a case that's *really* going forward. Thirty-thirty time is up." Eric was referring to the speedy trial section of the Criminal Procedure Law. There was OT, and then there was real OT, when the prosecutor had to act *now* or face dismissal.

"You know I'd go to Police Plaza if I could." The rules of evidence prohibited it. If Dana checked out the property and a question ever arose about the handling of evidence, she would become a witness at trial and taken off the case. Not good. This way, Eric would be the witness for the chain of custody.

He looked at her with his unique blend of adoration, intensity and confusion, finally muttering, "Fuck it," under his breath. Louder, he said, "Hell, the Plaza closes at five, so your thing has to be done now. I can do Denzel's stuff when I get back. I just have to organize these policy slips." He tipped his head toward the desk to indicate a mound of small paper slips from Jared's gambling case, a prosecution involving a numbers joint.

"Eric, you're a life saver." Dana touched his shoulder and smiled broadly—a genuine smile. She loathed batting eyelashes and coquetry, or even asexual greasiness. "Just get the bank records, okay? There's cash too, but don't bring that."

"Right."

"Thanks. That's my phone."

She dashed to get it. Rookies didn't merit a private secretary to screen calls. After the fourth ring, the receptionist down the hall would pick up and write one of those pink message slips. Dana could answer the phone now, blind, or let it roll and take a walk later to collect the message—a waste of time. In her ideal science fiction world, she would have the ability to intuit the caller's identity before answering. Or maybe the name could flash on a little screen when the phone rang?

Receiver to ear, in the split second before saying, "ADA Hargrove," she wondered if it was Kaplan or Reichert. She wasn't quite ready to return her calls, but she wasn't a person to hide from anyone.

"Hold the line for Mr. Reichert," said a female voice. Hold the line? She hated that. He wasn't from the executive wing or even a bureau chief, just a senior trial counsel. She dropped into her chair and swiveled, the receiver shoved between shoulder and chin while she inspected a painful, broken fingernail. Waited a full ten seconds. Finally, the man came on the line.

"Dana Hargrove?" The voice was deep in a forced, unnatural way.

"Speaking."

"You got my note?"

"Sure. You called about an hour ago? I just got your message."

"No, last night. You were in arraignments, weren't you?"

"Yes, but—"

"It was you then. You completely botched the Rios case. Didn't you see the note?"

"No. You brought one down? I'm sure it wasn't there."

"I had it sent down."

Had it sent. Of course. He was the type to *send* it down.

Not hearing her thoughts, he continued. "They tell me the case was adjourned for defense motions. Are you responsible for that?"

"Sure. There wasn't any reason to deal it away, and he wouldn't plead."

"Completely ignored my instructions! The case should've been dismissed and his property returned to him."

"Dismissed? He has a record. And the judge thought the forfeiture unit would be interested in the cash."

"Forfeiture? What does the judge know about this?" For a moment, panic infected Reichert's voice, but he recovered in the next heartbeat. "Oh. The farebeat. He thought we could forfeit cash in a farebeat? Who was the judge? Don't tell me. I know. Had to be Chomsky."

"Yes, but—"

"Chomsky. Judge, jury and executioner. He couldn't tell the forfeiture law from the tax code. You and Chomsky royally screwed up! I'm taking the case back."

Dana was on the verge of ignoring matters of rank. She'd taken enough. Who was he anyway? No more than a senior trial counsel, which meant he'd been a rookie just like her five or six years ago. "That won't be necessary," she responded coldly. "It's on for trial tomorrow. I can handle it."

"On for trial? There's no way you're gonna try this."

"Maybe if you'd just tell me what this is about—"

"It's over your head. There's an ongoing investigation. Something big. Even that's saying too much. I've put in a call to McBride about this. He's out of the office right now, but when he gets back we'll straighten it out. Just don't do anything on the case until I get the folder from you."

This last instruction was followed by an awkward silence in which Reichert seemed to get in touch with his long-submerged sense of etiquette. Finally, the surprising words, "Thank you," tumbled from his mouth. He hung up.

So. She wasn't to be entrusted with even the gist of this "big" investigation. So be it. She didn't intend to follow his orders. He wasn't her boss. If her bureau chief, Patrick McBride, yanked the case, that was another matter. For now, she still considered herself assigned.

The phone rang again almost immediately. "ADA Hargrove," she answered, still seething.

"Dana. It's Seth Kaplan."

"Where's Eric?" came another male voice from the door behind her. "He's supposed to be doing something for me."

"Hold on, Seth." Dana put her hand on the mouthpiece and swiveled around to see Jared—tie askew, jacket unbuttoned—striding through the door, the Penal Code and manila folders stuffed under one arm. "Hi, Denz. I'll explain in a minute."

"Sorry. I didn't see you were on the phone." Displaying the genesis of his nickname, Jared stretched his ample mouth across large white teeth in a sheepishly sexy grin. The resemblance to actor Denzel Washington was striking.

Dana turned back to her adversary. "You put me to shame, Seth. You beat me to work by almost two hours."

"Couldn't sleep."

"Me neither." There was unintentional intimacy in this confession. She laughed to cover her embarrassment. "I'll never get used to graveyard. So, what's up? I guess I don't have to ask. Your guy decided he wants to save the People some expense. Plead guilty and do his time."

"Fat chance. We're still going to trial, now or sooner. How's tomorrow?"

"I'm filling out the notification for the arresting officer as we speak. Let's see. What's his name? Margate." She grabbed a form and started to fill in the officer's name, badge number, precinct, and the time he was needed for trial prep in her office. If Eric called the notifications desk when he got back, there was a good chance Margate would receive the order in time to appear for trial tomorrow.

"Good. I'll put in the order to produce Rios. We just need a part."

"No small problem."

"That's where I was hoping you could help. You know there isn't a court clerk who would help a Legal Aid attorney."

"Sob, sob."

"You know it to be true."

"And we have it so easy."

"You have the power of the State behind you."

"I'm usually ignored."

"Hmm...I haven't noticed that."

"Okay, so I'm important and powerful. I do know a calendar clerk who owes me a favor."

"Now it comes out."

"And why should I use up a perfectly good favor on this case?"

"Pretty please?"

"Since you asked nicely. But you'd better come along. With two of us there and our little story about Chomsky it'll help."

"Okay. When and where?"

"Meet me at the AP-6 clerk's office at 5:45. We'll catch him right before he gets off work. There'll be less traffic."

"Okay. I have to send in the order to produce before five. Can we bank on this?"

"As much as you can bank on anything in criminal court."

"All right. I'm having him produced in AP-6 for tomorrow. See you in a while."

Dana replaced the receiver and looked across the room into Denzel's warm brown eyes, now with a slightly worried cast as he played percussion with two pencils on an empty square of desk. Seth and Jared...good looking, smart men everywhere, and all she had was this, the job from hell.

"I stole Eric," she confessed.

"Dana, how could you do that to me? I'm OT tomorrow and no time to prepare. I was on calendar all day."

"I'm sorry. It's just for a little while. He's running an errand to Police Plaza. I would have gone myself, but you know I can't check out the evidence."

"I just love looking like a fool in court. Love it—"

"He'll be back to finish your stuff. He swears! You know Eric."

" —a fool."

"Just do your Dr. Chandler tomorrow."

"Right."

"It's all an act. Speaking of our good friend, here he is. That was quick."

Still panting, Eric trotted up to her desk. "Faster than a speeding bullet." He pulled a small brown envelope from his pocket and dropped it on her desk. "Here's the goods. Hi, Denz. I'm more than halfway through those slips."

"Okay. I forgive you. I know Ms. Hargrove here distracted you." Jared suppressed a smile, not very well. Dana remembered he was the first to notice, months ago, when Eric turned sweet on her. "But halfway isn't gonna help a hell of a lot."

"Don't worry, Denz. I'm on it. I'll stay late if I have to."

In the middle of this, Mary Poppins walked in soundlessly and rolled her eyes at the three of them with her own peculiar unreadable look, either disdain or commiseration. Unlike Jared's nickname, Ellen's was spoken behind her back and possibly still unknown to her. She tiptoed to the desk, lowered her crisply-suited petite self into the chair and launched into her usual routine. Her habit was to scurry through the business of the day on mouse feet, oblivious to the rest of them, battling chaos with quiet, compulsive organization.

Dana checked her watch. A quarter past four. Ellen must have just finished the day shift in arraignments, and any minute now Tom would return from wherever he was, and their office would become a zoo again. Dana remembered he was likely OT, finally, on that assault case he'd been obsessed with, to the distraction of his officemates.

"Here, Eric," said Dana, picking up the notification form. She glanced at Jared and pulled back. "Never mind. I'll call the notification desk and copy these bank records myself so you can get back to the gambling case."

"You've proved yourself," said Jared. "I don't hate you any-more."

"But, Eric," she added, as the TPA was making his way to the door, "you'll have to put these records in the bureau safe later. And if my cop shows up tomorrow for trial, can you get the stuff out of the safe and hand it to him? That way we keep the chain clean."

"Sure thing."

On his way out the door, Eric brushed shoulders with Tom on his way in. Dana's third officemate was noticeably sullen and bedraggled. Mary Poppins raised her head and rolled her eyes at him with a quick, flat-lined smile, as Dana lifted a hand in the air and Jared asked, "How'd it go?"

The question wasn't necessary. Everyone knew. Tom shook his head and dumped a stuffed accordion folder on his desk.

"Acquittal?"

"Legal Aid had a field day with my witnesses," said Tom. "First, my complaining witness has to admit on cross that he had it in for the defendant. I mean, he looked like a fucking maniac the way he was talking about him. Then it turns out my cop is a sadistic sonuvabitch sitting back and watching them pummel each other before he tries to break it up. After all that, he arrests the wrong guy. Should've arrested the CW, even though he's the one got hurt. Next to him, the defendant looks like an angel. He gets on the witness stand and says so sweetly the CW started it. I had nothing on him for cross." Tom shook his head again, picked up one of his aging soda cans and took a swig.

Even Mary Poppins couldn't remain oblivious to this lament. She gave him an extra sympathetic eye roll, and along with Jared and Dana, offered words of condolence. Acquittals were common in the Land of Misdemeanors, not always because the young prosecutors lacked skill. Not many cases went to trial—most defendants pled guilty and took their meager punishments—and only a few of the trial cases were solid, like those against career criminals who were facing the maximum time, a year in jail. The rest of the cases were dogs, involving unreliable scuzzball witnesses, bad police work, or stale or missing evidence.

The four officemates fell into their individual worlds within the cramped space, the air buzzing with one-sided phone conversations, the metallic bang of file drawers, the rustling of paper. Dana applied her acquired skill of tuning out her surroundings and heard only the whirring of her own thoughts. After calling the notifications desk about Officer Margate, she pulled out the contents of the evidence envelope Eric had delivered.

Inside were eleven pieces of pink and yellow carbon paper, all customer copies of bank slips for deposits made on April 20, the day Rios was arrested. Each one from a different bank, and each with a handwritten figure in the box for cash. Large amounts, $5,700, $7,200, $6,700, on and on, no cents. One of the slips had the preprinted name "Bernardo Rios," six others had just as many different Spanish names, and the remaining four had no name at all. Maybe the blank ones were from new accounts, before individual deposit slips had been printed with name and address, and the others... Dana tried to think of a reason why a normal, law-abiding person might want only a name printed on the form without an address.

On a pocket calculator, she figured the total. $72,700, more than double the salary she would make this year, her first in the DA's office.

The largest single amount was $8,500, written on a ticket with the name "Luz Melendez" and deposited into an account at First City Financial. The address of the branch was printed on the slip. Melanie's.

The coincidence flew up to greet her. One of the pink

telephone messages on her desk was from Melanie, and she needed to return the call. They'd left things open about Saturday night.

Without further reflection, Dana picked up the phone and dialed Melanie's direct office line, allowing a thought to play in the back of her mind. Perhaps she could ask a favor of her best friend, her ex-college roomie. It was nearly five o'clock and the bank was closed to customers, but Melanie would be there. Two rings, and she picked up. "Melanie Avendaño."

"Hi, Melly."

"Dana. How are you?" She sounded at once surprised and distracted. Had she forgotten that she'd left a message to call?

"Not too bad considering I've had only four hours of sleep since Tuesday night."

"You poor thing. Will you be rested up by Saturday?"

"You still want me?"

"Sure, sure." Still distracted, almost hesitant.

"If Saturday isn't good for you…"

"No, of course it is." The voice came awake. "It'll be just the three of us, unless you want to bring someone along. Whatever happened to that acting student you were seeing—your sister's friend?"

The question proved that Melanie's brain was elsewhere. A month ago, Dana's younger sister Cheryl had arranged a date for her with a boy, a fellow classmate of Cheryl's from the American Academy of Acting. "Not for me, but maybe for you," Cheryl explained beforehand. The two sisters had distinct personalities and tastes, so Dana gave it an honest try. After two dates, the experiment ended in disaster, the details of which she'd fully disclosed to Melanie. "I sure don't want to go out with him again after the last time. You remember."

"Oh, yeah. We'll be looking for his name in lights. He was kind of into himself, wasn't he?"

"Putting it mildly."

"Okay. Noel and I want to see you on your lovely lonesome then. Is seven all right?"

"Fine. Can I bring something?"

"Don't bother. I'll cook something simple. Gotta go now, I have a ton of work and I haven't been able to focus all day…"

"Just one thing—"

"…you know how it is. One of those days when nothing gets done. What was that? I cut you off."

Dana paused, suddenly mindful of the pressures on Melly, but she pushed her hesitation aside. They were close enough to know that one was always ready and willing to lend a hand for the other. She only needed to ask. "I have a trial tomorrow and I was hoping you'd be able to look up some account records for me."

"Sure. But I have to cover myself with a subpoena."

"I'll get a judge to sign one tomorrow. What I need is the recent activity and the balance in a certain account." She read off the name and number. "The other thing I need is a little more difficult. A big chunk of cash was deposited yesterday morning. $8,500. Since it was so much, I thought maybe the teller would remember the person who made the deposit."

"First I have to find the teller. There were six windows open yesterday morning."

"So, it's impossible?"

"Not really. I just have to look at the tellers' cash sheets. The only problem would be if there was more than one deposit for $8,500."

"That seems pretty unlikely."

"More likely than you'd think. Anyway, none of this is too difficult. But don't you already know Luz Melendez? Isn't that your defendant?"

"That's the account name, but I think someone else deposited the money. I'm hoping the teller can remember the person, what he or she looks like."

"What is this, dirty money of some kind?"

"I don't know what it is, and if I did, I wouldn't be allowed to tell you."

"Oh, come on! You can't trust your best friend?"

Dana remembered her own reaction to Reichert's closed lips just an hour ago. But that was different, wasn't it? She and Reichert had taken the same oath, were required to abide by the same ethical code, and as colleagues, should be able to trust each other with investigative secrets. "You know I don't mean it that way. I have to play by the rules or it's my neck."

Melanie sighed, then laughed, sounding more like herself, breezy and warm. "I love you, Dana! Always taking everything so seriously. I wouldn't upset your rules. Listen, I've got to finish some work right now and half the tellers aren't here anyway, so I won't be able to finish this until maybe nine or ten tomorrow. Won't that mess up your trial? You'll be in court by then."

"If only things worked that smoothly around here. I seriously doubt I'll be starting the trial at ten. If I'm not in my office when you're done, you can leave a message and I'll call you from wherever I am."

"Okay. Don't forget my subpoena!"

"Don't worry." Dana said thank you and goodbye, determined to return this favor at the earliest opportunity and grateful to have a rare best friend, a person better than every fleeting acquaintance combined. And then she checked her watch, mindful of the minutes ticking off toward 5:45.

"Now *I'm* impressed," said Seth as they left the AP-6 clerk's office. Their footsteps echoed in the nearly empty corridor of the Criminal Court building as they walked through the residual stench and litter of cigarette-smoking lawyers and defendants, most of them gone for the night. "All you had to do is snap your fingers and say, 'roll over.' Do you have all the clerks under your thumb like that?"

She glanced at him sidelong and smiled mysteriously.

"Come on and spill it."

"It was really very easy. I came to his defense when a judge reamed him out over a mistake in the calendar. He removed a case when he shouldn't have. The judge had ordered the last-minute add on. The defendant was produced and waiting in lockup, but the clerk removed the case and the defendant was sent back. It was all my fault because I had an outdated calendar and I convinced him there was a mistake. Really, all I did was admit my error to the court and took the heat for him."

"So even prosecutors can make mistakes?" Seth's eyes were devious.

"Yes, but we always immediately atone for them. That's why we're the good guys."

They pushed through the revolving door, Dana ahead of Seth, and paused together at the top of the steps. "Someday we'll have to discuss this 'good guys/bad guys' concept of yours over a drink," he suggested. "That is, if good guys ever go for drinks."

"Everything in moderation."

"All right. I won't buy you more than one-point-five cocktails. But it's impossible right now. I think I'd fall asleep before your eyes."

"If I didn't fall asleep first."

"Which way are you going?"

"Up to Canal to take the subway."

"I'm going the other way. See you in the morning."

Dana waved and lilted off with a spring in her step, wondering at her excitement over Seth's almost-invitation. Something about flirting with a defense attorney seemed slightly treasonous, although she could think of no obvious reason. Would a subconscious infatuation cause her to throw the case tomorrow? For heaven sakes, it was just a farebeat! And she had enough sense not to allow her personal desires influence her professional judgment.

The Rios folder, containing photocopies of the bank deposit tickets, was squeezed snugly between the Penal Code and Criminal Procedure Law in her briefcase. Did Seth know about the money? They'd find out what everyone knew tomorrow morning.

3 » YANKED

WHEN MELANIE PICKED up the receiver, she needed a moment to come back. She'd floated through this day in a muddled haze with periods of roiling emotion. Something was forgotten, and Dana's voice served as a reminder. There'd been a dinner invitation.

In the act of remembering, Melanie instantly changed her mind. Perhaps it would be best to cancel.

She wasn't herself and more fully herself than ever before. She refused to be a stereotype. Her conviction on that point required her, in the act of changing her mind, to change it back to the original plan. She would *not* make excuses for herself. Saturday night would be perfectly fine to have a visitor, her best friend at that. There was still a day and a half to recover—or not, if the ultimate fact proved to be what she strongly suspected.

It had started Monday evening with a sudden flash of heat and lightheadedness. Her naturally pink complexion blanched, her honey-colored hair grew damp with sweat. Blackness rushed up to greet her as she dropped to her knees, lowering her head until it passed. Since then, she could think of nothing, concentrate on nothing but the nausea. On Wednesday at lunch, she felt only regret for the salad she'd prepared the night before. Opening the plastic top, an overpowering smell of cucumber hit, sending her running to the bathroom with the dry heaves.

All that on Wednesday, after a negative test result on Tuesday. "Wait seven days and repeat," said the directions. She would wait, maybe, until Friday.

The flu was just as likely in this season of early spring when virulent bugs were hopping. But this was a pat explanation, a feint. She knew. She'd never felt anything like this before.

"Hi, Melly."

"Dana. How are you?" Melanie should have been the recipient of her own, automatic question. Not well, she could have answered. Under the circumstances, it just might be best to cancel.

Reason guided that thought, and emotion immediately reversed it. Oddly, so unexpectedly, the nausea had vanished a full hour before Dana's call. Sitting at her computer, Melanie had been overtaken by another novel sensation, impelling her up from the chair to open the cabinet where she'd affixed a cosmetic mirror inside the door. A brief examination revealed a soft face, an involuntary smile, an ethereal light in her hazel eyes. Her body was fully infused with a woozy elatedness, a sense of universal connectedness and well-being. She laughed out loud at these thoughts, the words she'd chosen. Hokey and hippie! No way could she ever confess anything like this to her levelheaded friend Dana and get away with it.

This nirvana was merely an avoidance of responsibility, the thing she liked least about herself. She and Noel were smarter than the haphazard course they'd charted. "Just this once," became twice or three times, giggling afterward at their little slip-up. They realized full well the significance. Their desire for the consequence had been the silent instigator.

They were living their daily lives knowing exactly what they ultimately wanted. They'd established this common desire four years ago, when they first met.

Noel was the middle child of a huge family, eight brothers

and sisters, mother and father, countless aunts, uncles and cousins, the people he'd left behind in his native country when he set out in pursuit of a new life. Each time he spoke of them, she heard the longing in the throaty sound of their names on his tongue: "Santiago," "Mauricio," "Pilar." She'd met most of them during a brief, tumultuous trip to Cali, shortly after their marriage. But he hadn't been back for three years now, tied as he was to this country by a wife and a business and a lack of leisure time or money for travel.

With all those loved ones left behind, how could she ever be enough for him?

Melanie came from the opposite extreme. She was an only child, well-loved and pampered by a mother and father she adored, raised in a small house that seemed entirely too quiet.

From opposite worlds they'd found each other and shared a dream to create a large family together, as large as they could afford. And that was the problem. The money part of it, and the planning part of it, because they should have waited until Noel's business was on a solid footing and they were living in something better than their overpriced rental, a tiny one-bedroom apartment in Chelsea.

She'd told Noel of her nausea but hadn't yet conveyed her suspicions. She wanted the support of a positive test result to enhance her credibility. Admitting her own guesswork out loud too early might touch on the depth of her desire, and she was afraid of that. The disappointment. If not. She had no fear of Noel's reaction when she was sure enough to tell him. He would be ecstatic. He would shout and sing. He was that kind of man, filled with the joy and passion of life.

The financial part would just have to fall into place somehow. Noel's bookstore had been picking up in the past few months, bringing in a little more profit, another hundred dollars or so a month. And Melanie had gotten a raise (a rather small and disappointing one) along with her recent promotion to the position of assistant manager, business accounts. "Not much more than a glorified teller," she would downplay to others, nevertheless feeling a quiet surge of pride at her achievement. No longer a lowly teller, she now enjoyed her own computer in her own corner cubicle, windowless and cramped, but hers entirely: two white plaster walls, the third and partial fourth walls erected from maroon-fabric-covered, prefab partitions.

With her new title came new responsibilities, and her queasiness of the past few days hadn't helped. A pile of new account applications awaited entry into the computer database, orders for bankcards and checks had to be processed. She was glad for the switch from personal accounts to business accounts and didn't miss dealing with the general public. Now she was part financial planner, part salesperson as she explained the bank's varied services and accounts, tailoring a plan to a particular business need. But, in the evenings after the bank closed its doors, she felt more like a clerk, shuffling through mountains of paperwork and squinting at her computer screen.

At the moment, her immediate responsibilities were suddenly even less attractive, now that Dana had piqued her interest about a dirty account. Dana wasn't giving up any secrets, but there must be something interesting going on or else the DA's office wouldn't be asking for the information. Gladly, she pushed her work aside, postponing it for just a few minutes.

Although Melanie no longer worked with personal checking accounts, she could still access the database and bring up the information on her computer screen. Whether she should share that information with Dana was another matter. First City Financial handled outside requests for account records through its subpoena compliance unit, located in Melanie's building, the main branch. It was against bank regulations to disclose account information without a court-ordered subpoena, and she had no intention of violating the regs, technically anyway. Tomorrow she would give Dana the information over the phone in exchange for a promise to fax the subpoena that day. Once Dana got the chance, she could arrange to have the original subpoena served, and the SC unit would formally comply with a printout from the account.

Melanie was curious, and the excitement prompted a surge of new energy, riding on the coattails of her fading nirvana. She typed the number for the Luz Melendez account into her keyboard, sat back to let the machine "think," and leaned forward again when the information jumped onto the screen. The print was small. Eyes adjusting, she squinted hard.

"Hi, Melanie," came a voice at her back.

Reflexively, Melanie hit "Esc." The screen flickered, and the account information vanished under the First City logo on the home page.

"Did I startle you? I'm sorry." Juliet stood in the "door" of the cubicle, that opening in the half-wall. A coincidence? Not so funny that someone from SC would happen to pass by just when Melanie was stretching the rules. But she had nothing to hide, really. Only her intentions. She was authorized to look at any account she wished.

Melanie shook her head and laughed. "No, not really. Maybe just a little. It's so quiet around here."

"I think everyone left early but us."

"How do they do it? I have a ton of work."

"Me too. We really need more people in SC. The subpoenas keep piling up. I think the feds declared a new war on financial crime. Anyway, that's the reason I need to talk to you. This one." She stepped into the cubicle and handed Melanie a document. "It's for an account you opened up last month. Usually I can dig up the records myself, but they're asking for some unusual things, like did the company rep sign the signature card with his right or left hand? Did he have an accent?"

Melanie gazed at the paper, drawing a blank. "How'm I supposed to remember that kind of stuff?"

"I don't know. Do your best. I just have to warn you. The U.S. Attorney's Office called me about this one. Depending how you respond, they might have to subpoena you to testify."

"In court?"

"Grand jury. Just wanted to give you the heads-up. But it'll probably end up being nothing at all, like most of these."

"Okay, thanks."

"Thank *you*." With a grin and apologetic shrug, Juliet stepped back to the door. "Don't work too hard now!" And she was gone.

What was that tone in Juliet's voice, lingering in the air like stale grease? Nothing but her imagination, Melanie told herself. Still, it was odd to be handed two subpoenas within minutes of each other, both requesting information to help identify depositors. She had no way to judge the significance, only because she had no idea what went on in SC on a daily basis. One thing she did know. The subpoena Juliet had delivered was from the feds, but Dana worked with New York State, so the two of them probably weren't related.

Waiting a moment to be sure Juliet was well down the hall, Melanie typed in the Melendez account number again. At the top of the screen was the account holder's name and address, which was a post office box number. No telephone number was entered. The account had been opened just two months ago, on February 20, 1988, and the current balance was $3,876.58, not a very exciting amount. Thanks a lot, Dana. But then Melanie remembered that her friend still handled only misdemeanors. Maybe this was a misdemeanor amount of dirty money.

"Deposits; Checks; Other Charges; All Recent Activity." Melanie selected the last tab and pressed "Enter." She waited five seconds before the information rolled in, line after line of it until the entire screen was filled. She hit "Enter" for the next screen, let it fill up, and kept hitting "Enter," just to see how far this went, six repetitions in all. A lot of activity for such a new account.

She returned to the first screen and examined it in detail. Every two or three days, large cash deposits were made, $3,500, $5,600, $4,700. "Cash" simply meant that the funds were available immediately, so the deposited items could have included money orders, traveler's checks or bank checks. And the deposits could have been made at any of the twenty-five branches throughout the city. This database didn't contain that kind of detail—to learn more, she'd have to go digging. Curious, she punched in the command for total deposits. Nearly $95,000. Not a bad income for two months.

Daily, the money flowed out in large chunks in the form of checks in round numbers, along with a few small checks in odd amounts of dollars with cents. The data available to her included only the check number, the amount and the date cleared. If she wanted the payees, she'd have to search elsewhere. The total amount paid in checks equaled the total amount in deposits since day one, less the current balance, $3,876.58.

None of this would have been so terribly unusual if it were a business account. Melanie saw this kind of activity in many of the accounts she handled for large cash-generating businesses that made frequent deposits. Restaurants, boutiques, drug stores. Even Noel's store, but not nearly in the amounts here. Wouldn't they be on Easy Street if he brought in this kind of cash?

The Melendez personal checking account could belong to an unsophisticated business owner with a misguided faith in avoiding the IRS and state sales tax consequences. Or an illegal business. One way or another, Dana was most interested in the identity of the depositor, and for that, Melanie needed to check the cash sheets, to find the teller who'd taken the most recent deposit.

She cleared the screen, and just as she stood, the phone rang. Quickly, she sank back into her chair. The change in position had brought on a sudden dizzy spell. It took another two rings for the room to steady itself, and she picked up the receiver.

"Melly?"

"Hello darling."

"I'm closing the store now. I guess you were on the way out the door?"

"Not quite yet."

"You took so long to answer."

"Checking up on me?" There was a wink in her voice.

"Of course I am," he answered. "You're not feeling well." She loved the sound of his voice, a rich tone in a Spanish accent mixed with concern and connection. "How are you?"

"Fine. It's nothing. A little tummy ache, a little dizziness—"

"Now you're dizzy!"

"It's nothing really. But I can't leave this minute."

"I worry, you know."

"I appreciate it. But I'm a big girl. I have a few things yet to do. I'll probably make it home about seven."

"It's been a long day. You've been working since dawn."

"Eight o'clock."

"That's too much work for you. Try to get out of there now."

"Just a few more things. Now that you've called it reminds me, I have some work to do on the new account for Saludos Limitada."

"Don't worry about that. The man can wait one more day. Tomorrow." Like "*catarro*" with rolling "r's."

"It won't take but a few minutes."

"Please, querida."

"All righty. Let me finish up now and I'll be out sooner."

"Okay. See you at home."

"Bye-bye."

She stood again, slowly this time. Good, no dizziness. The task of looking through the tellers' cash sheets would take only five minutes, and it was best to do it now, when most employees were gone and she wouldn't have to explain herself. Then, despite Noel's concerns, she would spend ten minutes on the new Saludos account, enter the data, and rush the order for checks. Proper bookkeeping for the new concession in Noel's store couldn't be established until the Saludos account was up and running.

Now, at the end of her workday and after official bank hours, her husband and best friend took priority—everything else could wait a day or two, even Juliet's request. Off the top of her head, she couldn't remember anything about the account Juliet had been asking about anyway. She'd have to hope it would all come back to her in the middle of the night. As for the backlog of work on her desk, she would come in early the next morning and tackle it.

Out of her cubicle and down the hall, Melanie headed for the drawer under the tellers' counter where the completed cash sheets were stored. Pausing at the counter, she pulled a key ring from her jacket pocket, picked through the jangling mass for the tiny, distinctive key, and opened the drawer.

"Hello there."

She started. Her eyes shot up to behold Roberta Glade, VP, walking toward her from the other side of the counter. Melanie's boss was the personification of First City Financial with her striking, solid appearance in a granite textured skirt suit and lines of silver threading her black, boyish haircut.

"Hi, Roberta."

"Working late?" The woman's tone was pleasant, her smile benevolent.

"A little." Melanie's heart was still up in her throat, tightened against the words.

"I hope part of the reason is the quarterly report?"

"It's almost done."

"That's good. I hate to do this to you—I know I said Monday. But the powers-that-be are breathing down my neck for those stats. I wonder if you could get it to me tomorrow by the end of the day?"

"Sure, I can get it done."

"Good. I'll be able to study it this weekend and report to them on Monday. Thanks for your help."

She was off again, headed toward her office. Melanie had no complaints about her boss. Roberta expected a lot from her employees, but her commands were backed with mutual respect, professionalism and trust. Melanie had earned that trust, and so Roberta couldn't have thought twice about seeing her opening the tellers' drawer. There were a hundred and one reasons why she might be perusing the cash sheets.

The quarterly report flashed through her mind. She would have to make an extra push to finish it in time. Tomorrow was turning out to be a hell of a day.

She spread the six cash sheets on the counter and scanned them quickly, looking for an entry of $8,500. She found it on Dwight Berkeley's sheet. She checked a second time, just to make sure there wasn't another entry like it on another sheet. No, that was it. She would talk to Dwight tomorrow morning, first thing.

At 8:20 the next morning, just after Dana arrived at the office, Patrick McBride knocked once on the doorjamb and strode through the open door. Always on the move, McBride was known to visit the attorneys he supervised as frequently as he summoned them to his own office. Easily, he filled any room with his presence the moment he entered it, never soliciting attention but winning it naturally. There was something about the combination of attributes, his height, the obvious good health and boyish energy in middle age, the russet hair and rugged face. Whenever he spoke, a keen intellect, good judgment, and love of the law were evident. These were the qualities that had earned him the position of bureau chief of the largest trial bureau in the office.

When McBride entered, Dana wasn't alone. Jared sat behind his desk, poring over the evidence for his gambling trial as he waited for his witness, an undercover officer. Tom and Ellen hadn't arrived. With the boss coming through, Dana and Jared perked up in their seats.

"Dana, let's talk," he said as he approached her desk, grabbing and dragging a straight-backed chair along with him. He placed the chair backward in front of her desk and straddled it, placing his forearms on the chair back and leaning toward her. "Yesterday I assigned a farebeat case to you. Bernardo Rios. Ring a bell?"

"Sure. It's right here." Dana's briefcase, not yet unpacked, was on her desk. She pulled out the case folder and placed it in McBride's outstretched hand.

"So, you've already taken a look at it?" he stated more than asked, eyeing her briefcase obliquely as he opened the folder.

"Yes. Judge Chomsky offered ten days, but the defendant wouldn't plead—says he's innocent. Then the judge set a ridiculous amount of bail. So, I had it advanced for trial today."

Her boss flipped through the pages, looking at them as he talked. "So, it's on for today? Fast work. Where? What time?"

"Well, assuming my cop shows up, I'm meeting the defense attorney in AP-6 at ten to answer ready. Last night the clerk added it to the calendar. But you know how it is. Everything depends on the calendar and there's no telling what time the case will be called."

"I see." McBride slapped the folder shut and leveled his gaze at her with a serious, untroubled face, no disapproval in his eyes.

He was not the kind of boss to rule by censure or criticism but fully supported any hard-working rookie with a reasoned approach. "Now that you've done all this good work, I'm afraid I have to take the case away from you. Did you get a call about this from Bruce Reichert?"

"Yes, I did. I told him there were no instructions about this at arraignment, but he claimed he'd sent a note down. He was rather upset."

"Don't take it personally," McBride said with a smile and a wink, as if he could guess her opinion of Reichert and tacitly agreed with it. "I have to hand this case over to Financial Crimes. One of the ADAs there will go to AP-6 today and handle it."

"They're dismissing it, right?"

"I would assume so. That's not to say you've done anything wrong. In fact, everything you've done is a hundred percent right, if this case was just what it appears on the surface. But there's more to it."

"Reichert hinted around but wouldn't tell me anything." Dana heard the crankiness in her tone and instantly regretted it, although McBride's expression betrayed no disparagement.

"It has to do with another investigation. He told you that much, didn't he?"

"That's about it."

"Well, if you'll keep a lid on it, I can tell you only what you've probably already suspected—that this Bernardo Rios is one of their targets. Beyond that, believe it or not, even I don't have much more information." With that, McBride stood, picked the chair up with one hand, twirled it around and placed it to the side of Dana's desk, all in one neat motion. With the other hand, he used the folder to deliver a salute, said "Thanks" to Dana and "Knock 'em dead today" to Jared, and was out the door.

Dana sighed, muttered angrily, and caught her head in her hands, elbows on the desk.

"I'm shocked," said Denzel. "Was that an expletive I heard pass through your lips?"

"'Shucks,' I said. That trial was almost going to be fun."

"A farebeat case is fun?"

"It was different. This Rios had a lot of money on him and money in the bank, and there he was, jumping the turnstile. I wanted to cross-examine him."

"I guess Financial Crimes gets to ask him about the money, not you."

"No. They want to dismiss the case and give his cash back."

"Crazy. Must be something big going on. You think Patrick really doesn't know anything about it?"

"That part seems weird, doesn't it? But this Reichert from FC was tight-lipped, and somehow, I always believe everything Patrick says."

"I know what you mean."

They were interrupted by the unmistakable sound of a police utility belt in motion. Service revolver, night stick, handcuffs, memo book, ticket pad, flashlight, keys, and god-knows-what-else clattered on the waist of a blue-uniformed officer padding through the door on thick-soled rubber shoes. He ignored Dana and headed straight for Jared.

"He's not mine," Jared said, shooting her a look.

"Margate?" Dana asked.

The young officer swung around, a puzzled look on his face. "I got this," he said, holding up a wrinkled piece of paper. He took a step toward her. "Can you call ADA Hargrove for me?"

"*I'm* ADA Hargrove."

"Oh." He paused to let that piece of information sink in. "You're lucky I wasn't on midnights. I mean, I just got this when I came in this morning at eight. Dispatch said the notification for court just came in." He waved the paper. "You never would've got me if I was on midnights, like I was all last week. You're lucky

I'm even here. I just wanted to let you know that. Suits me fine though…"

"I figured you were on days. You arrested this guy on Wednesday at noon."

"Hey, I can use a day in court any time—"

"Well, you're not going to get a day—"

"—fucks up everybody else's schedule, you know. They gotta get someone to cover for me, but what do I care? I always like to come down here and see what all you lawyers are up to. I've got enough arrests to keep alla you busy. But none of 'em ever go to court. Whadda you do with all these cases? They should be coming up for hearings. I could tell you something about all my collars. I remember every one of 'em—"

"Listen," said Dana, standing up. Perhaps a few years in the subway system had affected Officer Margate's hearing.

"Like this one," he kept on, ignoring her. "This is about that Bernardo Rios piece-of-crap, isn't it? I coulda given him a ticket but I arrested him. You know why? He did the same thing, right in front of my eyes a couple weeks ago. Jumps the turnstile, then sees me standing there and pretends he's lookin' for his token. Just his luck I'm there again. And I remember him, you know?" He jabbed his temple three times with a stubby index finger. "I got a memory like a giraffe."

"That's great, officer. Really good work. But I have some bad news for you."

"Whadda you need to know? I can tell you all about it." He reached for the chair at the side of her desk. "Can I just sit?"

"No." The word erupted, louder than she'd planned.

He froze, hand on chair, looking at her. "What-who?" came from his mouth as he swung his head over his shoulder toward Jared and back again, a syllable for each head movement.

"No, I said. I'm sorry about this, but there's no trial today."

"No trial? No hearing either?"

"Nothing. Sorry. The case was just yanked from me." She wasn't about to tell him why.

Margate lifted a suspicious eyebrow. "Wha'd you do to the case? Fuck it up?"

Behind Margate's back, Jared sent Dana a warning look. Keep the lips closed, especially around an officer with a memory like a giraffe. Dana tamed her defensive instincts.

"Yeah. I fucked it up."

"He's gonna get off? That was a good collar!"

"Well, I'm sorry about that. It's a long story, actually, but I know you want to get back to work." She stepped from behind her desk and held a hand out behind the officer, gently coaxing him toward the door.

"I'm in no hurry, like I told you. What about some of my other cases? You have the Littleton case?"

"No." She advanced him forward, one slow step at a time.

"Or Wes Balmoral?"

"No. There's four hundred and fifty attorneys in this office."

"How about Dale Harts?"

"There *is* one thing you can do before you go back to work."

"Sure!" He smiled.

"I need you to return the Rios evidence to Police Plaza. Can you do that for me?"

"Sure thing."

It was her turn to smile. "Eric?" she called, leaning out the door. And she saw the welcome sight, the curly flaxen head, even before her TPA eagerly turned around and stood up, ready to save her.

4 »   FLEA

A NEW SOFTNESS in the spring air encouraged Dana to walk the mile from her apartment in the Village to the Avendaños' apartment in Chelsea. The sun had just set, and the streets were beginning to jump with Saturday night energy, people sharing the excitement of release from winter's tenacious grip.

Dana stepped out briskly in her ankle boots, feeling slim and unrestricted in stirrup pants with a long, loose sweater on top. Turquoise. Along the way, gray twigs of city trees were newly adorned in dresses of pink and white blossoms, and flowers had pushed up in the dirt squares around tree roots, sending the fragrance of new growth into the breeze.

Traveling west on Bleecker Street, Dana maneuvered throngs of NYU students taking a break from their studies. She passed the Village Gate where couples loitered arm-in-arm, then took a right onto MacDougal and headlong into the aroma of falafel, left again and past the Blue Note, over to Sixth Avenue, a basketball game, park benches, the smell of marijuana, crossed the street and took West Fourth, boutique windows, restaurants, an art gallery, then over to Seventh Avenue.

Immersed and surrounded, yet alone, she was just another stranger among her unknown companions of the weekend world, the atomic particles of the city. Warm bodies were close enough to touch, at once available and unavailable, letting their laughter and snippets of conversation suddenly blare in her ear and just as suddenly recede, selfishly snatched away.

The impossibility of belonging would be an easy subject of obsession if she didn't train her mind on something else. She thought of Cheryl. This city held real excitement for Dana's little sister, who might be out in the Village at this moment, laughing and carefree. Cheryl didn't work on Saturday nights, or maybe Dana was mistaken about this; her schedule might have changed, or she could be covering for another waitress at the diner tonight.

Just before going out, Dana had made her weekly phone call and was answered by Cheryl's recorded message. It was always a bit unsettling whenever she couldn't reach Cheryl immediately. The worrying was mostly for the benefit of their parents, who'd asked Dana to keep an eye on little sis. Beyond her obligations as a pseudo-guardian, Dana had to admit she was fascinated with Cheryl's lifestyle, a complete contrast to her own. It was a loose, bohemian existence, a surrender to the senses.

With five and a half years between them, the sisters had never been particularly close. The age difference had removed some of the competitiveness that might otherwise have arisen between two smart, pretty girls. Growing up, Dana had always been introspective, grounded, focused and driven in her academic goals, at times retreating from the outside world. Cheryl remained in the shadow of her older sister academically, but in some ways, was the quicker of the two. In high school, she breezed through her work without studying or taking the extra steps necessary to excel, more interested in boys and social activities, drama club and theater productions.

Cheryl's natural dramatic ability and musicality, a beautiful singing voice, had always been a source of pride in the family. When she turned nineteen, her talents became a source of driving ambition, to the distress of their parents. She dropped out of the private college she'd been attending near their family home in New Jersey and moved to Manhattan where she joined the ranks of Broadway wannabes, waiting tables to scrape by. At first, she'd stayed with Dana, who was in her final year of law school at NYU, but quickly found the monastic lifestyle of a law student such a downer that she'd moved into an apartment with a classmate from acting class.

No luck with Broadway yet, but Cheryl, unlike Dana, seemed to be having a good time. Maybe their parents should be worrying about their firstborn instead. On the surface, all was fine. Dana was a picture of success for a young woman of twenty-six. Her apartment was small but adequate and in the most picturesque neighborhood of the city. Her job was not as lucrative as an associate position in a private firm, but still quite prestigious and, she supposed, important, even if there were times when she felt like a single straw in the broom bent against a mountain of filth. Patrick had expressed more than mere satisfaction with her work, had given her praise and offered solid support.

She liked to remind herself how much she enjoyed her independence, her long-awaited freedom from law school, her new life in the real world. How would she describe it to someone on the outside? On a positive note, an appropriate adjective might be "exciting." The days were filled with shocking surprises, the grist of tomorrow's anecdotes. On the negative side, the dreadful specter of unknown catastrophe was a perpetual black cloud looming overhead, threatening to swallow her.

"Are you afraid of the criminals you prosecute?" Outsiders had asked this question many times, and she always answered, "No, not in the least." There was a belief in safety, not capable of direct proof. It was said that disgruntled ex-cons more often went after the witnesses to their crimes or their own attorneys rather than the prosecutor. And for now, all her defendants were misdemeanants, although many among them were capable of far worse.

Other fears preoccupied her. Fear of the judges and her adversaries, fear of failure. Her position was synonymous with constant uncertainty. Rookies were given only a few weeks of training before they were handed a stack of cases with the instruction, "Go!" That was real trust. The DA hired these recent law grads solely on the instinctive belief that they possessed enough good sense to make the correct decision in the blink of an eye, at least nine times out of ten.

When feeling low or insecure, she garnered strength from her membership in a club which, tradition had told, would surely move beyond the quagmire of misdemeanor court. All rookies were in the same boat, feeling the stress. The signs were there, different in each. There was Ellen's quiet compulsiveness. Tom's loud fretfulness and foul mouth. Denzel's incongruous mix of square-shouldered confidence and vocal admissions of fear.

Dana was aware of her own signs, largely through her fight against them. There was that tightness in her throat, tension in her neck and shoulders, stiffness of her facial muscles, all arising in moments of panic. To her rescue, adrenaline would rush in, punching the muscles into submission, imposing an impossible relaxation. Later, in quiet moments at night, she would look back and see herself in the situation of the day and imagine how all her internal workings must have been visible to others. But maybe not so obvious. Day by day, she got closer to mastering the power of illusion, and her legal strategies and speech usually came out sounding well despite—or maybe because of—the stress.

Nearing Melly's apartment, she searched backward for the beginning of her long train of thought and found Cheryl. Her baby sister was the third in a line of transplants from the suburbs of New Jersey, each attracted to the city for her own reasons. Melanie: to escape hovering, overprotective parents without traveling too far away. Dana: to prove she could survive the toughest city and the toughest job in the world, just because she was in the habit of making things difficult for herself. Cheryl: to follow a pipe dream of stardom on Broadway.

Different reasons for migration and different experiences upon arrival, especially when it came to men. Melanie had met Noel almost immediately and married within a year. Cheryl had been in love a dozen times and thrived on emotional drama. Dana, persistently alone, couldn't seem to break her pattern of window shopping and declining.

Before she'd completely satisfied her need for deep thought, Dana turned onto Eighteenth Street, and in the next minute, was standing inside the building vestibule, pressing the buzzer to 3B while glancing over her shoulder, watching her back.

"Who goes?" the familiar voice came over, distorted by the intercom system.

"It's me."

The buzzer sounded and Dana pushed into the door, opening on a stubby hallway with another door at the other end, leading to the stairwell. She bounded up the three flights, two steps at a time, and opened the door onto the landing.

Grinning ear to ear, Noel stood in the open doorway of the Avendaños' apartment. Dana said "hello" with a smile of her own and came up close. He touched her shoulder as she craned upward to receive the press of his smoothly shaved, musky cheek against hers. Dana wasn't short, five-foot-eight, but Noel was at least six inches taller. He looked down at her in silence with a daydream floating in his eyes.

"What's with the goofy grin? What've you been smoking?"

His eyes grew round and he drew in his breath, aghast, but said nothing.

"Noel," she chided. He had to know she was kidding. Acquaintances might be wary of her prosecutor persona, but not her best friends.

He laughed, proving her right.

"What's going on?" she asked.

"Maybe Melly should tell you."

Now she *knew* something was up. She stepped in and Noel closed the door behind her. From the other end of the short hallway, a beaming presence emanated.

"Not you too," said Dana, coming up for a hug. "Is someone going to tell me what's going on here?"

"I'm sick as a dog," said Melanie with a huge smile.

"You don't look sick in the least. I've never seen you so...I don't know. Did you do something to your skin? It's all dewy looking."

Melanie burst out laughing. "Now that's *really* sick. It must be a male conspiracy. Some kind of psychological witchcraft—"

"You're a little confused there. I'm not male, or a witch."

She laughed again. "I love it. Now I'm dewy *and* confused!"

"Then explain yourself. What's with the male conspiracy?"

"Men. They inject you with something that makes you feel like hell but you look great at the same time. Just so they don't have to feel guilty!" She laughed delightedly while Noel pretended to look hurt.

"Sorry, Noel. I couldn't resist. But you've got to admit it's pretty hilarious. All those stereotypes are actually true. Even Dana says I'm dewy and confused. Really! Oh my God." Her eyes suddenly changed. She threw a hand to her mouth and pushed between them, headed toward the bathroom.

A light entered Dana's eyes, a smile blossomed.

"Now look at *you*," said Noel.

"It's catching."

"Don't blame *me*." He backed up a pace.

"Not that! The smile."

"So that's how I looked when you came in."

"Exactly. And I think I know what's going on here. Just tell me if I'm entitled to congratulate you."

"You certainly are."

"Well, congratulations then."

Melanie emerged from the bathroom, a limp smile on her lips. "False alarm. Go into the living room you two." She made a pushing motion at them, but Dana grabbed her shoulder and gave it a squeeze. "Little mother!"

"Oh Dana. Now I really *am* sick. Get in there and sit down."

They shuffled four steps down the hallway into the space that served as both a dining room and living room. Dana sank into the single easy chair while Noel and Melanie took the two-person loveseat. Two end tables, a six-by-nine rug on the hardwood floor, and a small dining table with four chairs completed the furnishings. Tight and cozy.

Melanie immediately got to her feet again. "Anyone want wine? I'm not having any, in case you're worried I'm one of *those* kinds of women. I'm not the slightest bit tempted, so go ahead."

"Sure, I'll have a glass, but let me get it." Dana pitched forward, ready to stand.

"No, I'll get it," said Noel, jumping up. "Sit, Dana. Sit, mamacita." He took four steps from the couch to the kitchen. Almost everything in the apartment was four steps from everything else.

"Too funny you two." Melanie plopped down into the cushion again. "I'm not exactly an invalid."

"Admit it," said Dana. "You love it. If it were me, I'd take everything I could get away with."

"Don't give her any ideas, Dana," Noel bellowed from the kitchen. His back was fully visible through the doorless opening as he stood at the kitchen counter, working at the corkscrew. She considered the breadth of his back, the scope of his arms and length of his legs, a body that needed the freedom of open spaces. He was a giant impossibly squeezed into an elf's habitat.

She turned to Melly and saw what she'd first noticed upon

entering, the unmistakable dewiness and glow. If Dana weren't so happy for her good friend, she might have felt the sting of jealousy. What unbelievable good fortune! Four years ago, newly graduated from college, Melanie landed in this monstrous city, found a decent job immediately and a more than decent man the following week. Married him after barely a year of "courtship." At first, Dana had worried that Melly was jumping in out of loneliness and a need to replace the doting parents she'd left behind. And something else, an attraction to the dark and different, the exotic and mysterious.

But the more Dana saw them together, the easier she felt. Noel was a man possessed of enviable qualities: intelligence, compassion, industriousness. Nothing overt in Noel's behavior could be called mysterious. He was reasonable and steadfast to a fault, seven years older than Dana and Melanie and maybe that much closer to knowing what he wanted. He acted with calm, motivated by intellect, not passion. But the emotion was there inside him, Dana always sensed it, deep and intense, a side he exposed only to Melanie.

Dana's cheeks grew hot. The mystery, if it was there, resided in her own curiosity about Noel, something that drew her to him in a way that, sometimes, made her uncomfortable.

"How long have you known?" she asked, internally cooling her embarrassment.

"I've been feeling nauseous for almost a week, but the test wasn't positive until today. A drug store kit. I haven't been to the doctor yet."

"How can you be sure?"

"I know, believe me."

"Believe me, she knows," said Noel, coming toward her with two glasses of red wine. He handed one to her. "The baby is smaller than a flea, but she knows."

"Is that some kind of Colombian expression? Don't call our

baby a flea, darling."

"Bueno, an adorable little flea."

"That's better."

He sat down slowly next to his wife, careful not to spill.

Dana sipped, holding the wine glass in one hand, its large bowl resting on the insides of five fingertips, the stem poking down through index and middle fingers. The glass was warm, smooth and round, very large, filled halfway with the dark red liquid. She held the glass up, touching the side of it to her chin, letting the aroma rise into her nostrils before she took another sip. A pungent smell, a warm taste. Relaxing, indulgent. She looked up. As her lips met the rim, her eyes met Noel's. He gave her a brotherly smile. She shifted her eyes to Melanie, who continued her happy chatter.

"Anyway, the baby has to be bigger than a flea by now, don't you think? By my calculation, I'm at least three weeks pregnant, possibly three and a half."

"That *is* early," said Dana. "I'm surprised you have a positive test result already."

"The way I feel, the hormones are surging like mad. It had to be positive. I was surprised I had a negative test on the second day I felt sick."

"Do you feel like eating?"

"Sometimes I'm ravenous but most of the time the sight of food makes me gag."

"And you're cooking dinner for me? You should have canceled."

Melanie shook her head forcefully and waved a hand in the air. "Don't be silly! I wanted you to come over."

"Me too," said Noel.

"The adorable little flea isn't the only person in this world."

"Right, there's your spinster girlfriend too." Dana intended a joke, but her voice fell flat.

Melly laughed. "The way you exaggerate! Weren't you the one who called me the 'child bride'?"

"You'd just turned twenty-three."

"And twenty-six is over the hill, right?" Melanie turned to Noel, who sat contentedly listening with a tiny smile on his lips. "Isn't Dana the most beautiful young spinster you ever saw, Noel?"

He nodded, eyes shining, and took a sip of wine.

"You're so beautiful, Dana," she went on. "You're so striking. The picture of a Manhattan swinging single. I'm glad you still have time to come see your old married friends. What's this spinster business?"

"Just a lame joke." She was now a good way into her glass of wine, wearing down the edge of her pessimism, a hidden note that had surfaced against her will.

"Well, it's nothing you have to worry about. I'm sure you have a hundred and one prospects."

"They're not exactly lining up. Even if they were, I don't have time to date."

"There's always time for love," observed Noel. "You're saying no one interests you right now?"

"No, well, maybe there is someone I'm sort of interested in, but I don't know what to make of it. He's a defense attorney."

"I'm shocked," Melanie exclaimed with a big smile.

"Outrageous," said Noel.

"The way you talk about some of that breed they're the lowest of life forms, no better than germs."

"Sure, well, I'm trying to be more open-minded, but you don't have to worry. It's going nowhere." She thought of the telephone message she received yesterday morning: *Re: B. Rios. The good guys were good today. What's up?* Understandably, the reassignment and dismissal of the Rios case had piqued Seth's curiosity. He'd called her the minute he returned to his office from

AP-6. But she made herself busy enough for the rest of the day to avoid returning his call and facing the inevitable questions, the discomfort of holding things back, the worry she might imply too much in the things left unsaid.

Now she wasn't sure if Seth would ever renew his "invitation" for a drink, or if he did, whether she would feel professionally obligated to decline. Perhaps his interest in her had been a passing impulse. The hazy intimacy and loneliness of night court can suggest strange things, possibilities that would be out of the question during daylight hours.

She hesitated, considering a full confession of the heart, but steered away from Seth. It was easier. "Anyway, I think my prospects are limited to other lawyers. A lot of men find my job daunting."

"What does that mean, 'daunting'?" asked Noel.

"Threatening. They're threatened by my job. The minute it pops from my mouth, I see this look in their eyes, and then they say, 'Oh,' like that."

"Oh," mimicked Melanie.

"Oh," tried Noel.

"Exactly," said Dana.

"I don't understand that reaction," said Noel. "It's a very important job. Something to be proud of. Any man you are with should be proud of you." His dark eyebrows were pushed together in earnest.

"Well, thank you," said Dana, suddenly shy.

"And speaking of that job of yours, I couldn't *believe* what you did to me yesterday," said Melanie. "Sticking my neck out at the bank, and then you didn't even need the information!"

"Did you get in trouble over that?"

"No, don't worry about it. I'll tell you in a minute, but I have to check on the dinner. It's almost ready." She jumped from the couch.

"Can I help?"

"Not at all! You sit. There isn't enough room in the kitchen for more than the two of us anyway." She pointed to her stomach and laughed.

"Oh *please*." Dana's laugh was forced, covering her anxiety about having troubled her friend needlessly for the account information. Melanie must have been teasing. Dana knew that tone of voice. She couldn't really be mad, because now she was humming a gentle melody as she pushed back a strand of blonde hair fallen from a haphazard bun. She donned oven mitts and bent forward to open the oven door, making her hips visible under a long, loose skirt. An extra five pounds proved her love of cooking, and the rich aroma that escaped the oven was a sign of her skill and imagination in the kitchen.

Over the top of her glass, Dana's eyes turned to Noel. "How's everything at the bookstore?"

"Good. Couldn't be better. Business is picking up."

"That's great!"

"Finally."

"How long has it been now?"

"I opened two years ago. More than two years. You should come by and see. I've changed some things…"

"I didn't realize it's been that long. I haven't been there since the day you opened."

"I have more stock and new displays…well, you should see it." His eyes shone with pride as Melly's humming drifted in from the kitchen. Noel's bookstore was truly his own "baby."

"It's so great you enjoy your work."

"I couldn't ask for anything else. I'm surrounded by the masters. I can tell customers about them, and when the store's empty, I pick up a book and read. Carlos Fuentes, García Márquez, Vargas Llosa, Jorge Amado. Only the greatest literature. I have some junk too, of course." His eyes crinkled in self-mockery. "The business aspect is important too."

"And the business aspect is going well it seems."

"Let's say it's better. I even hired a part-time worker, my cousin Domingo. He's been here a few months now and needs some work. But this business will never make big money. People don't read so much as they should."

"Enough to keep you going, though."

"In Jackson Heights there's the demand for books in Spanish. A large Spanish speaking community. That's why I chose that location. It just took some time to pick up. And now I'm going to add other products—stationery and Spanish greeting cards and calendars. People always need that kind of thing—"

"Soup's on!" chirped Melanie, walking in with a steaming serving bowl. Dana transferred from easy chair to table, sitting at the single place setting on one side of the table, two settings on the other. The silver was heavy and real, the china delicate and elegant—wedding gifts—all the proper grownup stuff to which Dana had not yet graduated. The married couple bustled back and forth, retrieving other dishes from the kitchen while their guest sat helpless.

Before Dana could pretend to say "no," the host poured her another glass of wine. Melanie served the food. "We'll start with la sopa," she said.

"Melly is too good to me," said Noel, hand on his chest. With a straight spine, he leaned toward Dana across the table. "In my country, we always start the meal with soup, and Melly has learned all the best ones."

"But after that, we're mixing it up tonight. The rest is French."

They started on the soup, a variety of corn chowder, and after that, continued with salad, soufflé, ratatouille. The mixture of foods was improbable but uniquely complementary, each dish sumptuous and rare to Dana, who always ate quite simply. "This is unbelievable," she said. "This kind of cooking is beyond human possibility."

"Not beyond this human." Noel nodded his head sideways.

"Thanks guys. And thank you, Lord, for giving me a steady stomach tonight." She cast her eyes to the ceiling.

"Everything going down okay?"

"So far so good."

Dana took a big sip of wine, feeling good enough to dare an apology. "I'm really sorry, Melly, about the account and everything."

"Don't worry about it."

"I didn't think the case would be yanked from me like that, so soon anyway."

"So soon?"

This was the hardest part to admit. Her mistake. "Right after I got the case, a lawyer in another bureau of my office told me it was related to one of his cases and he was going to have it reassigned to him. He was going to call my boss, he said. He acted like such a jerk, I was sure my boss wouldn't listen to him, especially if I was doing all the right things to move the case forward. Turns out I was wrong, and now that I look back on it, maybe I was being a little unrealistic. Anyway, I'm sorry I put you to all that trouble. I hope you didn't have to do anything illegal."

"Is that a loaded comment or what? Straight from the mouth of a prosecutor."

"You know what I mean."

"I have a clear conscience. Nothing illegal or even a smidge improper. You would have sent the subpoena, right?"

"Right."

"And I didn't even get to the point of faxing any account records to you."

"That's true."

"I was covered, nothing against bank policy. But for some

reason I did feel strange snooping around, maybe a little nervous. I don't know. The real thing is, it was just getting interesting. I felt kind of like a detective. Maybe that's why I'm disappointed. I was dying to tell you yesterday, but you were in such a hurry. Don't you want to know what I found out?"

Dana hesitated, on the cliff of indecision. She had set every-thing in motion, feeding Melanie's curiosity, giving her the apparent authority to examine account information and gather clues about the depositor's identity. But Melanie already had the authority to gather this kind of information, otherwise it wouldn't have been so easy for her. Whether she should divulge what she'd learned was a different question, now that Dana wasn't on the case anymore and hadn't asked a judge to sign a subpoena. This was another one of those little gray areas where she wasn't sure of the rules.

"That's okay." Dana waved her hand in the air. "I don't want to put you to any more trouble about this."

Noel jumped right in, failing to sense the unease behind Dana's display of indifference. "The activity in the account was a little odd. Of course, there might be some legitimate explanations for everything, but we were interested to know your opinion."

Now Dana couldn't dismiss it again without calling attention to her dilemma. She was curious, and what did it matter? Melanie had certainly disclosed everything to her husband. "What was odd about it?"

Melanie perked up, a glint in her eye, frankly excited to be playing the amateur sleuth. "It was opened less than two months ago and already tons of cash has gone through it. $95,000! At least I think it was all cash, but there could have been money orders and bank checks too. I didn't look into it that far. The money just goes in, big blobs of it every two or three days, and comes out again. The deposits are always less than $10,000, so there's no need to fill out a CTR."

"What's that?"

"Cash Transaction Report. It's sent to the IRS for every cash deposit or transaction of $10,000 or more. The cash in this account doesn't stay there very long. A lot of checks are written, and the current balance is only $3,000 something."

"That *does* seem odd." Her mind's eye beheld a vision of Rios standing quietly in court, neatly dressed, not impoverished but not particularly well-off. Also not someone she would pick out as a criminal, but what did she know after nine months on the job? All types came through the system. He had a look about him that spoke of humility and honest hard work, a quality that likely contributed to Seth's belief in his story.

"I was saying to Melly that this might not be so completely strange," said Noel. "A lot of businesses deal just in cash and make a lot of deposits. I deposit my receipts a couple times a week. I don't like the cash lying around."

"But it was a personal checking account, not a business account," said Melanie.

"I've seen this kind of thing before," said Noel, "with my people and others. Some small business owners are very informal. Maybe you could say backward. They don't file the proper papers and they use personal checking accounts."

"And deposit four or five thousand dollars every few days? What do you think, Dana?" asked Melanie.

"I don't know what to think. But it does seem odd, especially since Rios had the deposit ticket for Luz Melendez."

"Who's Rios?" asked Melanie. Too late, Dana realized that Reichert might not like her to give out further details about his suspect. But what harm could Melly do with this information?

"That's the defendant in my case."

"So *that* must be him. The man who deposited $8,500 on Wednesday. Dwight, the teller, told me a man deposited the cash."

"What did he look like?"

"Dark hair, dark eyes, Hispanic looking, neat, maybe five-nine or ten. Sounds like a thousand people, right?"

"It could be him."

"So, what's this all about?"

"What kind of investigation is that other attorney doing, the one who took your case?" asked Noel.

The two looked at Dana expectantly. She just shrugged her shoulders.

"Come on, Dana. You're playing dumb, I can tell." Melly twisted her pretty mouth into a dubious frown.

"Really, I'm not playing dumb, I *am* dumb. I'm almost embarrassed to admit it. They won't tell me anything about the investigation—"

"So, it *is* a big investigation." Melly's eyes popped wide.

"I don't know how big or little it is. When I got the case, it was real little. Rios was arrested for farebeat."

"What's farebeat?" asked Noel.

"He jumped the turnstile in the subway."

"You can get arrested for *that*?" exclaimed Melanie. "I've seen a million people do it."

"Yes, you can get arrested, and he was, and all I know is he's related somehow to another investigation. Sorry. No big stories to tell. I'm just a little fish in the bowl." Dana's face drooped. Again, her innermost feelings had played a trick on her, surfacing when least expected to deliver the sting of humiliation.

Now, her imagination filled in the blanks. Reichert: complaining to McBride about that naïve fledgling screwing up his big investigation. *Can you believe it? She actually wants to try my suspect for farebeat!* McBride: politely defending his underling despite grave disappointment in her obvious blunder, and later, handling her with his smooth paternalism, gently pulling the case from her infantile clutch. *Believe it or not, even I don't know much about this investigation.* Believe it—not.

In her sudden silence, she felt the curious, concerned regard of her friends from across the table.

"Here, Dana," said Noel, "have some wine. We'll talk about something else."

"Do I look that bad?"

"You look bad. I mean, not bad. But that job—it must be getting to you sometimes." He reached for the wine bottle and aimed it in the direction of her empty glass. She'd been feeling the effects of the first two glasses, swimmingly happy, until this. Now, a third glass seemed impossibly too much, suicidal.

She put her hand over the glass. "No thank you, Noel. I've had enough." She laid her fork amidst the crumbs on her plate. "And this dinner was fabulous."

"I know what you need," said Noel.

"Some dessert?" asked Melanie.

"No. A good book."

"You're right," said Dana. "I haven't read anything good for a while."

"Promise me you won't leave here tonight without one. Maybe a García Márquez. Have you read *One Hundred Years of Solitude?*"

"No..."

Melly sent Noel a stern, sidelong glance that caused him to change his mind. "I know," he said. "Something lighter, something funny. *Doña Flor and Her Two Husbands,* or *Aunt Julia and the Scriptwriter.* I'll find just the one for you—"

"In English, I hope."

"Yes, in English." He laughed. "I'll give you something good, something funny, and you'll laugh and feel good in the morning and sing in the night."

5 » CONNECTION

"THIS IS DANA HARGROVE, everyone. She's on loan to us from Trial Bureau 90."

Not surprisingly, Bruce Reichert lacked the social skills to make a proper introduction, leaving Dana to guess the identities of the four people tucked around the table in the small conference room. Dazed and unsure, she merely nodded a greeting toward the center of the table.

Maybe, if she blinked and clicked her heels three times, she would rematerialize in her old office with Ellen, Tom and Denz, jolted awake from this nightmare. Everything had happened so quickly in the past twenty-four hours, she hadn't seen it coming.

Yesterday, the Monday after McBride yanked the Rios case, Dana expected to start a new week tackling her misdemeanor caseload. Mid-morning, after a dozen conversations with cops and witnesses, she received a phone call from Reichert—direct from the man himself, sans secretary. His voice was the last one she expected to hear. Even more puzzling, he seemed to have nothing new to say. On Friday, an ADA in his bureau, Evan Goodhue, had gone to AP-6, dismissed the Rios case, and arranged the return of the defendant's money and other effects—in short, everything Reichert had asked for. Yet, he seemed to be on a hunt-and-strike mission, searching for a new basis to criticize her short-lived handling of the matter, determined to inflict further pain and suffering.

"Evan just handed me the Rios file. I see a photocopy of the deposit slips in here." He paused, as if expecting an explanation. She stewed and said nothing. "So, you removed the evidence from Police Plaza," he accused.

"Right."

"After I asked you to turn the case over to me."

"It was still mine. Patrick had assigned it to me."

"But I let you know it was a big deal and I was going to be talking to him. I don't talk to someone's boss without extending that courtesy first. And now, I'm forced to do it again. This is something I should tell McBride." He paused for a reaction and got nothing. "Why were you messing with the evidence after I told you it was an important investigation?"

"I don't remember you telling me much of anything about this case..."

"I told you not to touch it, I know that."

She was seething, on the brink of hatred, an emotion she rarely felt for anyone. What was the point of this? Urges pressed outward at her temples. The urge to scream, to curse him out, to hang up. But survival demanded restraint. He was threatening to complain to her boss, and she hadn't a clue how much sway he had over McBride or how much influence he had in the executive wing. True, Reichert wasn't at McBride's level in the hierarchy, but he could still cause enough trouble for her if his own boss backed him up, creating a nice little incident to put in her personnel folder, a cloud on her reputation.

She held back, but her wall of restraint had a chink, allowing a little seepage of self-pride, self-defense. "As long as the case was still assigned to me," she explained, "it was my responsibility to prepare for trial."

Reichert laughed, a rat-a-tat burst of gunfire in her ear.

"What could you possibly do with these bank records in a farebeat case?"

She inhaled deeply before answering his question precisely. "His attorney said he wanted to testify. With his bank records, I had a better chance of tripping him up on cross. I already knew he had $3,300 in cash, and if he was evasive about his money in the bank, he wouldn't have been a credible witness. And if all this money was really *his* to spend, it made his theft that much worse, inexcusable."

A moment of silence hung between them, and then she heard "oh" in a blasé tone, a notch of adjustment in attitude peeking through underneath. Something she had said interested him, maybe even impressed him. She sensed it. That hunch gave rise to a modest rush of confidence which pressed her onward, if only out of a chance to completely win him over—or to show him up—leading her to take the next step, the one she would later come to regret.

"The best thing was," she continued, "I knew I could surprise the defendant with the amount of information I had about his bank accounts. I have a connection at one of the banks on his deposit slips and can get account information overnight."

"Hmmm." Reichert digested this information, no longer hiding the interest in his voice. "A connection. At a bank. You know someone at a bank? Which bank?"

"First City," blurted Dana, still caught up in herself. But then, just as quickly, the finger of doubt touched her. Too late.

"First City is one of the biggest banks in New York. Which branch? Who do you know?"

Oh my God, Melly. Never never never will I tell him about you!

When she didn't answer immediately, he kept on. "Is it someone in their subpoena compliance unit?"

"No, actually, I'm not sure exactly what her title is."

He paused and seemed to back off. "Okay, well, I don't want

to discourage meticulous trial prep. Next time, just think before you act. Okay?"

She resented his little bit of paternalism, but there was a grain of sense in his advice. After all, hadn't she failed to think of all the consequences before prepping the case—before blurting out the name of the bank? "Sure, okay," she said. He gave a hasty "good-bye" and hung up.

Several hours passed. The worst of her self-doubts seemed to be over when Patrick summoned her to his office. The reason was not given, but she knew it would be something bad. She felt it coming.

As she walked the long, wide corridor from her office to his, she passed cubicles bustling with clerks, TPAs and secretaries, hearing only Reichert's words and seeing his face—the one she imagined to go along with that imperious, unnaturally deep voice. Thin and angular with a beakish nose and hard lips like nails. Steely gray, deep-set eyes and a prominent widow's peak etched into his hairline. A tall man, thirty-three or thirty-four, head bent down and forward from a skeletal tower, stooped shoulders protecting a sunken chest—the only outward sign of insecurity, the source of his assumed voice and those little shows of authority. *I told you not to touch it, I know that.*

Perhaps his change of tone at the end of their conversation gave reason for hope. Then again, maybe he'd complained to McBride about her anyway. He'd been entirely too interested in her proposed trial strategy. It made her nervous. She must have done something wrong. In his investigations of financial crimes, Reichert probably issued subpoenas for bank records every day. He knew the rules. That must be it. In her zeal to prepare for trial, she'd breached a rule of procedure or professional ethics by trying to get the information from Melanie without a subpoena in hand.

By the time she knocked on the frosted glass pane of McBride's door, her heart was beating high up in her chest.

"Come in," she heard.

She turned the knob and stepped in. Patrick's desk faced the door, but he was turned sideways, profile to her, facing a visitor who was planted in a chair at the side of the desk. Patrick swiveled around to look up at her. "Why don't you close the door?" he suggested. She complied and stepped toward the empty chair in front of his desk, the one he indicated with an outstretched hand. "Have a seat. This is Bruce Reichert."

Some part of her had guessed as much without successfully cracking the false image in her head. This man, the real Reichert, was red-cheeked and stocky, tending toward plumpness, his hair dark and plentiful. Caterpillar-thick eyebrows met across the wrinkled bridge of his nose, then opened and separated as his brow relaxed over common brown eyes without a message in them. He didn't bother to stand but squeezed a grimace of a smile onto his mouth, making his cheeks go ruddier. Dana guessed that, if he stood, he might barely equal her height of five-eight.

She experienced an awkward moment of indecision, debating whether to extend her hand, not really wanting to. Since he failed to rise or make any gesture toward her, his behavior and attitude didn't warrant formality in return. She smiled grimly and said "hello" as she sat. Their introduction lasted but a few seconds, and just as soon as their eyes met, they disengaged and focused on McBride, their savior from further uncomfortable contact.

In the midst of readjusting her internal image of Reichert, Dana couldn't forget his tone and attitude during their telephone conversations. Now, from her brief glance in his eyes, she thought she detected a willful attempt at denial of everything that had gone before. But she couldn't be sure. His empty expression could just as easily be a sign of indifference left unchecked by a weak conscience.

Patrick was not one to waste time, and he jumped right to the point. "We just came back from the executive wing. Bruce and his boss, George Blaithe, dragged me over there to plead for extra help. Their investigation is heating up and they need another attorney. Bruce suggested you."

Dana caught her breath. She had imagined many things, but not this. She looked at Patrick, then Bruce, and Patrick again. "A transfer?"

"I'm afraid so. I didn't want to lose you, but Financial Crimes made a compelling pitch. And Bruce is impressed with the thought and work you put into the Rios case. I can't say I blame him." Her boss flashed a smile, meant to be reassuring. Undoubtedly, he saw the disappointment in her eyes, something she was trying hard to mask.

Reichert had remained unmoved with a grimace plastered on his face, but now he decided it was his turn to speak. "It's an exciting investigation."

"More interesting than street crime," admitted Patrick with good-natured self-deprecation.

Dana smiled nervously, not knowing how to respond but having enough good sense to avoid saying what was on her mind. Financial Crimes was a specialty bureau that investigated white-collar crime, embezzlement, fraud, money laundering and the like. Her work in street crime had been fast-paced and unpredictable, each case involving only a few witnesses, usually just the complainant and a cop, and not much physical evidence. Constant court appearances, frequent, short trials. But investigations in Financial Crimes were long, tedious and paper intensive. Dana knew exactly what her transfer meant: boredom, seclusion, lack of daylight, no glory. She would be exiled to a back room where she would shuffle papers or interview colorless witnesses like clerical workers and custodians of records. The big shots like Reichert took the cases to trial and stood in the limelight, getting all the credit.

"When does the transfer take effect?" she asked.

"Immediately," said Patrick.

"My cases...?"

"I'll reassign them. We'll just have to cover somehow." He shot Reichert a mildly disgruntled look, and Dana could imagine how their meeting had gone with the administrative ADAs in the executive wing. Patrick surely must have registered a complaint about the transfer, which created a shortage of manpower in his bureau. Dana's colleagues, already overburdened, would each be picking up a share of her cases. "You're getting my best rookie, Bruce." Had Patrick said as much during the meeting in the executive wing? "You lucked out this time."

"I'll take her across the street now," said Reichert, as if he were merely borrowing a law book from Patrick's office.

"Whoa! I know we said 'immediately,' but we have two or three hours left in the day and Dana has to straighten out some things." He turned to her. "I'll come by your office at about five and we'll talk about your cases."

"Okay," she said.

"Tomorrow morning then?" asked Reichert.

"Fine." Patrick stood and said, "Now get out of here you two," but he caught Dana's eye and winked.

Dana stood. Reichert stood, his eyes level with hers. "The team is meeting tomorrow morning, 8:30, Room 1202."

Her eyes darted to Patrick and returned to her new boss. Or *was* he her new boss? As an ADA assigned to Financial Crimes, she should be taking orders from Blaithe, the bureau chief, not Reichert, a senior colleague. But she could see he wasn't going to be viewing it quite that way. "I'll be there," she said, and turned to leave.

Walking back to her office, she took the corridor like death row, condemned and beset with panicky nostalgia for her lost life. A new set of images haunted her: Reichert's small brown eyes under the bulky eyebrows, impassively prodding her to follow orders. As she approached Eric's desk, Dana averted her eyes and attempted to scoot past, but as always, her admirer's antenna was raised and tuned to her wavelength. He looked up from the desk. "What's up?"

She stopped calmly in her tracks and turned to him. "I've been transferred to Financial Crimes."

Eric's milky brow knit in consternation. "Holy shit! That sucks. FC's across the street—we'll never see you again."

Dana just shrugged her shoulders.

He caught himself. "Sorry... I'm supposed to say 'congratulations.' It's a promotion, right?"

"Not the way I see it." She sighed and walked through the open office door.

Spurting a few extra obscenities, Eric stood, shook his head, and followed her like a lost puppy. "Is there anything we can do? You need help with anything?"

As it happened, all three of her officemates were back from court and at their desks. No place to hide. Perhaps it was the way Eric heeled or the misery etched in Dana's features, but Jared, Tom and Ellen could sense the significance of the occasion and perked up, demanding the news.

Dana looked at them one by one, realizing how close they'd become in their short time together, like refugees in a wartime bomb shelter. This was bad. Emotion clogged her throat and she bit her lip hard against it.

Her colleagues' commiseration was genuine and abundant, tinged with a small measure of jealousy. They were sorry she was distraught about the transfer but, as they all emphasized in a hundred ways, she should be looking at this differently. She should be excited and proud. A rookie in FC? The move was unheard of. Only experienced attorneys worked in the specialty bureaus. "But you haven't met this jerk Bruce Reichert," she reminded them, bringing on a new wave of condolences.

After a few minutes of this, she told them McBride would be here at five and she had to go through her cases. This news caused an immediate shift in the focus of their sympathies. Suddenly, there were copious, exaggerated shows of self-pity for the inevitable reassignment of Dana's cases and the impending increase in their caseloads. Don't give me your dogs, each of them warned. When in doubt, dismiss, Dana recommended.

Denz answered his ringing phone. Called back to reality, Tom and Ellen peeled away, returning to their paper stacks of victims, cops and perps. Dana had less than two hours to sort through her cases, writing notes with instructions where necessary. Her mind wasn't on the task, the printed pages a blur to her eyes, the voices of her office companions swelling and receding in the background.

With no sense of how far she'd gotten or had yet to go, it was five o'clock and Patrick came striding in. One look at the busy office and he crooked a finger, motioning her to follow him. They walked out the door, passed Eric's desk, and crossed the corridor to an empty corner.

"Looking through your cases?" he asked, just to ease into it. His eyes were concerned, fatherly.

"Trying to. All fifty-two hundred of them."

"Don't worry. Do your best. Attach notes about anything unusual and just leave the stack on your desk."

"Okay. It'll be my final challenge—stacking them so they don't fall over."

He smiled. They stood very close to one another, each leaning a shoulder up against the wall. Something about this job, this environment, made a professional sort of physicality and intimacy natural. She knew it would fade quickly, once their daily contact ceased.

"You're all right about this?" he asked.

She nodded.

"I have to tell you a few things I couldn't say in there." He nodded toward her office. "This transfer is a big deal for you. I want you to know that. They do some important cases in FC, and they need people with brains and skill. This move is an excellent opportunity for your career. It's already an accomplishment."

His words forced a smile from her. "Thanks. That helps. A little."

"I can tell you're disappointed. But the transfer is temporary. I've told them they get you for a year. Max. And when you come back, with everything you've learned over there, I'm sure I'll be assigning you some big cases. Felonies. No more misdemeanors."

"I'll be carving notches on the wall, counting the days."

"Let's just hope you don't change your mind about us. A lot can happen in a year's time."

He put a hand on her shoulder just long enough for her to feel the warmth. "Good luck." He turned away and took two steps, swiveled around again and walked backwards as he added, "Call anytime if you want to talk. About anything." He turned on his heels again and was gone.

During the brief introduction, four pairs of eyes were on her at once, the faces accepting of her if not friendly, unlike Reichert's which remained adamantly plugged into his mission. After the heat of this moment they quickly forgot her, and Dana became the quiet observer, catching and processing clues from their interactions with each other.

Every member of Dana's new team was male and older than her except for one, a young woman about Eric's age—a TPA, Dana guessed, based on her youth and her tendency to defer to the others. Most of the time her face was turned downward, partially obscured by a scrim of black, shiny bangs as she scribbled diligently on a yellow legal pad placed under her nose on the conference table. She was there to receive assignments and report her findings when called upon.

The oldest man in the group looked to be in his late fifties. Tieless, dressed in a sport jacket, polo shirt and slacks, he'd pushed his chair away from the table and sat hunched forward, forearms on knees spread wide, his hands in the air space between them, alternately rubbing palms or playing with a bulbous, gold and ruby class ring. He had the grizzled, seasoned look of a cop, probably a detective. When he spoke, his voice was deep and husky—a smoker's voice—jaunty and sure when it came to his area of expertise: the crimes and suspects under investigation.

The other two men, gray-suited, in their early thirties, were ADAs with about five years of experience. Clean-cut, confident, quick. One of them was prematurely balding, with a boyish face and a porcelain spot the size of a sand dollar on his crown, in the middle of his hair. The other was dark-haired and lashed, curls threatening at his temples despite the short haircut. Their experience at the DA's office had matured them beyond their years and polished down all the outward, rough edges of uncertainty, leaving a professional sheen. Although Reichert was their team manager, they were not his flunkies. Each possessed a well-defined sphere of influence and contributed suggestions for the progress of the investigation.

At the outset, just after Reichert had introduced Dana, the balding attorney turned to him and asked, "Is Jack coming?"

Before answering, Reichert plunged into an expanding file folder and pulled out some papers, his busyness a transparent cover up. "We're just talking about the money today. She doesn't have to be here," he said, his eyes averted.

The balding attorney looked at the dark-haired one and lifted his eyebrows, an exchange the team manager missed as he maintained his pretense of sifting through the papers.

With a little thrill, Dana figured something out. A female "Jack" could be only one person: Jacquelyn DuBois, senior trial counsel in the Special Narcotics Bureau. Dana had been lucky enough to have ADA DuBois as her small seminar leader during the training course for rookies last fall. Somehow, source unknown, Jacquelyn's reputation in the DA's office had secretly circulated among the rookies in her group. DuBois was in part to blame, having introduced herself straight off as "Jack," a name given her by the detectives in the narcotics squad.

Quite appropriately, the nickname fit Jack's toughness and tenacity, while at the same time it contradicted her outward appearance, the petite form and sweet, dimpled smile set in a cherub face of smooth, caramel skin. Hers was the kind of femininity admired by every young female attorney in a profession still dominated by men. Confident and tough, reasonable and articulate, she possessed the qualities to ward off any attack by the threatened male ego and to disprove every favorite derogatory term for a strong woman. In her seven years with the Special Narcotics Bureau, Jack had put away some of the vilest drug lords, taking special interest in the pushers who ruled the streets of Harlem, her old neighborhood, a place she'd escaped by using her brains, determination and hard work.

With her little discovery, Dana felt a glimmer of hope and interest, the first in the past twenty-four hours. It would be nice to work with Jack. And now she knew for the first time that the investigation involved narcotics along with the money crimes. Reichert's tight mouth had not divulged even this basic fact. She wondered how much the FC team and SNB would be interacting. A perceptible tension had filled the air when Reichert mentioned his failure to invite Jack to the meeting.

"Paul. What's new on the wires?" Reichert addressed the detective, who ceased twisting his ring and cut short an examination of his shoes to jerk his head up, eyebrows raised.

"More calls are coming into the apartment in Spanish Harlem from the two storefronts in Queens I told you about. In a week or so we'll have enough to apply for wires on the Queens locations."

"Lay it out for me."

The detective cleared his throat and coughed. "There's no question these sites are Cali Cartel; we've linked all of them to known operatives. And this new system they have for handling the cash—they've got it organized down to the penny. They're not keeping it in one place anymore after all the big seizures in the last couple years, the ten million here, twenty there. Too risky. They've been hit hard, and we're hurting their operation. So, it's a new shell game. They keep at least ten locations we know of, and they stash small bundles in each one, no more than a million here and there. They've hired more couriers to get the bills into the banks, zip, fast." He clapped his hands together and slid one palm off the other. "Most of this we're following with street surveillance. The calls coming in from Queens are like all the others. Talking about deliveries, all cryptic of course, you know, 'three vestidos are coming in,' that kind of bullshit. That reminds me. When are we getting another bilingual? Gilbert and Manny are wiped out, working double shifts."

"Administration promised next week."

"The sooner the better. Especially if you want to go up on the other phones. What does Queens say?"

Irritation crumpled Reichert's broad face, squeezing the two caterpillars above his eyes into one. "Don't worry about that. I'll take care of it. Evan, you were supposed to—"

"It's right here," said the balding attorney, pulling a manila file from a briefcase on the floor. Dana synthesized this new bit of information. "Evan" must be Evan Goodhue, the FC attorney who'd dismissed the Rios case last Friday. He handed the folder to Reichert, explaining, "This is the case I was telling you about.

Queens came begging for it. We gave it to them and dismissed our case. So now we've got some leverage and can ask for something in return…"

With a brusque swipe of his hand, Reichert interrupted Evan. "I can handle Queens. They'll let us come in and do the wires. They can't handle something this big. Now, Paul—"

"Why don't we work together on this?"

The voice was her own, Dana realized, as every eye in the room shot in her direction. Instantly, she felt shock at her own gumption. Here she was, brand new and operating on guesswork, yet speaking out on what seemed to be a major issue. A key had turned inside her, sending speech to her lips when she heard Reichert's cocky eruption, exposing his obvious desire to snatch all the glory. It was obvious to Dana anyway.

Even with her limited experience and knowledge of the investigation, she sensed a developing professional turf war. The conspiracy didn't fit nicely into a single jurisdiction, its participants committing crimes in Manhattan and Queens. Reichert's plan seemed to involve bullying the Queens DA into giving up his right to investigate or prosecute the crimes being committed in Queens. But didn't "Detective Paul" (Dana's temporary name for him) express concern about a shortage of manpower even as they were considering expanding the investigation into Queens? It seemed to Dana that a joint investigative effort would be more effective and efficient. Attorneys and detectives from the two offices could combine forces to gather evidence, deciding later where to indict and prosecute the case, in Queens or Manhattan. The same kind of cooperation was built into the system for narcotics crimes, handled by the Special Narcotics Office, which encompassed all five boroughs.

But what did she know? She could only guess at the politics involved in any interjurisdictional conflict between counties.

Reichert didn't speak immediately, apparently stunned at

her gall. Yet his look didn't convey disdain. More of a blankness, an expression she couldn't read. Her suggestion could have been unspeakably naïve or surprisingly insightful or neither of the two, something mildly annoying and easy to ignore since, after all, it had been spoken by Dana Hargrove, that green rookie transferee.

"An interesting thought," said Evan with a smile in the space of Reichert's silence. He gave Dana an approving look, then exchanged smiles with the other attorney while Reichert continued to stare blankly at Dana.

"Yes, well, it's a thought," said Reichert, his voice expressionless and drifting. Then, quickly forgetting her interruption, he refocused sharply on his previous train of thought. "Paul, any clues yet on Rojo's identity?"

"Not yet. All we know is Rojo gives the orders directing the flow of money. It could be a code name for one individual or a group. And we don't know how Rojo's orders get to the people carrying them out. It's all just, 'Rojo this,' and 'Rojo that.' The orders could be coming from Colombia on a phone we don't know about, or maybe this Rojo is right here in New York, under our noses."

"Maybe the phones at the Queens locations will give us something. Gather up your best conversations between the Manhattan and Queens sites and we'll go over them for probable cause. From what you're saying, we should have PC for the wiretap applications in Queens."

"How do you want to work this, Bruce?" asked Evan.

"You're going to have to take the bulk of it. I'm bogged down with this administrative garbage and dealing with Queens. What're you concentrating on this week?"

"I'm working on the progress reports and renewal applications now. All six of the Manhattan taps are about to expire, some this week, some next week. We still have to go over last week's surveillance reports, and I'll have to incorporate a lot of that information in the renewals." Evan listed his tasks in a level, matter-of-fact way, without complaint. His manner was easy-going but not careless, revealing a steady commitment and drive, in contrast to the irritating tenseness exuded by his senior colleague. "Besides the work on the wires," he continued, "there's all the other—"

"We have Dana now." Reichert turned to her and flashed a smile, the first time she'd seen a purposeful exposure of his teeth. They were large and slightly protruding. The quick turn of his head and the smile were smooth and automatic like a marionette, leaving a chilling image in its aftermath. He was looking at Evan again when he said, "You're going to be strictly on the wires from now on. I'm giving Dana the rest."

What "the rest" was, Reichert didn't bother to explain. He continued down the list on his mental agenda and changed the topic, turning his attention to the other ADA in the room. "Joe, are you getting everything you need?"

"Joe" was sitting with an elbow on the table, chin resting in the palm of his hand. He tapped a bulky nose with his pinky finger before lifting his head from its support and straightening his spine. "I'm getting everything of any significance. Everything you have, right Mineko?"

The TPA looked up from her yellow pad, her bangs brushing the top lids of her almond-shaped eyes. "Yes, except some records I got in yesterday. Eight new accounts. I'll go over them and give you the summaries tomorrow."

"Good," said Joe. He turned to Bruce. "But the problem is— and this has nothing to do with Mineko's work, which is very good—a lot of the banks are slow. The Cartel doesn't keep these checking accounts active for very long. They open a smurf account, use it for a couple or several months, and close it or just abandon it with a few dollars left. When a bank doesn't respond to our subpoena for more than a month, the account could be closed out before we get a chance to look at the records. When this whole thing comes to a head and we start the forfeiture action, we need current information on the accounts we're trying to freeze."

Joe's little speech identified him as an attorney from the Forfeiture Unit, not FC. Dana now recalled the touch of panic in Reichert's voice during their first telephone conversation, when she'd mentioned Judge Chomsky's theory about forfeiture. The judge had been right—in a way. The DA's office wanted to forfeit the cash all right, but they were interested in far more than just the $3,300 in Rios's pocket.

"I understand that one of the biggest culprits is First City," said Reichert, flashing Dana an oblique look.

"Right," said Joe. "It's a big bank with so many branches, almost half the accounts we've identified are there. Mineko and I have been hounding them, diplomatically of course. We walk a thin line, trying to push for the information without completely alienating them. A couple of times I considered a motion to compel production, but—"

"No, you can't do that," interrupted Reichert. "They'd countermove to quash the subpoenas. We can't get bogged down in a lot of motion practice on collateral issues."

"—it's too time consuming."

"Right, and you'd completely turn them off to us. It would backfire, and we'd never get the records on a hundred other accounts we need. Don't worry about it. Dana's going to be taking care of First City Financial. She has a connection there."

All eyes went to her. The floor dropped out beneath her chair. Internally she wrestled her facial muscles, fighting to control her expression. So, *this* had been Reichert's interest in her! He wasn't impressed with her trial strategy; he needed her "connection" at the bank. He wanted her to hassle Melanie about a pile of subpoenas. How could she do that?

"I don't know if I'd call her a 'connection.' I just know

someone there…"

"I believe that's the word you used," he threw back. "Anyway, your job is to help with the subpoenas. It's getting to be too much for Mineko alone. You handle all the subpoenas from First City and apply some pressure on your friend there—what's her name?"

Dana hesitated, averted her eyes, then turned to meet Reichert's unwavering, dark pinpoints directly. "Melanie Avendaño."

"Avendaño?"

"Yes."

"Contact her today or tomorrow, once you're familiar with the subpoenas. Mineko will fill you in on what we're looking for. And I'll leave it up to you two to divvy up the rest of the banks. Okay?" He slapped his palm on the table like a judge slamming a gavel, concluding a session of court.

The meeting was over, without Dana having any more than a vague idea about their goals. They were looking at a Colombian narcotics cartel, the Cali Cartel, that much was clear, developing a case for narcotics and financial crimes, possibly money laundering. They were hoping to forfeit dirty money deposited into what they liked to call "smurf" accounts. The deposit slips in Rios's pocket were obviously for some of these smurf accounts. And now the team had subpoenaed too many bank records for Mineko alone to analyze.

Dana felt small. Less than small. She would be another paper shuffler for Reichert, not much better than a TPA with, of course, her one distinguishing attribute—a connection at an important bank. She would be organizing mounds of paper, calling Melly, badgering her, maybe calling people at other banks as well. Was that all? Did Reichert find no value in her legal skills? From the little he'd said, it wasn't clear if he had larger plans for her. She suspected not. She had many questions and dreaded the answers but felt compelled to start asking, even now, as Reichert pushed away from the table and stood up.

"What, exactly, am I to do with these subpoenas, other than apply pressure at the bank?"

Reichert looked at her as if she'd asked whether the sky was blue. He took a deep breath before speaking, and when the words came, his mouth shaped them slowly, as if helping a novice lip-reader. "You are to analyze the records when they come in and look for smurf accounts. As I said, Mineko will fill you in on the attributes to look for, the signs that indicate an account is being used for money laundering. You have to summarize your findings and report to me and Joe. Got it?"

Dana nodded.

He slammed the table again. "All right folks. We know what we gotta do."

6 » COUSINS

NOEL SLICED THE packing tape with a box cutter, carefully retracted the blade, and pushed the tool into his back pocket. He pulled up the cardboard flaps, removed the crumpled paper, and ran his palm over the smooth, top layer of glossy covers. He smiled. Everything appeared to be in order; these were the titles he needed, no torn or bent covers. Opening a box of pristine new books was like opening the cathedral doors on a choir in full voice.

Glancing back over his shoulder, he saw the customer who'd been browsing in the fiction section, now standing at the counter, waiting to pay. He recognized the woman; she'd bought a hardcover novel from him last month.

"Domingo!" He called out to his cousin, not yelling, but just loud enough to reach the back room. Libros NOMEL was a small store, and the office in back, which doubled as a storage area, was only fifteen feet from the aisle where he knelt to unpack the box.

A young man thrust his head out the open door. "Sí?"

Noel tilted his head toward the counter to indicate his interest in attending to the customer. "Could you check these off the packing slip and arrange them on the shelf please?" he asked in Spanish. Domingo's English was halting at best, and Noel usually addressed him in their native tongue.

"Momentico," responded Mingo before disappearing again, sending a wave of annoyance through Noel. It was becoming a

84

pattern, this dragging of feet. The boy had been in the office for over an hour doing the bookkeeping for their new concession — stationery, greeting cards and calendars — and he was not fond of menial tasks like stocking the shelves.

As Noel rang up the woman's order, he lifted his eyes to see his cousin emerging from the office to begin the assigned task. Noel forgot his annoyance and eased into a friendly exchange with his customer about the book she had selected last month. This was the best part about owning a bookstore, keeping fresh on the latest novels and comparing impressions with other literature aficionados.

Conversation over, customer gone, Noel and Mingo were again alone in the empty store. Noel walked over, retrieved the packing slip from the floor and checked it while Mingo put two books on the shelf directly in front of them. "Those go in the classics section," instructed Noel. "Okay," said Domingo, his mind elsewhere. "Sorry." He removed the books and went to the next aisle.

Tension permeated the air between them. This morning before opening the store, Noel had asked Domingo — again — if he'd recently looked into the prospects at their uncle's factory back home. Although the inquiry was double-edged, Noel saw no reason to avoid the topic of Mingo's plans. Almost two months ago, the boy had dropped out of college mid-semester and traveled to New York on a temporary visa — just to satisfy his curiosity, he said. A traveling fever. He planned to go back, either to college or to work in their uncle's plastics factory. He didn't know which. He needed time to think. The opportunities in their country were so rotten, Noel should know.

But his visa had expired ten days ago. This morning, Noel hadn't been able to elicit anything more definitive from his young cousin. "Uncle Carlos would hire me of course, you know that," was Mingo's sure answer to Noel's question. "But it would be something in manufacturing, not in the office."

"Sometimes you have to start low and work your way up to get where you want to go," suggested Noel.

"But he's stingy with the good jobs. You remember; I worked there one summer. I swept the floors, all the plastic scraps. It stinks and it's dirty. I'd rather work in the office, or in design, something to use my brain."

Noel would be the first to agree that his cousin should be using his brain. He was a smart kid. "Go back to college, then. You shouldn't have thrown away that scholarship."

"Let someone else use the scholarship. College is no help if you want to open your own business. Uncle Carlos doesn't have a degree."

"Yes, well, you forget. He started in a factory as a boy. One of those stinking, low jobs. He worked his way up."

"With a little help along the way—"

"He did it on his own," Noel was quick to disagree.

"Take a look, Noel. New equipment three years ago, and more improvements last year. Everything up to date. Where did Uncle Carlos get the money to invest? You think Colombian peasants are buying more of his plastic wrap?"

"The economy is expanding—"

"Expanding. It's expanding, all right." He smirked with sinister implication.

"You can think what you like. Uncle Carlos isn't that kind of man."

He refused to accept Mingo's veiled accusation. Carlos was the brother of Noel's father, Ernesto, and Mingo's father, Diego. The three brothers were close and frequently got together with their large families in cramped, noisy gatherings. When he was growing up, Noel formed an image of his uncle as a great man, larger than life. He was heavy and tall, articulate and charismatic, with an expansive smile under the drooped awning of his black mustache.

Carlos's success was a shining aberration amid the extended family's meager circumstances. He'd started with nothing, just like his brothers, and had given birth to his manufacturing company from scratch, working it day and night, turning the red to black.

But Carlos was not the kind to swagger or boast of his profits. He practiced humility and restraint while exuding a comfortable measure of self-confidence. The same qualities and good fortune had not been bestowed upon his brother, Noel's father Ernesto, who crept and struggled and looked on in envy.

Although at heart Noel believed in his uncle, he knew that Carlos was able to afford his honesty because, as Mingo put it, he was stingy. He lived in a large, contemporary house—a middle-class structure by U.S. standards but luxurious to Colombians—preserving his money for his immediate family, a wife and three daughters. Noel had no memory of gifts or generosity from Carlos at family gatherings or birthdays, no interest-free loans without expectation of repayment. This was a wise sort of restraint, as Noel viewed it. The first gift or bailout would have led to the next, and there would have been no end to it if Noel and his eight siblings, Mingo and his five, had come to expect this kind of welfare.

However, family members could always go to Carlos for work. He wouldn't create a job for a relative, but if one was available, he'd canvass the family first. Usually the available jobs were not the most desirable, involving repetitive tasks and manual labor. But any kind of work was a good thing when there was so little in their world to choose from. A brother and sister of Noel, and a brother of Mingo, were working in the factory now.

With the blind certainty of youth, Domingo scoffed at Noel's defense of Carlos, as if Noel's age (an ancient thirty-three) and his long absence from their home country had left him behind in an innocent era. "You have to keep your eyes open, Noel. I've seen some things maybe you haven't. There's too much money looking for a pocket. It's a wicked business. They got to Carlos through Benita, I'm sure of it."

"That was M-19. The Cartel had nothing to do with it."

"But look what happened when Benita was released—that wasn't just a coincidence."

"Maybe so," replied Noel reluctantly. Mingo's implication was plausible. Benita, Carlos's youngest daughter, had been kidnapped for ransom three years ago. Kidnappings were everyday news in Colombia, but this was the first for the Avendaño family, and the shock hit hard when seventeen-year-old Benita disappeared. Her father had the means to pay ransom, and so, like anyone with money, Carlos and his family were targets of guerrilla groups like M-19, which used the ransom to help finance its armed revolutionary struggle.

Carlos told the family that Benita's kidnappers were M-19, but a rumor circulated that the Cali Cartel was involved. The drug lords were also engaged in kidnappings and worse, torture and murder, for the sake of coercion or retribution. Had Carlos struck a deal with the Cartel? Was he helping to launder narcotics money? Speculation abounded among Noel's siblings and cousins, who liked to point to the "evidence": within weeks of Benita's safe return home, Carlos's factory started to expand dramatically.

Why do you think I left Colombia? thought Noel upon hearing Mingo's accusations all over again. His exodus in 1983 had been motivated in part by the change he'd seen in many people, not just Uncle Carlos. Most people wanted to be left alone, to go about their business honestly and without fear, but guerilla groups and narcotics traffickers were making it ever more difficult to do so. "Economic opportunities" were relentlessly pushed, backed by physical force or threat. Dirty money seeped into everyday financial transactions, discovered too late. The sponge sucked and grew, absorbing droplets of integrity in the business community.

To the poor, the drug lords were benevolent gods, purchasing favor by "donating" a mere pittance of their wealth to impoverished communities: a new sports field, a free food program, a town festival. People Noel had grown up with were following the money, volunteering their services.

And maybe—although Noel would never admit it—he'd been the slightest bit tempted himself. He'd always lived under the burden of a self-imposed sense of obligation to his family, opening his wallet to his parents and every needy cousin, brother or sister. Financial problems had prevented him from finishing college, and his meager income as a copy editor for a textbook publisher was always gone before hitting his pocket. For so many people it was like this and usually much worse.

From such straits, a barrier cannot be erected against temptation. There was a new sickness, a get-rich-quick mentality that was, at base, foreign to his nature and sensibilities. And the justification for it didn't suit him either. "Everyone's doing it." And why not? If the norteamericanos wanted to fry their brains on drugs, let them. They were responsible. A business cannot thrive without willing customers.

"Maybe if Carlos had a decent position for me, I'd be down there," said Domingo. "But I've decided I'm not asking for one of his little jobs. And anyway," he averted his eyes and lowered his voice, "maybe I don't want to go back."

There. It was said. "Hmm," Noel responded, giving himself time to cool an impulse to vent his anger. Derision would not be productive in awakening the boy to practical considerations. After a moment, Noel said calmly, "You'll have to think about how you'll get a green card. It isn't easy."

Mingo shrugged. "I'm not worried." He turned away, putting an end to their conversation. They didn't speak for the rest of the morning.

Now, as they finished up with the new shipment of books, Noel saw an opportunity to raise the subject again. The store was empty, they were alone. Just what to say was the problem.

Mingo's reluctant admission hadn't taken Noel by surprise, but he'd been hoping against it. He didn't want a problem. So far, he'd been lucky. Out of all his cousins and siblings, Mingo had been the only one to show up on his doorstep. But he knew that one family member with illegal status often led to another, and it was easy to imagine a trail of relatives following Mingo's path, asking for help or work or money — the kind of scene he'd hoped to leave behind, he now realized guiltily.

At bottom, Noel didn't have a right to judge his cousin. Five years ago, he'd also come to the United States on a temporary visa and overstayed his welcome. From the moment he purchased his "vacation" to New York, he felt the lie. This wasn't simply a desire to travel, easily cured with a few weeks away. At his core burned an overwhelming urge to escape, to discover a world free of unsavory temptations and silently begging relatives.

But, upon arrival in the new land, his illusion of complete escape was dashed. The narcotics culture was everywhere, and its net snagged Colombians in New York just as easily as those back home. He couldn't be sure whom to trust. And he faced a new insult, something he hadn't anticipated, a subtle, insidious discrimination. *Colombian? You must be a drug dealer*, so many upstanding New Yorkers seemed to think, or even say out loud.

In those early days in the U.S., to survive, he became a liar. To get a job, he concealed his immigration status and his nationality, and as long as he lied, low paying work was surprisingly easy to get. He toiled and tried to forget his cage, the impossibility of returning to Colombia and reentering the U.S. Any such thought amidst the shifting images of family faces in his mind would bring a fierce sting to his eyes.

In seeming contradiction, the rest of his being relaxed from the lighter burden he carried in relation to them, now that his only worry was self-survival. How easy it was to abdicate the responsibility he'd been shouldering! Religiously, he sent cards and letters—but no money. They never asked, making it easier.

And before long, he had the enormous good fortune of meeting his future wife. He adored Melanie but couldn't shut his mind to a convenient truth—she held the ticket out of his legal limbo. His feelings were sincere, his motives not duplicitous, and he made sure she knew it. In 1985, less than a year after their meeting, they were married. He got his green card and could legally take a trip to his hometown and introduce Melanie to his family.

Back in Cali he found that, after all, everyone was surviving well enough without him. They warmly received the newlyweds and accepted Noel's new status as a married man with attendant responsibilities. His guilt about having abandoned them was eased.

Domingo's arrival had stirred up Noel's memories of his own beginnings in New York. From the moment they met at the airport in February, Noel could see through Mingo's claim to be "on vacation." He wasn't going back. And unlike Noel, the kid lacked maturity, making the situation that much more worrisome. There was a bounce in his lanky legs and a look of awe and excitement in that pure part of his face not yet grown out of childhood. He didn't look like a boy ready to ponder his future or map it out along practical considerations but was anxious to follow the beckoning finger of temptation into new adventures.

For the first few weeks, Melly and Noel put him up on the convertible sofa in their living room, but their work schedules kept them from seeing much of him. Mingo would creep into the apartment in the middle of the night and still be asleep when they tiptoed around him in the morning, getting ready for work. One day, he announced he'd found a room in Jackson Heights; he didn't want to impose on them anymore. They were relieved. His lifestyle clearly didn't match theirs. But they were wary. Vacationers didn't rent rooms. Mingo was planning to stay in the United States, and they wondered where he would get the money to live. He'd spent little while living with them, but any money he had would not last long on his own.

Soon enough, Mingo learned that carefree independence did not come without a price tag. Within a week he approached Noel, reluctantly asking for work. His request wasn't an unreasonable imposition. Noel had been thinking of hiring part-time help but had hesitated to take on the extra financial burden. Employing his cousin would serve both their needs, giving Mingo a little money and Noel the chance to experiment with having an employee, while avoiding the onus of a long-term commitment.

Noel had no doubt the arrangement would be temporary — Mingo was not the type to sustain an interest for long in the types of menial tasks available at Libros NOMEL, things like stocking shelves, taking inventory, ordering supplies. This theory proved correct, once Mingo got started on the job. He balked at his duties and performed them slowly, with apparent boredom.

While the boy's attitude didn't always please Noel, he might have been more concerned if Mingo acted differently, cheerfully performing the grunt work. Noel had watched Mingo grow up, knew of his intelligence, and understood the frustration of a quick mind left idle under the yoke of mindless labor. "He's just a kid," Noel liked to remind himself and Melly. "He'll learn and grow."

Noel's sense of responsibility toward Domingo battled his urge to convince the boy to return home. If his cousin was going to stay in this country, he needed to learn skills beyond those of a stock clerk, and Libros NOMEL offered few opportunities. Literature meant nothing to Mingo, so there was no sense including him in decisions about inventory. But he showed an interest in the financial aspects of running the store, in line with the accounting and business courses he'd taken in college. Since bookkeeping had never appealed much to Noel, he willingly passed some of that responsibility to his cousin.

Without eliminating the menial tasks, Noel added new assignments. Domingo counted the receipts at the end of the day, filled out bank deposit slips, and made runs to the night deposit box at a nearby branch of First City Financial. The nature of the surrounding neighborhood made Libros NOMEL largely a cash business. Domingo clearly enjoyed the feel of dollar bills in his hands and working with the old-fashioned adding machine on the desk in the office, neatly writing the resulting figures in the ledger. He was precise and careful. Noel watched and guided him, checking his work in detail, gradually relaxing his supervision. Everything was done by hand. Noel couldn't afford a computer, and the operation was small enough to handle this way.

After a few weeks of bookkeeping, Mingo hinted he wanted more responsibility, but Noel wasn't ready to give more to a boy of nineteen. He certainly didn't want to give Domingo any expectation of acquiring a share in the business. Libros NOMEL, named after Noel and Melanie, was as small in the grand scale of the world as the two of them. He had no desire to expand the store and had no illusions that the local economy could support anything bigger. It was just enough for him and Melly. He wanted to keep it that way and avoid the hands of relatives dipping into his till. These protective instincts vied with a persistent internal voice pushing him to nurture his cousin, to provide him with a good start in the world.

In the midst of this internal conflict, good fortune shined on him, solving the dilemma.

Mingo came to work one morning looking chipper. "I've made a business contact for you, Noel," he declared proudly. "I think you're going to like this."

"Tell me!" Noel was curious to know what his cousin thought of as a "business contact."

"I met a man, a Colombian, who owns a greeting card company. His name is Guillermo Restrepo, and the company is called Saludos Limitada. They manufacture stationery and Spanish greeting cards and calendars in Colombia. He's in New York, looking for stores to sell his merchandise, mostly variety stores and bookstores, so I told him about Libros NOMEL."

"Well, I hadn't really thought of selling cards…"

"They're high quality. He had some samples. I think you should see them. They'll sell easily!" Pride in his little discovery was evident. A true businessman at heart.

Noel's sense of purity was threatened. Selling a lot of knickknacks next to his books marred the integrity of his vision. But Mingo persisted, and Noel agreed to meet the man.

The next day, Guillermo Restrepo visited the store. The three of them chatted amiably in Spanish, starting with news from the home country and a comparison of the cities in which they'd been raised. Life in the mountainous capital city Bogotá was very different from Noel's and Domingo's hometown, Cali, a smaller city nearer the coastline.

Noel liked Restrepo immediately. He was forty or so, a lively, small man, who bounced on his heels and gesticulated broadly when speaking. He grew especially animated when showing off the products his company manufactured. "Look at this," he said, pulling samples from his briefcase. "We use only the highest quality paper and inks. Our stationery, cards and calendars are entirely Colombian made, using the talents of the best artists and poets. You help support struggling people back home when you carry these products in your store."

"Hmm," Noel reflected, looking through the samples. "They're very nice. Tasteful. Attractive. Well made."

"Yes," Restrepo encouraged after each adjective.

"The messages on the cards are well written. Not overly sentimental…"

"I can see you're a man of taste, with an eye for quality."

"Well, I *am* impressed. But I hadn't thought of stocking cards and stationery. I don't know if they will sell."

Restrepo smiled, the gleam of a salesman in his eye. Noel could feel the hard sell coming, but somehow didn't mind it from this man. "I can see it may be a little difficult for you to get used to something new," he said, "but I've taken a look in this neighborhood. The Spanish-speaking community is large, and there's no competing business selling these kinds of products for blocks around. I have a proposal that might ease your nerves. The deal is completely risk free. Domingo and I have talked about this at length. He's a bright young man, wouldn't you agree?"

"Yes, very bright."

Domingo slightly puffed his chest under the attention cast his way.

"So, what have you two been talking about?" asked Noel.

"I would agree to place a modest inventory in your store on a consignment basis. No need for you to pay me a cent up front. Whatever you sell, you keep a percentage of the proceeds. I'm willing to make it a sixty-forty split. You may keep forty percent of the sales price. Not a bad deal for you my friend, wouldn't you agree?"

"No risk to me, then? If I don't sell any, I mean."

"Not a penny out of your pocket."

"But what about damage? People like to handle cards and read them before deciding to buy."

Restrepo smiled knowingly and shook his head. "Nothing to worry about. A certain number are always damaged. The loss is worked into our cost. You have the same problem with books, do you not?"

"Yes, to a certain degree."

"Then you know how it is. A few are damaged, the selling price of the cards reflects it. The consumer pays. With this merchandise I'll be leaving you a list of suggested retail prices to cover these costs. So, how does it sound? You know, Domingo should get credit for the idea. He came up with the consignment arrangement." Restrepo, a foot shorter than Domingo, reached up to pat the younger man's shoulder.

"No, you're too kind Guillermo! It wasn't me. You suggested..."

"Nonsense. I wouldn't say I suggested it. I don't operate this way with my other clients. But it's evident to me you have a head on your shoulders, and I'll feel comfortable if you handle this account for me." Restrepo turned to Noel and asked, "You wouldn't mind, would you? I can see you're busy with the literature, and Domingo has expressed an interest in managing the accounting aspects of our consignment arrangement."

"Yes, Guillermo thinks I can handle it," said Mingo eagerly.

Seeing that face, hearing that voice, Noel was heartened, and he could not refuse. "No, I don't mind at all. I can see there may be some headaches I might not particularly care for. I mean, the risk-free arrangement is good for me, but it's difficult because everything must be accounted for separately."

"Exactly," said Restrepo.

Noel turned to his cousin. "You'll have to keep track of every envelope, card and calendar we sell, Mingo. The amounts we receive, the percentages, the sales tax..."

"And it would be a great help to me if he could handle the banking as well," interjected Restrepo. "I'll be returning to Colombia tomorrow; I come to New York only a few times a year to make sales. Domingo will have to set up a bank account for my share of the receipts. I like to keep dollars here so I can pay my North American suppliers for the steel and paper pulp I use in my plant in Colombia."

They laughed about the worthlessness of Colombian pesos; dollars were always coveted and hoarded back home. Noel could understand why Restrepo needed the dollars to stay here; North American companies certainly wouldn't be willing to accept anything besides dollars from a Colombian businessman. The arrangement made sense, and Noel agreed to it.

Guillermo produced a written contract, preprinted and executed with a scribbled signature on the bottom, giving Domingo authority to transact banking business for Saludos Ltda. Noel suggested that Melanie could help Domingo set up an account at First City, and Guillermo was pleased with the idea. They agreed to communicate by fax machine rather than telephone, all at the vendor's expense, since Guillermo needed to retain paper copies of business matters and the mail was too slow. Noel, feeling somewhat embarrassed and behind the times, admitted that he didn't own a fax machine. Guillermo said he would make arrangements to have one delivered and installed the next day, as long as Noel agreed to return it at the end of their business relationship.

By the time they'd finished the deal, Noel was completely satisfied with the new venture, seeing it as Mingo's little side business, something to keep him interested and busy without any financial risk, maybe even a modest income. A dollar here and there. How many greeting cards and packages of stationery could a small store like this sell? It didn't matter. Noel wouldn't lose a thing while Mingo gained accounting and business experience. The arrangement suited everyone. And if they sold enough, Noel could pay Mingo for the extra work out of his forty percent share. That way the entire account would be self-contained with no risk, no expense to Noel.

But it soon became evident that Domingo's enthusiasm for his new responsibilities meant a diminished enthusiasm for the old ones. The day after their meeting with Restrepo, the fax machine was installed in the back room, and Domingo spent an hour poring over the manual and sending test faxes. Later in the day, he visited Melanie at the main branch of First City in Manhattan to fill out an application for a business checking account. She gave him a supply of envelopes for night deposits at the branch near Libros NOMEL in Queens, where Mingo was already making deposits for Noel's business account. A few days later, the first shipment of stationery, cards and calendars arrived. Mingo dusted off some old shelving in the back, assembled it prominently near the front checkout counter, and arranged the inventory. In all, Noel was pleased to see the effort, but displeased to see that Mingo had ignored his other responsibilities for most of the week.

Now, as the boy reluctantly finished his current chore of shelving the last of the new shipment of books, Noel struggled to reopen communication. There had to be some way he could make an impression, impart some important lessons about certain obligations, certain dangers. Mingo had already shown a careless attitude about his illegal status in this country, and Noel, more than a little worried about his own liability in hiring an illegal alien, hoped he could imbue a sense of responsibility.

There were other considerations too, taxes and reporting requirements. Noel didn't know much about any of it, relying mostly on Melanie for many of his tax and financial questions. He was aware of his own tendency to float and dream, to remain immersed in art, culture and literature, the world of ideas. Figures on paper and financial matters didn't interest him, but he knew well enough he'd have to start spending some time on these things as far as Mingo was concerned. Noel wanted to help his family, but he wanted to do it the right way.

"I sold some cards while you were out this morning," started Noel.

"How much was the sale?"

"Not much. Seven or eight dollars. The money's in the side drawer, and I wrote down the amount."

"This system should work out, don't you think?" asked Mingo, referring to the accounting method they'd established between them.

"Sure. It's no problem keeping track of the card and stationery sales, as long as we keep getting such a small amount of business."

"It will pick up," Mingo replied confidently. "People will find out we carry these products and they'll be in here. Everyone needs greeting cards. And it will help your book sales too. Wait and see."

"Yes, well, you could be right. You're thinking like a businessman. It's a shame…"

"What's a shame?"

"Well, you're smart and full of energy and could do well for yourself in this country if you were here legally. You say you want to stay here, but your opportunities are going to be limited unless you become a permanent resident with a green card."

Mingo swiped the air with his hand and shook his head disdainfully. "A green card means nothing. I can do anything anyone else can. Half the people on the street are illegal. You worry too much, Noel!"

"And you don't worry enough. Do you know how many kinds of forms I had to fill out to start this business? Corporate forms and tax forms. Everyone wants to know your status. I couldn't have done it without a green card."

"Okay. I'll get one. It's easy enough."

"It's not easy at all. I don't think I can sponsor you. Only a citizen can sponsor you…"

"Like Melly did for you. Smart thinking." Domingo winked and tapped his temple with an index finger.

"What do you mean, 'smart thinking'?"

"Getting married. I'll do the same if I find it's necessary. Plenty of girls are willing to do it for money—or even for no money if they want a Latin lover. Watch me hook a local girl!"

"That's fraud. Against the girl and against the government."

"Oh, that's right. You weren't thinking about a green card. You got married for love." Domingo winked again with a sparkle in his eye. Perhaps it was meant as a joke, but he'd hit a sore spot with Noel, the obviously convenient union of his love and need.

Noel looked away, unable to compose a reply. But his reaction was enough to convey the hurt inside. Domingo had seen it and sensed that he'd gone too far. With an embarrassed laugh he said, "You know I was just teasing, cousin. Anyone can see how crazy you are about Melly. Everything else came second."

It was a sensitive, mature observation straight from Domingo's heart, the first to be heard in the new world. With great relief and surging pride, Noel turned his eyes into the light of a genuine smile on the familiar face, a person he knew and loved, his cousin, and yes, someone he could trust to do the right thing. Eventually.

7 »   SMURF

AFTER THE MEETING, away from a roomful of her superiors, Mineko was relaxed and easy with herself, not nearly as reticent as she first appeared. "Your office is down this way. I'll show you around." The task may have been assigned to her, but any orders had been given and received out of Dana's view.

Along the way, Mineko pointed out the important features of the bureau. Reception, copy room, word processing, library, lunchroom. She was warm and talkative, curious, unabashedly interested in learning more about the new team member, and maybe grateful to have another woman around, a female "boss." Despite their respective titles, TPA and ADA, they were already relating more like colleagues than anything else since they were closest to each other in the pecking order, what with Dana's low rank on the attorney roster and Mineko's superior knowledge of the investigation.

The short tour came to an end when they arrived at an open door. Mineko stepped to the side, held out her hand, and chimed "Ta-da!" inviting Dana to enter. "Yes. You guessed it. This is all yours."

The office was not much bigger than a windowless closet stuffed with used furniture—a file cabinet, secretarial-sized desk, and a chair on either side—but still it was more than she'd ever had, a place of her own. No more officemates. "This is lovely. I think I'll call it the Closet." She plopped into the swivel chair behind the desk, which held only two objects, a telephone and a green cardboard-covered blotter. With a push of her foot, the chair turned on its axis and made a half revolution before it bumped to a stop, chair back against desk.

Jammed up against the blank wall with her back to Mineko, her thoughts came loose, the things she hadn't dared to acknowledge consciously. This lack of protocol for her transfer to FC was predictable but alienating. A welcoming committee she hadn't expected, but where was the bureau chief, George Blaithe? Shouldn't *he* be the one to escort her across the threshold of her new office?

As if reading her mind, Mineko said, "George was sorry he couldn't be here." Dana swiveled around to face her. "He's busy this morning but said he would stop by this afternoon to welcome you." Mineko's ease was reassuring, the way she spoke of "George" so comfortably. After all, maybe it was better this way, to get a view of the bureau from the bottom up, through the eyes of a person who responded to the personalities in FC from a position closer to Dana's. Mineko's face was open, filled with a gentle, guiding empathy. At once, Dana felt she could trust her with any question or doubt that came to mind.

"What's he like? I've never met him." As she spoke, she toyed with the curlicue cord of the telephone. Lifting it, she noticed the imbedded grime and reflexively dropped it.

"He's always been nice to me. A good boss. But we don't see him much. At least I don't, except at bureau meetings. Bruce pretty much calls the shots in our case."

"How long have you been in the bureau?"

"It'll be two years this summer. In the fall I'm going to law school. Columbia." Pleasure at her accomplishment showed in her face despite the telltale effort to mask it.

"Congratulations! When you graduate, you'll be qualified to

shuffle more papers for Bruce Reichert."

Dana immediately regretted the sound of her comment, which she hadn't delivered with sufficient comic flair. But Mineko appeared to take it as intended: a joke, not a slight. She laughed and blinked, sending a shiver through the black satin curtain of bangs. "Analyzing bank records may not be very glamorous, but it's not so bad really," she said. "If you keep your mind on the overall picture, the money laundering scheme is interesting. And you're going to be doing stuff I'm not allowed to do, like going to court on those subpoenas."

"What's there to go to court on? Bruce told the forfeiture attorney... What's his name?"

"Joseph Paglia."

"Joe—not to do any motion practice on the subpoenas."

"I don't think he meant the nondisclosures. We always have to get nondisclosure orders up front, you know, preventing the banks from telling anyone they were served and they're giving information to the DA."

"Secrecy."

"Right. Bruce didn't give you the third degree on that?"

"On what?"

"On keeping your mouth shut. Maybe he saves that lecture for the TPAs. How we're not allowed to breathe a word about any of this to anyone, not even our boyfriends or mothers. He's worried my mother could leak our investigation. The Cartel would find out, close all the bank accounts, and split without a trace."

"Your mother."

"Right. My mother, who only speaks Japanese."

Dana laughed, remembering Bruce's circumspection—to put it nicely—during their telephone conversation. "I didn't get the lecture, but he said enough to let me know how he feels about it. Anyway, they lecture the attorneys like that during training, when we first get here. 'Heads will roll' if anyone leaks investigative secrets or grand jury evidence before an indictment is handed up."

"Funny how a lot of this supposedly secret stuff ends up in the newspapers," observed Mineko.

"Yeah. Funny, isn't it? Someone's always ready to blab for fame or glory—or a price. But we're not like that, are we?"

"Gosh no."

They smiled into each other's eyes, these women who followed the rules. Then Dana said, "A minute ago—sorry if I sounded a little down on the investigation. I didn't mean it that way." Mineko was shaking her head, waving her hand in the air. Dana continued, "This transfer took me by surprise. But I'm here now and ready to get down to work. So, what do you have for me?"

"I'll go get some of the records and show you how the scheme works. I'll be right back."

A few minutes passed, during which Dana examined the contents of her desk drawers, coming up with a leaky pen, a few paper clips and a couple of stray deli napkins, which she used to dust the empty desktop. She crumpled and tossed them into the dented metal trash can.

Mineko appeared at the door, weighted down with a large, unwieldy cardboard box. Dana sprang to her feet. "Whoa! Let me help you." She supported one end of the box and guided Mineko to the desk, where they let the load down with a slam. "You should have told me you were bringing a truckload."

"This is nothing. Wait 'til you see my cube. I practically can't sit in there anymore."

With one hand she pulled out a stack of photocopies, and with the other, flicked her bangs aside. It would become a familiar gesture, a sign of Mineko's focus and determination, those slender, porcelain fingers brushing against the perpetually falling curtain.

They sat down on opposite sides of the desk, and Mineko turned the papers sideways so they could examine them at the same time. The clipped batch consisted of bank statements, deposit tickets and canceled checks from a single checking account in the name of "Enrique Arraz." Before long, Dana understood the pattern they were looking for, something very similar to the activity in the "Luz Melendez" account, as Melanie had described it. Every few days, large amounts of cash were deposited into the Arraz account, usually in round numbers, each deposit less than $10,000. Checks were written against the account, also in large, round numbers, made payable to individuals and companies with Spanish names. Money flowed in and out again almost immediately, never resting for long.

"Look at the handwriting on the checks," said Mineko. "Notice anything?"

"Hmm. Something odd..." Dana leafed through ten pages, each containing photocopies of three or four checks. "The handwriting for the payee names seems different than the handwriting for the dollar amounts. The E's and the S's..."

"Yeah, and look at the T's."

"This is so strange. Two people wrote on every check. The same two people, because all the payee names look alike, handwriting-wise, and all the dollar amounts look alike."

"Maybe three people," suggested Mineko. "Look at Enrique Arraz's signature on each of those."

Dana leafed through the pages again. "You're right. The signatures look different than the other two handwritings, but you can't really tell, can you? I mean, the payee names and dollar amounts are printed, and the signature is more like a scrawl."

"But you can see the differences also in the thickness of the ink. It looks like different pens were used. I think they're different people too, just by the slant of the writing."

Dana thought a moment. "Enrique Arraz, the account

holder—he's another one just like Bernardo Rios."

"Who's that?"

Dana explained.

"He must be one of the couriers," said Mineko. "They run around all day depositing chunks of cash in different accounts. The couriers aren't necessarily the same as the account holders." Dana remembered the eleven deposit tickets, only one with Rios's name, and his likely deposit to the Luz Melendez account. "We think that most of the account holders are fictitious people," continued Mineko. "What does it take to open a checking account? A name, some ID, maybe a picture ID, and a social security number. Anyone can manufacture those things. You see here?" She pointed.

"Um-hmm."

"The address of the account holder is a post office box. They like to use boxes at the post office or those private mailbox places. And we've seen accounts in different names with the same address. So, each box is being used as a collection point for bank statements on several accounts."

Dana shook her head. "This is mindboggling! How many layers of people are involved in this scheme?"

"We don't know exactly."

"You have people who open the accounts who aren't the real account holders and use fictitious names. Other people manage the accounts and decide where the money goes—maybe several layers right there. More than one person writes on each check."

"And those people are taking orders from someone higher up."

"This 'Rojo' they were talking about at the meeting?" asked Dana.

"Possibly."

"Another layer. Then you have all these lowly couriers running around depositing cash. People like Rios."

"Right. So, did Bruce dismiss the case against Rios?" asked Mineko.

"How did you guess?"

"It's the kind of thing he would do. They're following as many of these couriers as they can, to find out who they report to."

Dana nodded in agreement with this bit of information, as if no one could ever disagree with such a sensible investigative plan. Inside, she burned with shame, remembering her foolish tenacity when Reichert asked for the case. A farebeat.

"I just didn't understand one thing about Rios," said Dana. "Why he had $3,300 in his pocket and would risk arrest by jumping the turnstile. Doesn't that seem odd?"

"Maybe not. Was that the exact amount?"

"As far as I could tell from the police report."

"That was Cartel money. He was probably on his way to deposit it. Maybe he just didn't have the money for the fare. These couriers are unemployed illegal aliens, gophers the Cartel can get for very little pay."

"I guess he wouldn't have thought of borrowing Cartel money for his expenses…" Dana was remembering Rios: neat, groomed, quiet, impassive. Under that façade, was he praying for an easy deal, a quick way out so he could get to the bank before it was too late? Was the fear of death coursing through his mind as he maintained his poker face, standing there next to Seth?

Seth. These last few days he'd been ever present in the substrata of her consciousness.

"No expense accounts for these little guys," said Mineko. "The couriers aren't told anything, but I'm sure they can guess who's behind it, and they know what the Cartel does with employees who step out of line. Once you work for the Cartel, they own you. And it's too risky for the managers to give them any specific information about the scheme, so this Rios was more valuable to us on the street, where we could follow him. If we arrest and interrogate him, we won't get any useful information and we can't prosecute him for anything juicy anyway. A waste of time. Bruce and the Don are looking for bigger fish."

"Who's 'the Don'?"

"The lead investigator. You know, he was in the meeting this morning. Detective Paul Donegan." Mineko smiled and bobbed her head knowingly. "I went through the same thing when I started here! Bruce isn't very good at introductions."

Dana rolled her eyes, letting them settle on Mineko's solid-dark irises, framed in oblique folds. Her eyes were intelligent and communicated a quiet confidence tempered with a measure of restraint and deference.

"Maybe we aren't the stars of social etiquette over here," admitted Mineko, "but at least it's a little less chaotic than the trial bureau. I hear that anything goes in misdemeanors. Is that true?"

Dana laughed. "The Land of Misdemeanors. It's another reality." Already, that other reality was beginning to fade. She thought of the telephone messages from Seth, one last Friday and another (just a "please call") yesterday, Monday. She hadn't returned the calls. What would she say to him? She could manufacture any story she fancied about her reassignment and the dismissal of the case. Almost anything was believable in the Land of Misdemeanors, where illogical things happened daily. But Seth was intuitive. He was sure to wonder what was up the moment he saw Evan, an obviously experienced attorney, handling a farebeat case in AP-6.

Everything was so damn complicated when all she wanted to do was return his calls, free from worry. She'd never hidden from another person in her life, but she was hiding from Seth, the last person she wanted to evade. It would be nice to explore his interest in her without the fear that he would see through whatever she had to say. Whenever she lied or became embarrassed, pink blotches of color sprinkled her creamy complexion, an involuntary reaction over which she had little control. But maybe there was another possibility, maybe she could steer the conversation away. "Oh, let's not talk about work," she would quip over the rim of her Manhattan.

No, it was impossible. She couldn't return the call.

"Who are the payees? The people and companies getting the checks?"

"I'd love to know," said Mineko with a sigh. "That's really a step above what I'm doing. Bruce and Joe and Evan are working on that. From what I know, some of them are Colombian companies, some Panamanian. Whether the companies are shells or legitimate, the Cartel uses them to launder the cocaine money."

"But wait a minute. How do you even know all this money is from narcotics and not gambling or fraud scams or even something legal? Just because you have Spanish names on these accounts and some Colombian companies..."

"You didn't know that *all* Colombians are cocaine traffickers?"

The male voice coming from the doorway alarmed her as much as the suggestion. Dana's head bounced up from the papers on the desk to see Evan standing at the threshold, wearing a small, barely suppressed smile squeezing a dimple into his cheek. Her alarm vanished. His face was round and exposed by the receding hairline, open and honest like the ceramic circle she'd noticed earlier at the top of his head.

"All right, all right! Don't look at me like that," he said. "Your maternal grandmother is Colombian, am I right?"

Dana shifted in her seat, beating down those pink blotches. "I guess all Colombians are linked to the Cartel...," she said, feeling the heat rise, but she was driven to go on, "...like all Italians are Mafiosi."

"Something like that. Hey, maybe we better find out what

Joe's been doing with all that money he forfeits. Straight back to the Gambino family!"

Now two of his dimples were showing, and Dana had to smile.

Evan passed through the door and took a few steps into the office, Dana's cozy cubbyhole. There wasn't room to advance further, or he'd end up in Mineko's lap. "Seriously, that wasn't a dumb question you were asking," he said. "But believe me, we have a lot more evidence than just names on pieces of paper." He came over to the box, picked out a stack of papers, and placed them on a flat palm like the tray of a scale, weighing them.

"Thanks a lot," said Mineko.

"You're welcome," he said a bit flippantly and slapped the top of her head with the papers. He turned his eyes on Dana, pointed to his bald spot and said, "Now you know where I got this. I just had to give Minnie one back." To Mineko: "Where'd you get that attitude? Always testing me. You know I'm jealous — the accounts are the best part of this case!"

The tension in Dana's neck and face relaxed as she marveled at the unsuppressed openness of her new colleagues, wondering if Reichert simply had the effect of bottling people up whenever they were in his presence.

"You're going to give her the wiretaps, aren't you?" asked Mineko.

"So quick, so quick! Don't mind her, Dana. She's just showing off. I was on my way to get a copy of the papers for you now."

"The wiretaps?"

"The applications for the wiretap orders," he explained. "They have summaries of the evidence in support of probable cause to tap the phones at the collection and distribution points. These are the places they stash and divide and deliver the cash and cocaine. You'll see it all laid out in there. Basically, the Special Narcotics Bureau started this case more than three years ago with a cocaine bust for a relatively small amount, only five kilos."

"Is it Jack's case?"

"How did you…? So, you know ADA DuBois?"

"She was my seminar leader during rookie training."

"Lucky you! Yeah, this was her case from the get-go. The defendant on the five kilos was Colombian, and SNB suspected a direct Cartel link. They decided not to arrest one of the defendant's lower level accomplices so they could tail him. He led us to other suspects and a cash house, where we seized three million in small bills."

"I heard about that one," said Dana, remembering headlines in the newspapers during her last year in law school.

"Could've been that one or any number of others. In the past few years there've been a lot of large cash seizures by state investigators and the feds. And a lot of large coke seizures, hundreds of kilos in warehouses. It was enough to put a crimp in supplies and jack up the price of kilos—the old supply and demand. Then the Cartel started noticing the cash seizures were more than a drop in the bucket and so, we think, they responded with trickier schemes. Now they don't leave the money sitting around. In the last six months we haven't made a big seizure, only a few in the hundreds of thousands."

"Next to nothing." Mineko rolled her eyes.

"Minnie's worried—she put in for a cut to pay her upcoming law school bills."

"Say, that's a legitimate state law enforcement expense," Dana tried.

Evan and Mineko laughed politely.

"Joe's handling all those forfeiture cases, right?" asked Dana.

"Right. He's been busy. All cash narcotics proceeds are forfeitable to the state."

"And the money ends up somewhere in state government?"

"It's directed straight back to us. All that cash is helping to fund this investigation. I think we even bought that chair you're sitting in."

"At Salvation Army," said Mineko.

"Hey, what did I say about that attitude?" Evan grinned. "You're forgetting the good stuff."

"Like the Don's wardrobe..."

"...like the, well, now, that's okay as long as he wears those spiffy new polo shirts while he's using the new surveillance equipment, the tape recorders, the undercover cars..." Evan was pulling down one finger at a time as he counted their acquisitions.

"That's incredible!" exclaimed Dana. "I wonder what the Cartel would think if they knew their profits were helping us to catch them."

"They probably *do* know," said Mineko.

"Yes, I'm sure they do, but they're not trembling in their boots. We're getting closer to them, that's for sure, but they still outnumber us and think they can outsmart us. They're a highly intelligent bunch, running a sophisticated, well-oiled machine with a hierarchy like a corporation. It's the Chrysler of the cocaine industry—"

"Please, *Chrysler*?" A shudder passed through the silky black curtain.

"What do I know about business? Anyway, you get the picture, Dana."

"So, where does Financial Crimes come in?"

"I thought you'd never ask. FC is handling the money laundering aspects of the investigation, which developed only five months ago, quite by accident. The Special Narcotics Bureau had gone up on a couple of wires and was doing some surveillance when things kind of snowballed. Their suspects led to new suspects, and the narcotics detectives noticed they were following people running around to banks. On the wires, they were intercepting conversations that seemed to direct the distribution of money rather than kilos. Still, Jack and her team didn't notify FC or ask for our help."

"I guess Bruce didn't like that," blurted Dana, remembering the tension in the air when Evan had asked if Jack was coming to the meeting. Dana's fascination with the internal politics of the DA's office coincided with her growing ease around Evan and Mineko. She had a hunch that they, like all good people, shared her aversion to Bruce Reichert. Certainly, they would let her in on the secrets of any internecine warfare.

Instantly, however, she realized that her impression rested on invisible underpinnings. She may have crossed a line. Her easiness slowly iced as Evan returned her comment with a noncommittal, lukewarm smile. "You could say that," he said.

Not skipping a beat, Evan continued his story: "Jack had a target named Alvarez who was arrested on an unrelated charge, an assault against his wife, and Special Narcotics didn't know about it. Alvarez had ten deposit tickets in his pocket for the fifty-five grand he handled in the day or two before his arrest. Luckily, an ADA in the Domestic Violence Unit thought it was odd and contacted us. We learned the defendant was Colombian, so we called Jack to see if she knew anything about him…"

"Oh, that's right. I almost forgot," interjected Dana. "Colombian citizen plus money equals narcotics trafficker."

Evan laughed. "You got it. Actually, the deposit tickets for several different bank accounts were the main clue. We were already aware of a federal investigation into a money laundering case like this. They call it 'structuring' under the federal law."

"So, why didn't you hand Alvarez over to the U.S. Attorney?"

Evan and Mineko exchanged looks. "There are plenty of Colombians to go around, believe me," said Evan.

More secrets? Or maybe just another sign of an acquired perspective. The first clue had been that oddly quiet brush-off to her suggestion at the meeting that they pool their resources with Queens. The second was Evan's careful response to her hint at bad feelings between SNB and FC. Now, a third clue, Evan's apparent unwillingness to give anything up to the feds. Was cooperation a dirty word?

Dana hesitated to delve further and said only, "Right," in response to Evan's explanation. "So, the way we know this is narcotics money is the surveillance on Alvarez?"

Evan nodded. "Just a few days before his arrest, detectives saw another suspect leave a known cash house and deliver a package to Alvarez. After the delivery, the narcotics detectives tailed him to several of these banks on the deposit tickets. They stopped following him the evening he was arrested, so they didn't know when Midtown South took him in on the wife beating. Not very odd in a city as big as this, where the head can't see the tail wagging. But now we're keeping tabs on a lot of these couriers, linking them to the cash houses. A picture of the overall scheme comes together when you combine these surveillances with known facts about the Cartel from past prosecutions and the crazy activity in these accounts. In just the last few months, Minnie has identified, what, more than a hundred smurf accounts?"

"A hundred twenty-three so far."

"How did you get so many?" asked Dana. "I mean, Alvarez is the only courier you've arrested with deposit tickets, right?"

"And now Rios," said Evan. "But you're right, we started with ten accounts, subpoenaed those, and it just keeps branching out."

"For example," said Mineko, "we'll subpoena the accounts of the payees of known smurf checks and find deposits from other smurf accounts. Sometimes the banks even give us leads by accident. They'll photocopy three or four checks on the microfilm that has the check we subpoenaed, and those other checks will be smurf accounts we didn't know about. They happen to be on the same microfilm because batches of smurf checks from different accounts often get presented for payment on the same day. Whenever we get new accounts we subpoena them, and those accounts lead to others, and it goes on and on..."

"Seemingly forever," said Dana.

"Into infinity."

Within the hour, infinity was upon her. She spent the rest of the day alone in her peg hole, the Closet. Immersed in paperwork, she foresaw more and more of it without respite.

In the afternoon, George Blaithe stopped by to welcome her with a big smile. He was a colorless, well-respected man, someone she would be seeing little of. No chance of developing a relationship like the one she'd had with Patrick, who'd always been accessible, interested and eager to help.

Who would be her mentor, the person to go to with her questions and problems? Mineko would be reliable and helpful, but Dana needed a senior attorney on her side. Certainly not Bruce. Possibly Joe, once she got to know him, but Evan seemed most likely. She worried about having blown that chance, stepping over the line with her comment about Bruce, implying his pettiness. *That new rookie Dana—she's potentially traitorous.* The depth of Evan's loyalty to Bruce was unknown, and so, for now, she had to remain wary of his seeming transparency, his expression of fuzzy friendliness, the open, round face and unadorned baldness. She'd been deceived by appearances before.

"Isn't Evan great?" Mineko had remarked the minute he stepped out the door. "Really fun to work with." Mineko should know, yet Dana sensed the existence of critical details Evan had left unsaid and might never reveal. She was still an outsider and possibly would remain that way. She had no way of knowing if her status would change.

She felt the distance between herself and the others now, as she sat alone, thumbing through her first stack of the drudgery to come.

Still, there was no need to rush things—it was only her first day.

8 » NONDISCLOSURE

TRUE TO MINEKO'S prediction, Dana was soon asked to make a court appearance. With excitement, she anticipated the rapture of a brief escape from her cubbyhole and the mountains of paper. In two days' time, she'd assembled a new group of suspicious accounts, and Reichert wanted action on them "now." He told her to meet with Joe on the "nondisclosures."

Why Joe? She didn't understand until she examined copies of old subpoenas, each one issued by Joseph Paglia. Beneath his signature was a court order prohibiting the bank from disclosing the subpoena to anyone, signed by "The Honorable Sandra K. Brick."

Moments after this discovery, Mineko walked into the Closet. "Welcome to the Forfeiture Unit," said Dana dryly.

A quizzical look, a flick of the bangs.

"I just figured out that Joe signed all these subpoenas," Dana explained. "Why aren't they issued by the grand jury hearing the money laundering crimes?"

"Because of grand jury secrecy," said Mineko. "Joe's forfeiture case is a separate civil action, so he isn't allowed to see any grand jury evidence. But if he issues all the subpoenas—then everyone can use the evidence."

"But *we* apply for the nondisclosure orders. Makes perfect sense."

"I don't know why. Maybe Joe can explain."

Dana would have to ask Joe, but first, she needed to have the subpoenas typed. She went to word processing and sought out Cathy, the typist assigned to Bruce's team. When introduced on Dana's first day, Cathy had been somewhat cool and aloof. Now, in response to the newcomer's first assignment, she wasn't any friendlier, but she quickly completed the task in a professional manner.

Dana gathered up the subpoenas and headed to the eleventh floor, taking the stairs down one flight. The Forfeiture Unit was tucked around a corner at the end of the linoleum corridor, a small suite of five offices, the largest one identified with the placard, "Joseph Paglia, Assistant District Attorney."

His door stood open. Behind the desk, Joe sat in rolled-up shirtsleeves, furiously scribbling on a yellow pad. When she knocked on the doorjamb, his eyes momentarily jumped up to meet hers and fell again to his work. With two fingers, he beckoned her forward while he continued to write.

Dana stepped in and halted halfway between door and desk, unable to sit. The office, three times larger than the Closet, offered less available space, most of it jammed with file cabinets, stacks of cardboard boxes and red expanding file folders. The two chairs intended for visitors supported their own haphazard skyscrapers of pads, papers and files. Her nostrils prickled from dust and stale cigarette smoke invisibly hovering, saturating the carpet, walls and furnishings. Joe wasn't smoking just then, but a recently dumped ashtray sat on his desk at arm's length.

He stopped writing and glanced up again, making a quick appraisal of his junior colleague. "This case is eating me alive," he declared with a small beleaguered smile. His eyes were tired, seemingly weighted by their dense lashes, and his brow glistened. He was sweating. The temperature in the room was pleasant, the extra heat generated by Joe himself. "Whacha got?"

"Sorry to bother you. I have some subpoenas for you to sign."

"Sure." He beckoned again. The two fingers. Taking the dozen papers from her with a brisk tug, he started to sign one after another without reading them.

"Do you want to know anything about these accounts?" she asked.

"More smurfs?"

"Yes."

"I trust you." His voice conveyed preoccupation but was not unkind. His tone lacked the chumminess of Evan's, but there was nothing in it to suggest annoyance. "Here you go," he said, handing them back, then, "Oh. I guess you'll need to see some sample applications." He stood, went to a file cabinet, and opened a drawer.

To his back, she said, "I was wondering why an FC attorney would make the applications, I mean, since they're forfeiture subpoenas..."

Joe stopped riffling through the papers in the cabinet and shot a look over his shoulder. "We're a team here," he said matter-of-factly, and continued to search through the crammed drawer. "Lately, Evan's been doing some of the nondisclosures as a favor to me when he's in court on the wiretaps. Now, I guess you're the logical person. You'll be having daily responsibility for the checking accounts."

He pulled some papers out and handed them to her as he talked. "The typing pool in FC has a copy of these papers on disk. Just make a new set with your name and add a little something about the accounts on these new subpoenas. Then sign the affirmation, take the application down to Part 64 and try to squeeze in when Judge Brick has a moment. She's the supervising judge on this investigation. She'll sign the subpoenas without much trouble." He sat down, pulled his chair up to the desk, and picked up his pen.

Dana weighed the papers in her hand. Joe looked up from his pad. "Don't worry," he added. "This is a breeze, and I hear you're good."

She scanned the first page. At the top was a declaration that Joseph Paglia made the affirmation "under the penalties of perjury." Ten pages followed, dense with evidence from the investigation and legal arguments. The last page was signed by Joe on January 5, 1988, almost four months ago, shortly after the team had started the investigation.

Joe's voice cut through. "I wish I could spend more time with you on this, but I'm trying to collect my thoughts. A witness will be here with his lawyer in fifteen minutes." He was polite, but there was an edge to his voice. He glanced at his watch.

She'd missed his signals and had lingered too long. "I...I'm sorry," she stammered, and made for the door, waving the papers in the air behind her. "Thanks for these."

"I'll bring you up to speed on a few things later, when I have more time," he said, pushing up a tense smile to meet her final, over-the-shoulder glance.

Well, it serves you right for not calling first. Her thoughts were sharp against the empty click of her heels on linoleum as she retraced her steps back to the Closet. Emotion rose within her; reason fought it back.

In someone else, the abruptness might have been a moat at the base of a tower. But in Joe, she'd detected more to his personality, an underlayer of warmth and amiability. Her own need for self-validation had caused her to imagine a personal slight in his perfectly upright, professional behavior. *Pull back. Look at the papers, use your own judgment, the rest will come later.*

Back at her desk, she read the sample carefully, a time-consuming task. Joe's statement had a level of detail beyond her knowledge. He'd described the hierarchy of the Cali Cartel from the chief operating officers in Colombia to the managers and distributors in New York; the meticulous accounting methods of each distribution group; the network of storage facilities for the cocaine and cash; the fleet of converted cars and vans equipped to carry and conceal heavy loads of cocaine; a list of recent seizures totaling thousands of kilos and millions of dollars; a schematic of the money laundering scheme; murders and other crimes of retaliation inflicted on wayward employees; and the common practice of abandoning cocaine, cash, and bank accounts if the Cartel suspected police activity. This last evidence was meant to impress the court with the need for a nondisclosure order.

The legal arguments were new to Dana, so she took a trip down the hall to FC's small library and spent another hour researching. She was beginning to panic. The morning was nearly gone, and this "breeze" of a project was taking precious time away from her work on the bank records. *Just make a new set of papers in your name,* Joe had said. But how could she sign something she didn't fully understand? She needed to be prepared for court.

Planning to photocopy the more important points of law, Dana shoved bookmarks into four fat volumes and carried them out of the library. Just outside the door, she stepped directly into the path of Bruce Reichert as he bounded along the hallway in the direction she was going.

He took up stride beside her, eyeing the load obliquely. "Doing a little research?"

"Just the cases in the nondisclosure application."

His eyebrows instantly crashed, forming a single, bushy line. "You haven't been to Judge Brick yet?"

"Not yet. Later today…"

He stopped dead, bringing her up short. "Later will be too late. Just run those papers through word processing. Cathy has it on disk. When you get the orders, ask the Don to assign one of his men to serve the subpoenas today, before bank closing." With that, Bruce stepped past her and quickly put distance between them.

His speed broke her engine. Dragging her heels back to the Closet, Dana felt the load of dead words in her four fat volumes. She let the books fall to the desktop, a gust of air sending papers over the edge like autumn leaves swirling to the gutter. She dropped into her chair, biting a quivering lip. That man pushed a button in her, made her see red, and brought her dangerously close to lashing out.

This dark energy would destroy her if she didn't turn it around and use it, build on it. She looked at her watch. In theory, the task wasn't impossible. Quickly, she analyzed the obstacles and unknowns. The Don might prove easy or tough, depending on whether, like some veteran cops, he was invested in his own ego and turf. Cathy might be a problem, judging from her coolness and vaguely hostile expression. Judge Brick, if true to rumor, was an unpredictable number, most days a prosecutor's judge, then wildly and unexpectedly swinging over to the defense.

Plotting the shortcuts and assuming the cooperation of these accomplices, she could make it happen.

Dana walked right up to Cathy with an apologetic explanation of the emergency and planted herself next to the desk. Cathy brought up Joe's affirmation on her computer screen. Her usual aloofness warmed slowly in response to Dana's humility and the pleasant, medium-low timbre of her voice as she dictated the necessary changes. Within half an hour, the papers were printed, and Dana signed them, uttering profound thanks.

Before leaving for court, she called the Don, gently interrupting his unexpected chattiness (welcoming her to the team, inviting her to visit him and the DA's detective squad down in their basement offices). She pleaded for help and he delivered. One of his men, Gilbert Herrera, would meet her in court to grab the freshly signed subpoenas and run to the banks before closing time.

Papers in hand, Dana rushed to the courtroom on the tenth floor of the building. It was about two o'clock, a potentially for-tuitous time if Judge Brick could be caught just before starting her afternoon session.

Outside the courtroom, things didn't look promising. The corridor was nearly empty, everyone already inside. Only one person lurked near the door, a slight, dark man with a face full of holes like a bubbling pancake on the griddle, ready to be turned. He walked toward her, smiling crookedly. She didn't know this man, yet instantly recognized him as any one of many defendants she might have arraigned in the past several months.

Instinctively, she acted oblivious and averted her eyes, focusing intently on the double door of the courtroom. But he per-sisted in his approach, coming up to her, very close, just outside the door.

"ADA Hargrove?"

She turned to face him, this ugly man with surprisingly blameless eyes. "Yes," she said, trusting.

"I'm Gilbert." He stuck out a hand.

"Oh...hi!" She took the hand, callused and scratchy. "Thanks for coming. How did you know me?"

"I guess it's my job to know people."

That and other things, she supposed, like the ability to remove the innocent light in his eyes when working undercover. She smiled. "Well, let's see if we can catch the judge."

They pushed the swinging doors in, he on the left, she on the right. The audience portion of the courtroom and the judge's bench were empty. Five people were behind the bar. The court clerk was at his small table to the right of the bench, the court stenographer was at her steno machine near the witness box, and a male ADA unknown to Dana was hunched over papers at the prosecutor's table on the left, nearest the empty jury box.

At the defense table on the right sat Legal Aid attorney Vesma Krumins, a former adversary of Dana's in one of her misdemeanor trials. Vesma's biggest claim to fame was the spectacle she'd created about a month ago in the arraignment part. Dana had been sitting in the unusually crowded audience section, awaiting the beginning of her graveyard shift, watching Vesma handle the last few arraignments before midnight. There was something odd about her. At the changing of the guard, Vesma unexpectedly stripped off a bulky outer layer of clothing to reveal a form-fitting oyster-colored dress underneath! A bouquet of flowers materialized in her hand as certain people in the audience revealed themselves to be members of a wedding party, including a tuxedoed Legal Aid investigator, her groom. Of course, all of it had been prearranged by the participants, but the other professionals in the courtroom were taken by surprise. The night court judge, a friend of Vesma's, came on the bench and married them in a five-minute ceremony, followed by tremendous cheers from the audience and a quick getaway for Vesma and her new husband. Left behind were Dana and the befuddled Legal Aid attorney, scheduled to carry on between midnight and eight.

This memory would have been enough of a diversion (how could Vesma possibly show her face in court afterward?) if it weren't for the presence of another attorney behind the bar, a man who sent a ping into Dana's nerve endings. Sharing the defense table with Vesma was Seth Kaplan. What luck.

Sitting in silence, the five people turned to look at the newcomer making those audible clicking noises as she came up the center aisle. Gilbert's rubber soles, the material of stealth, were inaudible. Seth's eyebrows were raised in obvious interest. Dana tried to avoid him—a futile idea—by turning right out of the center aisle, traversing a long pew, and turning into the far-right aisle to approach the bar. Gilbert continued to walk up the center aisle and took a seat, while Dana leaned over the bar to speak with the court clerk.

"I need to see Judge Brick. Is she coming?"

"On her way."

"What's going on in here this afternoon?"

"None of your beeswax."

The clerk's lips had not moved. Dana turned to see that parenthetically-defined grin and those lively blue eyes focused directly on her. She glanced back at the clerk, said "Thanks," and walked slowly along the bar toward Seth. "Why the secrecy?"

"I don't know. You tell me."

The door of the robing room opened, and in walked Judge Brick. "All rise," intoned the clerk. Those seated complied.

The judge was a tall woman, grown to giant proportions atop her elevated platform. She waved everyone down as she took her seat. "Call the case, Barry."

Dana took a seat next to Gilbert in the first pew as the clerk read the docket number and the two defendants' names. The stenographer moved her fingers. With a fluttery stomach, Dana checked her watch. 2:07. She could kick herself, losing the chance to edge in first! Seth's case might take two minutes or all afternoon.

Luckily, it turned out to be the two-minute variety. The case was left over from the morning calendar, on for a second call. Vesma and Seth each represented a codefendant in an armed robbery. During the morning calendar, everyone but Seth had been present, including the two defendants, who'd been produced from jail. Seth had been in another courtroom, summing up in a jury trial. Now that he was present, both defendants were absent. By mistake, they'd been sent back to Rikers Island during the lunch break. The case was scheduled for the court's decision on defense motions, but the court hadn't made a decision because the ADA had missed the deadline to file responding papers.

All in all, it was a familiar ritual of missed connections and delay as the clock ticked on the timecards of the six state employees inhabiting the vacuous courtroom.

"I'll give you a week, that's it," said the judge. "May 6. Time chargeable to the People." She cracked the gavel and stood, apparently on her way to the door, oblivious of Dana and Gilbert. Surprised at being ignored, Dana jumped to her feet, suddenly realizing that the judge had no reason to think she was waiting to see her.

Gilbert jumped too and opened the little gate for Dana, letting her walk through ahead of him and past the three attorneys who were heading out. The movement caught the judge's eye. "Mr. Herrera," she greeted Gilbert, who saluted with an index finger. Feeling small, Dana addressed the court: "May we approach, Your Honor?"

Judge Brick waved them forward and dismissed the stenographer. "You're here on the Cartel?" she asked once they were standing alongside the bench. The word "Cartel" nudged Dana's fear of betraying her secrets. She glanced over her shoulder and saw Seth headed for the exit, beyond earshot.

"Yes, Judge," said Gilbert.

"What's new with the Colombians? Put 'em all away yet?"

"All but one or two," he said with his crooked smile.

The judge turned to Dana. "And you are…?"

"ADA Hargrove from the Financial Crimes Bureau."

The judge lifted an eyebrow in appraisal and cleared her throat. "What do you have?"

"We're requesting nondisclosure orders on subpoenas for bank records." She handed the papers up, wondering if she should continue talking or simply let the application speak for itself.

The judge flipped through the papers without reading, too

fast even for a good scan. "Funny," she said, her eyes still on the papers. "I could have sworn you were Joe Paglia or Evan Goodhue."

Dana caught her breath until the judge raised her eyes, revealing the levity in them. Dana managed a smile. Without waiting for comment, the judge scribbled her signature on each of the twelve subpoenas and handed them back. "Take these over to Barry and he'll stamp them for you." She stood and winked at Gilbert before stepping away and swishing out the side door.

So that was it. Dana watched the court clerk apply the official court stamp. Gilbert checked his watch and said, "We've got enough time." As soon as the subpoenas were stamped, he took the bunch directly from the clerk, and with another one of his index-finger salutes, stepped away and padded briskly out of the courtroom.

The big day in court was over. Back to the paper grave. Dana's steps down the center aisle were slow and measured. Behind her, the court clerk was packing up. At the door she extended her arm, fingertips poised on the wood surface. Before pushing it open, she looked through the little rectangular window.

There, on the other side of the pane, Seth's eyes were drawing her in.

"Let's not talk about work," she said breezily over the rim of her Manhattan. She took a sip, and with affected nonchalance, surveyed the dim room from her perch at the bar. The tables, aisles and corners brimmed with laughing acquaintances, familiar mouths sipping well-deserved drinks. Mostly ADAs. Why had Seth agreed to meet her in this DA hangout? And why hadn't she thought of how it would look, being seen here with him?

But there were more important things to worry about, like

why she'd consented to meet him at all, knowing he would ask her about Rios. She wasn't here simply to alleviate her guilt over a few unanswered phone messages. Her true motivation could be felt now in the beat of her heart and the press of her sweaty palm against the cool glass.

"No, let's not," he mocked, and lifted his glass to pull a sip from the top. She watched him obliquely in profile. The beer left a thin residue of foam on his upper lip, which he patted gently with a napkin. She guessed that, if this had been a night out with the guys, he would have just licked that upper lip clean.

He turned his head to look at her directly. "I guess there's nothing *to* talk about. Stuff like this happens every day. A senior ADA from Financial Crimes takes a farebeat case away from a rookie who's then transferred to FC." He pushed away from the bar and swiveled toward her on the barstool, resting a hand on one of his knees, leaning slightly forward. His words and posture were politely insistent, a quality she'd admired in the courtroom. Not a screamer or a whiner like so many defense attorneys. Not pugnacious or falsely righteous, but quietly respectful and self-assured.

She hadn't told him about her transfer. "So, you called me again? I mean, after I transferred."

"Yes. You caught me. I confess. They said you'd transferred and swore they'd give you the message."

"I never got it."

"Or the next one?"

"No." She aimed a wrinkled brow at him. "Only the first two messages, when I was still in the trial bureau."

"Maybe I called a few times. I was confused." He laughed and scratched his head with evident embarrassment, a gesture that seemed genuine, like everything else about him. "And you're still gonna leave me in the dark."

"You're putting me in an awkward position, Seth."

"I know. I expected as much. All those state secrets."

"Something like that."

"Serves me right though, doesn't it?" He lifted his eyebrows and sipped again. "I'm not about to give you all of my secrets about Bernardo Rios. All those juicy things he told me in confidence."

"Unless you'd like to risk getting disbarred."

"That's not a bad idea. Maybe I could open up an aerobics studio."

"You're into aerobics?"

"You're shocked, I can tell."

"Not at all." She reexamined him briefly and discovered the source of his attractiveness. He exuded good health—not a common sight in the gritty, stagnant air of the Criminal Court building.

"I'm told it's not a manly activity. But the critics forget it's a great place to watch women jump around in skimpy attire."

"And maybe a place to meet a few of them."

"Well, that part hasn't really worked out." He smiled and scratched his head again.

They fell silent, and Dana was relieved to give her mind and voice a break. The barroom was smoky and noisy. Later, when she got home, her clothes would reek.

"So," he started again. "If we can't talk about work in a specific way, we can stick to the general things. That doesn't violate any rules, does it?"

"Depends, I guess."

"We never finished our conversation about the good guys versus the bad guys."

"Not much to talk about," she said, feeling looser now with a sudden gush of warmth in her throat and cheeks. "We're the good guys and you're the bad guys. End of discussion."

"Now, that's interesting. I always thought it was the other

way around. Haven't you heard of the tyranny of the state? Oppression of the individual? You represent the power machine with its vast resources, while I represent—"

Dana laughed out loud, her self-restraint quickly evaporating. "You can't be serious. Little me, part of a power machine!"

"You're powerful, woman. The power radiates from your eyes." His grin was delicious, but she didn't acknowledge the dubious compliment and looked at him askance. He went on. "You represent power. I represent the lowly and downtrodden, the ghetto dweller who can't hope to attain wealth and power, can't even make it to the middle class. He's a person who's been abused or neglected all his life and schooled in the laws of the street..."

A smile crept onto her lips. This had to be a joke, a farcical imitation of his colleagues who bought into those pat excuses. She'd never heard Seth talk like this in court. He always gave his clients a fully adequate defense but saved his zeal for the deserving few whose guilt was truly doubtful. Now, over drinks, he was only playing with her, flirting. There was a devious look in his eyes, quote marks embedded on either side of his grin. He was testing her, looking for a reaction, dishing out a good tease. She believed him to be the opposite of these ideas, a person with a deeply felt sense of right and wrong, shunning stereotypes and classifications. He was more like her than like them. Why else did she consent to meet him here? She would play along.

"A great speech," she said. "I've heard that one before, but not from you."

"You haven't been in the courtroom long enough, Class of '87."

"I could have sworn you were also an '87."

"'86."

"That's right, I knew that."

"Of course."

"You're handling felonies in Supreme Court now."

"Damn right."

"Then experience speaks. What about honesty and individual responsibility? I guess the poor are genetically incapable of developing those traits. Their only choices are drugs or crime. Or both."

"A typical DA response." His grin widened, then his lips pursed around the rim of his glass for another sip. He wiped his upper lip again. When the napkin was removed, the playfulness in his expression had vanished, replaced with the beginnings of a dangerous intensity. "Of course the poor are capable of responsibility. Most are honest. But it's the state that decides to prosecute street criminals in greater numbers than the big-time, white-collar and corporate swindlers, or the executives who cheat on their taxes and beat their wives."

"I don't think that's true, but I don't have the statistics. I'm not involved in the decisions about who's prosecuted. I just handle what my boss and the cops give me."

"But one of these days you'll be in the position to decide."

"I doubt it."

"I think you will be." His eyes spoke his assurance and she blushed, hoping the dim surroundings would hide her change in color. "You're an ADA going places, I can tell," he continued. "And you have to beware of how they're shaping you with a distorted emphasis on street crime."

"It isn't distorted. What about the white-collar criminals prosecuted by Financial Crimes? You forgot, I transferred. And what about organized crime? My office has brought a number of prosecutions." She hoped to sound sufficiently general and vague, without a hint of her current assignment. "These aren't your white-collar executives or your street criminals either."

"Those cases are a small percentage. Anyway, I don't represent those types of people, and I won't represent them even if I get good at this. The rich can afford the best attorneys. I hope to even out the ranks. My clients, the people who qualify for Legal Aid, are people who grew up in the slums and projects. Most of them never had a single person on their side. They need a voice, and I'm their voice. Their crimes can always be explained. Degrading circumstances have an impact on behavior. I might have been in the same boat if I'd been born into one of those types of homes. Without any opportunity or hope, what is there? If we'd been dirt poor, who can say that you or I wouldn't be tempted into a life of crime? Who can say?"

His ardor touched her, but only superficially. She was caused to think of her own modest upbringing, the way she'd financed her education with loans and part-time work. Sure, it was a far cry from the ghetto, but what about Jack and other people who'd overcome dire conditions? "You have a point, maybe. Who can say what we would have done? But look at all the success stories, the people who rise above their circumstances. Blaming the world and making excuses gets no one anywhere. What good does it do to make excuses for people who hurt other people? If you want to change society, you have to go to the source."

"Poverty."

"Declining morality and broken families. Personal responsibility is taught by the family…"

"Sorry. Poverty is the source. How can a single mother teach values when she's slaving away at a minimum wage job?"

"Or teach by example if she feels entitled to collect welfare indefinitely?"

"We're back to poverty. If I were a businessman, I might find a way to battle poverty. But I'm a lawyer, so I do this."

"And you're good at it and getting better. Soon you'll be every bit as good as the expensive lawyers who represent those rich, white-collar criminals." As Dana spoke she searched his eyes, looking for, but not finding, a splash of lightness, the ghost of his parenthetical grin. His face had become hard. "So, you think the poor should have the same chance as the rich to beat the rap. Is that how you want to use your talent?"

"That's my mission, though I wouldn't put it in your terms."

Dana shook her head. "I could never have a job making excuses for people."

"I don't make excuses for people. I try to hold onto their rights. *You*," he jabbed, "take rights away. You deprive people of their liberty."

"People who victimize others."

"People who've been victimized!"

Abruptly, their sparring stopped. They were unable to look each other in the eye, finding new interest in their nearly empty glasses. Dana finished her drink, set the glass down, and started to laugh. Look at them. Fresh out of law school and so sure of their own solutions to the crime problem. How absurd!

Seth joined in. They laughed freely, with a superficial ease that felt full of disappointment. Their eyes met, and she saw the health and energy that had attracted her. She saw the inspiration for her false vision that had blossomed from the lonely, other-worldly soil of night court.

But it wasn't the same between them, even after they changed the subject and explored lighter topics, ordered a second round of drinks and lingered over them for another hour. It wasn't the same and would never come close to the illusion. Not because of anything Seth had done or said, but because of Dana and who she was and what she could not become—and how she had misjudged him and had disappointed herself.

9 » DUNGEON

THE TRUE REASON for her transfer could be avoided no longer. *Contact her today or tomorrow, once you're familiar with the subpoenas.* Bruce had given the order on her first day, almost a week ago, and she'd been living with a creeping dread that he would soon discover her procrastination. Finally, he did notice.

She was at work with the door open when he stepped into the Closet and asked for an update on several accounts. The subpoenas had been served on First City before Dana joined the team, but the records hadn't arrived. "Call your friend," he demanded. On the way out the door, he tossed a grenade over his shoulder: "Now."

If it hadn't been for her transfer, Dana would have called Melly by now to ask how she was feeling and to thank her again for dinner, maybe also to suggest a time for their next get-together. But she'd been too "busy" to call. Now she regretted waiting so long. A week ago, she could have warned Melly about Bruce's ulterior motives without having to deal with the pressure of an immediate need for bank records. Now it was too late.

Was it better to start the conversation with business and get it over with? It would be so awkward and cold, as if she'd called only to ask a favor. Any personal stuff would sound like an after-thought. Better to start the other way around and ease into the difficult part. But when she got to the difficult part, the opening chitchat would seem like an insincere delay tactic.

If only it were just this one time. But Dana had a premonition of an endless imposition—countless favors she needed to ask and couldn't hope to return, favors that were different than the usual personal ones because they signified something beyond their seeming boundaries. The best friend—now a mere "connection."

Various openings were pondered, none of them just right, and all rejected as transparently self-centered. Finally she thought, to hell with it! She was giving Reichert too much power and control over her personal relationships. She wouldn't plan, connive or pounce. She would simply be herself and let her feelings guide her.

Taking a deep breath, she dialed the number. Melanie was at her desk and answered after the first ring. She sounded tired and peevish, not at all like herself.

Dana was concerned. "Are you okay? You sound, I don't know…"

"Like a bitch from the backwater. Don't ask me—it's an old family expression. Those ancestors from Arkansas."

"What's going on? You still have the nausea? The…"

"Nausea and dizziness and vomiting and fatigue and headache? Wait a minute. I might've forgotten a few."

"I had no idea…"

"Neither did I. We're supposed to be supermoms, right? Keep going to work, business as usual, and nine months later, grab a tree trunk and squat. What a fairy tale! It's only 9:30, and I don't think I can make it through the day."

Dana was momentarily at a loss for words. Where was the joy and excitement of last week? Her lighthearted, jubilant friend had never sounded so negative. "Oh, sweetie, I'm sorry you're feeling so rotten," she soothed.

"God, I *must* sound bad. You never act like that."

"I'm worried about you."

"I'll get through this. I'll survive. It's just a dreary Monday morning. You should see the work piling up on my desk. The worst part is facing the customers. I actually had to jump up from my desk in the middle of a new account interview and run to the bathroom."

"Just explain what's going on. They'll understand."

"Well, I did, and he didn't. He looked at me like, 'one of those women's problems.' Anyway, I hate to go on like this. I'm becoming completely self-absorbed."

"No, you're not. It's a big change. You're going through a lot, and being sick doesn't help. I can't believe with everything going on you still cooked dinner for me. I meant to call you last week to thank you again. The food was incredible, as always."

"I'm glad you could come. You know me. I always like to cook. Come over again soon. If I can't eat, I'll be happy just to watch you eat. You're getting too lean and mean with the job of yours."

Dana treated the comment as a joke and laughed. Nothing bad could be implied, even in Melanie's current nasty mood. "Nope, I'm not making you cook again. I'll wait on you next time. How about this Saturday for dinner? You and Noel, and I'll get Cheryl to come over."

"Okay, sure. Fix something bland for me. Just pour some hot water over instant oatmeal. That's about all I can eat."

"By Saturday you might be feeling better. But don't worry. Everything I make is bland. I don't know how to cook anything interesting. Maybe I'll buy something at the restaurant on the corner and pretend I made it."

"What time do you want us? Oh, wait, I forgot. Domingo was going to take us out this weekend. I think he said Saturday. I can tell him to switch it to Friday..."

"Why don't you bring him along?"

"We could do that. But I'll bet he still wants to take us out. It's kind of important to him. He's all excited about the new business concession he's handling at Noel's store. He's a lot easier to be around these days, so I think he's feeling good about himself. Happier. I told you that whole story, right?"

"Maybe a little." She didn't remember a thing.

"I can't really get into it right now…"

"Just bring him along, okay? I'd like to meet him. Come about seven."

"All right. Thanks. I'll see you then."

Melanie was about to hang up, jolting Dana out of her temporary amnesia. "Okay, but wait," she rushed in, "there's one more thing I have to tell you. I've transferred bureaus at work —"

"Transferred? You didn't say anything about it last week."

"It happened after I saw you, and it was kind of sudden. I can tell you all about it later, but I don't want to waste your time. My new boss asked me to check on the status of subpoenas we issued for bank records…at First City Financial."

Silence. Then, "You're asking me to go check on them?"

Dana searched for resentment in her friend's voice but heard none. Melly's question was needed to elicit the direct request Dana was reluctant to make. "Well, yes, if you could, and maybe just nudge them a little. My boss is anxious for the information."

"I'll see what I can do. I don't have much contact with subpoena compliance. You could call them directly, you know. Maybe that would go faster."

"I…could do that."

"But…," Melanie sighed deeply — knowingly. "I get what you're saying. Go ahead and give me the account numbers and I'll just run it by Juliet."

"Thanks." Dana massaged her throat to loosen the tension there and began reciting the names and numbers. It was a long list, and after endless minutes, when she was only a third of the way down, Melanie said, "How many more?"

"A lot."

"You know what? I might miss a number doing this over the phone. Can you fax the list?"

A brilliant suggestion, relieving some of Dana's pain. She took down Melanie's fax number and closed their conversation with a simple, "thank you," feeling despicable.

Pushing aside her low feelings, she reverted to pure mechanical function and neatly printed the list and a fax cover memo. In a blur, she made her way to Cathy and handed the task over with a "please."

Evan was passing by and noticed the exchange. He stopped by her side. "How's it going?"

She turned to him, frowned, and shrugged.

"That good, eh?" He laughed, bringing a smile to her face. "You done here?"

"Yeah."

"Follow me."

She thanked Cathy and went with Evan to his office. It was a cheerful place decorated with potted plants, framed prints and diplomas, even a light-colored Scandinavian throw rug placed neatly over the institutional dark gray wall-to-wall. Before this, she'd only breezed past his open door, never entering. Now, as she walked in and took a seat, her eyes rested on one object after another, appreciating the difference.

"I've lured you in here for a purpose," he said, sliding behind his desk and rummaging through some papers.

Her eyes came to rest on a bare spot of white wall. "I don't believe it," she said. Evan looked up at her, his eyes begging an explanation. "Did you paint your office?" she asked.

"Yes," he admitted.

"They let you do that?"

"I made a pitch for my sanity. The light gray color was

making me feel hung over."

"You painted it yourself?"

"You can tell."

"No, I mean it looks great. Everything's so light and airy. I'm just amazed—"

"That they trusted me? They trust us to charge people with things like murder, so I guess they can trust me to slap a little paint on the walls. I had to do it. I can't be questioning my sobriety fifty hours a week. Life's too short. Here." He handed her a thick packet of papers, apparently what he'd been searching for. "I filed this in court on Friday. The application for an extension of our eavesdropping warrants. It has the latest evidence we've gathered."

"Thanks."

"Just to keep you up on things. How's the paper trail going?"

"Moving along, I guess. Are you interested in seeing the summary I'm working on with Mineko?"

"I am and I'm not. I don't really have the time to do anything more than get a superficial handle on the bank stuff. My little end of this is keeping on top of the eavesdropping and surveillance reports and complying with all the legal requirements for the wiretapping. Didn't Bruce mention something at the meeting last week? You report directly to him and Joe. Bruce is following the accounts, looking for clues to find the bigger fish behind this scheme. Joe's developing the forfeiture case for all the bank accounts. When you have your report ready, see if you can lasso them both at the same time."

Dana nodded and pursed her lips in a grimace, a poor attempt at a smile. Life would be much easier if she were reporting to Evan.

An odd moment of silence stood between them before Dana made a move to go. "Sit," said Evan gently. She complied. "It can't be Minnie, so it must be Bruce. Am I right?"

Evan's meaning was clear, and she was astounded by it. Their eyes met in understanding. "Don't let Bruce get to you," he advised. "I've worked with him for five years. I know the bastard, and I say that with love in my heart." He winked. "Has he been barking the orders?"

"The few times I've seen him."

"You'll have to look past it. You can't take it personally. Let me tell you something that maybe you can't see right now." He leaned forward to rest his elbows on the desk, lowered the crown of his head into cupped palms, rubbed back over the bald spot, and lifted his head again. "Bruce is a damn fine lawyer. But he has a one-track mind. That track right now is this investigation. He wants things done, and he wants them done yesterday. I can't say it's a bad quality. It's gotten us to the point we're at today. In another month or two, we may be ready to slam these crooks with some heavy-duty indictments."

"If that's only a couple of months away, then my job will be finished."

He gave her a puzzled look. "Your job? You mean, analyzing the bank records?"

"Right."

He laughed. "Typical Bruce!"

"I've been hearing that a lot. 'Typical Bruce.'"

"He hasn't told you a thing. You think the only reason we got you over here was to wade through bank statements? We need that now, but later, there will be a lot more. You may not believe this, but Bruce thinks you have promise."

"He's told you that?"

Evan smiled slyly. "Not in so many words. You forget, I know him. He *has* told me he plans to take full advantage of your talents for all stages of the litigation. There will be witnesses to interview, and I'm sure, endless briefs to write when we get into motion practice on the criminal case. To do that, you're going to have to know all the evidence fairly well. That's why I'm handing you my summaries of the evidence." He paused, refusing to remove his eyes from hers, as if looking for a sign that he'd gotten through. "This is a big case," he said, more serious than she'd seen him yet. "It's the kind of case that makes careers. Just a few of us in this office, maybe two dozen of us, are up against the most powerful narcotics organization in the world."

"I guess I know that, and it almost makes it seem hopeless."

"It *is* hopeless. We don't kid ourselves about that. It's as hopeless as thinking we can eliminate muggings in Manhattan. But we can't let them all go free. We have to *try*, don't we?"

Dana nodded.

"And we'll make a dent, somewhere. Someone will fall."

"A bad person."

"A big powerful bad person or two, at least." His face brightened. "I know what you need. Have you been down to the Dungeon yet?"

"What's the Dungeon?"

"It's our little pet name for the dark and dank squad room in the basement."

"Oh, yeah. The Don invited me down, but I haven't had the time. I've been stuck in the Closet, shuffling papers."

"The Closet?"

"My office."

"Hmm. An apt description. Well, come with me then. You've got to get out of the Closet for a few minutes, and I have to go down and talk to the Don anyway." He leapt from his chair and Dana followed him out of the room.

Side by side, they strode down the corridor to the elevator. Evan's step was quick. Like most people in the DA's office, Evan was in perpetual fast forward, not from an innate physicality, but out of defensive habit against the ever-ticking clock. With his round face and extra inch at the belt line, Evan looked as though an easy chair and a stein of beer would suit him better than a sprint around the track. But all the same, he seemed comfortable with the pace he set, making it natural for Dana to fall in alongside.

She took the moment to reflect on the things he'd said. He was transparent after all, she was beginning to think. Nothing could be intentionally deceitful or surreptitious about him, especially now that he'd confessed his opinion of Bruce—all in a highly diplomatic way, of course, but still, he revealed more than was usually called for under the rules of office politics. And why had he done it? For her benefit apparently. Just to make her feel better. That must have taken some trust on his part.

In the elevator, Evan pressed "B" and they descended thirteen floors. The door opened on a noticeably grayer environment, the color and texture of airborne dust. The floors and walls were made of cool cement, and pipes of every diameter ran the length of the ceiling. A monstrous boiler hissed in a dark recess of the basement, a city block away.

"Lovely," said Dana.

"It has potential."

"Go get your can of white paint."

"Ha ha! Maybe we should consult the Don about the color scheme."

He led her through a maze, around corners and through interstices and steel doors until they entered an immense expanse of space, furnished with metal desks and wheeled chairs, haphazardly strewn partitions tacked with papers and photographs, tables holding stacks of cassette tapes, tape recorders, cameras, and other equipment.

Gilbert, wearing earphones, sat plugged into a tape recorder at a desk in the middle of the space. The Don was all the way across the room next to the wall, talking on the phone with his feet propped up on a desk. They were the only two inhabitants at the moment, although the space and its personal relics suggested an army of dozens.

"Almost everyone's out in the field," said Evan as they started across the room toward Gilbert. "The Dungeon is the headquarters for more than half of the DA's squad, and out of this lot, ten are assigned to our case."

Gilbert let out a roar as they approached. Doubling over in laughter, he took off his earphones, unplugged them and rewound the tape. "Listen to this," he said, pressing a button, letting the voices escape and echo in their cement crypt. Two men were talking angrily in Spanish, sounding nothing like the textbook tones Dana had heard on a "Learn Conversational Spanish" cassette she'd once attempted.

When Gilbert stopped the tape, Evan smiled and said, "Be sure to get every word into the translation!" He leaned toward a partition Gilbert was using as a bulletin board, lifted some papers and tore off a glossy magazine photograph of a woman dressed in three tiny triangles of pink cloth. Evan crushed the photo and tossed it into a wastebasket. "Get rid of this shit. Didn't you read the harassment bulletin?"

"There aren't any women down...here." Gilbert's eyes flickered toward Dana. "Anyway, it's just *Sports Illustrated*."

Evan balled a fist at Gilbert, a gesture that struck Dana as eminently dweebish. As they walked away, she asked, "What were they saying on that tape?"

"Hell if I know. I could make out only a few choice words, like 'hijo de puta.' My Spanish is limited to curses and blasphemies. Detective Paul," he yelled out. "Get off that phone! I'm coming to see you."

When they came close, the Don put his hand on the receiver and looked up. "At your service," he said dryly, and turned away again, continuing his conversation. While he talked into the phone, Evan shuffled through a pile of photographs on the desk.

"The Don has some new surveillance photos I want you to see," he said to Dana.

The Don hung up without a goodbye and said, "I've been wanting Dana to come down, but *you* I could do without." As he said this, he kept his blue eyes, pink in the whites, trained on Evan's face except for a brief, playful flash in her direction. Something about his manner reminded her of a time years past when her grandfather loved to tease her, making her feel uncomfortable. She smiled. The detective coughed, sending a spurt of venous color into his cheeks and up into his thinning hair.

Evan continued to rummage.

"Hey now," warned the Don. "Watch it with those pictures!"

"Is this the one?" asked Evan.

"Yeah, that's him. Right there he's walking into the bank." Dana looked over Evan's shoulder at the blurry black and white photograph of a young, dark-haired man with his hand inside an open jacket. She glanced again at the desk, littered with similar photographs, most of them ordinary looking men of all ages, shapes and sizes. A few women. All of them Hispanic—or was that her assumption, under the circumstances? Given the poor quality of the photographs, the people could just as easily be Palestinian, Italian or Native American.

"Great camera work," said Evan.

"I know. You could do better with your Brownie."

"What else you know about this guy?"

"We don't know his name—like it matters. No one goes by their real name anyway. We call him 'Niño' because he's so young. Maybe seventeen or eighteen. Here." The Don pulled out another photograph, apparently depicting the same youth, standing with an older man, shorter and stockier. "This is the meet I was tellin' you about. We've seen Niño with this guy a couple of times. This is how we got interested, because the older guy could be, I'm saying *could* be, someone important. We've been calling him 'Jefe.'"

"How important can he be, walking around in the open like that?"

"Exactly why I say, 'could be.' The important people are usually hidden. It's clear that Jefe isn't Rojo, but he could be a mid-level manager of some sort. He struts around in the open wearing a business suit, looking very legitimate, walking into Spanish bodegas. But we also saw him go up into the apartment on East 103rd, and a minute later we intercepted a conversation. Had to be him, because no one else was up there. And he's giving orders right and left, all in code, 'tres carros' go here and another dozen there, you know the deal. He wasn't on the receiving end. Strange, because we've only heard the people in that apartment answering calls from Colombia and receiving orders."

Evan pondered. "This is a new angle. What do you know about the businesses Jefe visits?"

"Not much. We don't want to stir things up by going in and asking questions. They could be fronts for stash houses."

"And what about identifying the accounts that Niño has been making deposits to?"

"That's a possible. If he happens to go into one of the banks where we have a contact, we can go in after he's been there and ask a few questions. One of his favorite banks is First City. You have a contact there, don't you Dana?"

Her eyes went to Evan, looking for help, but he was still studying the photograph. "I know someone. But she doesn't see the depositors because she isn't down on the floor with the tellers—"

"But she could back us up if we need to go in and question the tellers—"

"Sounds like a good idea," Evan cut in. He turned to Dana. "Do you think she would mind?"

"I'd rather not ask her. I mean, I've already burdened her

with a huge list of subpoenas—"

"You know, on second thought, I have a better idea," said Evan. "Banks can't give information without a subpoena anyway. We'll just prepare a subpoena with blanks for you to fill in, requesting, you know, 'the identity of the account or accounts into which money was deposited on thus-and-such date at thus-and-such time by Niño at the window of thus-and-such teller,' and don't say Niño but give a physical description of him. You've got the idea."

"Right."

"So, when you're in a position to see the deposit with a certain teller, you run in afterward and serve the subpoena. Once we get the name on the account, we follow up with a formal subpoena for records. Dana's friend doesn't have to get involved unless we have problems down the road getting the records. Make sense?" He turned to her, and she managed to hide an internal sigh of relief. "Sounds good," she said.

After tightening a few other investigative strategies, Evan and Dana took leave of the Don, making their way past Gilbert, who was still under his earphones, completely absorbed in another world. As they retraced their steps through the maze, Gilbert's intermittent bursts of laughter punctured the air above the hiss of the boiler, each one a faded report of the last as they got closer to the elevator bank. A short wait, a "ding," a final distant chortle, and entry. The elevator door slammed shut, closing out the Dungeon and carrying them swiftly up from the bowels of the building.

"She was very upset, and I can't blame her." It was a relief to unload some of this. What were sisters for? Having called Cheryl to invite her to the Saturday dinner party, Dana took the opportunity to launch into what was foremost on her mind. "How can I be in this position? Don't be surprised if they don't show on Saturday."

"Aren't you going a little overboard here? Melanie isn't like that."

"There's a whole story behind this—"

"I know. About matters you *cannot* divulge." The comment was a blunt reminder of their conversation a few days back, when Dana had mentioned her transfer to Financial Crimes while carefully avoiding any details about the Cartel investigation. Cheryl's blasé tone was all too familiar. It was the tone she always used to cover up her searing interest in Dana's work. The veneer was so transparent that Dana felt like advising her sister to give up her dream of an acting career.

Were the sisters really so different? Dana hid behind her intellectuality, shunning ego and sexuality while harboring a bit of the performer within her. Cheryl outwardly denied her intellect, failing to mask its acuity with her fluffy and cynical remarks. Each was attracted to aspects of the other while reigning secure in the polar territory charted for herself.

"Basically, yes," said Dana. "I can't divulge it, but the gist of it is that I've asked Melanie to help me get some information from the bank. I faxed her a list of some of the subpoenas we served, and a couple of hours later she called me back, nearly screaming. 'Did you know that SC is working on forty-five subpoenas from your office? Forty-five! They're doing the best they can.' She calmed down, but I've never heard her talk like this. I'm beginning to think my priorities are way out of whack, making her do this extra favor for me, especially now that she's pregnant and not feeling well. It's just that I'm under pressure from my new boss."

"You have to be up front with her about it."

"Okay, sure. I'll confess that I wasted her time on a case I should have known would be yanked from me by the jerk who later got me transferred just so he could use me to get to her and waste more of her time."

"Say—what?"

"It's a whole story, like I said."

"Forget it. Forget all of that and just ask yourself what's important to you here. What's *really* important to you?"

There was a sagacious kernel in this advice, coming from the mouth of a mere twenty-year-old, her little sis. Dana attempted to ignore it with her glib reply. "The investigation is important. My job is important. Melly is very important..."

"You said it right there..."

"My new boss, Bruce Reichert, is *not* important. Not to me anyway. That sounds very low."

"Who cares? You answered the question. The only 'very important' is Melly. So have a talk with her and get it straight."

"Sounds too easy."

"You two are a couple of stress candidates. Everyone's a little unreasonable when they're stressed out."

"Said so cool by a woman who thrives on stress."

"Yeah, well, all I have to do is sling hash and audition for tone-deaf producers. That's easier than being a prosecutor or pregnant. Anyway, I want you two to make up by Saturday so I can get a free dinner out of this. I've been living on leftovers from the diner."

"Don't count on a good meal."

"Oh, I know your cooking. By the way, I promise I won't mention that to a friend of mine I think you'll like. Maybe I'll bring him along on Saturday and he can make up his own mind about your cooking—"

Dana started to protest.

"Wait a minute! I think you'll like him. He's nothing like the last one. He's really very common and steady."

"Boring, like me."

"If you want to put it that way."

"Do me a favor, Cheryl."

"Just a suggestion—"

"I can't handle these kinds of suggestions right now."

"—something to take your mind off work."

"Keep him in your phone book for later, but not right now, okay?"

"As you wish."

10 »   JACK

AFTER THE HIGHS and lows of Monday, the rest of the week inched forward in monotony and tedium. Dana settled into an isolated existence, enclosed in her canyon of paper, receiving no hints from Bruce about her supposedly bright future on the team. He remained indifferent and thoroughly unimpressed with her work.

Then, on Friday, came a small shift.

Midmorning, having miraculously snagged Joe and Bruce simultaneously, Dana and Mineko delivered an update of their work. The meeting lasted all of five minutes. Bruce silently scanned Dana's written summary while Joe asked a few, well-placed questions.

Suddenly, Bruce's head jerked up. "Resner Aircraft Corporation. Tell me more about that." Dana explained she'd identified checks from twenty-one different smurf accounts made payable to that prominent U.S. company, a manufacturer of aircraft parts. It was the first U.S. payee she'd seen. All the checks were canceled on the same date, as if Resner had received them in one batch and deposited them together into its company account.

There was veiled excitement in Bruce's face, his small eyes pushed open and bright. "Nice," he said, as if he'd been handed a gift. "I'll follow up on Resner."

A second glimpse of his satisfaction with her work came as a surprise late in the day, the unexpected outcome of a panic-inducing phone call.

The caller was a defense attorney Dana knew from her days in the trial bureau. When she picked up the phone, he greeted her like an old chum. "Dana? It's Fred. Fred Marrero. I'm calling on this matter involving my client Stella Ramos."

The false friendliness was off-putting. Dana uttered a few pleasantries while her mind raced, trying to figure out the purpose of his call. Was this leftover business from the trial bureau? The matter couldn't be related to her work in FC, although the name Stella Ramos did sound familiar, like so many others that blurred under her eyes these days.

Marrero noticed her hesitation and helped her memory along. "You know what I'm talking about, Dana. Stella's checking account was subpoenaed. I called the ADA on the subpoena, Paglia, but he referred me to you."

Now the panic set in. Subpoenaed? How could he know? All the subpoenas were issued with nondisclosure orders.

There'd been a leak somewhere, and Joe must have figured as much when Marrero called him. Yet Joe hadn't warned her in advance before simply punting the call to her. What was she to tell Marrero? Nothing, of course.

She asked him to hold the line while she fished through piles of material on her desk, on the floor, in the file cabinet. After a tense minute, she found the subpoena and heaved a sigh of relief, noticing it wasn't addressed to First City but to a much smaller bank. Apparently, the clerks at that bank could not be trusted.

Picking up the receiver she said, "Yes, I've found it. You realize there's a nondisclosure order on this subpoena? The information shouldn't have been given to your client."

"Yeah, sure, but you gotta know there's a federal law requiring banks to tell their customers about any subpoena on their account."

"Only when the customer specifically asks the bank—"

"Stella asked the bank. She *had* to ask when—"

"But our court order overrides the bank regs anyway."

"You'd never win a challenge on that ground, Dana. I'd give you a run for your money if you want to waste your time litigating it. But that's not the issue. She came to me, asked me to look into this subpoena and protect her from the DA's squad. Why are you snooping around in her account?"

"That's confidential information, and how did she know to ask?"

"Don't give me that 'confidential' bullshit. You think your office is onto something new here? The feds have been doing this for years, sending out subpoenas for every bank account with a Spanish name on it, hassling the Hispanic community. All of it's drug money, right? I'll be next, I'm just waiting for it." Marrero was quick-tongued and angry. For show or for real? Dana could rarely tell. "Stella's just trying to make a living like you and me. She writes a check for her telephone bill and the bank freezes her account, won't honor the check, so she asks them what's up and they tell her the DA wants her money."

"They froze the account? Our subpoena didn't authorize a freeze!"

"You're telling *me*, Dana. I'm dealing with a moron over at the bank right now. If you pull your goons off, maybe he'll believe me. His name is Wade Jellison."

"I can call him and get the freeze lifted, but I don't think I can—"

"Let me guess. You're not gonna withdraw the subpoena. Doesn't matter, 'cause I bet they already sent you the records. So why don't you actually take a look at them? Stella makes maybe fifteen grand a year. She's an artist, a craftswoman, a single mom. She comes into my office with her two little kids and shows me her box of samples, trinkets she sells for pennies so they can eat.

Look at the bank statements. Little deposits and checks to pay the rent and utilities. She's no drug dealer. She's no money launderer. Use some goddamn sense and back off."

Dana promised to look into it and call him back. Everything he'd been saying was beginning to ring true. She remembered looking at these account statements and a few others, thinking they didn't fit the pattern—small deposits and small checks in odd amounts. She didn't know for sure without seeing copies of the actual deposit tickets and canceled checks, items they'd requested but hadn't received.

Bruce had instructed her to obtain all the bank documents before coming to a conclusion on any account, but she saw no reason to pursue this one, especially since the bank had improperly frozen the account. They should withdraw the subpoena, just as they should withdraw five others for accounts that didn't clearly fit the money laundering pattern.

She jotted down the six account names and numbers and made her way to Bruce's office, giving herself encouragement along the way. No cowering, no mindless execution of orders. She'd been hired to use her brain and good judgment.

Through a sliver of open doorway, voices emerged, female and male, clashing, in discord. Pausing outside, Dana knew the female voice immediately. It was a large voice for such a small woman, a smooth, median pitch, authoritative and rich with experience. Jacquelyn DuBois, senior trial counsel in the Special Narcotics Bureau. She was the person Dana had been hoping to run into ever since her first day in FC.

The thought crossed her mind she should turn back; it would be inappropriate to knock, to interrupt. But her desire to meet Jack, together with her sense of urgency over the maligned accounts, drove her to action. She rapped on the doorjamb. The voices ceased, and she stepped inside.

Bruce shot her a red-eyed look. "Can't it wait?"

"I'm sorry to interrupt, but something rather serious has come up…"

"So, you're the new recruit," said Jacquelyn with a smile bright as sunshine.

"Yes, I'm Dana Hargrove."

"I remember you from the seminar group."

Jack's recognition made her heart soar, despite a small fear that it meant nothing, or perhaps even something bad. *I remember her, that bumbling, clueless rookie.* But Dana took the best possible spin, returned the smile and said, in her most professional voice, "I'm looking forward to working with you on this case."

The two senior attorneys exchanged looks. "If you call this working together," Jack said dryly. Here it was—direct evidence of the rift. "We were just talking about togetherness when you walked in—"

"This is not a good time," Bruce interjected.

"Why not? Dana can help us wash a little dirty laundry, and I'm not talking about the money laundering scheme." She flashed Dana a look as if—did it mean?—she wanted to include her.

"Cut it, Jack. This is none of Dana's business."

"It certainly is. She's part of the 'team.' The formation of this team has been getting in the way of teamwork, and you've been avoiding it. Let's just get the ugly history out in the open, examine the slave ships and move on to coexistence. Maybe you don't believe it, but there wasn't any plan to sneak this behind your back. We were working the A felonies because we had all those targets on narcotics crimes, or at least conspiracy. We weren't ignoring FC. We were just doing our job. But you don't like to hear that. Any time we can't make an A we call you. Isn't that the truth?"

Bruce sat mute, the single fat caterpillar crunched into his brow. Underneath it, his dull brown eyes darted upward, unwilling to meet Jack's. His focus quickly dropped to his left

hand, clenching the arm of his chair. A gold wedding ring—
something Dana hadn't noticed until now.

Dana stood awkwardly, not sure if she should sit in the
vacant chair next to Jack as though fully entitled to hear this
conversation between her two superiors. She admired Jack's
openness but was equally alarmed by it. Bruce plainly did not
possess appropriate responses within his limited repertory. Nor
did he have the fortitude of character to deal with Jack's
exploration of his hidden animosities.

Jack's implication was clear. Bruce was suffering an attack of
inferiority and unable to admit it. FC was investigating money
laundering under a relatively new statute which classified the
crime as a C felony, carrying a lower sentence than the A and B
felonies for narcotics and conspiracy offenses. Why waste your
time on a C when you can prosecute for an A or B?

"The front office didn't share your view," said Reichert, his
voice more timid than Dana had ever heard it. He carried on,
gaining strength and momentum. "You can't look at the narcotics
crimes in a vacuum. The legislature enacted the money laundering statute for a purpose. It complements every type of
lucrative crime, and this office is committed to using the statute.
You can't let it sit. Almost every case this bureau gets is a referral,
and if the most important cases are hoarded—"

"I'm not in this for glory, you know that." A believable
statement. Jack's reputation preceded her wherever she went,
lending all the glory she needed.

"I'm not accusing you of that, but this whole thing is being
twisted back at me. Let's just get on with it. Why dredge up the
past? It's over and done with. Every time I ask for a little independence on the money laundering stuff, this comes back to me—"

"That's just it. There *is* no independence. Everything has to
be shared or we're cooked."

Bruce shook his head at empty space for a moment before

suddenly turning a blank stare on Dana, as if stunned into an awareness of her presence. "What do you have, Dana? Let's deal with it and get you out of here."

"Some of the subpoenas. I think we should withdraw them before the banks go to the trouble of sending the deposit tickets and canceled checks." She stepped forward, handed him the list and finally took a seat, glancing at Jack, her neighbor on this side of Reichert's desk. "We've looked at the bank statements and they don't seem to fit the pattern, and I've just gotten a call from Fred Marrero about the Stella Ramos account. He said—"

"I heard about this. Marrero's full of hot air," said Bruce, looking at the list. How had Bruce heard? Through Joe? Had the two of them decided to dump this on her? "I approved all these subpoenas," said Bruce. "I told Joe you'd take care of it. You should go ahead and look at everything before you make up your mind."

"What is it about the Ramos account that doesn't fit the pattern?" asked Jacquelyn. Bruce leveled angry eyes on her but kept his mouth shut.

"There's not much money going in and out. It looks like every other checking account of a person with a modest income. Marrero says she makes only about fifteen thousand a year with handmade arts and crafts."

"Dana, you have to learn to sift through the bullshit," said Bruce. "Half the people we're trailing cover their dirty money with a legitimate looking business. That's part of the scheme."

"But I thought our theory was that most of these names were fictitious. How does that fit with a real person who tries to pay her phone bill and gets her check stopped by the bank? If it was a Cartel phone bill, would she be consulting an attorney? Why would she call attention to herself in this way? There's very little money in this account. If it was Cartel, they'd just let it go."

Bruce cleared his throat. "Sounds like you've made up your

mind…"

"Sounds like a valid concern to me," said Jack.

Bruce ignored the comment. "These accounts aren't much use to us anyway if they don't have a big balance. Use your judgment. I'll leave it to you."

Stifling an urge to smile, Dana sprang to her feet before Bruce could discover the fallacy in his face-saving rationalization. By itself, the size of the account balance didn't matter. A lot of Cartel accounts showed a flurry of activity and dwindled down to nothing. Besides, no one was supposed to admit that the DA's office was in this for the money, even though forfeited funds were now a significant component of the investigative budget.

But she wasn't going to quibble about the finer points, happy to have scored another small victory in a battle of intellect, knowing that Reichert's estimation of her ability had risen a notch, even before he confirmed her thought with his final words: "Nice work, Dana."

"Thanks, Bruce," she said. On her way to the door she smiled at Jacquelyn, who shot off an easy, conspiratorial wink that outdistanced the time and experience between them.

Noel insisted on taking a taxi instead of the bus or subway, even though Melanie would have preferred to save a few dollars. Mingo's carefree style might have had its influence on her husband, but Melanie couldn't blame the boy entirely. Noel's recent slackening of financial restraint could be explained by his joy over the baby and his modest increase in income, two forces which, in Melanie's mind, should have worked the opposite effect, or at least should have canceled each other out. After all, their baby would be here before they knew it, and Melanie's position at the bank would be in question.

She liked to frame the issue that way, although there was

nothing at all uncertain about her position at First City. Her employer offered two months of paid maternity leave, which was standard industry practice, not liberal but not stingy, and she'd have her position back upon her return. The real issue was that unspoken temptation. What if she stayed home with the baby for six months or a year—would they hold her job that long? Didn't a baby need his mother exclusively for a few years, maybe until kindergarten?

Even putting these temptations aside, the unpredictable could hit them. Already the symptoms of early pregnancy had interfered with her work, causing extra stress in situations she normally took in stride. Screaming at Dana like that! Such shameful behavior. Her friend hadn't asked for much, just a walk over to SC with a list of accounts. Five minutes of her time. She would apologize to Dana without making excuses for herself because she hadn't any. Feeling lousy wasn't an excuse.

But what if the nausea and fatigue didn't stop? And how would she feel in her eighth and ninth months, big as a house? She might have to leave work early, take unpaid sick leave, and worse, what would happen if the baby had health problems? Why wasn't Noel considering these possibilities as he waved Mingo's money away, handing the driver the fare and a generous tip besides?

Throughout the short taxi ride she'd been silent, not angry or on edge, just quietly worried as Mingo and Noel rattled on in Spanish. This, the happiest time of her life, was sewn with a thread of unease and preoccupation. She was immersed in her thoughts, ignoring her husband and his cousin when she could be trying to pick out the parts of their conversation she understood. In her four years with Noel, her Spanish had developed to the point of understanding the basics, never the finer details. Often, she would miss the entire meaning of a sentence from an unknown word or two, making it just maddening when Noel was running on at breakneck speed.

But the stream was so relaxing and mellifluous that she loved to listen, especially when her mind was turned off to the hopeless task of comprehension. There was mystery and beauty in the sound, a feeling of being outside and different but special for being selected and included to share the secrets of a faraway world. Even now, in her state of preoccupation, a few of their words and phrases flowed into her cognizant center. They were talking about the bookstore and then about one of their cousins back home.

Noel enjoyed reverting to his native tongue, although he wouldn't admit it. She could feel his enjoyment and relaxation. She wanted that for him. From the start of their relationship, he'd made a point of always speaking English with her. "The United States is my new home; I can't ask you or anyone else here to speak my language." When she first met him, his English was excellent; now it was nearly impeccable, with a vocabulary that might even surpass her own.

It surprised her that he didn't impose his own standards on Domingo, especially when it became clear that the boy was planning to stay in this country. Maybe it wasn't so surprising. Mingo's difficulty with English gave Noel an excuse to lapse into Spanish, to let down his guard and feel a bit of home again. She couldn't begin to imagine that feeling of wrenching loss—to leave one's native country, forced to adapt to a foreign land, its culture and language.

In the Village, as they stepped from the cab, Melanie felt a surge of motherly hormones, washing her with euphoria, dissipating the fatigue and nausea. Oh, how wonderful it would be if these moments would only last! Soon, it would vanish, but for now, she felt great. At the front door of Dana's apartment building, Noel said, "I'm sorry, Melly. We've been leaving you out."

She waved him off with a foggy smile.

"I should make you practice your English, Domingo," declared Noel.

"Yes," he said, the only word he could completely count on.

"How will you ever learn, surrounding yourself with Colombians? It's a shame you can live in this country forever without ever speaking English. You'll be missing so much."

"He'll get plenty of practice tonight," said Melanie.

"Yes," repeated Domingo with a puppy dog smile, showing he didn't understand at all.

Her cousin-in-law was looking particularly sharp tonight in a well-tailored jacket of supple, dark leather, perhaps a little much for the warm May evening. It looked brand new and possibly expensive, although Melanie knew little about clothing. When he'd first set foot in their apartment this evening, she and Noel had marveled at the jacket, while Mingo sported a self-satisfied look and proclaimed his luck in having found it in a secondhand shop. His hair had been recently cut and styled, and his youthful jaw gleamed. Melanie was proud enough of this tall, lithe, well-groomed young man, whose intelligent eyes proved more about him than his spotty English. He seemed eager to make a good impression tonight, especially with the prospect of meeting two lovely young ladies.

She could have told him not to get his hopes up. Dana was too old for him, and Cheryl, at twenty, was just a year older, but possibly light years ahead in maturity. Melanie wasn't entirely sure. In the three months she'd known Mingo, everything between them had been superficially pleasant. They always approached each other full of smiles, making sweetly awkward conversation in her halting Spanish and his nearly nonexistent English, with Noel as interpreter. In her presence, he was always polite and well-mannered, sparked with that touch of eagerness and energy characteristic of the very young.

Because of the communication barrier, Melanie harbored a tiny misgiving about including him in the dinner party tonight. It seemed there were risks involved. He was an unknown. But she brushed the thought from her mind a moment after thinking it. He was family, and Noel had approved the plan, and that should be enough to quell any doubt.

As expected, her biochemical euphoria was fleeting, entirely absent in the elevator on the way up. When Dana opened the apartment door, Melanie flung herself into her friend's arms in a fit of unrestrained emotion. Puzzled, Dana returned the hug, while the other three—Noel and Domingo behind Melanie, Cheryl behind Dana—looked on. "I'm so sorry!" blurted Melly, teary-eyed, pulling away.

"For what? I'm the one who should be sorry—"

"There's no excuse for me. I just flew off the handle—"

Noel gave Cheryl a friendly wave over the shoulders of the two apologetic friends while Mingo caught her eye and smiled. Cheryl resembled her older sister in many ways—her slenderness and natural, upright posture, the crisp, articulate speech—except in the roundness of her face, which was more girlish, reflecting their difference in age. She made a subtly softer appearance than Dana, who was always the one to handle any situation requiring authority and decision. Cheryl's thick hair was slightly longer than Dana's and a shade lighter. She wore it loose. Whenever it fell onto her face, she had a habit of clawing it back along the top of her head with the pink fingernails of her right hand. That night she wore a cotton sundress in a vibrant floral print of yellow, orange and green, tied at the top behind her neck, backless to just below her shoulder blades.

She returned Mingo's smile. His charm was immediate and penetrating, and she couldn't very well avoid it. "I'm Cheryl," she said. "Dana's sister."

"I should have introduced you," Dana tossed back to Cheryl

over her shoulder, keeping an arm around Melanie. She'd forgotten that she'd never met Domingo herself. A confusion of bodies and introductions and handshakes and hugs ensued in the doorway. They all made it inside and scrunched up within a few feet of one another on futon chairs and pillows thrown around the studio apartment while Dana and Melanie continued their apologies.

"It's not any trouble at all, really," Melanie kept insisting, "and you're doing such important work. Please let me help."

"But I can't stand giving you extra work when you're feeling like this…"

"It's nothing really. Just give me a list whenever you have one ready. I'll run it by SC—it's right next to the bathroom and I'm always down there anyway."

"I wish I didn't have to do this, but my new boss is a Type A and he's constantly pressuring me…"

"I understand, believe me. Anytime you want, I'll ask those girls in SC. It's just that they're overworked."

"I'm sure they're doing their best—"

"They also get a ton of subpoenas from the feds—"

"I just need a status report to let my boss know we're trying—"

"Maybe another hug would help?" Noel jumped in, the corners of his mouth twitching.

The friends exchanged looks. "All right," said Dana. "We're over it."

"But I hope you know I'm glad to help," said Melanie. "Really I am!"

"Didn't you hear Dana?" said Noel. "You're done."

"We are," said his wife.

"Yes, we are," said Dana.

"Melly told me they're all Spanish names. Colombians, right?" asked Noel.

Dana shifted awkwardly on her pillow and said, "I'm not allowed to talk about it." On Monday she'd have to remind Melanie about those nondisclosure orders.

"Don't think I take it personally," he continued. "You should get all those bastards. They're ruining my country."

Domingo, who'd been looking on with large, shining eyes, interposed something that sounded like, "Nice apartment."

"Thank you, Domingo," said their hostess. "With five people in here, we have about an hour of air left, then the oxygen masks drop from the ceiling."

They all laughed except Mingo, who blinked and smiled from his cross-legged seat on a pillow. He seemed comfortable, although he hadn't taken his jacket off. He placed a hand inside the open edge of it. Dana's eye was caught, her breath trapped under a little stopper in her throat. In a slow, fuzzy motion, he turned his head toward Cheryl. The corner of the room where he sat was dim, his features shadowy. Cheryl seemed to smile at him.

Mingo turned his eyes on Dana, not revealing any more about himself. His hand was still inside the jacket, fishing for something. He brought out a small, gold box and leaned forward, stretching his arm out to her. "For you," he said, the "you" like "jew." From her side of their circle, with her eyes on the box, she stretched forward. Their hands met in the center of the room. She accepted the gift: expensive candies from a gourmet confectioner.

"Thank you," she said, looking up at him again. His face came into focus, dissipating the specter of a submerged image.

"Como te gustan los Estados Unidos?" asked Cheryl, leaning toward Domingo from the low futon.

He turned to her in surprise. "Bastante bien, gracias."

"Cuánto tiempo vas a pasar en Nueva York?"

"Estoy pensando en quedarme aqui un rato. No sé exactamente."

Their eyes were locked, Cheryl's full of pleasure at her

accomplishment—or was it attraction?

The others looked on in wonder, not one of them, least of all Dana, previously aware of Cheryl's proficiency in Spanish. And the evening progressed in the meld of Dana's full house—three in English, two in Spanish—with Cheryl and Mingo partially removed, intently creating their own little world.

11 »   *THURSDAY'S LIST*

"YOU'RE FAXING A LIST over today?"

Reichert startled her, coming up behind as she was about to step into the Closet. Dana turned to see him with a piece of paper in hand, poised to deliver it.

He had quickly caught on to her "system" with Melanie. It was the Thursday after the big apologies, and having faxed a second list on Monday, Dana was holding off as long as possible before burdening Melanie with another.

Her answer to Bruce's question—whether "yes" or "no"—would make no difference, so she replied simply, "What do you have?"

"Add these to your list."

"Okay." She took the paper and ran her eyes over it. Something odd. "Bruce?"

The caterpillar lifted and divided in two.

"Maybe I missed something, but I don't remember these accounts." The names were Spanish, but not individuals. Businesses. A short list of five.

"No reason you should. I wrote up these subpoenas one night last week after you'd gone home, and Joe did the non-disclosures."

She couldn't be sure if this was a jab at the length of her workday—which was already entirely too long—or a statement

165

that she was excluded from this aspect of the investigation. She assumed the latter. "So, these records should go directly to you when they come in?"

Bruce paused affectedly, as if her question took some thought. "Yes. Please." Turning halfway, he added "thanks" over his shoulder and was gone.

A milestone. "Please" and "thanks" all in one day. She looked at the list again but failed to recognize a single entry, none of the names jumping out as identifiable secondary payees.

As she pondered the possibilities, her phone rang. She hoped it was Cheryl. She'd left several messages with clear instructions to call back at any time of the day or night, home or office. There hadn't been a single opportunity to speak with her sister privately after the Saturday evening dinner party, and she'd been growing more anxious by the day to figure out exactly what had happened under her very nose in her own living room.

That evening had begun with a special time, the two sisters together in the kitchen before the company arrived. Cheryl's easiness and cheer calmed her nerves about a new recipe she was trying and her recent rough spot with Melanie. The sisterly closeness was heightened in the warmth of the first few minutes with the three Avendaños, until things slowly started to shift, the attraction between Cheryl and Domingo acquiring large proportions and eventually dominating the vibe in the room.

Dana was upset about it but couldn't say why. The boy seemed decent enough, certainly very young but respectful and polite as far as she could gather from his behavior and the few words of English he'd uttered. All evening it grated on her, watching the sparks shooting from their eyes while being unable to understand their conversation. They were a good-looking pair, an aura of sex hanging between them. Domingo's attractiveness couldn't be ignored, but it was not the kind that would have drawn Dana in. He was the type to make her instincts scream.

She leapt to answer the phone and was relieved to hear Cheryl's voice. Immediately she asked, "Where have you been the last few days?"

"Working double shifts. A couple of girls are out sick."

"I left you three or four messages —"

"And I left a message on your machine."

"It's on the fritz I think."

"Sorry, I didn't want to bother you at work."

"You're not bothering me." With the telephone receiver pressed onto her ear, Dana paced around her desk and glanced down at the list in her right hand.

"You're upset, Dana. What's going on?" Her tone was impatient.

"I'm not upset," she fibbed. "I just wanted to talk about Saturday. Where did you learn all that Spanish?"

"Now I have the proof!"

"Of what?"

"That you *completely* ignored me when you were away at college. I took four years of Spanish in high school. It was easy for me, nothing but easy A's. And then there was that foreign exchange student from Spain. My very good friend Miguel. I got a lot of practice my senior year."

"But you never used it after that —"

"I took that trip to Mexico, remember? But, no, I haven't really used it for a couple of years, until now that is."

"You're amazing. You've got to do something with those brains of yours."

"Not *that* again."

"What were you and Domingo talking about? I was the only one in the room who couldn't understand."

"Not much. His family, his home, his impressions of the United States…"

"And what are his impressions?"

"I don't know. All good. He doesn't come right out and say it, but it's pretty clear he wants to stay here. Last night he was saying—"

"Last night?"

"We went out to dinner."

"I thought you were working a double shift."

"It was a very late dinner. I have to eat, don't I? He's nice. Maybe it's kind of interesting to practice my Spanish."

"But he's so young."

"I don't know."

"Eighteen or nineteen at the most."

"He's at least nineteen, maybe twenty. He doesn't seem so awfully young. He has this way about him that's so...different."

Cheryl's tone said it all, tripping an alarm in Dana's head. "I don't think he's for you," she advised. "He's perfectly nice, I'm not passing judgment, but he's too young, too Latin American maybe."

"Whoa! Nuevo racist. Must be that job of yours..."

"I didn't mean it like that. He's a decent guy. But you two don't seem to fit together. I'm just doing a little looking out for you, the big sister thing."

"I can look out for myself."

"I'm not saying you can't. But sometimes you need an objective point of view. In this city, everyone needs an ally. I wish I'd had one when I first got here. It just strikes me that Mingo is a little immature, a little too into himself, and if he's staying in the country, I'm sure it's not legal. Hold on—" Evan had just walked past her door and she clamped a palm over the receiver, suddenly regretting she'd been speaking so loudly when anyone in the hallway might overhear.

Keeping the receiver to her ear, she walked to the door and shut it, letting the phone cord stretch out behind her. The Closet was so small that it reached.

"Okay, I'm back." She resumed her pacing.

"Stop worrying. Everyone is such a criminal to you. Even if he overstayed his visa, that isn't such a terrible crime."

"I wasn't implying that. Actually, I don't know exactly *what* I was implying." Someone knocked on the door and she yelled, "Come in." Mineko poked her head in, and Dana beckoned her to enter. "Look, Cheryl, I have to go for now."

"Don't forget to come up for air." It was the blasé tone that said the girl loved her.

"My little sister," Dana told Mineko after hanging up. "Whatcha got?"

Mineko placed a stack of bank documents on the desk. "These just came in."

"Thanks. Do you know any of these accounts?" She handed Bruce's paper to her.

Mineko flicked her bangs aside and examined it. "They look like names of secondary payees, but I don't recognize any of them. You got this from Bruce? It looks like his handwriting."

"Yup. He and Joe aren't letting us in on this part of the case. Except, of course, to make me hassle my friend at First City until we get the records."

Mineko didn't seem troubled by this revelation, which made Dana hear the bitterness in her own voice. She wasn't proud of it. "Good thing they're doing these accounts," said Mineko. "We have enough work as it is, don't you think?"

Mineko always had a way of putting things in perspective. Dana took the list from her. "You're absolutely right. I'm going to have Cathy type a few more onto this list and fax it over." She walked out and into the hall, passing Evan's open door on the way to Cathy's cubicle. He was at his desk, head bent over a document, reading.

She paused, considering whether to act on her temptation to ask. If she controlled her voice, it might be possible to remove the jealousy and pettiness from it and just get the question out. She was, after all, a member of the team and entitled to know what she could find out. Evan had said as much and more—she was expected to know all the evidence inside and out if she was to be of any use to them later down the road during courtroom litigation.

She backtracked, went up to his door, and knocked on the doorjamb. "May I interrupt?"

He looked up. His face brightened. "But of course. Do come in." His eyes met hers and then brushed quickly over her hair which she wore differently that day, pulled up in a twist. She handed him the paper, and his eyes dropped to it.

"Bruce and Joe subpoenaed these accounts and I'm just curious. I haven't seen the names before."

Evan pretended to think, but his look was transparent. Clearly, he recognized the names, and a self-conscious flutter of his eyelids told her he knew she could see through him. Of all the people she'd worked with, Evan was the most readable. His thoughts were telegraphed through that porthole in his bare cap, and his emotions beamed out to her through the two, blue-gray windows in the boyish face. The subtle workings of his eyebrows, forehead, cheeks and chin withheld nothing.

But she'd been surprised one day when she and Evan had been talking in Mineko's presence, and it later became clear that Mineko had misread one of Evan's wordless gestures. The episode prompted a thought. Maybe Evan's transparency wasn't universally discerned. Dana's ability to read the clues might just be a distinct form of communication reserved for the few, like sign language among the deaf.

"Aren't you allowed to tell me?" she asked, pretending.

"Of course I'm allowed. And maybe I'm even glad that Bruce doesn't like to tell you everything."

"Why is that?"

"Because then I get to tell you." His eyes opened wider on the "I," and again she could read him, but they ignored it. He continued. "You remember those pictures we looked at? The guy in the business suit, Jefe?"

She nodded.

"We think these accounts are controlled or set up by Jefe. But we don't know much else. It's a puzzle that doesn't seem to fit the rest of the scheme."

"They aren't secondary accounts?"

"They don't appear to be. They're primary accounts. We're following Niño and others to the bank when they make cash deposits. We don't know if these accounts are controlled by the same person or people who control the rest of the personal checking accounts, or if they're part of a separate scheme."

Dana held back the burning question, afraid how it would exit her mouth. There was a pause, allowing background noise to enter from the hallway, people talking, moving.

Evan's blue-grays saw the question in her eyes, and he answered it. "I think Bruce subpoenaed these accounts himself because he has such an interest in Jefe and he's eager to follow through. He thinks Jefe is a key player. I'm not so sure. You remember what the Don said: it's odd that the man is out in the open."

"Interesting." Dana rose. She'd gotten what she came for. "Thanks, Evan. Sorry to be a pest."

"You can be a pest anytime."

She spun lightly on her heels, aware of the image the back of her body might leave behind, and left Evan's office to find Cathy. But then she remembered it might be better to call Melly first and warn her to expect a new list in the next few minutes. She wasn't sure if Melly was picking up the lists at a communal fax machine that others could see.

Melly apparently hadn't understood the importance of

confidentiality, and Dana had given a gentle reminder earlier this week. Husbands and wives talk; it's inevitable. But how much had Melly divulged? At the very least, Noel knew that the names were Spanish, and he'd asked Dana about it in front of two other people the other night at her apartment, demonstrating just how easy it was to spread confidential information without really meaning to.

Melanie's inexplicable resentment vanished once the apologies were spoken, and now, quite the opposite, she was feeling a small thrill to be included in Dana's world of criminal investigation.

She couldn't fathom why she'd been so put out before. Sure, Juliet and the others in SC had been rather nasty to her the first time, but that was no reason to take it out on Dana. She should have given Juliet a piece of her mind instead. Now her interest was piqued again, just like it had been when Dana first told her about the Luz Melendez account, three weeks ago.

Dana's closed lips only heightened the intrigue. Melanie's imagination filled the vacuum with her own theories about the people behind those names on the accounts and their crimes. It became an escape, a way to get through the tedium and nausea of her day. The power of concentration was the key. If she focused very hard on her usual work, keeping a thought tucked away in a corner of her mind about the small reward awaiting her, she had the incentive to take care of business, efficiently, effectively, making the time pass more quickly, the seven months remaining until baby time.

Those other inevitable concerns could wait: the length of her leave of absence, the risk of health problems, the money troubles. Her mind so easily went to the baby. This life growing inside of her had overwhelmed her physical reality. Her thoughts would always start out positive and warm and excited and segue into the worries about health and money and the future without her immediately noticing the transition until she was immersed, almost obsessed—for how long? Minutes or more were lost at a time. A voice or a ringing phone would call her back to the work on her desk or computer screen.

She'd successfully transferred some of that energetic imagination to her tucked-away thought, her little reward, the bit of sleuthing, the Nancy Drew. That was exciting!

On Monday, when she got the second list, she'd jotted down the account numbers for herself before running down the hall to SC. After a little friendly prodding, she returned to her own computer screen to satisfy her curiosity. Nothing could be wrong with taking a look; she was authorized to see the information anyway, and (this time) she would heed Dana's warning (so foolish of her to have let that nondisclosure order slip her mind).

She wouldn't speak a word about the subpoenas to anyone, not even Noel. It would be tough to keep her mouth shut because she'd gotten so used to telling Noel about every little mundane and not-so-mundane detail of her life. Last time, she hadn't told him so much really, but afterward, they'd let their imaginations go wild about Dana's investigation. It didn't end well. Dana's discomfort was so evident when Noel asked that question last Saturday. They should have known better than to put their friend in such an awkward position.

It was just that they'd been so lax the first time, when Dana had been so trusting and had spoken so freely about the Luz Melendez account. But that was a time when Dana was still an outsider, before her transfer to another bureau and assignment to a top-secret investigation. Something very big! It had to be, Melanie supposed. She should have known better than to discuss it in front of Mingo and Cheryl.

When she made her own examination of the accounts, Melanie quickly discerned the suspicious pattern of activity. Gobs of cash in and out again. The accounts were being used to launder dirty money, narcotics money of course. Spanish names meant narcotics.

She was ashamed to jump to that conclusion, being married to a Colombian who was blessed with moral values that surpassed the Pope's. Since the stereotype hadn't been completely erased from her own mind, it made her wonder if Noel was doing enough to change the common perception. Clearly, he was bothered by the narcotics cartels and the bad name they'd given his country. Whenever he spoke of it, she saw the shame in his eyes.

And that's why he avoided the topic. There were times he would bite back the words when the subject was raised in his presence, letting narrow-minded people spew malicious speculation. She would be disappointed when he remained silent, wishing he'd speak up and set people straight. His articulate, diplomatic rejoinders to backhanded comments always had a way of revealing the bias and narrow judgment behind them.

But why should she expect him to speak up in defense, when the attack was unwarranted in the first place? His eyes were windows on the goodness inside. It was absurd even to place Noel and the Colombian narcotics trade in the same train of thought. The pressure was too much for him, she could tell, and sometimes he reacted by holding it in, telling himself it was best not to dignify a disparaging comment with a response.

One time he'd been so offended by a slur on his country that he blurted the popular justification espoused by many Colombians: "We're just supplying your demand. Without the drug-crazy North Americans, there'd be no cocaine trade." Emphatic and righteous. Correct too, but shallow and unethical and unlike him. Two wrongs did not make a right in Noel's book. His hasty remark was driven by defensiveness—and who wouldn't get defensive, hearing so many ignorant remarks, time and again?

What an unlucky coincidence that her best friend happened to be working on an investigation against Colombians. There it was again. That judgment. She'd come to this conclusion without any evidence of Colombian nationality. These accounts belonged to people with Spanish surnames handling enormous amounts of cash.

Looking at one of these accounts, Melanie was reminded of the day, several months ago, when a teller had come to her with a question. Should he fill out a CTR for a certain customer who frequently deposited large cash amounts, like $6,500 and $7,200, all less than the legal reporting limit of $10,000? Two days after taking a large cash deposit, the teller had seen the same depositor at another window, handing over cash. He became curious, looked up the account, and found a pattern. Was this account holder trying to get around the federal reporting rules?

Melanie had been uncertain and bumped the question up to the legal department, assuming it would be investigated and appropriate instructions handed down the line to the tellers. She hadn't heard anything since, and now she was feeling almost ashamed at not having taken a stronger, more ethical stance.

Where had she developed this attitude of "look the other way?" Possibly it had rubbed off on her from the bedrock of bank culture, money as a commodity detached from its source, assets as black figures on paper, unrelated to the people who generated them. This chance to help Dana seemed like a good opportunity to correct her uneasy apathy.

How she longed to call up Dana, invite her for lunch and just brainstorm openly over these accounts. Too bad about the confidentiality problem. It would be such an interesting pastime, a way to bring her even closer to Dana. Suddenly, this closeness seemed more important after glimpsing the abyss of a potential falling out. They'd pulled back from the edge in time. There'd been a slow growing apart over the past four years, an inevitable consequence of her marriage to Noel.

A husband may replace the best girlfriend in some ways, but not all. There were things she missed. College days had been the best, the innocent talk and laughter into the night, shared experiences about classes, boys, friends, career decisions. Melanie longed for some of that again, especially recently, and if she could pinpoint a time the feeling had taken hold, it was the instant she became aware of the growing baby inside. Inexorable change was at hand, a significant life change that would put all girlhood dreams in cold storage, a bequest to the next generation.

She and Dana had talked many times about children, how Dana wanted them but wanted to wait, how Melanie wanted them but didn't necessarily want to wait. The "child bride," Dana's loving nickname for her, was now twenty-six, nearly twenty-seven, not so completely young anymore but the first among her friends to be pregnant.

If Melanie had a question, she could always call her mother, who gave love and support and advice backed by experience. But a different kind of outlet was needed for these tumultuous emotions, the potluck of excitement and worry, anticipation, resentment, disbelief, and bursting joy. She could open up in this way only to another woman her age, and she wanted that woman to be Dana, her remaining link to a carefree past, the friend she'd shared so much with and—should she admit this?—emulated and admired. Dana, with the brains and the looks and the glamorous, tough job, at the forefront of things that really mattered. Melanie needed to expose her fears about the baby and be reassured by a strong woman like that, someone on a different course.

And so, on Thursday, when Dana called, Melanie was happy to hear from her, even though she knew that the main purpose of the call was work related.

"Whatever you did on Monday really helped," Dana said brightly. "We just received a stack of documents, about half of the accounts on the list. That's at least a week faster than we've been getting them!"

"It was easy enough, and I'm glad to help. I almost wish I could be a part of your team—maybe I'm getting a vicarious thrill out of this."

"It's nice someone is thrilled. Most of the time I feel only the drudgery. It never stops. My boss just handed me another list of five accounts he wants immediately. I'm adding a few to the bottom of the list and faxing it over in a few minutes. Can you pick up the fax, you know, somewhat discretely?"

Melanie leaned out of her cubicle to peer down the hall. "Sure, don't worry. I can see the fax machine from here." She heard a touch of panic in Dana's voice and wasn't offended by this reminder of confidentiality. She hoped her own words and tone were reassuring.

"Thanks a million. I really appreciate it."

Before Dana could hang up, Melanie jumped in. "I was thinking, why don't we have lunch sometime? Just you and me. No husbands or sisters or cousins or blind dates. Just like we used to."

"Yeah. Like we used to." A meaningful silence fell over the wire, in which they shared a retreat into the memory of their weekly luncheon dates from the days when Dana was in law school and Melly was new at the bank. Even after Dana started at the DA's office, they'd gotten together more frequently than they had in the past couple of months. First City was headquartered in the financial district, just three short subway stops from the Criminal Court building. For a while they'd taken turns meeting near Melanie's work, then near Dana's. Where had those times gone?

"You're busy, I know," said Melanie.

"True. You're busy too."

"True."

A pause. "Life can keep on getting busier, or we can find the time," said Dana decisively.

"How about next week?"

"Okay." Dana hesitated. "Not Monday. Monday's are always hell. Let's try for Tuesday. Is that a good day for you?"

"Sure. Twelve, or later?"

"I can't set a time right now. Let's talk Tuesday morning."

They agreed to the plan, and Melanie said goodbye with a smile on her lips, feeling reconnected and content. How amazing life was, to have everything one could possibly want! A wonderful husband, a baby on the way, parents who loved her, and the very closest of best friends. Sour moods were no longer allowed. A little nausea now and then could not ruin this euphoria. There were people she could count on to help her get through this.

Five minutes passed, and her ears picked up the familiar sound of the communal fax machine. She went to retrieve her message. The surrounding cubicles were either empty or busily occupied by oblivious tenants.

The cover page was already in the tray. "To Melanie Avendaño, From Dana Hargrove," the DA's insignia at the top. The second page, the list, squeezed through. She picked up the shiny paper, still warm, and placed it on top of the cover page in her hand. Her eyes scanned the list, not immediately focusing on the distorted print. Sometimes these faxes just weren't as clear as the original, and this one was partially handwritten, five lines hand-printed at the top, three lines typed at the end.

After a brief look, she decided to go back to her cube to examine it further. If it was indecipherable, she'd have to ask Dana for a better printout before giving it to SC. Also, if she could make it out, she hoped to do a little bit of sleuthing on her own with these account numbers.

Pages in hand, she turned and nearly walked into Dwight

Berkeley coming toward her. She gave a nervous greeting, hoping he hadn't seen her jump. He replied with a smile and a friendly "hello" on his way past. She was reminded of the day they'd spoken about the man who'd made the cash deposit to the Luz Melendez account. Wouldn't Dwight be amazed to know how she'd become involved in this investigation? It was her little secret.

Instinctively, protectively, she pulled the list close to her, hiding the written side against her maternal breast. As she walked back to her cube, she tilted the papers outward to peek down. Maybe it wasn't so fuzzy after all.

She rounded the opening in her partition, took another tentative step and was hit. A knot of sickness squeezed her insides, stomach acid erupted in her mouth, and a giant hand pressed down from above. Darkness rushed up. She lowered her head and dropped to her knees, fighting to stay in this world. Taking a deep breath, she dared to lift the paper to her eyes once more.

There, on the second handwritten line, blurry but indelible, a familiar name screamed at her: "Saludos Limitada."

12 » INITIATION

EUGENE QUITMAN MADE a favorable first impression and, under different circumstances, might have been able to maintain it. He was congenial, open and accommodating. The first part of his exchange with Reichert was conversational, easy and pleasant. Then the interrogation began.

Initially, Bruce's questions were civil in tone, becoming gradually more pointed and confrontational, causing that broad smile on Quitman's face to shrink slowly, millimeters at a time.

Dana said nothing, just listened. This was the ostensible purpose of her presence. She hadn't a clue what to expect. Minutes before the meeting, Bruce had called her to his office. On the way in, she saw Quitman sitting in a small waiting area in the hallway. Bruce told her he was about to interview an executive from a large paper mill headquartered upstate. He'd subpoenaed the company's bank records but hadn't compelled Quitman's presence by use of process. The witness was here voluntarily to lend cooperation.

Everyone else on the FC team was tied up, and Bruce needed Dana to sit in on the meeting, "to witness the witness." As a rule, no ADA should ever be alone while interviewing an important witness. There was nothing for her to study, no need for her to ask questions; she was only to observe and garner her own impressions of Quitman. Later, Bruce would test his own thoughts against hers.

She was stunned at this request, particularly since the witness was related to an aspect of the investigation Bruce had reserved exclusively for himself. He'd never actively solicited her opinions on anything other than her narrow, assigned field of investigation. Still, she could read nothing into it, no heightened regard for her opinion or implicit invitation to join the field from which she'd been excluded. This assignment was merely a consequence of circumstance. No one else on the team was available.

After this brief explanation of why he'd summoned her, Bruce picked up the phone and asked Cathy to escort Quitman into the office to join them. There were friendly handshakes. Bruce even remembered to introduced Dana. The three gathered in a small conference area of the room, Dana and Bruce taking the two chairs on one side of a low coffee table, Quitman settling into a small couch on the other side.

Niceties and service of coffee preceded any talk of business. Dana contributed a few remarks about the weather and city truisms just to avoid being another piece of the furniture. In this set up, without a desk or table to hide behind, her legs were on display. She saw Quitman's eyes go to them, and she pressed her knees firmly together.

It was about this time when they all eased into an agreement to use first names. Dana silently wondered at Bruce's uncharacteristic ease. When his job absolutely called for it—a matter of interview technique—he could drum up the pleasantries and a faux congenial air.

Quitman was a man of about fifty, nicely attired in a European business suit, trim and prematurely tanned for this Friday morning in May. Bruce asked some general questions about his business. Quitman spoke almost lovingly of his concern, Hanniger Paper, Inc., a prominent, reputable New York corporation. To Dana, nothing seemed to be further from the Colombian narcotics trade.

"I know you're a busy man, Gene, and we appreciate your taking the time to come in."

"Not at all. We're very happy to cooperate with your investigation."

"Good! Then let's get down to business, shall we? Did you bring along that information we talked about?"

"Yes. It's all right here." Quitman lifted a shiny black attaché case from the floor, laid it on the couch beside him and fiddled with the combination lock, making two unsuccessful attempts before getting it open. *Click* went Dana's internal camera. The witness was more nervous than he first let on. Out came four slender manila folders. "These are the records of all sales to the four companies you mentioned." He slid them across the coffee table.

Bruce picked up the folders and placed them neatly in his lap. He opened the top one and examined the contents—two sheets of paper—closed the folder, put it at the bottom of the pile and repeated the ritual with each of the next three. Silence stilled the air for the two minutes he took to get through them. Dana crossed her legs, cast her eyes down at her hands, looked at the framed diplomas on the wall, glanced out the window behind the desk. Finally, she allowed her eyes to alight on Quitman, who returned a fleeting but purposeful gaze with a broad smile.

Bruce closed the last folder. "This is it?" he asked, no longer smiling.

The first millimeters of shrinkage reduced Gene's amiability. "Well, yes. That's what accounting tells me. Those are computer printouts of all our past business with these companies, the items and quantities ordered, the dates, the amounts paid. The column showing the items they purchased might look like Greek to you, but I'm happy to interpret. We simply entered our own internal codes for the various kinds of bulk paper products…"

"But no details about the method of payment."

"Method?"

"Check, cash, credit, international wire order. The way they paid for the goods, the Hanniger employee who received the payments, the employee who deposited the payments, which Hanniger bank account was used for deposits of these payments, and so forth. You get the picture."

Quitman chuckled briefly and cleared his throat. "That's a very detailed kind of report you're asking for. I had no idea from our phone conversation you expected any more than what we usually keep on file."

"I did say, I remember distinctly, that we were interested in the financial dealings between Hanniger and these Colombian companies." Dana was momentarily diverted from her immediate function as an observer, drawn into a memory. *I told you not to touch it, I know that.*

"Well, yes," said Quitman. "I assumed you would want to know how much money these companies paid us for the products, and it's all there. Of course, you already have Hanniger's bank records from your subpoena. You should be able to piece some of it together from that, and I might be able to remember a few other facts, but frankly, we don't keep the kind of detailed reports you're talking about. Especially not for good customers."

"So, you consider these to be good customers?" He swatted the palm of his hand with the folders.

"As far as I know."

"Well, as the executive in charge of foreign accounts, it must be your business to know."

"That's...correct."

As Quitman's self-assurance wilted, Dana masked her astonishment at the transformation in Bruce. His tone had changed so completely, his questioning was starting to resemble cross-examination of a defendant on trial. Was Bruce considering a prosecution against Hanniger, its executives or employees? If so, Quitman wasn't aware of it. He was here to "cooperate."

Often, full cooperation could be had by applying a little pressure, the threat of civil or criminal penalties. What was Hanniger's alleged crime? Had these Colombian companies paid for Hanniger products with narcotics money? There were problems with this theory. Receiving criminal proceeds in a different form, twice removed from the street, didn't constitute a crime without specific intent of the recipient, or at least a criminal level of negligence. Dana was loath to believe that a reputable U.S. firm would knowingly accept narcotics money. It had to be unintentional.

She remembered her discovery of the link to Resner Aircraft Corporation. How many U.S. corporations had received Cartel money? Could the business transactions themselves be phony? Perhaps no paper products or aircraft parts were ever sold. But no, that was going a step too far. Bruce's favorite refrain was that the Cartel laundered its money in legitimate looking transactions. The four Colombian companies that Bruce now held tightly in his fist could be owned and controlled by the Cartel, companies that manufactured consumer products in Colombia and needed raw materials for their manufacturing process. Using narco dollars for their expenses, these companies expanded their operations and prospered in the legitimate marketplace, increasing the power of their Cartel owners.

Dana would love to know how Bruce had discovered the link to Hanniger, but he'd erected a wall between her and this part of the investigation involving North American companies. Resner was the exception, something she'd tripped over. She'd seen other corporate entities written on the payee lines of smurf checks, but they were all Latin American companies. Now she wondered if she'd recognize any of the names in these four folders, or if Bruce had discovered them independently, without reference to the evidence she and Mineko had been gathering.

Bruce seemed to realize he'd gone a bit far and was pushing his luck with Quitman. He backed off.

"I meant to say, Gene, I just need your help here. You have the experience and insight into Hanniger's business relations with these foreign corporations."

"Certainly, you can count on our cooperation." Quitman's smile came back in a more tepid version as he quickly averted his eyes and peeked at his watch.

"Like you said, some of this can be pieced together with the bank records. I have a sketchy map of the flow of money from these companies into Hanniger, but maybe you can explain a few things. Let me pull out some examples, and we'll go over them."

Bruce placed the four manila folders on the coffee table, went to his desk, picked up a neat pile of papers he'd placed there before the meeting, and returned. Quitman watched his movements warily, pulling himself up straight out of the soft cushions and resting his elbows on his knees, fingers intertwined. Bruce moved the coffee cups aside and set the papers on the table between them. "Some of these checks may be familiar to you —"

"I have no daily contact with the flow of money," interrupted Quitman. "The accounting department handles all receipts."

"I can appreciate that, but I imagine you have an understanding of Hanniger's procedures for handling incoming payments?"

"In a general way."

"Good. Then, generally, can you tell me what these numbers are, written at the top of each check? I'm guessing they were put there by a Hanniger employee before the checks were deposited."

Bruce slid the stack of papers closer to Quitman, who picked up the top one. Dana's eyes shot quickly to the next paper in the stack, now exposed. She didn't need a second glance to know it was a photocopy of three smurf checks.

"You're right about that," said Quitman. "Employees in the accounting department place those numbers on the checks to make sure the right customer is credited. Each customer account has a unique five-digit number."

"That's the number at the top of each of the computer printouts you gave me, right?" Bruce was resting his fingertips on the closed manila folders as he asked this.

"Correct."

"And the set of three numbers after the dash, that would refer to the specific transaction with that customer?"

"Correct again." Quitman returned the paper he was holding to the top of the stack on the table.

"So, I could easily link up the checks which were used to pay for each particular purchase by comparing the numbers on the checks with the computer printouts you've given me?" Bruce didn't wait for an answer, already sure of his hypothesis. "Like the numbers on these checks."

Bruce picked up all the papers in his stack except the bottom one. "All these checks—thirty of them—bear the number '66017-012' at the top. See if I'm right." He gave the stack to Quitman, who glanced through and nodded, while Bruce picked up the four manila folders and quickly checked their contents. "Here it is." He pulled a sheet from one of them and laid the folders on the table. "This customer, Servicios Escolástico, has the account number '66017,' and '012' must refer to the twelfth purchase in the list, let's see, $46,700 in paper products purchased on April fifth of this year. Seem right?"

Quitman took the printout, compared it to the checks, and nodded. There was no smile on his face now, and he didn't look up as he repeated his new, favorite word: "Correct."

While their guest was so occupied, Bruce sent Dana an oblique look. The room suddenly grew warmer. Was Bruce checking to see if she got it? Of course she got it, even as she sat stupefied with disbelief. She fought hard for a mannequin face as the realization hit her. A major U.S. company had received street dollars in payment for its products! No corporate checks buffered the link. Hanniger had received a bundle of smurf checks from accounts in the names of fictitious individuals, funded with cash from narcotics sales.

Quitman gingerly placed all ten sheets of checks and the Hanniger printout together in a separate stack on the coffee table. Bruce took a pointed look at the pile and relaxed into a comfortable sideways lean on his left forearm where it rested on the arm of his chair, placing his right hand on his knee.

Just as Dana fought to control an outcropping of emotion on her own face, she could discern the same struggle within Bruce. His eyes shone with the faintest emergent glimmer of cockiness. That energy was diverted into his left thumb, which rubbed against the fingertips of his left hand in a sustained, controlled motion, crushing an imaginary hard nugget of clay into fine, red dust, sprinkling down. The wedding ring glowed, its warm radiance intermittently caught by the light.

"I think you can see why I'm puzzled over this," he said. "Thirty checks, none of them from a bank account in the name of your client, Servicios Escolástico, all these little amounts—1,200 here, 1,500 there—all batched together to pay one big bill of $46,700. Is this how all your foreign clients pay for Hanniger paper products?"

"No, but let me explain—"

"Please do." Bruce stopped the crushing motion and leaned slightly forward, expectantly.

"Servicios Escolástico is a Colombian company, a publisher of textbooks and educational pamphlets manufactured in-house. Their representative showed me samples of their books, and we came up with a line of Hanniger paper products they could use. I opened the account. The textbooks are a good quality, used in schools all over his country. The company seemed solid. He showed me some impressive statistics—"

"Sure, okay, Gene, all right, but how did you come up with this payment plan?"

"Well, Bruce," started Quitman. The familiarity almost sounded like a joke at this point, but Dana believed he meant the opposite, hoping to shore up his strength. "Hanniger requires payment in U.S. dollars. Checks or drafts are acceptable, if they're in U.S. dollars. Servicios Escolástico chose to make its payment this way, in several smaller checks. The first time it happened, I questioned their purchasing agent..."

"You thought it a bit strange?"

"I suppose you might say that. I might not use that word, but..."

"What would you call it?"

Quitman rolled his eyes heavenward, searching. "Unconventional."

"Unconventional."

"Yes, so I *did* ask about it and had a long conversation with their purchasing agent, a man named Muñoz I believe, but don't hold me to that. A very sharp fellow, excellent English. He explained certain currency restrictions that hamper businesses in Colombia. Apparently, the Colombian government puts a ceiling on the number of dollars any one individual or business may buy for Colombian pesos. Manufacturers have difficulty purchasing American materials for their businesses and sometimes have to resort to creative financial arrangements." Bruce raised his bushy eyebrows. "So," continued Quitman, "this Muñoz said his company had affiliations with other businesses and individuals in the United States who maintained checking accounts in American banks and would, by arrangement, be sending payments to Hanniger directly on behalf of Servicios Escolástico. It seemed the perfect solution..."

"Perfect. I suppose he told you a little about these businesses and individuals his company was affiliated with?"

"Not much."

"Like what, for instance?"

"Nothing significant that I can recall."

"Nothing at all? How about the source of the money in these U.S. bank accounts? Did you ask about that?"

"No, not that I recall—but listen here!" Quitman was now actually riled, his anger completely breaking through his original façade. "You seem to be implying something entirely out of line."

Bruce was calm and even keeled. "I'm not implying anything. I'm asking some questions and you're giving some answers—"

"Implying I didn't do my homework here. I checked out this company Servicios Escolástico, and I saw their products, looked at their balance sheet, saw some official statistics, all in print with the sources. This is a legitimate company."

Bruce sat back with his hands up in the air, like the victim of a stick-up. "Whoa! I'm not doubting your sincerity here, Gene. But you've got to admit, it looks strange. Unconventional, as you say."

"Unconventional doesn't mean criminal."

"Who said criminal?"

"You're a prosecutor, aren't you?"

Bruce shrugged his shoulders in a gesture that said, *Yes, but so what?*

"Maybe I'm—to be perfectly honest, I might agree that it looks like Servicios Escolástico is guilty of some Colombian regulatory violation. But that's them, not us, not Hanniger. Are you trying to say we're subject to Colombian currency laws? I think not. I think not! I think Mr. Rei—Bruce—I think you're a little out of line here in what you're accusing."

"There've been no accusations. You've come in here to help us out, and you've been more than forthright. I greatly appreciate it, especially since all of this could have been done a little less friendly, with a subpoena."

Dana noticed the omissions from Bruce's veiled threat—the risk he would run in pursuing that strategy. The DA's office had two kinds of subpoena authority: a civil subpoena for a private office hearing investigating forfeiture, or a criminal subpoena for a grand jury investigating money laundering felonies. Either way, Hanniger's legal department undoubtedly would become involved, pressuring the DA for a promise of immunity from prosecution in exchange for Quitman's testimony. If the DA declined to grant immunity, Quitman would assert his Fifth Amendment right to remain silent and give nothing up. Bruce was trying to work around this dilemma by getting as much information as he could under the guise of friendly cooperation.

Was Quitman a potential defendant or merely a witness? More than likely, Bruce didn't know the answer to that question. He was straddling the line, trying to size up the situation, and Quitman was catching on to it, growing nervous and wary, beginning to believe he'd fallen into a trap. Only time would reveal the truth or fallacy of his belief. An indictment against Hanniger or Quitman would clinch the trap. But if Quitman ended up a star witness for the prosecution against Colombian bad guys, his memories of Bruce would be rose-hued, full of self-congratulation for having saved his own hide under the mantle of civic duty.

"I don't enjoy hauling people in with a subpoena," continued Bruce. "So, let's keep this informal, shall we? I have just a few more questions."

Quitman waved his hand in the air and dipped his head, as if to say, "Okay." With a flourish, he assumed a confident posture. Relaxing back into the cushions, he propped a foot up on the opposite knee and placed a hand on top of his ankle while stretching the other arm along the top of the couch. The man was not running.

Apparently, Bruce had handled the crisis well with his gently stated innuendo, better than Dana would have anticipated after seeing him dig a hole for himself, coming on too strong too fast with his usual brand of third degree, an ingrained tendency difficult to overcome. For now, he'd scored a tiny victory. The witness remained in his seat, willing to answer a few more questions, although Bruce's mind undoubtedly contained more than a few.

"Before you start the questions again," said Quitman, "I think it's my turn." His fingertips started to play piano on his ankle. "You haven't told me very much about this investigation of yours. Let me know what you're after, and maybe it'll jog my memory on some things." Dana smiled inwardly with embarrassment at his weak, belated attempt to acquire leverage.

"I'm afraid I can't tell you any more about this—"

"I mean," blurted Quitman, furiously playing the piano, "the first thing that comes to mind with Colombians is the cocaine trade, you know, with everything you read in the papers, but this is the Financial Crimes Bureau, am I correct? You don't investigate narcotics crimes, just money crimes, although I suppose money crimes can be related to narcotics too…"

"That's a sharp observation, Gene, but like I said, I'd be breaking my oath as a prosecutor if I gave you confidential information. I hope you can appreciate my duty to maintain the integrity of the investigation."

"Sure, no, of course."

"What I *can* say is, you're doing an important thing here. We need help from people like you."

The smile crept back onto Quitman's lips, and he said, "All right. I'm here to help and I have a little more time. What else is there? I think I've said just about all I can say about Servicios Escolástico."

Bruce picked up the single sheet of paper, the one left alone on the coffee table when they were considering the ten pages of checks from Servicios Escolástico. "We have just one more example to discuss with you," he said, looking alternately at Quitman and the paper in his hand. "The number at the top of this check is '41542-009'."

Quitman reached for the manila folders on the table. "I think I recognize that number—41542?—but let me double check."

While Quitman was so occupied, Bruce swiveled around to the side and faced Dana head on, making his first unambiguous acknowledgement of her presence since the start of the meeting. His movement was so unexpected, she instinctively recoiled as he leaned toward her with outstretched hand, the paper taut in his grasp, its cutting edge directed at her.

He wasn't simply showing it to her. He was telling her, without words, to take it. Why now? What did he want? Should she take a quick look and hand it back, or did he want something more, a stronger, united front against the witness on this one? Was it now "we" instead of "I"?

She took the sheet, and he immediately turned back to face Quitman, abandoning the paper to her care. "Found it?" he asked.

"Yes." Quitman replaced three folders on the table, retaining control of one. "This is it. 41542 is our account number for Saludos Limitada."

Dana's nerves muffled the sound of Quitman's voice. She was aware only of Bruce, the change in his behavior. When Quitman said the account name, Bruce flashed an oblique look in her direction, his eyebrows mashed into the single caterpillar, giving her the distinct impression he wanted her to do something with this paper. She'd glanced at it when he first handed it to her, but she couldn't remember what it contained. She looked again, trying to focus, to remain calm.

"What kind of company is Saludos Limitada, as far as you

know?" Bruce asked the witness. The name, mentioned a second time, jarred a memory. It had been one of the handwritten entries on the list she'd faxed to Melanie yesterday. Now she held in her hand a photocopy of a single check dated April 27, 1988, bearing the account name, Saludos Ltda, and a post office box address in Queens, New York. The payee, Hanniger Paper, Inc., and the amount, $32,546.89, were typed on the check, which bore an illegible signature, written with dramatic embellishment. On the bottom was the imprint of the bank, First City Financial.

"They print greeting cards, stationery, calendars, that kind of thing. Again, I met a representative of the company, a Mr. Restrepo, who was most personable and gave me details of their operation. I saw samples, read their literature and saw invoices for their sales in several countries. You know, now that I'm remembering these people, I just can't believe you're investigating them. These are polished businessmen, all of them at these four companies you're looking into. I just can't believe this—" He looked at Bruce, then Dana, and back again. "Well, I guess you have your reasons."

"Again, we can't get into those reasons. But Dana and I do want to go over this example of one of the transactions." Bruce tipped his head in Dana's direction and leaned back in his chair with his arms crossed.

The ball was in her court. All a test? Her stomach churned with a combination of loathing and nerves. *You won't have to say or do a thing*, he'd said, *just witness the witness*. Oh, and one other thing: a spur-of-the-moment performance for his entertainment.

There was no time to fume. She had to act. The test was not so difficult, the questions suggesting themselves with just a little thought.

"On your printout, what is the amount for the ninth transaction, number 009?" she asked Quitman.

"$32,546.89."

"Then they paid for the Hanniger products with just one check, this check." She handed the photocopy to him.

"Correct," he affirmed, looking at the paper.

"That's what confuses us," she said, in feigned complicity with Bruce. "Maybe you can explain."

"What's to explain? One transaction, one check."

"This company, Saludos Limitada, is a Colombian company, right?"

"Correct. They're incorporated in Colombia."

"So, they're subject to the same currency restrictions as the other company, Servicios Escolástico?"

"That's correct."

"Then you must have wondered why they were able to pay their entire bill with a single check, a company check drawn on a United States bank, rather than dozens of personal checks like the ones Servicios Escolástico used to pay for your goods."

Quitman looked at her, blinked and smiled as widely as he had during the early moments of the meeting, signaling that Dana's question was easy for him, too easy and perhaps naïve on her part. "There wasn't much to wonder about. Servicios Escolástico sells its products only in Colombia, but Saludos Limitada sells its products worldwide and has a large market in Hispanic communities in this country, especially in the New York metropolitan area. So they generate income in U.S. dollars and maintain a bank account here. It's that simple."

"I see," said Dana and nothing else, as the two men settled back into their seats, looking pleased with themselves.

When Quitman left, Bruce asked her to stay; he wanted her impressions. "By the way," he began, "nice the way you picked up at the end." She was flabbergasted but anxious for the sour taste in her mouth to dissipate. She had to work with this guy and didn't want to be angry.

Whenever she stood back and took a rational look at the objectives of their investigation, her inclination to accuse Bruce of the worst motivations usually fell by the wayside. In this instance, he may have felt forced into a split-second decision to pass the questioning to her, a necessary change in strategy occasioned by his own mistakes. Maybe she should give him credit for that much. He recognized the need to soften things between him and Quitman after he nearly sabotaged his own effort with a harsh approach. Dana's tone of voice may have been gentler, but their position remained strong, two against one.

If he'd thrown in a test for Dana as well, it was a relatively easy one he knew she could pass. Quitman thought he'd come out on top, but his transparent relief at finding a suitable answer to Dana's question only heightened the suspiciousness of the other transaction with the thirty smurf checks.

In the aftermath of Quitman's departure, Bruce and Dana carried on their conversation half-standing, propped against desk and chair, respectively. Joe poked his head in the half-open door, was invited to enter, and enthusiastically joined in. He paced the room with his hands stuffed in pants pockets, suppressing the urge to break the unspoken rule against smoking in Bruce's office. The men treated Dana as an equal, answering her questions and listening to her opinions. A corner had been turned. Dana had passed her initiation and was now a full member of the team.

They discussed their impressions of the witness, including Joe's option of using Quitman in a forfeiture case. She asked how they'd learned about Hanniger, and they told her. It had been a month before she joined the team when Mineko uncovered smurf checks like the ones Bruce had used during the meeting. They'd subpoenaed Hanniger's bank accounts, and informally, without a subpoena, asked company representatives to identify Hanniger's corporate customers from Colombia. Bruce was referred to

Quitman and had taken it from there.

"All of that's bullshit, you know," Bruce told her. "That stuff about the currency restrictions. Those regulations exist all right, because the Colombian government wants to build a stable currency by preventing flight of its cash. But Colombians are using the currency restrictions as a convenient excuse to hide narcotics money."

"How?" asked Dana.

"You tell her, Joe."

"I've interviewed a few witnesses," said Joe, "Colombians who have large investments in the U.S., like mutual funds and brokerage accounts. They funded their investments mostly with smurf checks. These are wealthy people who could be Cartel connected for all I know, but even if they acquired their wealth honestly, they claim they can't legitimately purchase U.S. dollars with pesos, so they have to resort to middlemen who deal in dollars on the black market. They give pesos to these middlemen, who purchase the smurf checks for them."

"But they have to suspect the money is dirty when they see these strange-looking checks," said Dana.

"Exactly. That's what we think, so I'm developing a forfeiture action against them. The biggest problem will be proving the knowledge element. They all have the same story. They never ask about sources and just assume the checks represent legitimate income of hard-working Colombian immigrants in the U.S., people who want to send money home to family members and exchange their dollars for pesos through these middlemen."

"Hard working, indeed," muttered Bruce.

"So, Quitman was either lying, or he just put an innocent spin on what Muñoz said about his 'affiliates' in the U.S.," suggested Dana. "Servicios Escolástico got those thirty checks on the black market in currency."

"That's the most innocent explanation," said Bruce. "It implicates the Colombian company only in violations of currency regulations and, maybe, an attitude of 'look the other way' to ignore the evidence that these checks represent dirty money. The alternative explanation I see is that Servicios Escolástico is owned by the Cartel, and any black market 'middleman' is just a Cartel operative, using narcotics money to pay the company's debt."

"And you're thinking that the same kind of payment system happened with Resner Aircraft—"

"Exactly."

"But Saludos is a different story. They've gotten around this currency market cover by selling products in this country. Or, is all of that a sham too?" she asked.

"We don't believe so," replied Bruce.

"So, you've actually found out something about the company's operations in this country?"

Bruce and Joe exchanged looks before Bruce turned to her and said, "I guess you haven't been brought up to date on this part of the investigation."

"No. Well, I remember the name from the list you gave me yesterday to fax to the bank. But before that, I'd never seen it in the bank documents we've been analyzing. I guess you learned about Saludos from Quitman."

Bruce cleared his throat and folded his arms across his chest. "It was just a coincidence, really, that Saludos happened to do business with Hanniger. Quitman gave me the company name when I asked him to identify Colombian companies. After that, the check I had today and a few others showed up as items deposited into Hanniger's bank accounts when we received the documents on the subpoenas. But before we got this information from Hanniger, we knew about the Saludos checking account at First City. The Don and his crew have been following one of the mules. About ten days ago, right after the target made a deposit,

Gilbert ran into the bank with a subpoena and got the account name. We followed up with a subpoena for the records but still haven't gotten them. And that's why the name was on your list yesterday."

"Interesting," said Dana, her thoughts leading sequentially from Gilbert, to the Don, and to her trip down to the Dungeon several days back—had it been more than ten days already?

13 » NIÑO

MELANIE RECOVERED JUST enough to find her chair, sit down, and place the paper on the desk. She rested her forearms on either side and hunched over the list protectively.

When she dared to fix her eyes steadily on the page, her panic returned. Not just the name but the manner of its placement seemed deliberate and sinister, designed to make her notice and react. Prominently displayed as Number Two on a short list of eight. Wasn't the handwriting on that line just slightly bigger than the rest? A masculine hand. It must have been written by that man, Dana's boss.

What was Dana trying to say with this? What did she know?

Already there were so many names, maybe hundreds of names in this investigation, and Dana couldn't be on top of all of them. The investigative plan was engineered by her boss. Hadn't she complained about being left out of the loop?

But she'd also hinted at her growing involvement in the investigation. Whatever she *did* know, she wasn't allowed to tell. Secrets. Confidentiality. *Can you pick up the fax, you know, somewhat discretely?* Sneaky. And then there was her reluctance about lunch. Couldn't commit to Monday, not even Tuesday. Nothing firm. They would have to talk Tuesday morning.

So many little signs of avoidance. Dana simply couldn't face her best friend, except to fax the list over, fax the list, fax the list…

Let's put a fax machine between us and play dumb. *I'm not allowed to talk about it.* "It" was what Dana knew about Saludos, and what Melanie had to figure out. "It" must be something bad or the name wouldn't be on the list.

Melanie was sure she'd never mentioned the name to Dana. But the DA's office had investigators, methods, informants. They'd surely found the connection. Noel's business was now tied to this shady company and its crimes, whatever they might be, seeping into the cracks of his daily activities.

Dana, of all people, should know he was incapable of any crime. He was innocent — but innocent of what?

Melanie examined the handwriting again, now so obvious and prominent, not fuzzy at all. There was something forced and unnatural about it. A masculine hand that usually produced a scrawl had made a purposeful effort to form legible, block letters. Dana could have asked a secretary to type the list. She could have rearranged the entries or removed this particular name. It was a warning: *I know something — I know, I know.* What kind of message was that? What was Melanie supposed to do? Warn Noel? Play along as if nothing was going on? Or demand the truth from her friend? Whose side was Dana on anyway?

Melanie covered her eyes with her hands and pulled in a deep breath. Gradually she became aware of her surroundings, the tight walls of her cube, the hum of the fluorescent light overhead, the opening in the panel at her back, voices, a copy machine, a ringing phone down the hall.

She spoke to herself in a calming voice. These rampant, venomous suspicions were so unlike her, a person who always found the positive side in every situation. Primal, animal panic was to blame. This whole thing was ridiculous. The answer was quite simple. Whatever Dana or her boss suspected, the bank records would prove them wrong.

What could this account show but deposits from a small

concession at Noel's store? A modest amount of cash and a few checks for eight or ten dollars, payable to Libros NOMEL. How suspicious could that be? If there were other deposits, they had to be from other retail stores that sold Saludos products. Maybe these other stores were involved in crime. Or maybe a customer of Libros NOMEL had paid with a check from one of those dirty accounts Dana was studying.

An explanation was there, waiting to be uncovered. All Melanie had to do was push SC for a quick response to the subpoena, and the whole matter would be cleared up in days.

She rose with the list in hand, took a step toward the hallway, stopped, and looked back at her computer screen. It wouldn't take a moment to find the explanation for herself before going to SC with the list. Maybe this was Dana's message. This is what Dana wanted her to do.

She dropped into the chair and typed in the account number. This was the reason she'd come back to her cube in the first place. Why had she delayed? She'd gone into a kind of shock, her brain frozen in a holding pattern.

While waiting for the account to appear on her screen, she reached for the glass of ice water on her desk. The ice was nearly melted, the external surface of the glass sweating. Early May, already so hot, and the air conditioning system was still dormant. She pressed the cold wet surface against one cheek, then the other, tabbed over to "All Recent Activity," and pressed "Enter."

Soon, the very active life of the young account spilled onto her screen. She hadn't looked at it since she'd first done the paperwork almost a month ago. The screen held ten lines—only a few days of activity. She pressed "Enter" again and again, the terror rising high in her chest. Cash deposits, checks written. Numerous and large, each in the several thousands of dollars.

Only yesterday, Noel had proudly reported to her that he'd sold about $250 worth of Saludos merchandise to date, better than expected. Mingo, in charge of the accounting, had quoted that figure to Noel, who'd passed it on to Melanie at the end of the day. About $250, a "decent" amount.

The sight she now beheld could only be described as indecent. To sum up the proof, she pressed the button for "Total deposits." $254,168.95 in less than a month. It seemed that an astronomical number of "greeting cards" had been sold.

Dear, sweet Noel. Her immediate feeling was embarrassment at his ignorance. What, really did he know about this? What *could* he know? This was Mingo's pet project. Had Noel done nothing to supervise him?

Today was Thursday, May 12. First City mailed account statements on the third of the month, and the Saludos statement should have arrived at its post office box address. That statement contained half the entries now displayed on her screen. Why hadn't she thought of this before? Noel and Domingo didn't have access to that post office box unless the Saludos representative had given them a key. She seriously doubted they had the key.

Still, Mingo was authorized to conduct telephone banking, to track deposits and withdrawals and the balance on the phone. He was a signatory on the account. Noel was not. How could Noel supervise his cousin when he had no access to the information? So typical of her husband to ignore the dollar signs as he floated euphorically on his high cloud of literary works.

But this? How could anyone miss this much money? Certainly not Mingo, the boy who loved style and excitement. Was he just an easy mark for the Cartel or an active participant? It seemed to her now that there was no way Domingo couldn't have known about this. And there must have been something in his behavior at the store to give Noel a clue, to tip him off...maybe even an offer of easy money.

She thought of Noel's recent nonchalance about financial matters. Not a worry in the world. *Was this the reason?*

Sickness gripped her insides. By her own hand, at her husband's behest, she'd created an instrument of crime, the bank account of a crooked business, while secrets were kept from her, very big and terrible secrets. Her head spun with a strange curiosity, driven by an image of dark, clandestine behavior. All at once she was beset with an urgent desire to know every detail of every minute of her husband's daily life. Deception and betrayal, their possibility, simmered and hissed, a new feeling, previously unimaginable.

Deception didn't fit Noel's character, but neither did complete blindness to this absolute evil invading his own turf. Right under his nose. Had there been temptation? Had she supplied the justification? She and the baby and the need for money?

This was insanity. With a shudder of shame, she rejected the idea of Noel's involvement. Idealistic, intellectual, sensitive Noel tempted by money and the world of crime? If one look in his eyes didn't acquit him, the ridiculousness of the so-called plot certainly did. A man trying to hide a criminal scheme from his wife would never ask her to open an account at her place of business where she could freely, at will, examine its contents.

The black cloud passed over again and she suddenly supposed it was possible, and not beyond imagination, that a certain type of man would be willing to use his wife—a trusting and loyal wife—counting on her to remain silent and protect him when the authorities came calling...

Again, her imagination was running away with her. The answer she'd hoped for was not revealed in the figures on her computer screen. The total amount was obscenely enormous and shouted "crime." She felt unclean just looking at it and pressed "Esc." She dropped her head to the list again, the words staring back, begging for action. Tears threatened and receded. Minutes passed.

In time, the paralysis of indecision suggested a strategy. Why should she do anything at all? This business of prodding SC was only a favor. No one could fault her if she didn't help her friend this one time. No one said she had to give SC this exact list, the faxed one. She could make up her own list, lacking one name.

But this plan solved nothing. At most, it would slow the progress toward the inevitable. SC already had the subpoena, and in time, would send its response to the DA's office. Dana would see the quarter of a million, put it together with the rest, and then decide, if she hadn't already decided, whose side she was on. Noel's fate was in Dana's hands, and along with it, Melanie's life.

She couldn't sit. Action was called for. She needed relief from this pain, the dizziness and pressure of relentless, unwanted thoughts.

After a time, an idea surfaced. She plotted a map and wrote a play, a set of lines with appropriate inflections. It would work as a temporary fix, one that would give her time to come up with a better plan, if one existed, and the fix could always be undone if her hand was forced.

She knew what to do and resolved to do it regardless of the consequences, which surely couldn't be worse than what she was imagining now. She would get up and do it.

She folded the list in half, hiding its contents from view, and stood up. She clutched the folded paper tight to her side as she stepped out into the hallway, looked left and right, and calmly placed one foot in front of the other. Her eyes and ears were open to any human presence along the route between her cube and the subpoena compliance unit. The few people who passed her along the way received her wan, trancelike smile in greeting. She passed a row of cubicles, two offices, the elevator bank, the ladies' room, and pushed open the glass door into the legal department, which contained the four cubicles assigned to the SC unit, Juliet and her staff of three.

Melanie said, "Knock, knock," and stepped into the opening.

Juliet looked up and smiled but said nothing. She didn't need to ask Melanie's purpose. This would be the third time she'd come to inquire about the status of the DA's subpoenas, and Juliet had already begun to accept it, grudgingly at first, now gratefully, because she was no longer being hounded directly by attorneys and paralegals at the DA's office. In the final analysis, she preferred to deal with a colleague at the bank instead of an outsider. She didn't quite understand why Melanie was doing something that wasn't strictly in her job description. But why not? Let her be the go-between. Let her handle the lists and the phone calls. It was actually making Juliet's job easier.

"Me again," said Melanie, shooting a quick inspective glance at Juliet's desktop. Subpoenas and photocopies of account records littered its surface. She didn't know where to look or how to look without being obvious. She experienced a moment of amnesia. She'd forgotten her plan and didn't quite know how she was going to accomplish her mission.

"What are they crying for this time?"

Melanie unfolded the list, but she wasn't going to let Juliet see. That was it. She held it up in front of her face, careful not to expose its contents. "A *huge* list." She flipped it closed again.

"Don't they get it? We're doing the best we can, and I'm short-staffed. Grace is sick today, and Sarah just started her maternity leave this week. She didn't want to wait until she popped." Juliet raised her eyebrows and made a funny, lighthearted grimace of helplessness, something halfway between jealousy and comic disdain. Single, childless, and in her late thirties, Juliet might never have the chance at motherhood.

Melanie would have liked to use this reference to Sarah as an opportunity to mention her own condition and engage in small talk about it—something easier than the task at hand. In her seventh week and still not showing, she hadn't yet told anyone at work and had decided to wait until the pregnancy was obvious. She'd seen the subtle ways some of her superiors changed their behavior toward pregnant women, as if the big belly replaced the brain. She didn't want that, not yet.

Melanie responded with the lines she'd mentally rehearsed. "The assistant DA I'm dealing with? I always tell her you're overloaded; you're doing a phenomenal job under the circumstances."

"I need all the help I can get." Juliet eyed the list, and Melanie clutched it tighter. "What do they want? I haven't even had a chance to *look* at some of the subpoenas they served us in the last two weeks." She picked up a stack of papers on her desk and slapped them down again for emphasis.

Melanie caught her breath and worked to control her voice, which threatened to emerge high-pitched and shaky. "You know…there's a ton of them on this list," she waved it, still folded. "Maybe I can make it a little easier. They're going nuts about a few of these accounts. I could just pull those out for you, if you give me all the subpoenas you haven't gotten to yet."

"You mean, prioritize?"

"Right. I'll make two stacks. I'll find a few that will really make them happy and put the rest in a second pile, to do later."

"Be my guest." Juliet's hands flew near and far to the four corners of her desk, gathering papers she'd laid out in her own, inscrutable system. "Here you go." She handed Melanie a thick, untidy wad.

"I—I'll just go sit in Sarah's cube to go through these."

"Okay." Juliet nodded in agreement and turned away, resuming her work in such a rapid shift of attention that Melanie hesitated a moment, stunned at the ease of her lie. Now, if only… She set off to do her work.

Sarah's cubicle, cater-cornered from Juliet's, was not entirely private. From its threshold, a small sliver of the opening into

Juliet's cube was visible. Melanie walked all the way in, pulled out the rolling chair from its parked position tight under the desk, sat down, and placed the stack of subpoenas and Dana's list in front of her. She glanced back over her shoulder to make sure she couldn't be seen in this position.

The desktop was clean, sparsely fitted with a computer terminal and keyboard, vacant "in" and "out" trays, a coffee mug, a cup of pencils and pens, and a flip-over desk calendar opened to Sarah's last day, Friday, May 6, 1988. A wedding photograph. Indulging in a moment of avoidance, Melanie gazed at the happy couple, their pedestrian faces shiny and posed, Benjamin in tux, Sarah in a white lace dress with a lengthy train swirling out from behind and neatly fanned at her feet. In their late twenties, married just two years, they lived in a little house in the suburbs and were having their first baby. Nothing alien or illicit would ever upset the clockwork of their lives.

She pulled her eyes away and turned to the subpoena at the top of Juliet's stack, bracing herself to see "Saludos Limitada." It said "Angel Orinda" instead. Breathing out, she slid the paper off the top and placed it face down on the desk. Angel Orinda was not on Dana's list and would be the first in the "to do later" pile. The "to do now" pile was predetermined in Melanie's mind and would contain no more than seven pieces of paper.

As she made her way through Juliet's stack, separating the two categories, her pace quickened with a growing sense of panic. It wasn't here. Juliet had already sent out the records, they were being delivered to Dana this very minute. As she turned each one, her eyes automatically sought out the line with the account name on the next. She was halfway down, then three-quarters of the way, then near the bottom when she found it, second to last.

The sight of it crystallized her purpose. The subpoena was dated May 3 and signed by an ADA named Bruce Reichert. Dana's boss? Had Dana known about this since May 3? Last

Saturday, the 7th, they'd all been over at Dana's apartment for dinner, making small talk and laughing and Dana had known. She had known.

It was convenient, after all, that Sarah was out on maternity leave. Melanie hadn't thought it would be quite so easy. She scanned the desktop, looking for the best place, and spotted the plastic "out" tray, which had four little feet, one at each corner, creating a tiny sliver of space underneath. She took another quick glance over her shoulder to the cubicle opening. All clear.

She took the Saludos subpoena, sandwiched it between two others from the "to do later" pile, turned them upside down and shoved them more than halfway into the space under the plastic tray. Sarah would be gone for two months at least, and no one would miss them—unless Juliet was in the habit of making a photocopy of everything as it came in. But, no, Juliet was too busy to create this extra work for herself.

Melanie folded Dana's list twice, making it a quarter of its size, and put it in a pocket of her skirt. The waistband was now so tight! She stood and picked up the two piles, one in each hand, ready to put on a smile for Juliet.

She supposed there were consequences. "Obstruction of justice" came to mind. But this was only temporary—she could return the subpoenas at any time. For now, they were "misplaced." If they were found and she was asked about it, she had an excuse. There were so many of them, a few must have gotten caught under the tray. No one would know, and she would have time to think, to find out some things—to ask Noel?—before she planned the next step.

Back in her office after the Quitman interview, Dana was having difficulty concentrating. She was taken by the rush of excitement after participating in the interview of a major witness and being accepted, finally, as a full member of the team, entrusted with vital information, consulted for her opinion.

But the feeling was not entirely happy. Insinuated within her mood was a distressing unease, like a lapse of short-term memory in the midst of a conversation, a phrase on the tip of the tongue, inaccessible. Three fragments of information had floated to the surface of her consciousness. They circled and hovered, suggesting an elusive connection.

The first: Bruce's revelation about the discovery of the Saludos account. She remembered that day in the Dungeon a couple of weeks back, the plan to tail Niño to First City and follow up with a subpoena to learn the name on the account. Bruce had followed up with the subpoena for account records, and it was on the list she'd faxed to Melanie yesterday.

The second: Quitman's description of Saludos, a company that sold greeting cards, stationery and calendars in the New York metropolitan area. Where had she heard that before?

The third: A blurry surveillance photograph of Niño, a dark-haired youth, body in motion, head slightly turned, a hand inserted into the opening of his jacket.

She had to see that photograph again.

It was easy enough to call the Don and ask for another look at it, but what was her pretext? She wasn't involved in that part of the investigation, and the Don knew it. Why did she need to look at the photo anyway? Why indeed? She could hardly answer that question for herself, suspecting only that another look might solve the mystery of her unease.

By five o'clock, the distraction had turned into a disturbing restlessness. She would wait a bit longer, then take a trip to the Dungeon. Friday nights, most people went home early unless they were on trial or had other pressing business. By six, the place would be quieter. The investigators would likely be gone, or if working a swing shift, out on the road or sitting the wires.

Not that she was hiding from anyone, but she had no credible explanation for her curiosity. If she ran into any of the investigators, she would just have to improvise. The Don was always joking, wasn't he? "Why don't you ever come down and visit us, Dana?" It was a Friday evening, time to knock off business, time for a little socializing—that would have to be her excuse. She knew it might look strange, out of character. But she had to do it.

At six straight up, Dana closed her office and walked the long linoleum corridor to the elevator bank. Halfway down the hall, Mineko emerged from the section housing her cubicle. With affected nonchalance, Dana lifted her hand and said, "Good night!" before ducking into the ladies' room. A minute later, feeling like a fool, she poked her head out again. Coast clear.

She made it into the elevator alone, pressed "B," and rode the thirteen floors down, stopping twice on the way to pick up employees she didn't know. They got off on the first floor, and she rode the next level down to the basement on her own.

Behind her, the elevator doors joined with a metallic clang, echoing with crypt-like finality. Cold gray cement, the hiss and click of distant machinery. She started out through the maze and found she knew her way. This place had made an impression. She remembered the girth and dirty shade of every pipe along the upper walls and ceiling, running like tracks toward her fate. This is how she felt. She didn't know why.

Arriving at the door to the investigators' quarters, she opened it and stepped inside. Shouldn't it be locked? She hadn't thought of that possibility. Someone could still be here. Some, but not all, of the lights were on, lending a shadowy cast. She looked out into the immense space, apparently devoid of living creatures but scattered with the evidence of recent occupation, like a convention center after the event. A few areas were hidden by partition. She supposed that undercover detectives had their methods of remaining concealed, even in their own environs. She stood still a moment and waited. Not a rustle.

Her goal was distant, on the other side of the great expanse. Tiptoeing like a burglar, she passed each desk and partition with a beating heart, confirming as she passed that she was alone. There, against the far wall, was the Don's desk. A nearby fluorescent fixture gave enough light to see.

Silly to think that the photograph would still be there after all this time, but somehow everything else on the desk looked the same. Telephone here, tape recorder there, surveillance reports and photographs strewn everywhere in between. Dana scanned the desktop visually, and seeing nothing, gingerly lifted items and sheets of paper with sensitive fingertips, careful not to disrupt the haphazard arrangement. Who could tell? The Don might have his own peculiar filing system right here on the desk. These investigators never seemed to be organized, but when you asked for something, they could retrieve it in a snap.

She jumped at a noise behind her. Was that a footstep? She turned to look and saw nothing. All dead, quiet, except for the sounds of the machinery that maintained this enormous building.

Still, the feeling of being watched wouldn't leave her. What had led her to this? Ashamed and ready to abandon her mission, she swung around toward the desk one last time and there it was, eye level, tacked to the bulletin board on the wall. Right there in front of her nose, and she'd missed it.

Carefully, she removed the tack and brought the photo closer for inspection. It was exactly as she remembered it. Black-and-white, out of focus. A slender dark-haired youth, well-groomed as far as could be discerned from the smudged features, wearing a dark jacket that could have been made of leather. In fact, that was the problem with the photo. The jacket was more crisply in focus than the subject's face. It was a handsomely tailored jacket, possibly expensive. The youth's head was slightly turned to the side in a blur of motion, and his hand was inside the front opening of the jacket, as if he was about to extract something.

And there he was again, sitting on a pillow in her living room, his head turned slightly toward Cheryl, with his hand fishing inside that sharp-looking jacket. He extracted the small, gold box and said, "For you," with a charming, heavy accent. She'd accepted it, nearly accepted him. There was no mistaking him now.

14 » CHINESE

"QUERIDA. WHY DIDN'T you call? Are you all right?" Noel stepped around the counter to meet his wife as she walked into Libros NOMEL. He looked surprised, as well he should.

She remained alert to anything in his expression beyond surprise, the smallest indication of a hidden agenda. "I'm fine," she said. "I had enough of the office and left a little early, that's all." From the half dozen customers in the store, a few of the curious interrupted their browsing to glance at her, then at him.

"I'm glad you quit early. You've been working too hard." He kissed her forehead, put an arm around her shoulder, and escorted her to a chair behind the counter. "Here. Take a seat."

"Most people leave by five on Fridays anyway," she continued. "Why should I kill myself?"

"Or the baby. I've been worried about you since last night. Are you sure you're not sick?"

"Just the usual. There's been less vomiting, actually." She sat in the chair he offered, wondering what would come next. She couldn't avoid what was between them much longer.

Last night had been excruciating. She'd meant to tell him about the list, but ended up holding it in. They'd engaged in their usual evening routine, side by side in the kitchen cooking dinner, sitting across from one another at the table, eating and chatting about mundane things, cleaning up afterward, Melanie washing,

Noel drying.

Of course he could tell something was amiss. She sensed him sensing it, every time she looked away. She had difficulty meeting his eyes because of the things she was tempted to read into his. She was avoiding the subject because once it was opened, everything he said would be second-guessed and searched for possible lies. The thought of beginning this process was unbearable.

"I'll close up early and we can go home," he suggested.

"No, don't do that. I'll be happy just to sit here." She glanced at her watch. Almost five-thirty. Noel usually kept the store open until at least seven on Friday nights to catch the after-work crowd. Now that the weather was nice, people were out on the streets, postponing their return to tiny apartments.

She glanced around the store, her eye at a level just above the countertop. The shelves had been rearranged since the last time she'd visited, three or four months ago. Near the counter toward the front of the store was a new display of Saludos products. Mingo was nowhere in sight.

"Where's Domingo?"

Noel chuckled, his eyes flitting toward her and away again. A sign of embarrassment, she could tell. He leaned on the countertop, his forearms supporting his weight as he gazed out at the inventory. "That boy is hardly here anymore. I'm having trouble keeping track of him." He shook his head.

"I bet he shows up for payday."

"Yes, he likes to be paid, but I haven't paid him for a while. He's not interested in the store, only the card business. He's very protective about it, and I don't bother him. He comes at certain times to get messages from Colombia on the fax machine and to take care of the bookkeeping. He was here a few minutes ago. He divided up the Saludos money, gave me a share, and left again without saying too much. He might be on his way to the bank now, making the deposit for the end of the week. You know, for the cards."

For what else, if not for the cards? Was Noel trying to convince her or convince himself?

"How is the card business going these days?" Against her intentions, the sarcasm broke through. This was not the way to do it. She knew better.

Noel noticed the tone and gave her an odd look. "It's going well," he said formally, adding nothing else.

"Are those the cards over there?" She pointed but didn't wait for an answer. "Let me take a look." She pushed up from the chair and let her hand rest momentarily on Noel's back as she brushed past him and around the counter, on her way to the display.

She paused in front of it and scanned the merchandise. A lovely arrangement. Tasteful artwork, pastels, watercolors and oil paintings reproduced on glossy covers of calendars and greeting cards, flowers and geometric designs on the borders of stationery. A rosy, fairytale world. She chose a card, opened it, and read "¡Felicidades!" and a short poem she couldn't understand completely, something about the joy of new life. "Are there any blank ones, without a message inside?" she asked.

"At the bottom," he pointed, walking toward her behind the counter.

She selected one and flipped it over to inspect the back. No price was printed, just the company's mark, Saludos Ltda. She turned to face Noel, who stood very close now with just the counter between them. She felt the warmth and pull of his body as she always had, but still her voice played tricks on her. "How much is this one? They must be very expensive." She felt instant shame, but if he noticed it, his eyes revealed nothing. His handsome, almost angelic, face was filled with bewilderment and concern under raised brows as he gazed back into her hard look.

"Not much," he said flatly. "That one's a dollar-fifty. You

want it? I think we can afford it."

"Yes, please," she said glibly and skirted the counter to the end, rounded it, and took her chair again. "I want to write a note to Dana. That was a big deal for her, cooking dinner for all of us last weekend."

"Good idea. Give her my thanks. Está listo?" he asked a customer who was approaching the counter, book in hand. Noel took the book and praised the customer's good taste in literature while Melanie admired his animated profile.

Maybe this was the way she was intended to appreciate him, from afar, never very certain of just who he was. Did she love *him*, or her impression of him? What were impressions anyway but feelings and intuition, gleaned from probable messages conveyed by the eyes and mouth and hands, the warmth or chill of touch? Were these things enough? How could she ever really hope to know someone who'd grown up in a different country, spoke a different language? In this moment, a shocking belief seized her with a certainty that felt like truth: their trust was built on an illusory store of intangibles, nothing more.

She continued to evaluate Noel as he smiled and finished chatting with his countryman, completely at ease with himself. He entered the sale on the cash register, making a mistake with the change and catching himself with an apology. He'd always been that way, open and interested in people and books and ideas, clumsy and unfocused with money and the practical organization of life's activity. How could she possibly doubt his goodwill? It was something she just knew about him, something that everyone just knew. And if she was wrong...well, then maybe she couldn't count on anything in life, not even her own existence.

"I'll be right back," Noel said to her as soon as the customer had gone. She watched her husband walk between the aisles and enter the office at the rear before she turned her attention to the open, blank card on her lap.

Dana was the one she should be worried about. For nine or ten days, maybe longer, Dana had suspected Saludos of criminal activity and hadn't said a word about it, maintaining her precious ethics and ironclad confidentiality. If she really wanted to, there were ways to get around secrecy without violating the rules, especially if people she cared about could get hurt.

Melanie and Noel just weren't important enough to Dana. She could have dropped a hint, left a clue, anything to warn them and give them a chance to extricate themselves before it was too late. Nothing for days or weeks, and then the name on the list. A warning? But too late! How did it look now after weeks of banking activity, the account gobbling and spitting out more and more cash every day? Melanie had taken one look at it and suspected her own husband. How must it look to outsiders? Dana herself might be the most suspicious among them, unable to shed her prosecutorial point of view.

Melanie picked up a pen from the counter and started to write: "Dear Dana." She stopped. The ink was deep red, something she hadn't anticipated, and the two words shocked her like the spill of blood. There was no way to communicate her crushing disappointment in the woman who'd been her best friend, a woman she admired, sometimes envied. A few lines on this note card couldn't do it.

What was the next step for them? Would Dana telephone, acting like it was business as usual, asking for the documents on that list? Would they have pleasant conversation over lunch on Tuesday, parting with painted smiles and kisses on cheeks? How long would the masquerade go on?

The red pen was poised. "Dear Dana," she'd written. Flipping the card over, she drew a red heart around Saludos Ltda, and slashed the heart from top to bottom with a thick red line, intersecting the "u" and the "d." She opened the card again and began to write: "It was such a lovely dinner you had for us. And how nice of you to insist that Domingo join us. He's kicking himself for not bringing samples of the cards he's selling in Noel's store. I told him later how much you would like to have one to show your colleagues at the office." She ran out of space on the inside, closed the card, and turned it over to continue writing on the back. "So here is a sample. I hope you like it. Forgive the doodling. Love to you always—"

"Melanie." Noel's strong grasp stayed her shaking hand. He tried to pull the card away, but she crumpled it in her fist before he could get to it. She yanked her hand away and started to rip the card into tiny pieces.

"Querida. What happened? You're crying."

"No, I'm not." With a balled fist, fragments of paper inside, she swiped at a tear threatening to fall. "I'm just angry at myself. I ruined the card."

"Don't worry. I'll get you another—"

"I don't want another one!"

"They're cheap. Let me buy you another one."

"No, please don't."

He bent down and put his arm around her shoulder as she felt the heat of more eyes on them. "I can tell you're not feeling well," he said softly. "Let's just close up, and—"

"No, I'm fine, really. Close at the regular time."

"You're sure?"

"Yes, and let's go out to dinner tonight, after closing." *And I'll tell you everything then, and you'll explain it all, reassure me with your good heart.*

"Good idea. I can hardly wait. At least we can close a little early."

"But you're doing good business," she was whispering now. "Look, here comes someone." A woman approached the counter, carrying two books.

"Está lista? Algo más? Quizás una tarjeta?" He motioned

toward the card display, and the customer shook her head, no.

As Noel handled the sale, Melanie dumped the pieces of paper into her lap, poked through them and ripped the larger ones into tinier pieces, then deposited the entire mess into the trash can under the counter.

Noel had not been far off the mark. At that moment, Domingo was on his way to the bank, making a quick stop on the way.

He'd learned the routine and performed exceptionally well this month, proving himself, demonstrating his keen memory and sharp powers of observation. Hadn't missed a faxed instruction at the prearranged times, hadn't missed a pickup, hadn't missed a deposit. Hadn't missed his small weekly rewards in the small brown envelopes. The pay was little, but still more than Noel was offering, and if he established a good track record, who could tell? He might go higher places in this business.

This evening he was scheduled to return to the same apartment building, four blocks from the store. He was familiar with the neighborhood but still made his usual visual canvass of the area, stopping briefly outside the door of the building and taking a mental picture of the scene: the street lined with parked cars, a man talking on a pay phone at the corner, neighborhood residents sitting on the stoops, children playing, people walking, two women squeezing the fruit on display outside the deli. He spotted three cars double-parked on the block, a white delivery van, a red sports car, a square brown sedan.

Secure in his anonymity, he entered the vestibule, pressed the button for 3G, and said "tarjetas" into the intercom. The inner door unlocked with a buzz. He pushed it open and walked up three flights of stairs, taking two steps at a time. After a single knock on 3G, he heard the footsteps inside and sensed an eye on the other side of the peephole. The man remained hidden behind the door as he opened it halfway to let him in.

The next part went fast, as usual. Mingo pulled the bills and change out of his vinyl, zippered, night-deposit envelope. The man counted the money, added it to a thick stack of fives, tens and twenties, filled out the Saludos deposit ticket, and placed the whole amount with the deposit slip back into the vinyl envelope. Mingo always saw the same man but said nothing to him and did not know or ask for his name.

With the envelope inside his jacket, Mingo was on his way. The First City branch he used for the after-hours deposits was another five blocks away. This was the third Friday he'd made a night deposit, in keeping with his practice of storing the entire week's receipts from sales of the Saludos products at Noel's store and combining that money with the rest of his pickup to make one deposit. The other days he made pickups and deposited them at different branches of First City and other banks throughout Queens, Manhattan, Brooklyn and the Bronx.

He was getting to know the city all right, plenty of sight-seeing, a regular tourist. He'd gotten lost more than a few times but always found his destination in time, saving himself from near panic. It wasn't wise to ask for directions, even from fellow immigrants, and he didn't speak enough English to ask anyone else. He always kept his cool and eventually found his way on his own. He prided himself on his level head in the heat of potential trouble and supposed it was a good attribute to have in this business. It could take him far.

On the way to the First City branch he kept alert, aware of his surroundings without making an obvious inspection. A casual stop to look at his watch, eyes raised, scanning. Another stop at a traffic light, an absentminded turn of the head. Everything normal, unremarkable.

A half block from the bank he slowed his pace and extended his radar. A simple task was ahead of him, a drop into the night deposit box, a convenience maintained for owners of businesses dealing in cash. Like Mingo's business. Surveillance cameras were trained on the box. He knew and didn't care. Those cameras were inside every bank he'd ever entered and by now he was on videotape all over the city. Just one of the risks of the business. The other risks were greater, the ones he tried to avoid, like nosy police officers, a possible undercover surveillance, or worse, enemies and flunkies of his boss alike.

With just a few steps to go he halted, catching a familiar object in his peripheral vision. He turned his head slightly, and without a direct look, tried to get a read on it. Across the street sat a square brown sedan, double-parked. Two men inside. Had they turned his way? No, they were just talking, a middle-aged man and a young one.

The vinyl envelope burned his chest. His thoughts raced, trying to bring the earlier picture to mind. The car was the same one he'd seen a few minutes ago near the apartment building, he was sure of it. Had the men been inside it then, or had the car been empty? Now he couldn't remember, and he hesitated, doubting the acuity of his mental image.

Panic engulfed him. His first major mistake! Quickly, he walked past the bank, planning to return later this evening after he'd had some time to think.

Once he'd calmed down, Domingo realized he wouldn't have the chance to return until much later. At the soonest, he might go back to the bank sometime in the middle of the night. He wasn't about to miss his second date with Cheryl Hargrove, not after the way she'd begun to warm up to him.

The first time they'd gone to a restaurant, but this time she'd invited him to her apartment for dinner. Her roommate would be away. That meant something, didn't it? He was about to get lucky.

She fascinated him and even had a mind like his in some important ways. Quick and bright and interested in fame and wealth, but not willing to pursue her goals along conventional paths. Already convinced of her success, she would make it to the top, whether it was her singing or dancing or acting or all her talents combined with that face of hers, that body.

Cheryl was nothing like her sister, although their features were surprisingly similar. Dana, an older, more conservative and sober version of her younger sibling, didn't interest him at all, especially after he learned from Melanie that she was a lawyer working for the city. A government post of some kind. He hadn't bothered to ask for details because she immediately struck him as rather boring. He had no interest in the law, and his youthful overconfidence easily suppressed the budding thought that he might have to hire a lawyer for himself one day.

What he was doing was wrong, he knew, but he'd lined up his excuses like bowling pins, always leaving one standing after the others were knocked down. The money part of the business was clean and easy, far removed from the drugs. If people wanted to buy and sell cocaine, that was their business, something he would never think of doing. There was no stopping them and they would keep doing it whether he deposited the cash or not.

All he wanted was a little something for himself. Millions of dollars were flying in this city, and he just wanted a tiny piece of that, enough to start his own business. He would extricate himself from the Cartel as soon as he'd earned his chunk, no hard feelings, nothing owed on either side. Never mind those people who liked to joke that the only way you can retire is in a box, one with metal bars or a wooden top.

With that lump of cash pressed close to his heart, Domingo stopped at a small grocery store to pick up a bouquet of flowers for Cheryl. To pay for them, he dug out a slender fold of cash from his front pants pocket—his own money—and peeled off a few worn dollar bills.

He caught the subway into Manhattan, heading toward midtown on the west side. Cheryl had told him her address, and it was seared into memory. This was how he operated, avoiding paper evidence. Without much trouble he found the building, conveniently close to the theater district but far enough away to avoid the scruffier elements. It was a walk-up with an aging, pre-war façade, the lobby shabby but clean.

Cheryl buzzed Mingo inside the front door and was waiting for him at the top of the second-floor landing when he emerged from the stairwell. Her face was bright and expectant, ready for adventure. It was the quality that had attracted him the most.

"Flowers!" she exclaimed in English, her tone vaguely mocking. "How nice."

He handed them to her, and she kissed his cheek. With her kiss, he caught the scent of an alluring fragrance. "Come on now," she said gleefully. "You know the word 'flowers,' don't you?"

"Flowers, yes. Flores. Eres más linda que las flores."

"You're hopeless. *¡Imposible!* Nunca vas a aprender Inglés!" She smiled, proud of herself, just as happy to lapse into Spanish. It made her feel smart and impressive. They had talked a few times about her helping him with English, but whenever she made the attempt, he always reverted to Spanish. After only a few hours together on a few occasions they'd fallen into a confirmed habit.

The landing where they stood belonged to four apartments. Cheryl touched his arm and nudged him toward the single open door. Inside, she shut it firmly behind him.

"This is it," she said in Spanish. "Go in and have a seat. I'll put these in water."

As if he hadn't understood, he followed her into the kitchen. She looked over her shoulder at him and laughed. "I guess I have a—what's the word?—a shadow."

"You do look lovely tonight," he said, allowing his eyes to slip down the length of her body as she stood on tiptoe and reached up to a top shelf for a vase. "I can't get it," she said, turning to him with a pout.

"Let me help." He came very close and looked into her deep brown eyes, long enough to feel a melting heat. Unfastening his gaze, he tilted his head back on his neck to search for the desired object and shot his arm up to the cabinet shelf. The movement caused the front opening of his jacket to widen out from the bottom where the two sides were zippered together at the waist. Instantly aware of the bulging inside pocket, he quickly grabbed the vase and brought it down, almost letting it slip from his fingers. "¡Cuidado!" he exclaimed, more to divert her attention than from worry about the vase. He held it safely in his hands now, with the insides of his arms squeezing the jacket shut.

"That was close," she said. "You're lucky you didn't break my one and only vase."

"What would have happened to me?"

"There would be consequences. No, that's not the word. Punishment. Severe punishment."

After filling the vase with water and depositing the flowers inartistically, she made a pistol with her fingers and stuck it in his back, encouraging him to leave the kitchen. "This way," she growled in a low voice.

In the living room, Mingo glanced around at the seating possibilities: a lumpy, two-person sofa, a wooden rocking chair, a worn easy chair. Everything secondhand, acquired without thought for décor. He decided on the couch, hoping she would follow.

"Wait a minute," she said. "Don't you want to take that jacket off? It's hot in here." She reached for the lapel, fingertips touching it momentarily. Suddenly her hand was removed, sheathed in his tight grasp. A streak of alarm crossed her face. He relaxed his clutch and gently guided her hand away.

"Good idea," he said with a little laugh, releasing her hand. He turned sideways, unlatched the zipper at the bottom and slowly pulled out the arm on the side without the package, turned his back to her, removed the other arm, and pulled the jacket off. He neatly crossed the sleeves inward, folded the jacket lengthwise and in half again with the package inside, and laid it on the easy chair. He turned to her. "Now…"

"I guess that's your favorite jacket," she said.

"You guessed it." He took her hand and led her to the sofa. They sat, knee-to-knee, partially facing one another, his arm along the back of the sofa, fingers nearly touching her shoulder.

"Dinner will be here soon," she said, not pulling away.

"You mean, you're cooking it now." He thought her Spanish might have failed her.

"No, it will be here. I didn't have time to cook. I ordered Chinese delivered. You like Chinese? I love it."

"Then I love it too."

She laughed, her eyes playful. "Do you do that on purpose? You have such a way of saying things…" Her dress was sleeveless. His fingers started to glide over the smooth, bare skin of her upper arm, stroked the spill of chestnut brown hair on her shoulder, brushed it away to find her neck, and cupping the nape, gently pulled her toward him, their lips meeting, opening—

The telephone rang, shrill and loud. Cheryl jerked away and placed her hand on the arm of the sofa as if to push herself up. She changed her mind and stayed put. "I'd like to say that's my agent calling, but it's probably my sister. She left me this message earlier … Well, let's just see who comes on."

The fourth ring cut off abruptly and Cheryl's outgoing message started up on the machine. "I'm probably not here, so leave a message." A long, drawn-out beep and the line opened up to a moment of hesitation before Dana's voice came on: "Cheryl, you *have* to be there. If you're there, pick up. I told you it was important. This is *extremely* important. Call me back." A heavy clunk preceded the dial tone.

"Sounds like it's important," said Mingo. "I know that word."

"Your English is improving. But you don't know my sister. It could be important, or it might not be. She's gotten so dramatic and negative, ever since she got that job of hers."

"Melly said she's a lawyer?"

"Right. In criminal law."

"She defends criminals? I thought she worked for the city."

"Yes, she works for the city, but she doesn't defend criminals. What's the word for that? She puts them in jail..."

Mingo's eyes darkened. "She's a prosecutor?"

"Yes. That's the word. She's a prosecutor, and lately she's been working on some big investigation into financial crimes. Everyone thinks it has to do with drug money, but you can't get a word out of her about it, everything's so secret. The way she looks at people now, it just makes me shiver! Like everyone's a suspect. That job is doing something to her... Wait, there's the buzzer."

She headed for the front door, Mingo watching her.

Cheryl's sister a prosecutor?

Cheryl pressed the button on the intercom and asked who was there.

In money crimes?

"Delivery," sputtered a scratchy voice.

Those men in the car—was she having him tailed?

He eyed Cheryl as she dug deeply into a purse on the small table next to the door. Her hair fell forward onto her face and she clawed it back with long, raking fingernails. The gesture was raptor-like and ominous. Mingo started to sweat. She was shaking the purse now, keys and coins and cosmetics jangling. She lifted its open mouth and peered inside, aggressively thrust her hand in and extracted some bills. Her attractiveness had vanished, and the thought of slippery Chinese food made him queasy.

Mingo stood, pulled the fold of bills from his pants pocket, and removed a twenty. That should be enough. He started for the door, froze, and clutched at his chest in panic. He'd nearly forgotten his jacket! He spun around and retrieved it.

Cheryl was opening the door as Mingo put on his jacket and zipped it all the way up over his sweating chest. He patted the bulge on the front, left side, just to be sure. Coming up behind her in the narrow entryway, he put his hand on her shoulder just as the white-aproned deliveryman was handing over a large brown sack spotted with grease, emitting the distinct aroma of soy sauce, sesame oil and garlic.

Before she could pay, Mingo shoved the twenty into the man's slight, bony hand. "I'm sorry, I forgot something," he said to Cheryl, speaking fast in his native tongue. "I'm very sorry, forgive me, I have to go…"

"Thank you," said the little man with confusion on his face, eyes darting from Domingo to Cheryl to the bill in his hand, hoping to confirm that a generous tip was intended.

"Wait! Can't you eat first? At least?" cried Cheryl.

"No, I'm sorry," he said again. The deliveryman took a step backward, turned, and scuttled toward the stairwell. Cheryl held the bag in one hand, her ball of paper money in the other, staring at Mingo in disbelief. He kissed her hastily on the forehead and followed the deliveryman out, calling again over his shoulder. "I'm sorry. Thank you!"

Down a flight of stairs to the vestibule, Mingo hesitated at the glass door to the street, watching the deliveryman hop on a bicycle and pedal away. Seized by lingering unease, he stood on the edge of time, waiting a minute or an hour, he didn't know how long, before pushing the door open.

Where to turn? Parked cars lined the one-way street, and a

single car drove past at a high rate of speed. His eyes followed the taillights. Was that a square, brown sedan? Or was it black or navy? Were there two heads in the front seat? It had been dusk when he first saw it, and now, in the dark of night, under the streetlights, everything looked different.

He shook his head and took off at a quick pace in the opposite direction. Only a few hours ago he'd been tough and self-assured. Invincible. Now look at him. Just one deposit went wrong and he was a quivering coward. Turning a corner, he saw nothing to dread on the busy avenue. Carefree people, oblivious to his concerns, strolled happily on this warm Friday evening in May. What was happening to him? He threw his head back and drew in a deep breath.

Everything would work out. He had nothing to worry about except this bulge next to his heart. He couldn't hang onto it very long or they—the people worse than the police—would come looking for him. He could make the deposit tonight, but maybe it would be safer to wait until absolutely sure that the heat was off. He could always explain it later. His superiors would approve of a little prudence, a little caution. After all, the bank didn't credit Friday night deposits until Monday, so how could he be faulted for a short delay?

It was better for them if he avoided arrest with the money and account information in his possession. And he had other information that could hurt them, could lead the police to people far bigger than himself. He knew about the fax machine. The Cartel was using fax machines because the police couldn't legally intercept the messages—the eavesdropping law had lagged behind technology. His knowledge gave him a certain power, didn't it? He also knew about the apartment and could identify the man there, and the methods for pickup and deposit, the banks he visited. He knew a lot. And what about Restrepo? An important man in the Cartel, and Domingo could identify him, help the police to catch him. By now Restrepo had gone back to Colombia, but he was sure to return.

Considering everything, it wouldn't be in the Cartel's interest if he were to be picked up by a curious, suspicious prosecutor like Cheryl's sister. He kicked himself again for his blunder. Both women had invited him into their apartments. And he'd given each of them gifts!

He wasn't sure how long he would wait. On Monday there would be another faxed instruction, another money pickup, several deposits expected of him. Would he feel safe before then, maybe by tomorrow? Or should he wait until Monday and deposit all of it in one day?

And then, the idea came to him. Maybe he could beat everyone, the detectives and the Cartel. He was carrying more than $9,000 in his jacket right now, and on Monday morning he'd be picking up another forty to fifty grand for deposits into several accounts. Altogether, it was more than he could make in two years of honest labor back home. A lot for him, but a mere pittance to the Cartel.

How long would it take the managers to catch on? He still wasn't sure how they checked up on his night deposits. For day deposits, he would return the stamped teller receipts the following day. But he got no stamped receipt for the night deposits; confirmation came later in the mail to that post office box he couldn't open. How would they know on Monday morning that he hadn't made the Friday night deposit? He could make his usual pickup, add it to the wad in his jacket, and disappear. A clean break from his lowly post, time to move on to the next step in his life plan, a little earlier than expected.

He walked the streets of Manhattan a long time into the night before taking the train back to Queens. He had a lot to think about. The money was attractive, but it was a dangerous game. He didn't fool himself about that. The danger excited him one moment, sickened him the next. Was he really cut out for this? But what was his life? He had nothing to his name but that infinite family of his, siblings, parents, cousins, aunts, and uncles, all poor and struggling except Uncle Carlos, who'd handed him this gift in making the arrangements with Restrepo. *Go see that bright young nephew of mine.*

But the gift didn't come free, it was a test of skill and intelligence and courage. A challenge. He was a chosen one, Domingo Avendaño, and he scraped at the silver lining in it, like a drowning man clinging to a stray plank of the sinking ship.

Tomorrow he would go to Libros NOMEL, maybe even help Noel out with the books. He always needed help on Saturdays, his busiest day, and Mingo owed a lot to his cousin, the man who'd helped him get started in this country. A little help on the weekend wasn't much to repay the debt, but maybe someday, when Mingo had his own business, he would treat Noel and Melanie to all the best, take care of them like they'd taken care of him. Good people, so good but so naïve.

Yes, tomorrow morning he would go to the bookstore. He would need a place to stash this bulge on his chest. The closet? A high bookshelf? The washroom? Taped to the back of the toilet tank. That was the place. He couldn't keep it in his apartment the whole weekend. They knew where he lived. He'd keep his eye on the street, his ear to the ground, and decide if those undercover cops were fact or fantasy. In between, he'd do something nice for Noel, work on the books, stock the shelves, and smile at the customers, keeping a corner of his mind open to develop a plan. He needed a plan. And he'd have the whole weekend to think, to decide exactly what he was going to do.

15 »   EXTRICATION

TWO MINUTES OF her life were gone, sucked into a black hole. Released from the Dungeon, she came into herself again in the lobby of the Criminal Court building. The afternoon crush had dwindled to a light mix of attorneys and court employees headed out, free to enjoy their weekends. Dana would not be enjoying hers.

On her way to the subway, she remembered the moment she held the surveillance photo in her hand. Nothing else. She couldn't be sure if she'd tacked it to the bulletin board the way she'd found it. She couldn't remember if she'd been calm or hasty as she retraced her steps, if she'd sensed watchful eyes from dark corners, if she'd waited a long time for the elevator to deliver her up into the light.

Of the people who were important to her, the first to come to mind was Cheryl, not Melly. Of her responsibilities, personal and professional, Cheryl was foremost, not work. Family, it turned out, was more important to her than anything else, friendship or career. An image persisted all the way home, and later, as she sat by her telephone, leaving messages and waiting for a return call: Cheryl and Domingo, gazing at each other with eyes under sleepy lids, foreign words rolling sensuously from their tongues.

She was responsible for introducing them. She'd invited this man to her apartment, a criminal suspect in the biggest drug cartel in history. He'd sat on her pillows and chairs, eaten her food, flashed his faux innocent smile. *For you.* Played her for a fool.

But who was the real fool here? Didn't he know who she was? It seemed likely he didn't. Why would he attend a social evening with a prosecutor investigating suspicious bank accounts? Melly and Noel obviously hadn't told him about the conclusion they'd drawn—all on their own—that she was investigating Colombian narcotics money. She remembered Domingo's vacant expression when they mentioned it. Apparently, he hadn't understood a word.

By the time Cheryl returned her call, she'd convinced herself that Domingo couldn't have known what she did for a living. It was 9:30. She'd already left two urgent messages on Cheryl's machine and was contemplating a third when her phone rang.

Cheryl's voice was quieter, less buoyant than usual, and Dana suspected she'd been crying. "Now that my date ran out on me, I have time to find out this very, very important thing you want to tell me."

"Who was your date?"

"Who do you think? The very sexy Domingo Avendaño. He turned out to be a complete creep, unbelievably rude. He ran out of here for no reason at all, right when the Chinese food came. No explanation. 'Lo siento, lo siento.' God, it makes me sick. Hey, you want to come over here for Chinese? It's good reheated."

"Maybe he hates Chinese food."

"Ha ha! He said he loved it. Everything was going fine 'til you called and left that message…"

"You were *there*? Sitting right there listening to me?"

"Sure. Things were getting hot right about then. You think I'm going to interrupt all that to take a call from my sister?"

"Knowing you, no. Fine. I really appreciate that, the two of you making out while I'm talking on your machine. What did he say about it?"

"Oh, don't get so sensitive. I just explained—sorry about this Dana, but it's true—you're getting so melodramatic and morose these days, living in your little world of crime. And on top of that, checking up on me every other day—I didn't tell him that part— but I said it probably wasn't anything too important that couldn't wait. Why did you call anyway?"

Dana didn't need to ask for more detail. It was clear that Cheryl had said enough to make Domingo run off, likely never to return. "It wasn't...maybe it wasn't all that important."

"I knew it."

"I mean, I've been so worried about you."

"With Domingo?"

"Well, yeah. Maybe I just wanted to give you another one of my big sister lectures."

"I knew it."

"But see, Cheryl? I was right, wasn't I? Give me some credit. There was something strange about that boy and I saw it."

"A lucky guess."

"Not luck. Insight."

"The luck of a nosy snoop." Her grumpiness couldn't mask the note of appreciation in her voice. "Sure you don't want to come over for Chinese? At least he paid for it."

"That was nice of him. But no thanks." She manufactured an excuse. "I've already eaten and I'm really tired. I had a tough week. I'm going right to bed."

"You're acting like an old lady." Cheryl wasn't about to let Dana go to bed. She'd enjoyed her little cry and had gotten all her resentment against Dana out of her system. Now, she was in the mood to talk.

Dana wasn't so inclined but quelled the urge to cut her off, wanting to encourage the openness. It had been slow in coming, their developing relationship. Cheryl talked on and on, about her job at the diner, her acting classes, her aspirations and forthcoming auditions, even about Mom and Dad. Dana listened and spoke little. She was comforted, transported from her troubles for about an hour until she said a gentle good night and hung up.

It was frustrating, not being able to talk freely. She would have liked to confide in Cheryl and ask her advice. Despite her youth and capriciousness, Cheryl possessed a keen intelligence, common sense, and a slightly different take on things, qualities that would have been of help right now. But Dana couldn't take the chance that something too sensitive would slip out, further jeopardizing her career.

The hours were long, Friday night into Saturday morning, and she spent them in her dim living room, no thought of going to bed, mentally exploring every angle.

The possibility that Melanie was involved in crime was quickly crossed off the list. Dana knew her too well for that. The possibility that Noel might be involved was not immediately rejected. And *if* he was involved, to what lengths might Melanie go to protect him?

Dana knew very little about the power of love. She'd been in love, yes, but her own loves hadn't come close to the magnitude of Melanie's attachment to Noel. Such intense emotion could lead a person to do—what? Maybe not commit a crime but something less, a passive acceptance of her husband's crimes...as long as they weren't too horrible. Financial crimes.

But the DA had nothing on Noel. Domingo was the one, the only proven bad boy...or was he?

The Don and his team had been following Niño for weeks, but how much had they seen? If he was making only occasional deposits, he could be handling the receipts from Noel's store, while other people were depositing the drug money without his knowledge. For that matter, what evidence did she have of any illicit funds in the Saludos account? She'd seen only one transaction that appeared legitimate. A single company check paid to Hanniger Paper, Inc., no smurf checks, no phony excuse about currency restrictions.

She was left with nothing but a name on a list she'd faxed to Melanie, a name Bruce had supplied. Surely he suspected more about Saludos, but why should she rely on his judgment? He was willing to suspect anyone based on the slimmest of evidence. She thought of Fred Marrero and his client, Stella Ramos. *Wait until you get the account records before you decide.* Listening to Bruce, Dana had almost forfeited the meager funds of a struggling single mom.

She had to find out immediately what was in the Saludos account and couldn't risk asking Melanie for the records. One thing about Melly was clear. She knew *everything* about Noel and Libros NOMEL, the bookstore they'd named after themselves, and therefore Melly knew, at the very least, that Saludos products were sold at the store. To see that name on the list…the shock must have been tremendous. The shock of knowing that Dana knew…what?

Dana didn't know what to believe about Melly and Noel. As for Domingo—she simply had an inexplicable certainty of his complicity with the Cartel.

A gut certainty. Despite the possible innocent explanations. An unshakeable belief without any evidence to back it up. Was it just the look of him? The slight bit of cockiness? The mystery of the language barrier? The fact that his gesture, as he sat in her living room, was so very much like that gesture in the photograph? She wouldn't dare try to argue a case to a jury based on so little: a fuzzy surveillance photograph and a suspicious account, deemed suspicious only on Bruce's say so.

It was then she remembered a very important, forgotten bit of evidence. Her mind had closed it off, and she hadn't seen it again on her spy expedition to the Dungeon: the photograph of Niño with the man they called Jefe. A business-suited man believed to be an important player. A definite bad guy, tailed to a known cash house, intercepted on the wires giving orders for deliveries.

The Don found it significant that Domingo had met with Jefe, and she could rely on the Don's judgment. His hunches were backed by years of experience on the streets.

Jefe was a seemingly legitimate businessman, making the rounds to Hispanic proprietors in Queens. A string of connections was suggested: Noel, a proprietor selling Saludos products; Domingo, a cash courier for Jefe; Mr. Restrepo, the Saludos representative who'd met with Quitman. Were Jefe and Mr. Restrepo one and the same? If Bruce suspected as much, he hadn't let on after their meeting with Quitman.

These odds and ends were enough to confirm her gut certainty about Domingo, but they said little about Noel. After Melly, he was the last person she would ever suspect of crime. His relationship to Domingo alone meant nothing. *You should get all those bastards, Dana. They're ruining my country.* Just a cover up? Not likely. She'd never known him to concoct anything. Always straightforward and in earnest.

But how well did she really know him, this man from a foreign land? Their communication never went deeper than permitted by the unspoken rules of proper social intercourse between a man and his wife's best girlfriend. Superficially pleasant conversation, wholesome innuendo. Was a dark nature lurking under a plausible façade?

Everyone lied, some better than others. In her job, Dana had learned that the best liars were the ones lacking a conscience, people who lived on a different moral plane than the rest of humanity. Like the scrupulously honest, they always looked truthful, their faces and gestures never giving them away. Could Noel be one of those? It didn't make sense. There were too many verifiable facts about his life.

But appearances didn't look good for him. How could

Saludos use his store as a front without his knowledge, or at least his suspicion? If Domingo really was a cash courier, he would be gone frequently. How did this square with Noel's claim that Domingo was working for him in the store? And Noel couldn't have agreed to sell those products without personally meeting Jefe, the Saludos representative.

Had Noel taken a tempting offer, a little extra cash to play along? Money he needed for his growing family? If so, Melly had to be aware of it. The two of them were inseparable, all-knowing about each other, able to guess without being told. And Melly had access to the Saludos account records. Hadn't she taken a look? Now, after fitting the puzzle pieces together, Dana didn't need to see the records. She knew. The account contained huge amounts of narcotics cash.

Noel and Melly. The likelihood of their knowledge, at the very least, was growing stronger in Dana's mind. She couldn't confirm their innocence or their guilt. She didn't have the evidence. Yet she'd lost her intuitive certainty of their innocence.

As the night wore on, she waffled and despaired and cried. There were reasons to believe the worst, reasons to believe the best. She'd developed no plan for preserving her friendships, nor a strong conviction that those friendships were worth preserving. She would remain in this state of limbo until she knew all the facts.

Should she ask Melly directly? It would jeopardize Dana's job and career. And for what? To tip off people who were committing crimes? Or to warn a close friend, an innocent, unsuspecting, pregnant friend, that her husband and his cousin were up to no good?

One rule was very clear. An assistant district attorney violated the ethical code by investigating crimes in which friends and acquaintances were suspects. An obvious conflict of interest. Investigative and charging decisions would be discredited because the ADA was inclined to protect her friends.

Even if the investigation weren't compromised, it couldn't look good for the DA that one of his assistants had socialized with a criminal suspect. If her boss knew, he would kick her off the FC team, or worse. Maybe she deserved a boot from the office altogether, along with charges filed against her at the ethics committee—an investigation into her actions, censure, suspension or disbarment.

Her obligation was clear. She should tell Bruce immediately and ask to be taken off the case. Could she do it without revealing the suspect's identity? Bruce was bound to badger her into saying Domingo's name, and after that, his relationship to Noel and Melanie. The Don may have figured out the family relationship already, but if not, Dana wasn't going to serve Noel up on a silver platter. What if Bruce delved further? What about the dinner party, Domingo's budding romantic relationship with Cheryl? If he asked these questions, Dana feared she would lie, and lie badly.

More than anything, she feared Bruce's emotionless face, the judgments and opinions coursing behind those small, inscrutable eyes. It would be better to approach the bureau chief, George Blaithe, the man with whom she exchanged an occasional "good morning" in the hallway. She could explain the conflict of interest in a single sentence without revealing identities. But Blaithe was sure to involve Bruce, who would pursue her with his one-track mind and use her like he'd done before. *Dana has a connection at First City*. Now she had a connection to a suspect. How convenient for him! She'd be another Quitman. *I appreciate you being forthright, especially since all of this could have been done a little less friendly, with a subpoena.*

Dana had to find someone else to confide in. She thought of Jack DuBois, her conspiratorial wink. Patrick McBride, his fatherly pats on the shoulder. Evan Goodhue, his warmth and openness. People with experience and good judgment. But they all worked for the same boss, the DA, and were all bound by the same ethical code.

Maybe the only option was to do nothing at all, go about her business as usual and play dumb if asked. "No, I don't recognize him. Such a fuzzy picture. You say it's Domingo Avendaño? Sure, I've met him once—he's related to a friend of mine." Could she pull it off, suppressing those pink blotches on her cheeks? Maybe if she truly believed there was no conflict of interest. *He's related to a friend of mine, a friend and his wife who couldn't have committed any crime.*

This was the key to her peace of mind, her ability to go on. She had to uncover the evidence to prove their innocence—to herself. Maybe there was yet time to do this. It had taken her until tonight to make the connection between Domingo and the fuzzy surveillance photo—who was to say this realization wouldn't hit her until later in the week? She could do some digging before then. It was the weekend, an opportune time to get started. She could poke around in the Dungeon again, maybe even look in the offices, Evan's, Bruce's and Joe's. The building was nearly empty on the weekend. They should all be at home, and who would know?

She became convinced there was no other way. The clock was ticking. The longer she waited to tell Reichert or Blaithe of her conflict, the worse it would look for her when the truth finally came out. And it *would* come out, of that she was sure.

At 3:30 a.m. Saturday morning, she reached this tentative plan. There was time left to get a few hours of sleep. She picked up a novel and sank into a large pillow on the living room floor. She scanned a page, dragged her eyes back to the beginning, started over again, and put the book down. This was the pillow he'd sat on. *For you.*

She stood, turned on the television, and chose the large futon chair, pushing back into the cushions. Nothing to do now but rest. Praying for sleep, she hadn't a doubt that, if it came, she would be up again at dawn, ready to return to the office.

When they left the store, she said she'd changed her mind. It would be too much for her to sit up nicely at a restaurant. She was too tired. They could eat leftovers at home.

She was really thinking that she didn't want to risk being overheard in public. She kept this thought to herself.

At home, she sat on the couch while Noel reheated the meal and brought it to the table. "Did I ruin it?" he asked when she hardly took a bite. It was then that the emotion surfaced, her lips started to quiver, and she burst into a teary exposition of everything she knew.

His eyes widened in shock as she told him about the money in the Saludos account. "How can that be?" and "What shall we do?" and "I've been such a fool!" were the repeated refrains. She saw his pain and was drawn into complete alignment with him. How could she have entertained even the smallest doubt about him?

If only Noel would see her point about Domingo. For some reason, he couldn't bring himself to believe in his cousin's knowing complicity. "Someone else must be making those deposits. I see Domingo every Friday evening, counting the card money, dividing out my share, taking the rest to the bank. He may be lazy when it comes to menial tasks, but you can't say anything worse about him. He's a bright kid, too sensible to ruin his life that way. We've talked about the Cartel before, how bad it is for everyone. He would *never* work for people laundering the money. Someone else is working for Restrepo, making those deposits. Domingo and I have been taken for fools."

Nothing she said would make him believe otherwise. It was

all stubborn pride. Noel had invested too much effort in the boy to believe he would throw his future away so stupidly. But she didn't have the proof to contradict him. Her memory of the figures on her computer screen was cloudy. She'd been too shocked at the sheer amount of money to notice any of the details. Noel's theory could be borne out if there were a few small deposits consistent with income from the Saludos products, interspersed with the larger, round-numbered deposits.

She simply didn't know. She suggested that they confront Domingo and ask for the truth. Again, she was met with a surprising answer.

"No," he said, more strongly than before. "I told you he couldn't have done this; I know him too well. But even so. Let's just say he committed a crime. Just for the sake of argument. Do you think he'd tell us, 'yes, I'm working for the Cartel'? Whether he's guilty or innocent, his answer would be that he knows nothing about it."

She had to agree and nodded "yes."

"There's only one thing we can do," he said. "We'll get out of this business altogether. I'll tell Mingo we're discontinuing the Saludos concession. Send a fax message to Restrepo, tell him to remove his merchandise, or better yet, we'll mail it all back to him. The business isn't working out for us. Sorry. That's it. And I'll stand over him while he sends the fax. I would do it myself, but I don't know the number."

It was a plan, surely. A sensible plan. One that should have soothed Melanie's nerves.

But she had a fitful night's sleep and awoke Saturday morning drenched in a sweat of terror to add to her usual morning sickness. Noel was suggesting that they directly contact an associate of the Cali Cartel by fax, telling him to back off! It was dangerous.

Shouldn't they enlist the aid of the police or the DA? Didn't they need protection? She asked him these things over breakfast, in between her efforts to ingest a piece of dry toast and milk.

"No, querida, we would only endanger ourselves more. The Cartel wouldn't like us to run to the police, especially since I've seen Restrepo and could describe him to the authorities. Trust me. We'll make this look like a logical business decision. I owe them nothing. They shouldn't bother us anymore."

But Domingo. He might owe them something. She held this thought in as she pondered Noel's sudden confidence. His refrain of the night before—"What shall we do?"—had quickly fallen by the wayside, replaced with these definite opinions and methodical plans.

In a way, his self-assurance calmed her. She wasn't in any state to make decisions, and his strength would get them through. In another way, his behavior pricked her nameless fears. An unwavering stratagem against powerful criminals was not the sort of response she would have expected from Noel. Indecision, feigned confidence and trite reassurances might have been more in character.

But this was a situation like no other, and it called for immediate action. She would have to trust his judgment, his innate understanding of Colombian culture and character. He knew better than she how this man Restrepo would react.

After Noel's final, decisive words, they finished their breakfast in silence. Now and again they touched hands over the tabletop and caught eyes in a crush of awareness. The importance of this day. The difference of this day. When he was ready to go, she simply followed him. Without question, he allowed it. She was of a mind to stay by his side all day long, and she wouldn't think of leaving him.

As close as they were, Melanie had never been this clingy. Saturdays, while Noel worked, she liked to fill her day with enjoyable activities he wouldn't mind missing: clothes shopping, meeting girlfriends, or visiting her parents in New Jersey. But today, she felt a dependency born of fear. There was the lingering doubt that nothing, not even his sensible plan of action, could save them from a dreadful unknown.

On the way to Libros NOMEL, and during the first hours of business, they wondered openly whether and when Domingo would show up. At 10:30, he strode through the door, wearing his favorite leather jacket despite the warm, spring morning, already well into the seventies. He looked surprised to see Melanie behind the counter but greeted her cordially.

"Primo," he addressed Noel. "You have work for me?" in English.

Despite everything, Noel smiled with approval at Mingo's use of English and his offer of help after so many days of lax inattentiveness to anything other than the fax machine and Saludos merchandise. "Yes," he said, coming around from behind the counter. "More than enough."

Mingo held a hand up to Noel like a school crossing guard. Abandoning his meager English, he let the next words flow out in Spanish. Melanie understood the simple phrases: "Wait a minute. Let me take off my jacket and use the washroom first." He started toward the back of the store.

When Mingo was out of earshot, Melanie said, "Let's tell him now. We have to get this over with."

"All in time," said Noel. "We have customers."

During the next hour, as customers came and went, Domingo stayed in the back office, working steadily on Noel's bookkeeping. At a moment when the store was clear of customers, Melanie insisted it was Noel's opportunity, and she nudged him toward the back office until he stood in the open doorway, looking down at Domingo, sitting at the desk. Melanie scooted behind a nearby bookshelf, out of view but able to overhear.

"I've been thinking, Domingo," said Noel in Spanish. "I'd

like to discontinue selling the Saludos products."

"Oh?"

"As you know, I wasn't sure about it from the start, and now I think it's been detracting from the literature. In my mind, the small income hasn't made up for the look of it."

Domingo said nothing. Melanie could feel the tension in the moment of silence, as if Noel was taken by surprise at his cousin's failure to protest. Noel continued: "Please, I'd like you to send a fax to Restrepo, telling him we'll send the surplus merchandise back to him. Or he can have someone pick it up along with the fax machine. It's all in good condition."

"As you wish," said Mingo.

"You don't mind?"

"Not at all. It's your store. You make the decisions."

"Then you can put the ledgers aside and take care of it now."

"Oh, but I can't," Domingo rushed to say.

"And why not?"

"No one is in their office on the weekend. We'll have to wait until Monday. I'll do it Monday morning. How's that?"

"I suppose that's the soonest—"

"Yes. They wouldn't get the message before then anyway."

"All right then."

Noel retreated, head low, bumping into Melanie. She led him away from the door and into the reference section in a corner far from the back office. "I guess that's the best we can do," she said, hoping for reassurance.

"Yes, Monday morning."

"He didn't seem surprised or upset. He didn't object."

"No. I told you, Melly. He doesn't really care because he's not involved. It's clear to me now. He doesn't know a thing about them."

"Maybe you're right."

He gently cupped her cheek with his warm hand and kissed

her nose, making her smile. "Don't worry. Let's go back out front."

Dana started for the office a little later than she'd planned. 9:15. She'd awoken on the futon at 7:00 with a stiff neck and beating heart, a reminder that it wasn't a usual Saturday. She took a very long shower and extra minutes in front of the mirror trying to fix her tired face, then lingered over coffee.

Every minute of her usual morning routine was slowed with the weight of a shameful image of herself snooping in other people's offices. She reminded herself there was nothing illegal or unethical about it. As part of the team, she was entitled to see the evidence. Evan and Bruce, more than once, had come into her office to rummage for something while she was out. Rather impolite, but it was done.

Perhaps it was even more than impolite, a disrespectful act, for a junior ADA to snoop in a senior's office. She could think of a few convenient excuses to cover herself if caught, but still, she had the uneasy feeling her actions could be perceived as far more than disrespectful. It was a feeling that Bruce and the Don had purposefully concealed certain information and locked it away from her view. This would take more than just pushing a few loose papers around on desktops.

In the subway on the way down, she thought of Evan's face and his words of inclusion. Hadn't he assured her that Bruce wanted her to be familiar with every aspect of the case? And hadn't Evan initiated the first trip to the Dungeon, including her in the conversation about Niño? She was authorized to see the evidence. Absolutely authorized.

In the lobby of the DA's entrance to the Criminal Court building, Dana removed her small, leather folder with employee identification and shield as she walked up to the guard at the

desk. During business hours, a show of ID was the only require-
ment for entry, but on evenings and weekends, all employees had
to sign in at the desk.

Dana placed her open identification folder on the edge of the
high desk and picked up the clipboard with the sign-in sheet, a
ballpoint pen dangling at the end of a dirty string. The guard
briefly turned away from the "Taxi" rerun playing on a twelve-
inch, black-and-white television set, and without a word of
greeting, glanced at her shield and signaled his "okay" with a
raised hand before turning back to the tube.

Dana put her ID folder back in her purse, checked the clock
on the wall, and entered the time, "9:34," on the next open line,
about a third of the way down. She started to print "ADA Da—"
but froze and dropped the pen, letting it dangle on the end of the
string. Something had caught her eye.

The top line bore the distinctive scrawl of ADA Bruce
Reichert. 9:10. Funny, but predictable. The man with the one-track
mind was working extra hours on the weekend. To most ADAs
the weekend was sacrosanct; they'd earned their meager
government salaries by putting in a killing fifty-hour week. But
Bruce. It made sense.

She could still go into Evan's office at the other end of the
hall, well out of Bruce's view, and she could visit Joe's office on
another floor, and of course, the Dungeon in the basement. She
picked up the pen, held it poised for a moment, and dropped it
again. Something told her to check, just to make sure.

She lifted the top sheet to look at the one underneath, bearing
the names of all employees who'd entered before 9:10. Her eye
went immediately to three of them at the bottom, all in a row:
Detective Paul Donegan, 8:47, Investigator Gilbert Herrera, 8:55,
ADA Evan Goodhue, 9:00.

Thoughts whirred and tumbled. What were they up to?

She blacked out her entry with a thick layer of ink, turned

and scurried out the door. The guard was laughing and didn't seem to notice.

16 » CONFRONTATION

A CHANGE OF PLAN was needed. Dana briefly considered and dismissed the idea of returning to the office the next day. Something big was up, a new stratagem or investigative plan. Something so big that they might be back at the office on Sunday.

She was left with the only remaining option. To call Melly. But she had to be sure Noel wasn't around, just in case he was involved. Saturday was the best day to catch Melly at home, when Noel was at the store. Dana worked up the courage to call, but the phone rang until the machine came on. She hung up without leaving a message. Later in the day she tried again, twice, with the same results. Finally, it was too close to dinnertime to call. Saturday night and Sunday they'd surely be together.

She lived through these hours in her apartment alone, with little food or sleep. Monday morning brought no further enlightenment. The face reflected in her bathroom mirror was battered by stress and sleeplessness. Could she get through the day, business as usual? Could she pull it off?

She got to the office at 8:30, and at 9:00, made a purposeful trip down the hall. Along the way, she waved at Evan inside his office and Mineko inside her cubicle, said good morning to Cathy at her computer, Bruce outside his open office door, and George Blaithe, as he passed her in the hallway. It was like any other day, nothing out of place.

Having made her appearance, Dana went into the Closet and shut the door. She sat down at the desk and looked at the phone. Now, at last, she could speak to Melanie. Struggling to control the fluttering high in her throat, she straightened her spine, pulled in a deep breath and picked up the receiver. Her fingers dialed Melanie's work number. After three rings, with a bump, the call was transferred. After the fourth ring, a woman answered, "First City Financial." Dana left a message, requesting that Melanie return the call.

Now what? She turned to her work and tried to concentrate. It was a useless exercise. Numbers, deposit slips, and Spanish names tangled on the pages, fused and congealed. She got up, opened the door, came back to the desk, and arranged a pile of papers. Looked at her watch. Only fifteen minutes had passed since her tour of the hallway. She rose again, went to the open door and stood there, listening. All the usual sounds. She closed the door, sat at the desk, lifted the phone, and dialed Melanie's number. Three rings and a bump. She hung up. No reason to keep leaving messages, to reveal her anxiety.

Dana looked at her watch and set a time limit. If no return call by 11:00, she would ring back. She picked up the evidence summary she'd been working on last Friday, barely able to remember a word on the page. She looked at the phone. It made sense to try again, just in case Melanie had returned to her desk without receiving the message. She dialed the number. Three rings and a bump.

She hung up, went to the door and opened it. The cubicles within her view were occupied, but somehow, things seemed quieter. Evan's door was open, but she couldn't see inside. Cathy was down that way. Dana headed there now, thinking of an excuse on the way.

"Cathy, did I leave my evidence summary with you? The one I asked you to type last week?"

Cathy stuck her hand in the plastic bin marked "Hargrove" and came up empty. "Nope."

"Maybe I left it in the library. Thanks."

Dana walked the long way around Cathy's cubicle to afford herself a view inside Evan's office. The door was wide open, the office empty. She continued down the hall toward the library, walking past Bruce's open door. He was gone too. Bruce and Evan, gone. She took a walk through the library and passed the empty conference room.

They could be anywhere of course. In the men's room. In court. Down in Joe's office. On the way to meetings. Or down in the Dungeon, refining their plans with the Don and Gilbert.

She returned to her office, closed the door, and tried Melanie's number again. Three rings and a bump. This time she let it ring through, and the same female voice came on.

"Is Melanie Avendaño in today?"

"Yes, she is."

"You're sure? I..."

"She certainly is. I'll tell her you called. Your name please?"

"That's all right. I left a message earlier. Thank you." She hung up and buried her face in her hands.

Melanie was reluctant to leave the shelter of Noel's arms. He gently pulled away. "Don't worry, querida," he said, sounding vulnerable and more like himself.

She wanted to be with him when Domingo sent the fax to Restrepo, but she couldn't afford to take a sick day from work. They'd also decided she should check the account records one more time, to test Noel's theory of Mingo's innocence. With a final kiss, they parted to take their separate commutes to work.

What a time for the morning sickness to surge! Uncomfortably squeezed on a bench of the subway train, she sat with her arms crossed over her abdomen, bent over at the waist. The symptoms were different, arising from a place very deep inside. At breakfast she'd eaten only a few bites of toast, not exactly from nausea but a lack of desire to eat. She was exceedingly thirsty, crushed with fatigue, heavy, slightly dizzy, and damp in every place that touched the plastic seat and her neighbors' bodies.

The straphangers in the aisle involuntarily jerked toward her and quickly away, like actors in a silent movie. When the train slowed, they swerved like hawks gliding on changing air currents. She could have been dead or in another world. There was a faint stench of decay emanating from a person nearby — or from herself. Was it the impurity invading her body? Already she'd been a delinquent mother. For two days at least, the baby had been forgotten.

By 8:15 she was sitting in her cubicle, searching her computer screen for confirmation of Domingo's innocence. She found none. All the deposits were very large, all cash, ranging from $6,300 to $9,700. All were in round numbers except for the deposits made on Fridays, which included cents. $8,764.35 and $9,127.49. Nothing on Friday the thirteenth. Why had he missed his deposit last Friday?

She wasn't shocked by this confirmation of Domingo's involvement. Her subconscious memory of the account activity had already confirmed it. She thought back to the first days, when she wholeheartedly welcomed him into her home simply because he was a member of Noel's family. Now, he meant no more to her than any stranger from a foreign land, a person she didn't understand and with whom she couldn't communicate.

If he was guilty of a crime, he should be tried, convicted and sent to jail. She had no reservations about that. Her only concern was for Noel. He would suffer with this knowledge of his cousin's errant ways, but not for long. She believed the two had never been close. There was the age difference for one thing. Noel's emotional investment was more akin to pride than a close bond of love. He would get over it. He had to get over it to save himself.

She dialed the store. No answer. Noel had a longer commute and wouldn't arrive until 8:30 at least. She would try again in a few minutes, hoping to catch him before Domingo came in.

Her mind went blank for an instant, and Dana popped into the void. She'd concentrated so hard on Noel all weekend, she hadn't thought of Dana at all. Now that the evidence so clearly pointed to Domingo's guilt, the extra hurt of Dana's secretive knowledge stabbed her. Dana had known or suspected all of this for a long time, likely suspected her and Noel too, and hadn't said a thing, guarding her precious evidence.

Would Dana call this morning, asking for the subpoenaed documents? Should Melanie call first and demand a showdown? She could fight for Noel and knock down every unproven suspicion. But why was the burden on *her* to come forward with an explanation? She was so very tired, and everything was so unfair. She recalled without remorse the "misplaced" subpoena and had no intention of "finding" it, as long as Dana refused to reveal what her team was planning.

Twenty minutes later, when Noel answered the phone at the store, she told him what she'd seen in the account. "All the deposits are big, Noel. Even the ones on Fridays. You know what that means, don't you?"

"Well, it doesn't really prove—"

"Many thousands of dollars in each deposit."

"Thousands?"

"Yes."

He fell silent for a moment, then said, "Don't worry, querida." His voice was particularly unconvincing.

"You have to be careful."

"Don't worry."

"You'll call me after the fax?"

"Yes, I will. Of course I will."

"And tell me how it goes."

"Every detail. I expect him shortly. This will be over very soon. Now take care of yourself."

"And the baby."

"Yes. Kiss the flea for me."

"I love you."

"Te amo."

She replaced the receiver, kissed her fingertips, and rested them on her abdomen. She stood, feeling heavy, skin of lead, and very thirsty.

At the water cooler she stood swaying, drinking several cups, then made her way to the ladies' room. There, she found something strange. A spot of fresh blood on her clothing. Confused, she sat down on the lounge in the anteroom to the lavatory. She could lie down here, rest for a while and go back to work.

But no, it wasn't worth it. The stress had become too much for her. She needed to take this day at least and rest completely, try to get everything else out of her mind. She would go home, call Noel, clear her thoughts, call her obstetrician, and rest. She needed rest.

It was 11:00 by the time the receptionist at First City acknowledged that Melanie had gone home. She was sorry, but that information had not been given to her until just now.

Dana dialed Melanie's home number. After four rings, the answering machine started up, but Melanie interrupted it with a groggy "Hello."

A phone was ringing nearby. Then her own voice announced the Avendaño residence.

Melanie fumbled the receiver up to her ear and heard, "Were you asleep?"

"Yes, but that's okay."

"I didn't want to wake you up—they said you went home sick. Are you all right?"

It was Dana, her very good friend. The familiar, warm and welcome voice floated into the plane of Melanie's half-dream state. A concerned friend. "I'm tired and feel very strange. I need some rest."

"You should see a doctor."

"I'm going later. She's not in her office 'til three." Melanie sat up in bed. The plastic telephone receiver, the rumpled bedclothes, the events of the weekend and this morning—all of it came clear in the sunlight spilling through the cracks of the curtain. The genuine sound of Dana's voice had tricked her, and now she must be on guard. "Thanks for the call, but I'll be okay."

"I'm sorry you're feeling so bad. Remember how we talked last week about having lunch?"

"Right. Mondays are always awful for you."

"Usually that's true, but today I have some time. I guess you wouldn't feel up to it."

"No, I wouldn't."

"Maybe I could—do you need any help? Can I come over and make you some tea or something?"

"Dana..." Melanie debated. She couldn't stand this anymore. The bad excuses grated on her, bringing out the sarcasm and evasiveness that weren't her true self. She and Dana had never been this way with each other, always open and real. "Let's just cut through this, okay? I think I know why you're calling."

Dana hesitated before speaking. "We have to talk about something."

"Yes, we have to talk."

"Now's a bad time for you. You're sick—"

"I've been sick for weeks. This is nothing, I'll get over it. There's another thing I might not get over unless we talk. So, go ahead and say what you need to say."

"I can't on the phone. I'm in the office. Can we meet? I can come up there."

She couldn't have Dana in her apartment. What if Noel called to talk about the fax?

When they'd last spoken at 9:45, the fax hadn't been sent. Domingo had come in at 9:30 and ducked into the back room for a few minutes—just long enough to pick up his usual morning message. On his way out the door again, Noel reminded him of their plan. Domingo replied, "Yeah, cousin, as soon as I get back. Restrepo isn't there yet anyway."

It was not a good sign. Melanie could see through it, and she warned Noel, "You know what he's doing, don't you? He's going to pick up money. He has no intention of sending the message!" Noel didn't want to admit it. He believed Mingo would be back soon and would follow through with their agreement. Well, maybe he would. She had to hope. But she didn't want Dana in her apartment when Noel called with the news, one way or the other.

"Let's meet somewhere else."

Dana suggested a diner near Melly's apartment.

"Noon?"

"All right. I'll be there."

Before leaving her apartment, Melly called Noel. Domingo had not returned.

A brief greeting, a flicker of eyes. Dana was stunned at the change in her friend since the last time she'd seen her, a little over a week ago. Every shining, vibrant feature had become dull, the pink cheeks sunken and gray, the honey-gold hair tarnished, hazel eyes the color of an overcast sky.

They took seats across from each other in a small, two-person booth. Their nervous energy joined the surrounding din of a dozen conversations and the clinking of thick china and cheap silverware. "You look sick Melly. I feel bad about making you come out."

"You don't look so great yourself," was Melanie's rejoinder. "But we have to do this. You've been keeping secrets from me—"

The waitress arrived, set two glasses of ice water on the table, and removed her pad from pocket, pen from behind an ear. Without looking at the menu, they ordered standard diner fare, just to send the woman on her way. Milk, wheat toast, and chicken noodle soup for Melanie, coffee and a grilled cheese sandwich for Dana. As soon as the waitress had gone, Melanie drank half the glass of water.

"I haven't been keeping secrets. You know I'm under an obligation to keep a lid on the investigation. But beyond that, the name on that list, whatever it is you might be thinking..."

"Come out with it. You're hiding something."

"I can't hide something I'm not sure of! I didn't know anything at all until Friday night. Why do you think I need to talk to you? I'm still trying to piece this thing together."

"So, you figured *something* out but you can't tell me what it is because you're not allowed to talk. Is that it? Maybe we can just play a guessing game. I'll say what *I* know, and *you* just nod your head yes or no. That way no one, not even that sweetheart of a boss of yours, can ever accuse you of revealing secrets in a public place." Unaccustomed to her own sarcasm, Melanie displayed her self-consciousness with a rising voice and a hint of color in her pallid cheeks.

"Okay, calm down," Dana said in a subdued tone. "You're

getting so upset, it can't be good for you—" Her voice broke with unexpected emotion. Tears threatened. She wasn't going to cry. She'd planned to do this with absolute control, walking the tightrope with no slips, influencing Melanie with the aura of informed authority and the hint of vast knowledge, a trap to get her to spill everything. A deceptive plan, transparent and so obviously bollixed.

They were given a moment to settle their emotions as the waitress plunked their food down in all the wrong places, coffee, soup and sandwich for Melanie, milk and toast for Dana. When she'd gone, they sorted out the plates in silence without looking at one another. They each took a sip of their drinks but didn't touch the food.

"No," said Dana, finally. "I don't want to play a guessing game. I'll tell you the things I know if you'll tell me how to interpret them. I'm working blind here. I can't think what to do unless I have some facts. You have to help me figure out what's going on. I mean, I'm asking you to do that. Do you think you can?"

"This is just another game. It's a negotiation. 'I won't tell you this until you tell me that.' Well I can't say *what* I'm going to tell. You're the one from the DA. You're the one who investigates people and puts them away. You're the one with the information. What do you know about Saludos Limitada, anyway?"

"Very little. Only the things I'm sure you already know. It's a company that manufactures greeting cards and Noel sells the products in his store. I know it has an account at First City and my boss subpoenaed the account records. I know that Domingo makes deposits to the account. That's really about it." She purposefully avoided mentioning Hanniger Paper and the meeting between Domingo and Jefe. Those things were far too sensitive.

"That's it? That's everything you know? And based on that,

you're assuming the worst—a huge criminal conspiracy or something. All that stuff you won't tell me about."

"You've already guessed what I haven't told you."

"Drug money and a Colombian cartel. There, you made me say it. From my own mouth, not yours."

Dana nodded in agreement and hung her head low. She took another sip of coffee and looked up again, meeting her friend's eyes. "But you've seen the bank records. I haven't. You tell me. Tell me the account shows money from greeting card sales, nothing else, and we can stop this conversation right here."

Melanie emitted a few stumbling sounds, groping for a defense on that point. There was none. "Apparently it's a very successful greeting card company." She shook her head and raised her eyes to the ceiling, as if to indicate the height of its "success."

"How much? What were the total deposits last month? Thousands?"

"Hundreds..."

"Hundreds of thousands?"

She nodded affirmatively. "Tons of money going in and out."

They fell into silence and pushed the food around on their plates. At last, Dana said, "That doesn't look good."

"For who?"

"Domingo. He's been making the deposits. As for Noel—"

"It doesn't look good for him either, right? Is *that* what you're saying? It's Cartel money and my husband and his cousin are both Colombian. End of story, right? You don't really need any more evidence. Now I know what you've been thinking all this time. At least two weeks, right? That subpoena was dated May third. All this time and you haven't told me what you know. You even invited us to your apartment! Was that part of the investigation? To check out Domingo? To see if we'd confess over a good glass of wine?"

"You've already made up your mind, I can tell. What does it matter what I say? I knew nothing until last Friday. I didn't even know the name Saludos on Thursday when my boss gave me the list. It was Friday when I found out the other things, what kind of company it was and Domingo making the deposits. I tried to call you all day Saturday and you weren't home."

"You could have tried the store. Oh." She paused. "I know. You didn't want to speak to Noel, the Colombian suspect."

"Wait a minute. Step back and look at it from my perspective, from the outside. He sells the products at his store. He must have dealt directly with a salesman from Saludos. Domingo works at the store and makes the deposits. What am I supposed to think?"

Melanie stared back at her hard, incredulous. "What are you supposed to *think*?" Her lips started to quiver and water sprang into her eyes. "After all these years? I'll tell you what you're supposed to *think*. That we're good people! That you know in your heart we're honest!"

Dana blanched, all the air and sound sucked away. A horrible, irreparable mistake! She reached for her friend's hand on the table, but Melanie pulled back. "Take Mingo. Go ahead and take him and do what you have to do! I wish he'd never come. Don't you see, Dana? None of this happened until he came. *He's* the one! Noel didn't know a thing. *I* didn't know a thing. And you doubt us. *You* doubt *us*..." She shook her head in disgust and the tears fell.

"I'm sorry, I'm so sorry," Dana implored as Melanie slid along the bench, trying to get away, to get herself out of this place. She pushed down on the edge of the table and stood halfway, coming down again with a clutch at her abdomen, a grimace and a small cry. She crumpled and doubled up on the bench, leaning sideways on one hip with her shoulder against the wall.

A gasp broke from Dana's lips. She bolted from her side of the booth and squeezed in on the other side, placing a hand on the stricken woman. Eyes closed, breath shallow, skin clammy. Unconscious.

Dana jumped up and searched the crowded room, silently screaming for help, getting nothing. Panicked and helpless, she looked down again at the partially reclined figure, hips tilted upward from the seat. On Melanie's skirt, a circle of bright red blood the size of a saucer crept outward, growing larger, gently absorbed by the thirsty, cotton fabric.

17 »   EXPOSURE

NOT ALLOWED IN, Dana paced the waiting room and hallway, returning to the row of payphones in the visitor reception area every ten minutes to try the two numbers again, Melanie's apartment and Libros NOMEL. No answer.

The emergency ward was busy, individuals and couples isolated by their personal tragedies. Anxious relatives, doctors, nurses, frail and bandaged patients, the smells of disinfectant, floor wax, medicine, sickness and grief. Mixed into the stew, the most prominent ingredient was the phantom of Melanie's voice in a repeated refrain: *You doubt us. You...doubt...us.* The cry before the fall.

One person alone was responsible for putting Melly in the hospital, and that person was pacing the floor, sick with shame, powerless to force an answer to a ringing phone.

After an hour that seemed like several, a doctor found Dana and gave a brief report. Melanie had suffered a bad miscarriage, lost a lot of blood, but would come out of it fine in a few days. "Are you a friend of hers?" he asked. The young resident might have been about thirty but was aging fast under the stress of long hours in the emergency ward. He looked at Dana as if what he planned to say, and the way he would say it, depended heavily on her answer.

"Yes, I am."

"Emotional support is the most important thing right now. She seems very upset. Have you contacted anyone who needs to know? A boyfriend or husband?"

"I've been trying to reach her husband. I need to talk to her about that. May I speak with her?"

The doctor's trembling pupils were fixed on Dana in a sleepless stare. Trouble with a husband—an everyday story. "She's awake but very weak. You can talk to her for a few minutes, but don't tax her strength."

Good advice, but delivered too late.

He pointed the way. Dana entered a room with three beds, tiptoed past two of them without noticing the patients, and went up to Melly in the third one. She lay with half-lidded eyes, hair and face pale as the sheets, an IV tube running into her arm. Drawn and weak as she appeared, her face conveyed a sense of release and surrender to her loss. *She seems very upset*, the doctor had said, but there was little evidence of this. Perhaps he'd given her pain medication, enough to bring on the illusion of contentment.

But she was not drugged. When she spoke, it was with a slow, quiet and clear voice, very focused on what had happened and what she needed. "Have you told Noel? Is he on the way?" The sound was chilling, such a marked contrast to her tone and words at the diner a short time ago. The doctor, after all, was an intuitive genius to have seen the real Melly underneath. *She seems very upset.* He must have seen right through Dana too. His sunken, dark-circled eyes, the trembling pupils in sleepless REM, had picked up all the bad things she'd done to put her friend in the hospital…

"I've been calling your apartment and the store," Dana said, conveying what little she had left to offer. "He didn't answer."

"The store?" Her brow compressed into grooves over the bridge of her nose.

"The phone rang and rang."

"Sometimes he's busy with a customer. You have to keep ringing."

"I did. I've called four or five times. I counted twenty rings. I don't think he's there. Maybe he closed the store to go out for lunch."

"He never does that. Maybe the phone isn't working. Something's wrong."

A small silence, Melanie's hard intensity growing inside. "Something is wrong," she said again, pronouncing each word distinctly.

"Don't worry. You have to rest. I'll call again, and if he doesn't answer, I'll go out there myself. He has to be at the store, right?"

"He went into work and I called him there this morning. The phone must be broken. It has to be that."

"I'm sure it's nothing to worry about. My phone acts up at least once a month. It happens all the time. I'll get him and we'll be back. I'll try to hurry." Her words rushed out with breathless shame as she took a small step backward, anxious to go, yet drawn to stay. Melanie looked so helpless there, like she was fastened to the floor by the pole with the IV tube running into her arm. "Melly…I'm so sorry about the baby."

Melanie turned her head away, toward the window, and with her free hand, the one without the tube, she wiped at her eyes. Her voice emerged, changed again, soft and tremulous. "In a way it will be better, not to feel so sick anymore. We'll do this another time. Right now…well, this just isn't the right time."

Emotion swelled inside Dana, and she reclaimed the step she'd taken in retreat and walked right up to the edge of the bed, gingerly placing her hand on her friend's shoulder. "If I could do anything to take back what I said, how I acted… I didn't mean any of it, didn't believe any of it…" Tears surfaced and spilled, falling on the bed.

Melanie turned back to face Dana, her own eyes full of tears, her face transforming gradually, taking on a beatific light, a gentle smile. "I never gave up on you."

That look, the trust, broke Dana a little more. "You're too good, Melly. You're too good to be wasting your time on someone like me."

"Then stop wasting my time and go get my husband. Deliver Noel to me."

Dana lifted her hand from Melanie's shoulder, touched her forehead like a mother checking for temperature, and was ready to depart, to go to work. "Rest up. We'll be back before you know it."

On a subway train headed for Queens, it occurred to Dana that she hadn't been to Noel's store since the day of its grand opening, over two years ago. She hadn't asked Melanie for directions and hoped she could find it.

Her memory of it was clear: the proud little face with two large windows for eyes, the bold black letters of LIBROS NOMEL for brows, the passage between the windows and front door a mouth and nose. She kept the address in the tiny book she carried in her purse, and although she didn't know Queens well, she recalled the name of the subway stop and believed she would remember the way from there. The store was only a block from the metal staircase that descended from the elevated tracks to the street.

She looked at her watch. Already 2:30, and she hadn't called the office. This was a very, very long lunch hour indeed, but the office just hadn't crossed her mind since she'd left at 11:45 for her fateful lunch date. Her superiors, and the explanations she owed them, were the least of her worries at this moment.

More troublesome was the thought of facing Noel under these circumstances, delivering the bad news. She couldn't shake her feeling of guilt, the certainty she'd been at least in part to blame. The baby was gone, a victim of the stress and terror Dana had stirred up with her baseless accusations.

She didn't doubt that the same thought might occur to Noel, who would wonder why she'd been with his wife in the middle of the day at the moment of Melly's unfortunate, sudden illness. Undoubtedly, Dana's married friends had been openly guessing at her knowledge and wondering at her betrayal. Melanie had thought that Dana knew about Domingo for more than two weeks, even on the night of her dinner party. Noel must be thinking the same thing, angry that she didn't warn him of Mingo's criminal activity.

But all of that would have to wait. Naturally, it would be pushed aside in the wake of her terrible news about the miscarriage. She owed it to Melly to find Noel, to give him the news, and to deliver him to his wife.

Her head filled with planned words and comforting noises as she alighted from the train, telling herself this must be, this had to be, the stop. Yes, she remembered the platform, the newsstand, and the stairwell down, just over there—but didn't all the elevated stops in Queens look about the same?

Halfway down the steps, high enough to look out over the block ahead, she could see clearly that she'd arrived at the right spot. Near the end of the block on the other side of the street, bold and beautiful on the face of the building, were the prominent black letters in relief: LIBROS NOMEL.

Satisfied with this confirmation, she refocused on the path before her and descended the stairs quickly. She pushed through the turnstile and out the door, crossed the street, and made her way down the block, weaving in and out of the slower moving pedestrians. Why were people so slow when you needed simply to walk down the street?

She was near the end of the block and coming up on the store when the people in front of her grew in number, their wall of resistance thickening, becoming positively dense. It was a small crowd of a few dozen spectators right outside the store, immersed in rapidly flowing Spanish. *Something is wrong,* she heard Melly say.

Heart pounding, Dana started to push through. She halted with an urgent desire to turn and run, to escape! What was this? She hadn't the time to think. Something bad had happened, causing these people to stop and gawk. An accident, a fire, a robbery? Was Noel all right? But her immediate impulse was one of self-preservation. She was tied up in this somehow, she didn't know why or how, but there was something waiting for her on the other side of this crowd.

Ashamed once again at her selfishness and her primal instinct for survival, she straightened her spine and started to push through. She should be thinking only of her friends, Melly and Noel. She'd done them wrong, and they were more important than any of her personal concerns right now, more important than... She emerged at the front of the crowd to see two uniformed cops guarding the front door. A yellow police tape was strung across the entryway between the display windows. This could mean only one thing. A crime scene. Panic and flight mode reignited.

She tamped down her reaction, took a deep breath, and found the rational side of her brain. These patrolmen who were strangers to her would need to see her ID.

She fished in her purse for the little leather folder, imagining what could possibly be awaiting her inside, the big bad thing about to be revealed. It couldn't be as simple as an accident or a fire or a robbery. All of this was about Domingo, it had to be. *None of this happened until he came. He's the one!* And if Domingo was the one, he'd bestowed some form of tragedy on this little bookstore. The Cartel might have come calling, and Noel might have been threatened or injured or worse. She had to get inside.

Between the two cops, she picked the baby-faced one with the softer features and approached him with her leather folder open at eye-level to display her shield. "May I cross?" As she made this little show of authority, she realized that her affiliation with the Manhattan District Attorney might not hold much sway here in Queens. He wrinkled his brow and scrutinized her ID longer than she thought necessary. Finally, he nodded and shrugged a "go ahead." He'd needed to make his own little show.

Awkwardly, trying to preserve her modesty in the tight skirt of her business suit, she kicked a leg up and over the tape, straddled it, and pulled the other one over, avoiding any contact with the tape. About five feet ahead, the front door was propped open, and she could see people inside, a few in uniform, a few in business suits, a few in casual attire, an enormous amount of activity it seemed, entirely too many people for one little store and Noel not one of them.

What was this? She stepped forward, through the open door, and scanned the confusion, looking for him. Maybe he was in the back. Maybe she should ask. She walked in, looking for a friendly face, someone to ask. No one seemed to notice her, including the two people now almost directly in her path a few feet away, a man and a woman in business attire, their backs to her and their heads bent low in consultation over a very important, solemn matter. They broke apart and raised their heads in profile. She gasped. They turned to face her.

"Dana!" Evan's blue-gray eyes caught hers, and there was nowhere to hide.

"Hi Dana." The conspiratorial wink, the flash of ivory teeth. It was Jacquelyn DuBois.

Startled, Dana stumbled backward, but her knees buckled.

Evan lurched and grabbed her elbow. "You okay?" Her face must have looked like ashen death. Her mouth was open, gagging on syllables that wouldn't form.

She averted her eyes. Here was Evan, standing in Noel's store in the middle of the day. The "wordless communication" they shared—all a fantasy. There'd been no telepathic visions to prepare her for this.

There was a shimmer in her peripheral vision, an aura of wavering images like a mirage. "Dana." Evan's voice broke through, his hand sliding from elbow to forearm. He squeezed it. "Look at me." She did, and he dropped his hand. "Everything will be all right. Trust me." The face was round and open like his eyes, letting her in. No judgment or accusation. Just complete acceptance and inclusion. She'd had this illusion before.

She turned to Jack, the woman she idolized, and saw the same things. No disdain or condescension.

These two had been keeping secrets from her but wanted to include her now. Completely. Could she trust it? They had a lot of explaining to do.

In a blink of clarity, she understood fully why they were here and what they were doing. She didn't need to ask. If she hadn't been overwhelmed by a personal dilemma, she easily would have anticipated what was going on behind that police tape before crossing the line. Of course it was them! These were the people conducting this investigation. Of course.

With a small measure of calm restored, she scanned the room and saw what she'd been blind to only a minute before. Cardboard evidence boxes were everywhere, detectives picking through the bookshelves, behind the counter, labeling items, putting them into the boxes. This is what they'd been up to all weekend. Preparing an application for a search warrant.

Her voice returned to her, clogged and thick. "I guess...," she cleared her throat, "I guess you made that deal with Queens." She smiled wanly.

"Yes," Evan confirmed with a smile. "We're working this together. Your idea. Remember?"

"Another one of those little things Bruce didn't tell you, I'm sure," interjected Jack in a cool tone. She stepped toward them and assumed a solid stance, arms folded across her abdomen, legs firmly planted a foot apart, her two-inch heels bringing her only to the height of Dana's shoulder. Powerful, with benevolent authority. "Like some other things. Some very *big* things, right Dana?" Her smile was kind, her brown-eyed wink omniscient. Jack and Dana united against Bruce.

Dana gathered in Jack's look and glanced at Evan to find that his expression had turned mildly sheepish. And then she knew. She knew that they knew. Everything. Not just a suspicion or a hunch. They knew all about her and Noel and Melanie and Domingo and probably about Cheryl and Domingo, every detail of it. How long they'd known she couldn't tell, but there was no doubt in her mind.

"I know he can be an S-O-B, honey," said Jack.

In the heat of mortification, Dana again felt the urge to run. The third time in the past several minutes. Evan saw her pain and seemed puzzled by it. He reached out, touching her briefly and lightly on the shoulder. "I'm sorry, Dana. We'll get all of this straightened out later, I promise. But right now, Jack and I have to supervise the rest of this search."

The call to work snapped her awake and got her back on track. "Where's Noel?" she demanded. "I just took his wife to the hospital."

Her two superiors looked concerned. "What happened?" asked Jack.

"A miscarriage. She lost a lot of blood. She'll be okay, but Noel has to get to the hospital."

"A shame...," said Evan. "Hmm—now I get it. You haven't

been in the office this afternoon, have you?"

"No."

"Bruce stayed behind. He asked me to handle the warrants because he was going to call you in and have a talk."

"A talk. How sweet." Very interesting, but she didn't have time to think about Bruce right now—she had a single reason for making this trip to Queens, and they weren't answering her question. "Where's Noel?"

"Gone," said Jack.

"Right. We don't know where he is."

"How can you not know? He was here this morning."

"True, the Don had his eye on him this morning," said Evan. "The crew was set up outside here while we were in Judge Brick's part getting the warrants signed, and he filled us in when we arrived."

"Then he must have seen Noel leaving. Didn't anyone tail him?"

"He left with Niño out the back door, sometime around one o'clock, we're not sure exactly when. We didn't set up in the back because the alley is too narrow and doesn't provide any cover, so we lost the tail. A customer was banging on the front door before we realized they'd closed shop and locked up. About 1:30 or so we entered—had to break the lock, but Judge Brick gave us that authority in the warrant."

"Did you check his apartment?"

"We've got someone watching it. As of ten minutes ago he hadn't shown up. We don't think he'll be going home, not for a while anyway."

Dana was numb. Did this mean he was aiding Domingo? She was trying to raise the courage to ask Evan if he suspected as much when Jack cut off the opportunity.

"Listen, you two," she said, glancing at her watch. "I'm making a final round here, then going back to the office. We've been here, what? Forty-five minutes, an hour? Still no coke or narcotics records."

Dana mentally checked her own timetable. She'd left the hospital about a half hour ago. She must have been calling an empty store after Noel had gone, but possibly also after the investigators had entered with the warrant. What would she have done if a detective had answered the phone?

"I'm surprised Bruce called me on this one," continued Jack.

"Hey, you can't accuse him of keeping *everything* from you," said Evan with a crooked grin.

"I take that back. Maybe I'm not so surprised. He's good at keeping me up to date on things that waste my time. I'll be sure to thank him personally for the invitation."

"Here comes the Don now," said Evan, nodding toward the detective making a beeline toward them from the back of the store. "You might want to check with him before you go, just in case he found anything new."

Detective Paul Donegan, halfway between them and the back office, seemed to notice Dana for the first time and paused mid-step, but the hesitation was gone almost as soon as she remarked it. She guessed he'd been the first one on the team to find out about her connection to the people in this store. Meeting her here would be awkward for him, she knew, but he wasn't about to let it interfere with his job.

"Dana," he said when he'd joined them, tilting his head toward her by way of greeting. His forehead was pink around the gray, thinning hairline. He coughed, hand to mouth, then spoke. "Nothing much new to report from the last fifteen minutes. I'd say we've about exhausted the possibilities."

"Any cash yet?" asked Evan.

"No. Even the cash register was cleaned out. Niño ran off with about fifty-seven-odd grand when we add the money he usually deposits on Friday with the cash he picked up today.

There's some duct tape stuck on the back of the toilet tank, so we think he might have been hiding it there. We figured the amount from the two faxes he received this morning. He was in a hurry to get out of here and left the messages behind, but there's nothing else from an earlier date in there." He motioned toward the back office.

"That's another thing that helps Noel, correct?" asked Jack with a quick, oblique look at Dana.

"Right," said the Don. "Seems that Niño was pretty good about destroying or hiding the faxes once they came in."

"Not good for us," said Evan. "Evidence-wise that is."

"Sure, well, we're hoping something will turn up at his apartment. I'll make a stop over there in a few minutes and see what Gilbert and his crew found so far. Some of these couriers hang onto the messages they receive, figuring they're a kind of insurance. He could have the faxes stashed somewhere, and they'll have information about the pickup locations and accounts."

"But they'll be in code, assuming you find them."

"Nothing we can't handle." He smiled and coughed. "Put the instruction together with a surveillance and, bam, there ya go."

"I don't suppose you expect to find anything about kilo deliveries?" Jack inquired in a blasé tone.

"Nah. Doubt it."

"Okay, that's it for me," she announced. "Can't get my fix here, so I'm gone." She saluted with two fingers, took a step toward the front door, but stopped next to Dana. "Let me just say this before I go." Jack leveled her gaze at each one of them in turn, ending with Dana, where she left her eyes. "I just learned about all of this—the bookstore, the Avendaños, the works—at ten o'clock this morning. Dana, if you'd been assigned to Special Narcotics under my supervision, I would've handled this differently. And I'm not talking about the decision to go in with the search warrants this afternoon. The plan isn't working out so hot, but—"

"Hey, we've gotten some valuable information," defended Evan.

"And tipped off a few bad guys in the process, but sure, I'm not faulting Bruce for this. It was a legitimate tactical decision and could have gone either way. I'm talking about the other thing, and you know what I mean, Dana. You *all* know what I mean."

"Bruce had his reasons," said Evan. "I didn't know about it very long before you, Jack," he flashed a look at Dana. "It was Friday, late. And I didn't agree with his reasons either, but—"

"But *I* would have done it differently. That's all I'm saying. Dana, if you ever need to talk about anything, you know where to find me. You've got my shoulder to lean on," she patted it, "but you might have to bend down a little to get to it." She released a robust laugh that pulled a smile from Dana, and with a final wave, she was gone.

Dana turned to Evan. "I'd better go too. Melanie needs someone with her right now."

"Yes, you should go." Evan was looking at her in a way that reestablished their connection as the Don drifted off without a goodbye, called away by one of the men he was supervising.

"What should I tell her—about Noel? He's absolutely not involved...you have to know he's not involved in any of this. He couldn't be."

"No, I know that, but actually, to be fair Dana, I can't say the possibility has been excluded entirely. No, wait!" He held up a hand against her incipient protest. "We don't think he's involved and we're assuming as much. If you think about it, the Cartel can't possibly lure every honest person over to its side, or even threaten them all into cooperation. They do it in a way that looks legit, just so they can set up more bank accounts to dump the narcotics money. We think that's what happened here, without Noel's knowledge. If there was any bad guy it was Domingo, or maybe he was just a stupid kid looking to make a few bucks and got in over his head." Evan paused and rubbed his forehead. "But, to be honest, it doesn't look good for Noel, taking off like this..."

"He's not running because he's guilty. There must be another reason. Maybe he's scared."

"You're right. We're exploring the possibilities. The second fax Domingo received today contained a threat. The Cartel was onto him for not making his deposits. There was a veiled reference to an Avendaño relative in Colombia. The message was partly in code, and we don't understand all of it yet. But Domingo might've been so scared that he confessed everything to Noel, who decided to help him out. Not a wise move, but understandable given the family relationship. Or maybe Domingo forced him to come along as a means of protection. We're hoping Cartel operatives didn't pick them up."

"What do you mean, 'pick them up'?"

Evan took a deep breath and placed both hands on her shoulders. "They don't take kindly to couriers who try to get over on them."

"So, they're out to hurt Domingo."

"Or worse."

Dana looked at the floor and shook her head. "I don't think I'll tell Melanie that part."

Evan removed his hands. "Not yet anyway. Let's see if we find them."

She raised her eyes to his again. "If you get any information about Noel, will you call me? I'll be with Melanie."

"Sure."

She pulled a notepad from her purse, wrote down the main number for the hospital, and ripped out the page. "They've probably transferred her out of emergency, but the operator will know the room."

"Okay."

"I have to go do this now."

"I understand."

"We'll have to deal with everything else later."

"Okay."

She started for the door.

"Dana?"

She turned to face him.

"At the office—it won't be as bad as you think. Trust me."

On the way back to the hospital, she tried to compose a few gentle words that would lessen the impact of her awful news. But the distraction was too great. A string of ugly scenarios buzzed in her head—all the humiliating possibilities.

Bruce, Evan, the Don, Gilbert, and Joe—some or all of them— had been talking about her behind her back. When had it started? As early as the first day? *Paul, see what you can find out about Dana's friend, Melanie Avendaño.* Or later? Very likely they'd tailed Niño to Libros NOMEL, got the name of the owner, and figured it out from there. *Noel Avendaño? Sounds familiar.* Bruce's one-track mind would have remembered the name of Dana's "connection" at First City.

And after that, something worse—the investigators probably tailed Niño to her apartment or on his dates with Cheryl. The Don's jaw must have dropped at that one. *Wow—what's Bruce gonna say about this?*

A fine topic for whispering and intrigue. If Evan had been in charge, he would have confronted her directly to ask what she knew. A straightforward, honest approach. Jack would have handled it the same way—if she'd been let in on the secrets.

But they'd been kept out of the loop. The entire sneak attack must have been engineered by Bruce, possibly with the Don's help.

It smacked of the way Bruce thought: If we confront her, she'll just protect her friends. To get at the truth, we have to set the bait. Let's keep that surveillance photo of Niño out in the open. Make her ask the Hanniger exec about Saludos Limitada. See if she squirms. Oh, and here's a good one. Put Saludos on a list and ask her to fax it to Melanie Avendaño. See if she jumps at that one. Will she come to us then and confess everything? Or will she run and hide?

Not very different from her own tactics. Hold back what you know, lay a few hints about your suspicions, and trick your best friend into spilling the truth, whatever that might be—a full confession of guilt or a full defense, not to be believed without supporting evidence of innocence. Presumed guilty. Dana's tactics. The same as Reichert's.

Turning to look out the train window, she gazed beyond the patchwork of bleak rooftops in Queens to a world apart from the commuters surrounding her. Now, more than ever, she understood the extent of the damage she had wrought. What would it take to restore her relationship with Melanie? Every action or inaction, every word out of her mouth would be doubted.

What could she say to comfort a woman who had lost her baby and now faced the disappearance of her husband? Hiding the facts would only make things worse. Dana would have to be truthful but compassionate, optimistic without being unrealistic. She didn't know if this was wise or if she was even capable of the task.

Above all, she would assure Melly of her loyalty to Noel should any of her colleagues harbor lingering doubts as to his innocence. And more than that, she would stick by Melly's side in this time of illness and distress—but only if she was needed or wanted.

18 »   RETURNS

MELANIE WAS INCONSOLABLE, one minute telling Dana to go away, the next minute clinging to her. The clinging eventually won out. Luckily, they had privacy. She'd been transferred from emergency to a double room, the second bed unoccupied.

At about five o'clock the phone rang. Dana answered it, grateful for the interruption. Evan's voice came over calm and gently optimistic. He had good news, but not the news they were hoping for.

After Dana had left the store, investigators found a memo, handwritten in Spanish. It was headed: "May 16, 1988, By Facsimile, To: Guillermo Restrepo, Saludos Ltda, From: Noel Avendaño, Libros NOMEL." After many scribbled lines and cross-outs, the final draft was roughly translated: "We no longer wish to continue our business relationship. Please remove your merchandise and fax machine from Libros NOMEL as soon as possible. If they are not removed within three days, we will arrange to ship them to you."

The Don assured Evan that a Cartel subordinate would never direct this kind of simple, straightforward message to his superiors. The tone was too pure and the content too literal to be anything other than what it appeared to be—the effort of an honest man to disassociate himself from a bad element.

The new evidence spoke well for Noel, if indeed it had been

written by him. Evan suggested that, when Melanie was feeling up to it, she should bring samples of Noel's handwriting to the DA's office, to compare with the memo. She would be the best witness to identify his handwriting until, of course, Noel showed up.

Until Noel showed up. The words assumed the inevitability of the outcome, conveying an optimism that Dana passed on to Melanie. The corners of her mouth turned up slightly, lifting her gray, sunken cheeks and putting a spark into her dull eyes, now puffy from crying.

Soon after Evan's call, Melanie's parents, Mr. and Mrs. Vanderveer, arrived from New Jersey, overshadowing Dana's presence with their fretful demonstrations of concern. The mother was a plump woman who lavished love on her Melly with grandiose gestures and a large voice. The father was a fit, energetic man who incessantly questioned his daughter about the procedures and medications and tests she'd been subjected to.

Dana remembered them from better times, jolly and easygoing people, yet intensely protective when it came to their only child. Melanie was happy to see them but certainly not strong enough to endure the burden of their unreserved grief and worry, making it just as well when a nurse entered the room to administer medication and suggested they leave for a time to allow her some rest.

When they stepped into the hallway, the parents suddenly focused on Noel's absence and asked Dana about it. She explained in generalities as best she could, a trying task met with their incomprehension and rapid-fire questions. Dana reminded herself she was sparing Melanie the trouble of telling this story, but by the time she was through, she was very much in need of rest herself. At eight o'clock, she abandoned her bedside post to Mom and Dad, who planned to stay the night. If all went well, Melanie would be sent home the next day.

When she got home, Dana fell into bed fully clothed, allowing long-absent sleep to wash over her. Fear, despair and tension could keep her awake only for so long—she hadn't slept more than a few hours in the last three days. Her slumber was black and paralyzing.

Near midnight she almost missed the ringing telephone on her bedside table. It started as a distant sound inside the deep well of her dream, gradually rising to the surface.

The initiator of the call didn't give up. "I'm sorry to wake you," Evan said when she finally picked up, her voice rough with sleep.

"Has something happened?" she asked.

"Yes, something I thought you should know. Something important."

She sat up in bed, tugging at her crumpled business skirt which was hiked up to the top of her thighs. The bedside clock said 11:55. This was not a dream. This was Evan, usually so light and upbeat, calling her in the middle of the night, sounding strangely intense and dark. "They found Noel?"

"No, they haven't. He hasn't returned to his apartment or the store. He's still out there somewhere."

"Then...Domingo?"

"Yes. Domingo. They found his body just an hour ago, in an abandoned apartment in Queens. He was murdered...execution style. A large caliber bullet in the temple at close range. The time of death is estimated between one and three this afternoon."

Dana could say nothing.

"You going to be okay?" he asked.

Silence.

After a moment she said, "So what does this mean for Noel? They weren't together, so he must have gotten away. He must be all right."

"That's one possibility."

"I think I'll hope for that one."

"Me too." Evan paused, as if waiting for more questions, reluctant to hang up. "Am I going to see you at the office tomorrow?"

The office. Tomorrow was Tuesday, just another workday. It seemed impossible to return to the place that had spawned a game of cat and mouse, manipulated her perceptions, and now held sway over her future, both personal and professional.

"I suppose I have to face Bruce sometime."

"Keep an open mind and listen to what he says."

"Right. It won't be as bad as I think."

"I couldn't have said it better myself."

They said their good-nights, and Dana was left alone, cloaked in a different reality tinged with blood and fright. A boy she'd invited to her home only a few weeks ago was now dead, murdered. A nineteen-year-old boy.

What had been going through his mind when he became a courier for the Cartel? Was he just a dumb kid, enticed by the money, unaware of the ruthless power of these men? Or was he fully keyed in, more devious than he appeared? Devious and knowing perhaps, yet stupidly overconfident, thinking he could pull one over on them, making a fatal mistake.

She doubted that Melly and Noel had really known him very well, and now that he was gone, they would never fully understand him. Maybe, in the final hours of Domingo's life, Noel had learned a few things about his cousin. They would all know more when Noel returned.

Images of Domingo, his handsome face pierced and bloody, kept her awake until finally, in the hour before dawn, a light sleep tugged her into a brief oblivion. She would not achieve perfect and complete rest again until Noel was found.

* * *

In the morning, early, she went to the hospital. The news had to be delivered in person, not over the phone.

The elder Vanderveers were disheveled and bleary eyed from their night on the uncomfortable chairs crammed into the small space at bedside. Dana sat on the edge of the bed, and in the calmest voice she could muster, with compassion, repeated the little bit of information Evan had given her. She was aware of the tiny tremor in her lower lip as she spoke.

Mrs. Vanderveer reacted vocally, and her husband tried to calm her while Melly blanched and gasped softly, remaining quiet and pale with shock. Her mother wailed, filling the air with declarations of doom. What kind of animal would do such a thing? What now must they imagine of Noel's fate?

Dana silently examined the subtle changes in Melly's features, betraying a mind at work. She was absorbing the devastating news and moving on to a small negotiation. Her baby had been taken. Domingo had been murdered. With these deaths, she would strike a bargain with the unseen powers of reason and order. She'd made her sacrifice, and now, she should receive something in return. Noel must be returned to her, safe and sound.

Seeing a faint light growing in Melly's eyes, Dana said, "I think we have hope…"

"Yes, we do."

All four of them lapsed into a moment of silence broken by a sniffle from Melanie's mother, who pulled a tissue from her purse and used it noisily.

Dana stood and said, "I'm sorry everyone, but I can't avoid the office any longer. I have to get back."

"Go on. I'm okay. If the doctor lets me out of here this afternoon, Mom and Dad will take me home." The parents smiled broadly, indicating their desire and willingness to take over. In a way, for the time being, their only daughter had returned to them.

"And besides," said Melanie, "at the office, you'll be a bigger help to me, and…"

And a help to Noel. Dana caught her look and knew exactly what she meant, knew that Melanie still had faith in her loyalty, maybe even a stronger faith because it was something she needed right now. Dana would meet her faith with a renewed, undivided commitment.

"Call me the minute you hear anything. Even the smallest thing, anything at all."

"I will. You know I will."

As if in a time warp, Dana made tracks straight from her subway stop to the state court building that housed Trial Bureau 90, across the street from the Criminal Court building where most of the DA's offices and bureaus, including FC, were located. Stepping off the elevator at the fifth floor, she savored the familiar, cleaner air of this isolated enclave, removed from the bustle of the larger building.

The corridor from the elevator to TB 90 looked and felt the same as it always had, acquaintances along the way acknowledging her with a smile or a wave as if they hadn't noticed her absence. In this rush of sensory input, all second nature, she mentally skipped the preceding month. This wasn't a return after an absence. It was a Tuesday morning, just another workday in TB 90. Dana had a problem, and when she had a problem, she always sought out her bureau chief, Patrick McBride.

Her instincts led the way. She hadn't thought much about it beforehand. She could have gone to any of the other senior attorneys on the team, people with excellent judgment and years of experience. Jack was the first to come to mind, the woman who'd offered her shoulder. But Dana didn't need a shoulder to lean on and didn't simply wish to commiserate with another person who'd been wronged by Bruce Reichert. She needed objectivity and feared that no one else on the team could provide it, not Joe, Evan, or the Don, not even the distant George Blaithe.

Patrick was the only choice. She went to him now automatically, like in the old days when she would stride into his office with a troublesome misdemeanor case in hand, contained on a few sheets of paper inside a manila folder. She wished the case she now carried in her head and heart could be as easily enclosed and summarized and disposed of.

At the glass door to TB 90, the receptionist buzzed her in. "Hi Dana! How's everything in FC?"

"Fine. Just great. Nice to see you!" She didn't linger, hoping that further encounters would be kept to a minimum if she quickly made her way down the long hall to Patrick's office. She hadn't factored this part in—seeing the familiar faces, imagining the effect they would have on her and the difficulty of engaging in light chitchat, hoping her trembling lips and moist eyes wouldn't give her away.

She nodded and waved to a few others with a smile etched on her face while maintaining an assertive pace. But up ahead, standing in the middle of the corridor, were two people she couldn't ignore quite so easily. Eric and Jared.

Dana's former TPA took one look at her and brightened. "Dana! You're back from the dead!"

She paused and beamed a frozen smile at them. "Hey guys, what's new?"

"Same old thing," said Jared. He readjusted his gaze to scrutinize her face more carefully. "Say, what are those idiots in FC doing to you?"

She shrugged, forced a laugh and said, "We'll have to catch up later." She stepped out past them, saying, "I can't really talk now—have to see Patrick."

"I knew it. She's coming back, Denz!"

"Stay here with us, Dorothy," said Jared in his best Cowardly Lion voice. "We all love ya!" Looking back over her shoulder, she gave a genuine laugh this time and moved on.

Patrick's door was open a sliver. She peeked through. He was on the phone, sitting sideways to his desk. She knocked on the frosty glass pane and pushed the door open another few inches. Still talking into the receiver, Patrick looked up and pulled her in with a beckoning motion. Inside, she closed the door behind her, crept forward and sat in a chair across from him at the desk.

He soon finished his conversation, replaced the receiver, and swiveled around to face her head on. "Dana. It's good to see you. We miss you here." He smiled and said nothing more, waiting for her. His words, as always, seemed to reflect his thoughts exactly, consistent with his demeanor and facial expressions. Nothing hidden or disingenuous about him. And so, she believed he was happy to see her and that she had been missed.

She also remarked the absence of other trite openers: "How are things in FC?" or "What can I do for you?" Perhaps he'd been expecting her visit. Everything that was about to happen in this conversation between them was to be initiated by her.

"Patrick, I'm sorry to bother you, but I need your help on something. Your opinion, is what I mean." She halted sooner than she expected, already breathless, and swallowed to release some of the tension in her throat.

"I hope I can help." He fell silent and waited, making it more difficult.

"I don't quite know where I stand in FC, and I'm afraid I've made some bad decisions. Things that involve the professional code of ethics and my oath as a prosecutor." There. She'd gotten the worst out. Anything could be imagined from that.

Patrick scrunched his brow in serious thought. "Does it have to do with your acquaintance, the man who's a target of the investigation?" And there it was, *his* worst, but he'd gotten it out with a face that looked unchanged from the effort. His tone was calm and matter-of-fact. He wasn't ashamed to possess this information about her.

She was surprised at her own reaction to this revelation. She was not ashamed that he knew, nor was she shocked at his knowledge. It made sense. "What did Bruce tell you?"

"I assume you're now aware of everything he knows."

"Correct."

"Then I see no harm in relating our conversation. He came to me sometime last week and explained that a target of the investigation had been tailed to your apartment and a few days later was seen at a restaurant with your sister. Bruce had learned that the suspect was related to close friends of yours, a married couple, who weren't targets of the investigation and likely were unaware of the suspect's crimes. He gave quite a bit more detail than this, but I'm sure you know the story."

"Yes, but I wasn't aware that Bruce knew all of this until yesterday."

"He told me as much. His purpose in seeing me was to test his theory of your involvement—or rather, lack of involvement. He wanted to talk to me as someone who'd known you professionally for a longer time than he had. A character reference, basically. His intuition was that you knew nothing of this person's crimes and weren't even aware that he was a suspect. Your acquaintance with him was a mere coincidence, based on your relationship with his relatives. I agreed with Bruce wholeheartedly that this was the most likely interpretation. Number one," Patrick hooked his index finger with that of the other hand, "you're impeccably honest, and number two," he hooked his middle finger, "you would've told Bruce of a possible conflict of interest if you knew that your acquaintance was a criminal suspect."

Dana's eyes fell to her hands before she forced herself to look up and meet Patrick's steady gaze. "That's just it. Number two. When I figured out that Domingo was a suspect, I didn't tell Bruce, or anyone, right away."

"How long did you wait?"

"I figured it out last Friday evening. And, actually, I still haven't talked to Bruce about it. You see, Domingo is dead. He was murdered yesterday afternoon, and I heard the news last night."

Patrick's eyelids fluttered and he briefly glanced away. "I hadn't heard."

"Yes, well that isn't my excuse for not telling. My excuse, if you could call it that, seems inadequate to me now. I was certain I had to make a decision between my job or my friends, the married couple, Melanie and Noel. As of last Friday, I knew very little of the evidence, but when I started putting it together, I began to suspect they were involved. I was acting like a prose-cutor, not their friend. I was aware of two or three suspicious facts, and I decided I needed more facts to determine whether they were guilty of a crime. I ignored everything I knew about them, all my years of knowing them, in favor of a surveillance photograph and a bank subpoena and my imagination." Her lip started to quiver, and she had to stop, internally steeling the muscles of her face against the emotion.

"My God, this has been hard on you."

"I suppose...yes, it *has* been hard. I didn't want to be placed in the position of being used as a witness against my friends. So, instead of going to Bruce, I felt I had to test my suspicions. I wanted to find out more from Melanie, to figure out if she and her husband were involved, before I decided what to do. My doubt about her caused Melanie terrible pain. I know now what a big mistake I made as far as she and Noel are concerned..."

"I'm sorry."

"Now I'm doing the best I can to make amends. Meanwhile,

as I say, I haven't gone to Bruce, but I'm planning to see him right away. I just wanted to stop here first to…"

Patrick looked at her straight on, waiting attentively with his hands on the desk, fingers interlaced. Why *had* she stopped by? With his years of experience, Patrick could clearly see through her façade to the core of her ethical dilemma. He could supply both the question and the answer. But he wasn't volunteering his opinion or advice—she would have to work it through for herself. "I guess I came here to test my thoughts about the conflict of interest problems. I know it's not right for me to be involved in an investigation against an acquaintance or a friend. But now that Domingo is dead…well, we can't prosecute a dead man."

"Correct. Your conflict of interest died when he did."

"And for the period of time I knew about him, from Friday through Monday, nothing different happened in the investigation because of my relationship to him. I didn't make any investigative decisions affecting him. So, I guess I can safely say I didn't violate the professional code."

"That sounds about right."

"But what about Noel and Melanie? They won't be prosecuted, but the money laundering scheme involved Noel's bookstore. They could be witnesses in a prosecution, and it's awkward. I don't know if it technically violates any ethics rules, but it doesn't look quite right."

"That gray area. 'The appearance of impropriety.'"

"Right. I can just see a defense attorney trying to imply I've influenced witness testimony with my personal relationships."

"But you could handle that." Patrick winked.

"I suppose I could. So, there's really no reason I can't go back to FC, back to the Cartel investigation…" Her voice trailed under the burden of unspoken thoughts, the raw emotion unrelated to the law or professional ethics. She lacked a compelling justification to beg out of the Cartel investigation, and maybe she'd come to Patrick hoping he could supply one. But now, at the end of her reasoning process, he'd offered nothing new. She had no real reason..."except that it's so difficult to go back now after what happened, the way Bruce handled it." She didn't attempt to mask the bitterness in her voice and eyes.

Patrick gave her a look full of understanding. "It must have been tough to learn that he knew all about it without telling you."

She nodded agreement. "It's especially tough because I realize I was acting just like him. I was going to interrogate Melanie and try to squeeze all the facts out of her without revealing what I knew about her and Noel. It wasn't fair, and I don't like myself for it."

"I wouldn't be so hard on yourself. We have to do a lot of squeezing in this business."

"Sure, we have to act like we have a stack of evidence against suspects when we question them. But that isn't the way to treat friends. Or colleagues."

Patrick raised his hands like he was under arrest. "Then I guess I'm guilty too!"

Dana smiled, and he dropped his hands. "I'm not blaming you for anything," she said. "After everything that's happened, I wasn't surprised when you said Bruce told you about it. I don't see this as your obligation or responsibility."

"Thank you for that, Dana. As you can see, even bosses get caught in these conflicting obligations to job and friends." Dana smiled broadly, glad to have a friend in her former boss. Patrick continued, "He came to me asking for confidence until the matter was out in the open, and I felt obliged to promise it. My word is my word. But I did try to persuade him to confront you directly with the information he had. As the supervising attorney on your case, it was his call. He saw it differently than I did."

"I think most people would have seen it differently."

"Well, now, not that I'm going to stick up for everything he did, but he had some valid reasons for handling it his way. He could have started an internal investigation and ruined your future professional life with the specter of that investigation over your head. These things are supposed to be kept secret, but invariably they get out, and no one is quite the same afterward regardless of the outcome. After the internal investigation cleared you, the temptation would have been to take advantage of your personal relationships and use you to gather evidence about your friends. But he didn't want any of that. He fully believed in your innocence and decided to wait and see what came from you. Just let the investigation run its course and give you the opportunity to establish your innocence through your behavior. That's the kind of irrefutable proof you can't come up with once you're accused and put on the defensive."

A moment of silence fell between them as Dana absorbed Patrick's words. "I see your point, but it still doesn't feel right."

"Because Bruce Reichert is Bruce Reichert?"

She felt a prick of shock at Patrick's first open allusion to Reichert's odious personality. Her eyebrows may have risen in surprise, but she nodded slowly in agreement.

"All I can say is," Patrick continued, "I have respect for the man and his judgments. He called you right. And he told me he wanted to keep you on his team. In the month you've worked for him, he's come to respect you and appreciate your abilities. He could have come to me and said, 'Take this rookie back—she's nothing but trouble.' But he was looking for ways to keep you on, ways to avoid the conflict if he could."

"All right. I appreciate you telling me all this. Still, it would be difficult to work for him now, after everything that's happened. I haven't decided yet if I can continue to be effective on the Cartel investigation."

"I think you have a right to choose. But don't let me encourage you to stay in FC!" he warned with a gleam in his eye.

"Eric's been keeping your seat warm for you. He sits behind your desk from time to time, just to absorb your lingering aura."

Their eyes locked and shone together. "I'll keep that in mind," she said with a grin.

"And the rest of us would like to see you back too."

As Dana stepped out of Patrick's office, she felt calmer and empowered with the knowledge he would take her back willingly. Perhaps that was one of the reasons she had sought him out—to explore her options. She had choices and wasn't beholden to Bruce Reichert. Everything was up to her. She could shape her own professional life, a moral right she had believed in all along, she realized now. Patrick had recognized and affirmed it.

Making her way across the street, she thought of Patrick's comfortable face and how easy it was to talk to him. He listened and allowed her to pose and answer her own questions in a way that hardly made her realize it. A good boss. It would be so easy to go back to him and her old cache of officemates.

She walked into FC at about eleven thirty, almost exactly twenty-four hours after she'd left for lunch the day before. So much had happened in a single day that she felt like a weary climber of Everest, returning to Base One, still not home.

Not seeing Evan or Mineko on the way, and without stopping at the Closet, Dana walked directly to Bruce's door and knocked. "Come in," he yelled from behind the closed door.

When she stepped in, he looked up from paperwork on his desk, his thick eyebrows lifted high over those pebbles for eyes. He looked at his watch and back at her. "You're late," he said with a small, twitching smile. Unusual. She could swear he was attempting a joke, something to lighten the air.

"Sorry," she said, closing the door behind her. She approached the desk and sat across from him, still feeling uncomfortably close despite the large expanse of cluttered desktop between them. "I'm not just late. I'm very late. I should have come to talk to you yesterday morning."

"Why yesterday?"

Could he not know why? But of course, he was waiting for her to explain. He still didn't know when she had made her discovery about Domingo.

"On Friday, after the meeting with Quitman, and later when we were talking about the case, something about Saludos jogged my memory. That evening, after you were gone, I put things together and figured out that Domingo was 'Niño.' I suppose I should have told you yesterday morning that I knew a suspect in the investigation. But I started worrying that my friends might also be considered suspects."

"And you didn't know whether coming to me would betray your friends?"

"That's part of it." She couldn't explain it all in detail again. The worst part, from Reichert's perspective, was encompassed by the question he had asked.

"You know you were skating the line here? You could have seriously hurt this investigation, not to mention your career." He delivered this terse lecture like the report of a machine gun.

"I realize that now," said Dana. "As it turned out though, investigative goals weren't compromised. But the best thing would have been to deal with it out in the open. Immediately."

Did he pick up her innuendo? Nothing in his face registered it. She wouldn't hint around any longer. Now, at last, was the time for openness. "Maybe I'm a little late, but I think you're a lot later. You should have told me what you knew when you first learned it. Everything could have been explained. Melanie and Noel didn't know what Domingo was up to, and they aren't guilty of any crime. But the way you handled it was very unfair to me and nearly cost me important friendships."

Reichert's small eyes expanded to their widest extent in surprise at her bluntness. His mouth groped for words before finding them. "I'm sorry things turned out this way for you. When I was first confronted with your possible conflict, I had some hard choices to make. I assumed the best and hoped you would do nothing to disprove my assumption. You didn't disprove it, but the way events unfolded, you weren't given a proper opportunity to come to me. I don't hold it against you. I can understand your concern for your friends. Maybe you don't agree with the way I handled it—other people on this team certainly didn't—but you should know that the decision was made with your best interests in mind. I hope you don't hold it against me."

Dana forced a smile, not knowing quite how to respond. It was a relief to hear this new forthrightness and honesty, but it didn't seem like enough. Why wasn't it enough?

Bruce felt the silence and groped for words again. "At least ...please accept my apology."

Dana considered. This was what she wanted from him. Her eyes searched his and saw the person behind them. "Okay. I accept your apology."

"Good."

With this out of the way, they both understood what the next item on the agenda ought to be. Reichert took the initiative. "Your work here has been good," he said. "I hope you'll want to continue on and see the investigation through the entire process of indictment, trial and conviction. Technically, I don't think we'll be violating any rules if you stay on the team. I understand Evan told you about Domingo?"

She nodded and asked, "Do you have any news about Noel?"

"Nothing yet."

She pursed her lips hard against the worry that continued to gnaw at her. "I appreciate your wanting me to stay on, but I'm afraid it would be very difficult. I know you'll still be looking into matters that affect my friends, including what went on at Noel's bookstore and with the Saludos account."

"You're correct about that." He sighed deeply and sank down into his chair, as if resigned to a losing battle about something that, to Dana's surprise, seemed to matter to him. "I know McBride will be very happy to have you back."

"He's told me I'm welcome to return, but I'd rather stay on in FC."

Bruce looked startled. "I thought you wanted to—"

"Yes. I have to get off the Cartel case. It just wouldn't look or feel right with my friends as potential witnesses. But I'm asking for another assignment in FC. A different case. It would be nice to build on the experience I've been getting in financial investigations and put it to use. That is, if you think I'm up to it."

"No question you're up to it. I'll talk to Blaithe about it. There's just one problem. One favor I'll have to ask."

Dana looked at him with a question in her eyes.

"The Cartel case is really heating up and it would be difficult to replace you right now. Very *unfair* to *us* if you were to leave." His eyes twinkled and Dana responded with a smile, wondering how she could possibly be sharing a joke with this man. But something had changed between them in the last few minutes. A clearing of the air. "The favor I'd ask," he said, "is for you to continue on just until the time we make arrests, maybe only a month from now. By then we should have all the bank evidence in order, and we'll have the time to find a replacement for you. And you'll be off the case if your friends are ever called as witnesses at trial. Seem fair?"

"Seems fair."

"Good." He slapped the desk with the palms of his hands. "Then we know what we gotta do." A smile flickered across his lips, and he lowered his head once again to the papers he'd been

working on when she entered. Back to the one-track mind.
Dana stood and retreated without a goodbye.

19 »   WAITING

LATER IN THE DAY, after calling McBride with her regrets and meeting with George Blaithe about a new assignment, Dana was settled in again with her pile of bank documents when Evan knocked on the doorjamb. She glanced up and gave him a tepid smile.

"I guess this means you're staying. You look thrilled."

"It's just temporary. George says he'll have another assignment for me in about a month."

"You asked to get off this case?"

"What else could I do?" she asked with a shrug and dropped her head, refocusing on the piece of paper in her hands.

"If it were me, I'd be doing the same thing."

"But it isn't you, or four hundred and forty-nine other attorneys in this office." She didn't look at him as she said this.

With her eyes still downcast, she felt him draw near and lean across her small desk. He placed an index finger under her chin and lifted it up, forcing her eyes to meet his. "No, it isn't anyone else. Just little old you." He removed his finger and coaxed a smile out of her with the grin on his face. "But it could have been anyone, and I'm sure it's happened before."

He took a step backward, closed the door, and plunked down into the chair, letting his forearms run the length of the armrests, grabbing the ends. "You can ask anyone here and they'll have a story. A defendant who sent flowers to the office with a little note, 'thanks for the great deal.' Or a friendly neighbor who turns out to be a pedophile. Or even a friend who's a victim or a witness for the DA's office. It's a huge city, but a small world."

"I can appreciate all that." She sighed. "And I'm sure I'll get past being angry about it—angry at Bruce. I guess I'm just complaining to try and keep my mind off what's really bothering me."

He knew and didn't have to ask, but he did anyway. "Noel?"

"Yes. Any word?"

"Nothing that I've heard."

"I have a feeling I'll be asking that question every hour on the hour until he shows up."

"I'll be sure to let you know anything as soon as I hear it."

They fell quiet. Evan made no move to leave. As the seconds ticked, he gradually acquired the appearance of a permanent fixture in the Closet. Dana felt no discomfort. Evan's presence always lightened the air and painted her walls white, like his own bright office. He seemed relaxed and at home, jacketless, in white shirtsleeves, his tie slightly loosened at the neck.

"You know," she said, "I'm still in the dark about a lot of things. I don't understand why Noel ran."

"Be glad to elucidate." And Evan started to tell the story of the things that had been withheld from her.

Last Friday evening, the Don and Gilbert tailed Niño from Libros NOMEL to an apartment building, a stash location, where he apparently picked up some cash. Later, as he approached the night deposit box at First City, he seemed to spot the tail and panicked, walking away without making the deposit. The investigators tailed him to Cheryl's apartment, where he stayed for about twenty minutes.

"Did you know about that?" he asked.

"Yes, I did. Domingo left Cheryl's place when she started talking about me, telling him I was a prosecutor investigating money crimes. He never knew exactly what I did for a living before that."

"No wonder the visit was short. You realize we'll be calling Cheryl in for questioning?"

"I thought as much. It's not a surprise. Is it all right if I prepare her for the shock?"

"Sure."

"I still haven't told her about Domingo. I'll lay everything on her at once."

"Okay." Evan continued. After they tailed Niño for most of the evening, it became clear he wasn't going to make the deposit, possibly because he still feared being watched. When a target gets nervous, he's likely to abandon the criminal scheme or destroy evidence or both. The Don wasn't sure what Domingo would do. He might inform his superiors, or he might disappear. They had to consider searching his apartment and Libros NOMEL to preserve evidence.

But the team faced a typical dilemma. To search or not to search. The lesser of two evils had to be chosen: if they didn't search, they risked the destruction of useful evidence; if they searched, they risked tipping off the bigger criminals, who would feel the heat and destroy more evidence or change their mode of operation.

The Don called Bruce at home late Friday night, and a decision was made to prepare applications for search warrants over the weekend. They planned to tail Domingo Monday morning, and if it was business as usual, they wouldn't search. But if he'd disappeared or wasn't making his Monday deposits, they would be ready to go in with the warrants. In favor of the search, the Don was very hot on Niño, thinking it possible that the kid, the way he was running in and out, could have been using the bookstore as a mini stash location. Plus, the Don strongly suspected the use of a fax machine since Niño didn't seem to be getting his instructions over the phone. The telephones at the bookstore and Domingo's apartment had been monitored with pen registers that recorded the numbers of all incoming and outgoing calls. There was nothing remarkable about the phone activity.

"Wait a minute," Dana stopped him. "You had court-ordered pens on these phones? For how long?"

"About ten days or so. But remember, Dana. I had no idea about your relationship with the Avendaños until Friday. I knew all about Niño and the store and everything else, but not about you. Bruce didn't want to spread it around. He had to change his mind on Friday when we were considering the warrants, so he called me at home Friday night, told me the story, and asked me to come in on Saturday."

"I never knew anything about the pens."

"I wasn't hiding them. It just never came up in our conversations."

Dana pushed the shock of this new revelation aside and let Evan finish the story.

Bruce weighed the options and decided it made sense to execute the warrants. They stood to recover forfeitable cash plus a fax machine and hard copies of faxed messages that could help the team understand the way the orders were given. The downside wasn't risky for the continued sanctity of the investigation. Bruce believed they wouldn't tip their hand much. This business with Niño, Jefe and Saludos had been a diversion from the main thrust of the investigation—the identification of "Rojo."

The FC team now believed that Rojo was a code name for an entire money distribution unit within the Cali Cartel, headed by a couple of powerful managers who oversaw the flow of money through hundreds of smurf accounts. The Rojo unit was entrusted with the cash proceeds generated from kilo sales made by one of the cocaine distribution units. The team had no reason to believe that Jefe's group, which ran a scheme to infiltrate legitimate businesses, was directly connected with Cartel employees in the Rojo group, which laundered cash through the smurf accounts. So, the reasoning went, a lot of police activity at Libros NOMEL wouldn't necessarily cause alarm within Rojo.

Monday morning, Judge Brick signed the warrants, authorizing a break-in if necessary. The team sent new investigators to tail Niño all morning; they didn't want him to recognize the Don and Gilbert in the brown sedan they'd used to tail him on Friday night.

Niño arrived at Noel's store about nine thirty and left a few minutes later, went to the usual stash location, and made a pickup. The rest of the morning he loitered here and there, not visiting any banks, finally returning to the bookstore at about twelve thirty. Something was up. The team was made ready.

Meanwhile, Bruce called Jack to tell her of the plan. He didn't want to alienate her any further on the outside chance the team had misinterpreted the clues and Niño was somehow involved with kilo shipments. Of course, as it turned out, Jack thought her time was wasted, and as a result, Bruce had further mending to do on the FC-SNB relationship.

Bookstore business was slow that day. A few customers were in the store when Niño returned at twelve thirty. Those customers left shortly after one. The team prepared to go in, awaiting the signal from the Don.

"What about Noel and Domingo? What was the plan...?"

Evan gave her a knowing look. "We were only going to arrest Domingo...unless we found something in the store..."

"...to give you probable cause as to Noel."

"Right."

Just then, a prospective customer walked up and tried the door. It was locked. The customer knocked, put a hand to the glass pane, and peered in before walking away. This was something new. The team had never seen Noel close the store in the middle of the day and thought it possible he was still inside with the door locked. They sent a few uniforms to the back while the rest of the team went in through the front, knocking and calling out first, then breaking the lock. No one inside. In the time between making the decision to go in and seeing the new customer at the door, Noel and Domingo had left out the back, their trail gone cold.

The search yielded very little and did nothing to confirm the Don's theory about the bookstore as a possible stash house. They found two faxed messages, both cryptic and in code. The first was an instruction to pick up $48,000 from the usual stash location and split it among seven bank accounts. The second was a threat about Domingo's failure to make the Friday deposit of $8,900, with a reference to "Tio Carlos" in Colombia. Possibly a relative of the Avendaños, but they didn't know if he was a Cartel operative or a potential victim, a way to get leverage over Niño. The Don believed Niño had panicked so badly he left these two faxes behind unintentionally. He'd been diligent about destroying or hiding all previous faxes—the search of his apartment yielded nothing.

The time stamp showed that Domingo received the second message, the threatening one, when he returned to the store. The current theory was that he became fearful enough to tell Noel about it and to demand his help. Motivated by their family connection, Noel went along. Domingo's murder was an act of retribution or a warning or both.

The team didn't know why Noel wasn't killed alongside his cousin. Possibilities abounded. He might have split from Domingo and had gone into hiding. The Cartel may have kidnapped him to collect a ransom from Tio Carlos. Or Noel could have been killed at a different location.

"I don't believe in the latter possibility, but it can't be ruled out," said Evan.

"Poor Melanie." Dana shook her head.

"How is she?"

"I called the hospital a few minutes ago. She'll be going home this afternoon. I'll stop by her apartment this evening after work."

She picked up a pile of papers and started to stack them, a mindless activity to conceal a storm of emotion inside. Evan remained seated. She didn't want him to go, but neither could she face him directly.

Everything was so neatly in place for her at work. She'd had her talks with Patrick and Bruce and George, and her professional future was intact—but what about Melanie? There was nothing for her friend now but waiting and hoping.

Dana tried to focus on her hands, but her vision blurred. Tears ran down her nose and dropped onto the big green cardboard blotter on her desk. Evan stood and came around to her side of the desk, pulled her up from her chair, and took her in his arms. The feel of him so close was a shock in itself, to discover how much she desired this surrender to the consolation he offered.

She returned the hug, laying her wet cheek on his shoulder with her nose buried in the soft, white cotton shirtsleeve. Evan smelled good, like warm skin in the sun, and he felt big as a bear, enclosing and strong. They held one another until her tears soaked his shoulder. She pulled away and wiped her eyes.

"I'll let you get back to work," he said gently. He touched his damp shoulder and glanced down at it before meeting her eyes again. "A little accident at the water cooler." They both smiled.

"Thank you, Evan," she said. "Thank you for everything."

He stepped sideways around the desk and toward the door, pausing with his hand on the knob. "I'm glad you're sticking around. I was worried you might go back to 90."

He turned the knob, placed his free hand on his chest, breathed in deeply and exhaled, his eyes on hers. Swinging around the door, he backed out of the Closet, and closed the door on the way out.

After three years of sharing this apartment with Noel, Melanie now saw it for what it was. Plaster walls in need of paint, scuffed hardwood floors with worn throw rugs, furnishings squeezed into the tiny squares and rectangles, the sound of footsteps on the ceiling from the apartment above. The flip of a switch next to the front door illuminated the entry hall light, but in the living room, she had to crook her arm under the shade of the table lamp to turn a stiff knob. Why hadn't she noticed this inconvenience before? In this, their shared space, Noel overshadowed every tangible object within it.

She stepped into this apartment as if returning to the home of friends or relatives she'd visited long ago—a place vaguely remembered, each object bursting into memory as her eyes fell upon it. The presence of her parents only heightened the odd sensation. Their company reminded her that time was not recoverable. There was no going back, no chance to remake a life free of mistakes. Her mom and dad could not possibly offer what was now missing from inside these walls containing the hovering spirit of her marriage.

Her parents did everything for her, like she was their seven-year-old with the chicken pox. She loved them and was grateful but wished them gone. She wanted to be alone but equally couldn't face an empty apartment. She needed her privacy to cry but needed them here to prevent her from breaking down. She wanted Noel.

Dana called frequently, at least three times a day. Melanie was grateful for that too, but also annoyed and more anxious every time she hung up the phone. Never any news about her husband. Without any reason for it, she blamed Dana and her office for his disappearance. With shame, she turned these feelings around and began to regard Dana as her savior, the person who would ultimately bring the news of his well-being.

On the fourth day after leaving the hospital, she convinced her parents to go home, and Dana came to replace them on the convertible loveseat in the living room. The first night was a Friday night, and they stayed up late talking, "Just like college days," said Melanie through her tears. She loved and hated Dana, wanted her company and didn't want it, wished her to leave and wished her to stay forever—only until Noel returned.

She wanted and needed nothing, really, but Noel.

In the weeks that followed, Dana worked hard, caught up in the team's preparations for a massive sting to include a dozen search warrants, the indictment of some thirty individuals identified as members of the "Rojo" unit, the forfeiture of seized cash, and the attachment of dozens of smurf accounts. Forfeiture proceedings were also planned against secondary payees of money from smurf accounts, companies like Hanniger Paper.

Joe assigned some of the written work in the forfeiture case to Dana, who collaborated with Mineko analyzing and organizing the bank records, developing flow charts to follow the money. It was nice to have a female colleague within this bastion of men. The two women worked well together and kept things light with their banter and small comforts—coffee and Danish from their favorite deli in the morning, cassette tapes of gentle classical music played in the late evenings when they worked after hours.

With such intense concentration on Rojo, the team put the Avendaños, Saludos, and Jefe on the back burner. A few things were not ignored. On separate occasions, Cheryl and Melanie were called into the office and interviewed by Reichert. Dana sat in on these interviews.

Cheryl had been thrown by the news of Domingo's murder

and was no longer her carefree self. Shocked, embarrassed and ashamed of her involvement with him, she would heal in time. For now, she had nothing to add to the investigation. She'd been completely ignorant of Domingo's daily activities and criminal acts, even his thoughts and plans on the subject of money other than his clear desire to get ahead financially. Bruce didn't doubt she was telling the truth.

Melanie, often teary-eyed, related the events of the days before Noel's disappearance, including their discovery of Domingo's criminal activity after Dana requested the bank records. She supplied Bruce with copies of Noel's handwriting, which were compared to the scribbled memo found in the bookstore. Without a doubt, Noel had written it, confirming Melanie's story of his plan to send a faxed message to Restrepo in Colombia.

Melanie implored Bruce to state his belief or his best guess as to Noel's whereabouts.

"Anything is possible," he said with characteristic terseness.

"What Bruce means," interjected Dana, "is that we just don't have enough information now to make an intelligent guess. We don't want to forecast doom, but we don't want to create false hopes either."

"The worst is that he's dead, is that what you're saying?" she demanded tearfully.

"It's possible," said Bruce.

"But the best is that he's hiding, and he'll come back when it seems safe."

"Right there too."

"If you don't believe in the worst or the best—"

"We just don't know at this point," said Bruce.

"Then there's a middle ground, isn't there? Another possibility."

"Yes," said Bruce. "It's possible he's been kidnapped for

ransom or retribution or both. We don't think it's likely because they've already satisfied their vendetta against Domingo, but there's a small chance. We need your help on this. What do you know about a 'Tio Carlos'?"

"That must be Noel's uncle in Colombia," Melanie explained. "Noel always speaks highly of him. He's an entrepreneur and owns a factory that manufactures some kind of plastic products."

"Has he contacted you since Noel's disappearance?"

"No. Why?"

"He seems a likely person who could pay a ransom for Noel's return."

"You're right that he probably has money. I heard Noel and Domingo talking about it once. But he hasn't contacted me. If Noel was kidnapped, Carlos would *have* to contact me, wouldn't he? I mean, he'd have to find out from me if Noel was missing. Otherwise, he might think they're lying to him. How else could he confirm it?"

Bruce and Dana exchanged looks. They'd shared the same speculations. But there were ways the Cartel could easily prove they had Noel, and Carlos might not want to take the chance of placing Melanie in danger by contacting her. They did not repeat these theories to Melanie. Nor did they mention another theory — that Carlos himself was a Cartel operative who'd done something traitorous for which he had to pay with Noel's death or a heavy ransom.

Dana noticed that even Bruce could see the hope in Melanie's eyes and didn't want to dash it. "What you're saying makes perfect sense," he agreed. Melanie shook her head affirmatively and retreated inward with her small nugget of hope.

Bruce asked her to provide Carlos's address in Colombia and she agreed to get it for them. He told her the DA's office didn't have the jurisdiction to engage in an international investigation, but he would contact the Justice Department to see if the feds had any current information about Carlos or a possible ransom plot.

"But let me say this," Bruce said at the end of their conversation. "When everything is considered, it remains a very good possibility he will show up. Safe."

Two weeks passed, and something did turn up. A clue. At an automated teller machine upstate, cash was withdrawn from the Avendaños' joint checking account. Noel was alive!

Melanie was ecstatic but frantically impatient. Dana convinced the Don to send investigators to the town where the withdrawal had been made. Their search turned up nothing but more questions. There was no video camera at the ATM, leaving the possibility that a thief made the withdrawal with a stolen bank card. Melanie was advised not to get carried away with her hopes.

But she did.

And they all waited and hoped.

20 » DELIVERANCE

AT 8:27 ON A bright June morning, Dana heard the phone ringing even before she crossed the threshold to the Closet. She rushed in. Briefcase in right hand, she picked up with the left.

"Dana, what are you doing?" demanded Evan without a "hello."

"Drinking coffee and doing my nails. What do you think? Where are you?" She hadn't seen him in his office on the way in.

"Drop the nail polish and come down to the Dungeon."

"Give me a few—"

"*Now.*" Click.

She threw her briefcase in the chair. This was clearly it. Something important. Something about Noel. She rushed out the door and down the corridor to the elevator. Evan's voice had been excited—in a good or a bad way? Good, decidedly good. The Don must have a new lead, a clue, some evidence. Why else would they be meeting in the Dungeon?

As she pressed the illuminated "B" on the elevator panel, she wondered if this was related to a recent development in the case. Two days ago, by a fluke of good luck, Guillermo Restrepo had been arrested. Although the Saludos bank accounts had been cleaned out and abandoned, Restrepo had returned to New York to do more of the same, posing this time as a representative of a Colombian candy company. A bad move for him. Detectives spotted him in Queens, dressed in his neat business suit and carrying an expensive briefcase containing "corporate" literature.

Restrepo was now in custody, held without bail pending grand jury action. The team had more than enough evidence to charge him with money laundering, and also had a circumstantial case against him for the murder of Domingo Avendaño based on wiretap evidence proving he'd given the order.

In the basement of the Criminal Court building, Dana wound through the maze, arriving at the closed door to the headquarters of the DA's squad. She hadn't been down here since that terrible night she'd gone snooping around the Don's desk. With a pounding heart and moist hand, she turned the knob and pushed the door open.

Voices wafted from the distant end of the room near the Don's desk where a group of men huddled, most with their backs to her. As she approached, their identities grew clear: Evan standing on the left, Bruce sitting next to him, the Don perched on a corner of his desk, and Gilbert standing on the right. Even Joe was there, partially hidden from view, sitting behind Gilbert. Apparently, everyone was in on this important development.

When she was halfway there, Evan glanced up. He turned to the others and said, "Here's Dana." She picked up her pace. Like the sides of a curtain they parted, Evan stepping to the left, Bruce rolling his wheeled chair to the right, and there, sitting in the middle of the group, was Noel.

Dana halted, gasped, and ran the last few steps to him. Noel stood and caught her in his arms. He was trembling and less assertive in his physicality than ever before. She pulled back and looked at him. Noel. My God, he looked shaken!

Around them, the others had fallen silent. To break the tension, Bruce stood and said, "Here, Dana, sit," motioning for her to take the chair he had just vacated. She did as she was told, while Noel, slow and tentative as an old man, lowered himself into his seat.

It was then that Dana noticed the details of the change that had come over him in a month's time. Always tall and muscular, he now looked gaunt and skeletal, as much as fifteen or twenty pounds lighter. The spark had gone out of his eyes, sunken in black holes, and his dark olive complexion had turned the color of pasty oatmeal.

Bruce looked at Dana and said, "Mr. Avendaño arrived at the office about twenty minutes ago, asking to see you. He was sent down here to see Detective Donegan. The rest of us just got here, but we were waiting for you. I'm sure Mr. Avendaño doesn't want to go through this more than once."

"I appreciate that," said Noel. He turned to Dana. "I wanted to talk with you before I call Melly."

Bruce said to Noel, "We're all here because we have an interest in what you might know and how it could relate to our investigation. But if it's too much of a crowd scene, a few of us can get lost."

"I don't mind," he said. "Just let me talk. I have no secrets. I'm tired of hiding and I need your help. I don't know if I'm doing the right thing for my wife and baby."

Dana blanched and Noel saw the change. "What is it, Dana?"

"Melanie lost the baby the day you left. She's all right now. Physically all right. I've been staying with her."

"Oh my God." He slumped down into the chair and hung his head. A moment passed and he lifted his eyes. "Maybe it's not surprising, the way things were going, all the stress." He became quiet and reflective for a long time, as if he might not be able to continue talking.

"You okay?" Dana asked.

Noel nodded.

Bruce reached for a cup of water on the desk. "Here," he said. Noel took a long drink, finishing it.

"Can you start from the beginning?" prompted Bruce. "The day you disappeared. What happened that morning?"

Noel took a deep breath, frowned, and began speaking, slowly and with great difficulty.

That Monday morning, he'd arrived at the store about 8:30 and almost immediately received a call from Melanie, who was at the bank studying the Saludos account activity. She confirmed what he feared but hadn't been able to admit—that Domingo was laundering narcotics cash. He didn't know where Domingo had gotten all the money, but he suspected that instructions had been sent over the fax machine installed by Restrepo's people.

Noel regretted his failure to oversee the Saludos concession. He'd been happy enough to give Domingo free rein with a business project that was too small to hurt the bookstore financially, even if his young cousin made mistakes. Every morning, soon after arriving at the store, the boy would receive a fax message. After that, he would go out for most of the day and return in the afternoon, occasionally doing some work for Noel. At the end of the day, he would count the receipts from the sales of Saludos products and send a message by fax to Colombia.

Once, when Noel asked him about the messages, he explained it very simply. The evening message listed the item numbers sold and the sale prices, and the morning message was Restrepo's confirmation of receiving that information. The explanation seemed to make sense, and Noel didn't question it.

"What a fool I was," he muttered, shaking his head as the investigators and attorneys looked on. Dana, too, was stabbed with shame. She knew what it was like to be fooled by appearances. "When Melanie found all that money in the account, we decided I had to get Restrepo's merchandise and fax machine out of our store."

Noel drafted a memo to Restrepo. He sat alone in the empty store that morning, unable to do anything but scribble words and cross them out, trying to compose a message that was firm but not too threatening, something that made him look naïve so Restrepo wouldn't suspect he knew of the criminal scheme. Care had to be taken, for he understood now, despite his earlier denials, that he was pitted against evil, powerful men. Murderous men.

Domingo strode into the store at about 9:30 and barely said "hello" on his way to the back room. All was quiet. Noel hadn't yet opened to the public. A few minutes later, Noel heard the fax machine, and a minute after that, Domingo emerged and headed for the front door at a brisk pace.

Noel asked him to fax the memo to Restrepo, or to give him the number so he could do it himself. Domingo was curt and explosive: "When I get back. Restrepo isn't there right now. He's the only one who can see to it." The excuse was transparent, but Noel didn't challenge his cousin. He let Domingo walk out the door.

"I started to doubt whether my plan was such a wise idea. The message to Restrepo might provoke retaliation. Mingo was the one I should be kicking out. But..." Noel was afraid to instigate a confrontation with this new person he saw before him, not the usual cool and confident Mingo but a nervous, edgy and volatile man with a crazed look in his eyes. Noel didn't know him anymore, couldn't reconcile his behavior with the image he once held of his cousin in his mind and heart.

He opened the bookstore and tried to treat the day like any other, hoping an answer would come to him. At about 12:30, Mingo returned. He glanced around the store, saw two or three customers browsing in the aisles, and quickly retreated to the back office without a word. Intermittently he appeared in the open doorway, scanned the store with his eyes and retreated again. Finally, when the customers had gone, he rushed to the front door and turned the bolt lock.

If he looked crazed before, now he was frantic, near hysteria, sweating, panting like a dog. "I'm being followed. The men are outside." He grabbed Noel's arm and pulled him into the back room.

"Who?" demanded Noel.

"This time it's Restrepo's men, not the police."

"*This* time?" Just as Noel was about to demand an explanation, the fax machine spewed another message. Mingo snatched it up and scanned it, terror growing in his eyes. "Now I understand," he said. "It's not just the missed deposits..."

Noel was dumbfounded, unable even to think of the next question, but Mingo spoke, driven by fear. He admitted to being a cash courier for the Cartel. He'd failed to make a few deposits because he was being tailed. On Friday he thought it was the police, and this morning he believed it was Restrepo's men.

"You were thinking of keeping that money?" Noel asked. "For yourself?"

No, no, no, he denied at first, but seeing the doubt in Noel's eyes, he changed his story. It was tempting, he admitted, and maybe he'd been thinking about it. Fifty or sixty grand was nothing to the Cartel. But that wasn't the real reason Restrepo's men were after him. "Uncle Carlos is trying to shut them out."

Incredulous, Noel grabbed the faxed message from Domingo's hand. His eyes immediately found "Tio Carlos" on the page. "What is this? What does this mean?"

"You think I just happened to bump into Restrepo in New York? He's the contact man for Uncle Carlos. The cocaine money has been going through his factory for years. Carlos gave me to Restrepo—maybe he was forced to do it, I don't know. It didn't matter to me, I needed to make a little money."

"Carlos would never give his family to the wolves!"

"After Benita...what could he do?" Carlos was a good man,

Domingo agreed, but his daughter came first. After that, he was in over his head. Benita's safe return three years ago opened the floodgates for narcodollars into the plastics plant, improving and modernizing equipment, increasing the company's productivity and profits—with a hefty percentage going to the Cartel. Lately, Carlos had been taking measures to extricate himself. The details were unknown to Domingo.

Now, all he had was this cryptic faxed message from Restrepo with the final, sinister instruction: *Sabes lo que debes hacer*—you know what you have to do—if you want to right the wrongs of the Avendaños.

Domingo was out of his mind with panic. His only thought was to run, and for that matter, Noel better run too. Any family member was a sitting duck. "They want to send a warning to Carlos. They can kidnap or murder one or both of us. Here, we'll leave out the back door! Those thugs out front won't see us."

"I'm not going," said Noel. "What have I done to them? Nothing."

Domingo wouldn't listen. He ran to the cash register, swept out the bills and coins, and returned to the back room. "Here," he said, pushing the money into Noel's jacket pocket. "Take this. You'll need some money and you shouldn't use this dirty money in my pocket. Take it and come!"

Domingo pulled him by the arm and opened the back door. Noel resisted, but in the next instant, his will didn't matter. The open doorway was blocked by two enormous, armed men. One of them grabbed Domingo, the other grabbed Noel, and they whisked their prisoners through the alley into the back seat of a waiting car.

The first man entered the back seat and pulled Domingo in after him. The second man pushed Noel in next to his cousin, closed the door, and got in the front seat next to a third man, the driver. They sped away. The man next to Domingo ripped open his jacket and pulled out the money. "Where did you think you were going with this?" He laughed and stuck the gun into Domingo's lower ribs. The man next to the driver was turned to face Noel in the back seat. "You make a move, a bullet will rip right through this seat into your heart! Anyone looking in the window will think you're taking a nap."

A long drive, maybe not so long, Noel couldn't remember. His mind's eye held only the guns, very big and black. He didn't see much of them while in the car but was soon given a better view when they arrived at their destination, an abandoned building in a deserted section of town. Inside that building, Noel would experience his living hell.

A few junkies loitered in the foyer and common hallways which stank of urine, unwashed bodies and rat droppings. Glazed, uncaring eyes witnessed the three armed men pushing two others inside. Maybe just an everyday occurrence in this neighborhood. The captives were prodded up to a second-floor apartment in the back. Once inside, there were more demands. "What did you think you were doing with this money? You Avendaños are all alike. All trying to get over on someone!" Domingo begged for his life as the men laughed. His executioner said, "Sorry, not your lucky day. Restrepo sent us to deliver this message."

An explosion. Half of Domingo's head was gone.

Noel almost lost consciousness, fully expecting the same fate. The man at his side clenched his upper arm in a steel grip and pressed the muzzle of a gun against his temple.

"Restrepo sends another message," he said, pausing with a grin on his lips, delighted to see Noel squirm. The metal of the gun felt hot. But the man didn't shoot. He spoke: "Restrepo wants you alive for insurance. Who knows when we might need you to help us keep Carlos in line? Meanwhile, the heat is on, thanks to your cousin. Don't go back to the bookstore. Consider it gone.

Don't talk to anyone about this, not even your wife. Don't talk to the police. If you do, you're next."

And they left him there with Domingo's warm body and hovering spirit.

By the time Noel finished, he was crumpled in tears. Dana pulled her chair close alongside his and put her arm around his shoulder. "Where have you been all this time?" she asked when his sobbing was under control.

"A hundred places. Homeless shelters. Camping upstate. I didn't have much money."

"You withdrew some money…"

"Yes. I had to. I felt like a thief. I didn't want to take money Melanie needed. But I also thought it could be a way of telling her I was all right."

"Did you think of writing or calling? Somehow getting a message to her?" asked Joe.

"Of course. Every day I thought of it. But I thought the safest thing for her would be if I stayed far away. I didn't want to bring this danger home to her. I didn't know how long I would have to stay away. Restrepo's men ordered me not to talk to her. They might think I was trying to get her to convey a message to the police…"

"Do they know of Melanie's relationship with Dana?" Bruce asked, shooting a look in her direction.

"They didn't say. It was all general threats, don't talk to anybody, not even your wife… I was afraid it was a threat against her. Please, what should I do?"

"You've heard that Restrepo has been arrested?" asked Evan.

Noel nodded. "I saw it in the papers. That's why I'm here. I'm hoping things might be safer and maybe I can help—you can use the information I have in convicting him. I'd like to help, but

I have to be sure Melly will be kept safe. We need protection." He looked at each of them in turn, with a shining hope in his eyes.

Bruce cleared his throat and assumed his official persona. "This isn't a federal case. The state has no witness protection program, if that's what you're thinking about. And we can't give any assurances of your safety. It would be unrealistic for me to make those kinds of promises. We don't have the resources to put a watch on you twenty-four hours a day. We aren't even sure how to quantify the kind of danger you might be in. We don't know if Restrepo still has people loyal to him out on the street."

As Bruce spoke, the emergent light in Noel's face slowly faded.

"I will say this, however," Bruce continued. "You're right that Restrepo's arrest could mean you're safer. We have enough evidence to put him away for a while. He's being held without bail. We're going into the grand jury later today, and I don't need your testimony right now to get an indictment. We've yet to see if the case goes to trial. If it does, I'll need your testimony then. Meanwhile, if you come out of hiding, it's best to try and keep a low profile. You might even consider relocating. The city is a hotbed of Cartel activity." Bruce's left thumb fiddled with the gold band on his ring finger. "I'm sure it must have been hard on you hiding out like that, away from your wife. You face a personal decision now whether to reunite, and you'll have to decide without having full knowledge of the risks."

A silence fell over the group. Noel laced his fingers in his lap and examined his hands in thought. When he spoke, he addressed them all, but looked only at Dana: "I know what my decision is, and that's why I've come. But I won't force my will on Melanie. I have to talk to her first."

"Of course," said Bruce.

"And I'd like, if I could, I'd like to talk to her here in your offices. I don't think I've been followed—it's been too long—but I can't shake the fear. I don't want to go to the apartment and have her worry later that I've brought danger to our—to her home, if her decision is not the same as mine."

"Understandable," said Bruce. "Dana? Why don't you give Mrs. Avendaño a call?"

My connection at the bank? She almost said it. Her eyes twinkled with irony, but she doubted Bruce would pick up her thought. They'd come a long way and were past all of that now. "Yes, I'm very happy to do that."

"And tell them at the front desk to send her down here when she comes in."

"The Dungeon?" she asked skeptically, looking around at the gray walls, concrete floors and snaking pipes. "I don't think so, Bruce. I have a better idea."

Bruce raised his bushy brows over eyes gleaming with an odd mixture of pride and amusement. Nothing in those eyes gave her cause any longer to dread the thoughts or judgments harbored within.

She stood, leaned toward Evan, and whispered in his ear. Evan shrugged and smiled.

"Why not?" he said.

Melanie's decision wasn't difficult to guess, judging from the high flush in her cheeks and shining expectant eyes when she burst into the reception area at FC. "Where?" she asked. Dana took her hand. "This way."

Despite all the excitement, a shock was in store for her— Noel's haggard appearance and his frightening tale. Eclipsing it all would be the joy of reunion and the hope of making a new beginning together.

Seeing her friend's face, Dana had these thoughts for the man on the other side of that closed door: How can you really be uncertain about her decision, Noel? Sitting alone in that room, waiting for her, you must know that you and Melly will be leaving this place together, going home, wherever the two of you decide to make your home.

In the hallway, Dana caught Evan's eye before she opened the door for Melanie. Letting her friend slip inside, she caught only a glimpse of a blurred union and a cry from two throats before she quickly closed the door again, shutting them away from the world, muffling their sound. This must be a very private reunion, no surveillance or eavesdropping allowed.

Evan was waiting, expecting her to come to him. She did.

"I'm honored," he said. "But why? Out of this huge building, why did you choose my office?"

She smiled and dusted an imaginary piece of lint from his shoulder in the same spot that had soaked up her circle of tears a month ago. "Because it's the sunniest, most cheerful room in this dump. It's a happy place."

"Well then, maybe they'll make it even happier."

"I'm sure they will."

Evan looked at his watch. "This could take a while. I'll just have to go get happy somewhere else. The world doesn't stop for lovers, you know. I have some business with the Don, so I guess it's back down to the Dungeon for me."

"Don't forget your paint can."

He smiled and rubbed his bald spot. "That will have to wait."

"I have to get back to work too. Bruce and Joe aren't going to let me escape this Cartel nightmare until I finish my summary of the accounts and another pleading or two."

"So eager to get rid of us, are you? Don't let me stand in your way."

But neither one of them moved. Evan seemed to be searching for a parting remark, coming up with nothing. Shifting his weight from one foot to the other, he inched backward, hesitated, and said, "I was thinking, what are you doing for dinner tonight?"

She looked at the ceiling, pondered a moment, and met his eyes again. "Eating."

"Funny about that. Me too." He bobbed his head in agreement, his brow pressed down hard over the blue-gray eyes as if considering the most serious business matter. "Yes, I'll be eating too. So, I'm just wondering...do you want to eat together?"

"At dinnertime?"

"Yes."

"That's after work, right?" she asked in a somber tone.

"Correct," he acknowledged, beginning to look worried.

"I thought so."

They fell silent and stood with crossed arms, looking at the ground to see what there was to be seen.

At once, as if on cue, their eyes flicked up, caught and held. Two mouths twitched with suppressed emotion and broke into goofy grins. They were helpless to contain it. Their grins stretched into radiant smiles, and they burst into laughter that lasted until Dana's eyes were filled with tears.

OPUS NINE BOOKS

All works published by Opus Nine Books are dedicated to the nine members of the family headed by John and Kate Swackhamer at 3 South Trail, Orinda, California — a large world under one small roof.

CPSIA information can be obtained
at www.ICGtesting.com
Printed in the USA
LVHW052259030220
645691LV00001B/159